WHEN STARLINGS FLY AS ONE

Also by Nancy Blanton

The Earl in Black Armor

The Prince of Glencurragh

Sharavogue

Brand Yourself Royally in 8 Simple Steps

The Curious Adventure of Roodle Jones

Heaven on the Half Shell

WHEN STARLINGS FLY AS ONE

A Novel

NANCY BLANTON

EDB

ELLYS-DAUGHTREY BOOKS

FERNANDINA BEACH, FLORIDA

Ellys-Daughtrey Books

P.O. Box 15699, Fernandina Beach, FL 32035

Disclaimer:

Certain characters in this book are historical figures, however, they may participate in events and interact with characters who are fictional, products of the author's imagination. Any resemblance of these characters to individuals living or dead is coincidental. For more information about this, please see the author's note in the book's backmatter.

Published by Ellys-Daughtrey Books

P.O. Box 15699, Fernandina Beach, FL 32035

http://ellys-daughtrey.blogspot.com

ISBN: hard cover 978-1-7335928-1-9
ISBN: paper cover 978-1-7335928-2-6
ISBN: e-book 978-1-7335928-3-3

Library of Congress Control Number: 2021902577

Printed in the United States of America

Cover Design includes licensed images by Urška Batistič, iStock 1296138333, and Albert Beukhof, Shutterstock 1865205265

For Marilyn Paul Cook
My precious friend and runner in the night

And for Bonnie Jayne O'Keeffe
The undisputed Queen of Joy

From the Author

Thank you for choosing to read When Starlings Fly as One. First and foremost, this is a work of fiction based on factual accounts. It is not a classic hero's journey, but a story of war, struggle, spirit, and survival—a story of two sides.

I have respectfully used the names of real people to help the reader connect the story with the history. Any descriptions of individuals, their speech, mannerisms, relationships, or their interactions, are entirely imagined. I had no way of knowing what they were truly like or how they thought or behaved. I have created them for the purpose of telling a story. Any resemblance of these characters to individuals living or dead is purely by accident or coincidence, and not by intention. For more details, please read my author's note at the end of this book.

I hope you enjoy the story.

Acknowledgments

I am keenly aware of the many people who have been a part of this book, whether they knew it or not. First and foremost, it would have been impossible to write without the support of my husband Karl Shaffer, for his love, patience, and humor; and the inspiration of two remarkable and beloved women, Marilyn Paul Cook and Bonnie Jayne O'Keeffe.

I am also grateful for the support and encouragement of my sisters, Daphne Berry, Bonnie Rossa, and Gayle Baxley. My dear friend and fellow author Andrea Patten is and has always been at my side since they day we met, with ideas, connections, encouragement, and positivity. And coffee.

Eddie and Teresa MacEoin, who live in Bandon, County Cork, Ireland, and first introduced me to Rathbarry Castle—among other places—are forever at the top of my list for their support, kindness, knowledge, endless generosity, and joyful spirits.

I also wish to thank Larry Bienemann, Haley Connor, Terri Dean, Caryl and Jack Ferry, Janet Hartig, Trienah Anne Meyers, David O'Keeffe, Gail Vivian, and the members of Amelia Indie Authors.

Recognizing that my work also depends largely on the researchers and writers whose books and articles inspire, inform, and excite, I thank them especially for uncovering the Irish side of things that long was ignored as the victors wrote the histories. I am grateful for the stories and the rich threads of fascinating detail.

On 22 October 1641, a rebellion in Ireland triggered the onset of a decade of civil war, invasion, and conquest. The colonial authorities thwarted an attempt to seize Dublin Castle, but could not prevent Catholic insurgents from capturing strategic strongholds in Ulster. Over the winter and spring of 1642, the rebellion spread to engulf the rest of the country.

~ *Jane Ohlmeyer & Micheál Ó Siochrú*
Editors, Ireland 1641: Contexts and Reactions

Characters

VOICES

Merel de Vries: a Dutch orphan and shipwreck survivor who is taken in by Lady Carey and later works as companion to Mistress Dorothy at Rathbarry Castle

Tynan O'Daly: horse marshal for Sir Arthur, Merel's Irish love interest

Teige O'Downe: i.e. Teige-an-Duna MacCarthy, Prince of Dunmanway, clan leader in charge of the Irish forces besieging Rathbarry Castle

MAIN INTERACTING CHARACTERS

Sir Arthur Freke: owner of Rathbarry Castle, Commander-in-Chief of Rathbarry Garrison

Dorothy Freke: Sir Arthur's wife, lady of the castle

Lady Carey: castle resident who employs Merel as her companion and maid

Jayne O'Keeffe: Merel's friend, maid to Mistress Coale, later to Lady Carey and Mistress Dorothy

Cormac MacCarthy Reagh: Head of the MacCarthy Clan for the Province of Munster

Donough MacCarthy, Lord Muskerry: titled clan leader and member of Irish Parliament, cousin to Teige O'Downe, brother-in-law to Cormac McCarthy Reagh

SECONDARY CHARACTERS

Lord Arundel: owner of Arundel Castle, military ally to Teige O'Downe and MacCarthy Reagh

General Garet Barry: commander of the Confederate Munster army

Captain Edward Beecher: Bandonian officer assigned to command Rathbarry Garrison

Mistress Coale: noblewoman dislodged from her home in Ross by the Irish

Elinor: Rathbarry's head cook

Lord Forbes: Scottish military leader sent from Kinsale to relieve Rathbarry Castle

David Hyrd: garrison soldier, Jayne's love interest

Mr. Millet: Sir Arthur's agent and groundskeeper

Barry Oge O'Hea: a lieutenant for Teige O'Downe

McMahony: Sir Arthur's neighbor and intermediary for Teige O'Downe

Mr. Sellers: herdsman for Sir Arthur

SOUTHWEST IRELAND

MUNSTER

- WATERFORD •
- LIMERICK •
- LISCARROLL •
- MALLOW •
- FERMOY •
- BLARNEY •
- YOUGHAL •
- **CORK** ●
- COBH HARBOR •
- KINSALE •
- BANDON •
- KILBRITTAIN •
- TIMOLEAGUE •
- CLONAKILTY •
- KILSARKAN •
- ROSS •
- RATHBARRY CASTLE
- GLANDORE •
- SKIBBEREEN •
- CASTLEHAVEN •
- BALTIMORE •

THE SEVEN CASTLES OF CARBERY BARONY

TIMOLEAGUE

CLONAKILTY

ARUNDEL

INCHYDONY ISLAND

CLOHEEN STRAND

DUNGORLEY

6

7 DUNWORLEY

5 DUNEEN

4 DUNNYCOVE

ARDFIELD

3 DUNOWEN

1 DUNOURE

2 DUNDEADY

RATHBARRY CASTLE

THE LONG STRAND

ROSS

WARREN BEACH

GLANDORE

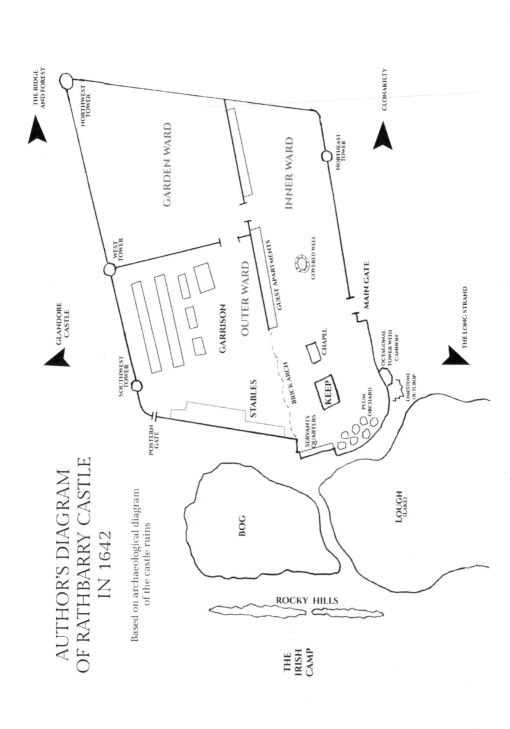

AUTHOR'S DIAGRAM
OF RATHBARRY CASTLE
IN 1642

Based on archaeological diagram
of the castle ruins

THE RIDGE
AND FOREST

GLANDORE
CASTLE

CLONAKILTY

THE LONG STRAND

NORTHWEST
TOWER

GARDEN WARD

WEST
TOWER

INNER WARD

NORTHEAST
TOWER

GARRISON

OUTER WARD

GUEST APARTMENTS

COVERED WELL

MAIN GATE

SOUTHWEST
TOWER

STABLES

BRICK ARCH

CHAPEL

KEEP

OCTAGONAL
TOWER WITH
CANNON

POSTERN
GATE

SERVANTS
QUARTERS

PLUM
ORCHARD

LIMESTONE
OUTCROP

BOG

LOUGH
(LAKE)

ROCKY HILLS

THE
IRISH
CAMP

1

Rathbarry Castle

County of Cork, Province of Munster
February 14, 1642

Just after sunrise, Tynan O'Daly woke to the skirl of warpipes, a familiar and yet disturbing sound rising with the frigid mist. It wasn't for entertainment the piper played, but to compel the clans and ignite the ancient spirits within them. The sentries in the castle towers shouted alarm, startling the curs and the hunting hounds to frenzy. He jerked into his doublet and ran for the courtyard.

Sir Arthur Freke crossed the wide court to the hexagonal tower where cannons were fixed, Captain Beecher and Mr. Millet behind him. Tynan followed, while the ensign and other soldiers of the garrison ran for the north tower. The sounds stirred castle residents and servants to curiosity and soon they filled the surface of the eastern wall from the north corner to the southeast, the sharp scent of salt air rising from the roaring ocean behind, the damp wind tossing their hair. At the far end, Merel and Jayne huddled against the wall, a blanket pulled tightly around them.

The sentries pointed Sir Arthur's attention to the northeast, a rounded hill just greening from an early sprout of grass about a half-mile from the castle. There on the highest rim, the brightening sun sliced through the mist to illuminate a white flag, red-bordered and flowing in the wind, and a red insignia at its center. Sir Arthur looked through his spyglass, then handed it to Beecher.

"It's the red stag, sir. The MacCarthy coat of arms," Beecher said.

"How many men do you count?"

"Five men, breast plates, two with red sashes."

Sir Arthur took the spyglass and adjusted it. "The largest man. Has to be that John Oge Barry who came to speak with us. I think I recognize my neighbor McMahony, as well."

The flag and breastplates glinted with sunlight whenever they moved, and the five men soon spread by equal paces across the width of the hill-top. The warpipes skirled and droned and then settled into an eerie, insistent wail—an attack. The piper marched to the far left of the field as the five men descended on the slope in wide, uniform strides.

"They're coming toward the castle, all five of them in line. Are the snipers at ready?"

"Yes, sir," Beecher said. "But those men are well out of range."

"And I am sure they know it. Look, they're moving forward again. The moment they come within range..."

The men advanced thirty feet, and then on the hill's rim behind them, another man stepped up. He was very tall, his breastplate and silver helmet gleaming. A long and broad red sash flapped boldly behind him like a ship's sail in fair wind.

"Who is that?" Sir Arthur asked.

"Teige O'Downe," Tynan said.

Sir Arthur lowered the spyglass and turned to look at Tynan. Beecher stared at him as well. Tynan returned a flinty glare. So what, if he was just the stable marshal and not a ranking soldier of the garrison? He knew better than any of them who these people were and what they were about.

"How do you know that?" Sir Arthur asked.

"Because I know him. Everyone around Dunmanway knows him. He owns the castle there. People call him Teige the Hospicious because he shows great hospitality to his guests, and treats them generously."

"I know what hospicious means, O'Daly."

Aye, he supposed he had that coming, but sometimes English folk needed reminding that the Irish were as civilized as they. "Sir, what I mean to say is, he's lord of the crooked valley, the prince of that region they call Glenna-na-Chroim, a blood relation to the MacCarthys all over County Cork."

Sir Arthur and Beecher looked at each other, then back at the towering figure on the hilltop. After a few moments, O'Downe began to descend the hill, and as he moved, so moved the five men before him, farther and farther toward Rathbarry. He stopped and remained very still as the warpipes keened. Then suddenly the piper stopped, and the only sounds were the wind and the raging tussle of the red and white standard. O'Downe held his arms at his sides, palms up, and raised them wide until they were level with his shoulders. Instantly a thunder shook the earth, and a great dark line appeared at the rim of the hill, and then it grew darker, heavier, and then wider and wider still, until it became clear that the line was not one thing but many—soldiers in close formation, hundreds of them, dressed in earth-colored cloaks and woolens, marching up and over the hill.

And forward they came, solid as a mudslide—dusky, heavy, rumbling in their march, the clatter of pikes, swords, clubs, and muskets adding to the terrible sound and the frightening spectacle of so vast the unified Irish army. On and on they came, until the dark line blanketed the entire hill.

"Merciful God!" Sir Arthur said. "Captain Beecher, how many men did Mr. Sellers count when he saw the Irish marching on the strand?"

Beecher, built like the trunk of an oak and with as much humor, replied flatly, "Sixty men, sir. In two companies."

"Yes, as I thought. And how many would you say stand before us?"

"Eight hundred, sir. At the very least, eight hundred, maybe a good thousand."

"But I've never seen such a gathering of them before. Where have they all come from?"

"O'Downe is a respected clan leader, sir," Tynan said. "When he summons, men come to him in tribute from all parts of the barony. It is their sworn duty."

"He is a wicked man, to do this," Sir Arthur said.

"Forgive me, sir, but in truth he is not. Men follow him willingly, and with pride. With such numbers he could easily march, overrun the castle, and it would all be over in a matter of hours. But he values life, and strikes only when alternatives fail."

"I should hardly call this a mercy, O'Daly. You risk impertinence. What he intends is terror."

"Aye, sir."

Beecher grumbled. "He has no artillery, that's why he doesn't charge. Let our cannons cut him down."

"That day may come, but not now. Let him have his spectacle, as long as that's all it is. We must conserve what we have until we know support comes from the Bandon garrison," Sir Arthur said.

"As you wish, sir." Beecher turned, cast a scornful look at Tynan, and then left the wall.

Tynan looked toward the north tower and waited until the two huddled women felt his gaze. Jayne was first to turn to him, her eyes wide and red-rimmed, her lips trembling. When Merel turned, she showed no such fear. She stared back at him—concern on her face, yes—but question in her eyes and something more. Her chin was tucked, and her eyes narrowed—an air of determination.

Here was the truth of what was before them, and the reason the others had left yesterday. Rathbarry was besieged by the Irish. Somewhere in that line of men on the hill stood Jayne's brother, likely a brother of his own, and a neighbor, and a childhood friend. People he'd known all his life. Not as soldiers in an army, and not as enemies, but relatives however distant. Where would he stand if he took up arms as a soldier among them? Or, being employed within an English-owned castle as he was, how would he face them should he have to stand against them? Did his blood not rise at the sound of the warpipes?

For half an hour the Irish covered the hill, and every soul in Rathbarry Castle climbed the towers to see their mighty show of power and hear the threatening marches. When at last the dark line began to recede, none could question the truth of circumstance. Women cried. Some men begged for the fight, while others saw the disparity in numbers and demanded immediate surrender.

Sir Arthur, Captain Beecher and Mr. Millet entered the keep, and the usher Jenkin closed the door with a firm and solid thump.

JANUARY

1642

2

Merel

Rathbarry Castle

It's little wonder that a small, plain girl of no consequence easily escapes notice. A minor stir begins if I cannot be found when tasks are required, and though I've only stepped behind a tall chair, the work is quickly assigned to another—I am free. Hours pass without concern as I wander through hay fields, explore the pond's muddy edge, or take comfort in the limbs of an ancient yew. Along the strand, the ocean spray stings my cheeks and keeps me from duties almost until dark. But then, offering only a fresh sprig of fragrant rosemary from my palm, Lady Carey inhales of it deeply and forgets her companion was absent at all. I curl at her feet like a dog.

Yet, my lady shifts in her cushioned chair, smooths the silver-streaked strands at her brow, and expels a heavy sigh. Without being asked, she explains to anyone who is near. "A precious jewel, is this child. She isn't mine, you know, and I wouldn't have taken her on, but what was I to do? Those eyes captured me at first. Like a Cavalier spaniel, don't you think? And her hair has just the slightest hint of red, like the Blenheim variety. My dear little Dutch orphan. I couldn't manage without her."

If that was not yet enough to shame a young woman before strangers, Lady Carey was only warming to her words. Like an automaton on a rich man's clock she clicks into action. She coughs loudly, rearranges the lap of her skirts, and lowers her voice to a confidential tone.

"My son—he's a major in the king's army, you know—he'd collected me at Cobh Harbor as I returned from a visit to London only a day before a frightening tempest enraged the Irish Sea. My little Merel was a passenger on a Dutch trader. The captain had meant to collect beef provisions for those poor souls in the Indies. You know, they have the most atrocious conditions on those islands, fearing the Spaniards at one side or the natives at the other will cut their throats at any moment. I can hardly ponder why anyone should choose to live there.

"But those people were destined to go hungry, weren't they? Because the supplies would never reach them. A terrible gale swept the ship upon Poor Head, a most treacherous spot in the harbor if the captain isn't wise to it. He and most of the crew were saved, but her ma and papa, Lotte and Pieter de Vries," —at which point Lady Carey would dab her eyes with a lace handkerchief— "they had sailed all the way from Harlingen only to be trapped by their own cargo and drowned." She'd pat my head. "Isn't that so, Merel, dear?"

My mother had allowed me to run barefoot on the slick, wet planks of the ship. She laughed when I fell and so, though I might have bumped an elbow or a knee, I laughed, too. When Mama laughed the clouds fell away from the sun. "Hold up your hand," she said one day when we sat on the deck and watched the sea skirt by. Her hand was warm and smooth as she spread apart my fingers. "Oh! Remember? We shall need both hands now. Which finger will you choose?" I picked the smallest one, my left pinky. "No, no, Merrie. I knew you'd forgotten. We used that one last year. Now we celebrate your tenth year, so you must pick the one we saved especially." I'd hardly thought of it as the year passed, but then it came to me: the pointing finger on my right hand. She kissed it and held it to her cheek. "Exactly so. The perfect one. This finger foretells your success in life. You'll be strong and confident. You'll seek solutions to problems and will find them. But mind: never push so hard for what you want, that you push away what you love."

Lady Carey chatted on. "When the storm had passed, my son led me along the wharf to board our carriage, and there she stood by a stack of old barrels, alone, filthy, and most confused. The captain was near and informed us of her name and her circumstance. She had no one to look after her and was destined for homelessness and beggary if I didn't take her—and wasn't the captain glad to be relieved of his charge."

My stomach took a turn each time Lady Carey told the tale, leaving me only slightly grateful that I hadn't perished in the ship myself. Always there came like a wave across my mind the wood cracking, cold water gushing, my open eyes plunged into dark terror. The physical memory of impossible cold caused my hands to tremble. They had flailed in the water with nothing to grasp. I'd been a daughter, beloved, and suddenly I was nothing and fated to be reminded of it daily. For a decade. I wished I'd stayed in the field a bit longer or knew a proper path beyond the castle wall that would take me—where?

We'd come to Rathbarry Castle in south Munster four months previous at her son's request. He feared for his mother's safety even before the Irish rising at Dublin last October. As a favor to his fellow officer, Sir Arthur Freke collected Lady Carey and me from her home near Fermoy. "Freck-Ah," he told us at once. "Please pronounce it correctly or my wife will have her fits."

At first, Lady Carey took to the castle as if she were a queen and Rathbarry her court, but Sir Arthur's wife Dorothy cared not for her dominating presence. Besides, the castle was already crowded with Sir Arthur's mother Ann, his son Percy, his sisters Mary and Ann the younger, and his brother Thomas who also served as Sir Arthur's estate steward.

Lady Carey soon found herself relocated to her own apartment across the courtyard from the keep. She was welcome in the castle for mealtimes and social occasions, and could join the other ladies in the solar for reading or sewing—if Mistress Dorothy was not present.

Perhaps to relieve her boredom, Lady Carey had taken to dressing me like a doll. I had grown to four feet, seven inches, almost, but my lady was head and shoulders taller and still saw me as a child. The little maid garments I'd worn for years were cast aside. Now I was to wear fine embroidered clothes and even jewelry. On Twelfth Night, when the wise men brought gifts to the infant Jesus, she gave me a pearl necklace. "My mother gave these to me when I was first allowed to dine at table instead of in the nursery. I sat just next to my father," she said.

"I am nearly twenty years now, my lady." To which she replied, "Those latchet shoes are simply frightful. Look at them, caked with mud from the bog. Where have you been, dear? You must burn them. We shouldn't have you about looking like a ragamuffin, and not after all the fine needlework I've done on those skirts. I shall have the cobbler make you a nice pair of lace-up boots."

It was no use trying to convince her I was a grown woman, but the dolly dresses did have their advantages, especially when one wished not to escape notice, but to be noticed most profoundly. If I walked in the castle yard, and particularly near Sir Arthur's stables, I might draw the gaze of his Irish horse marshal, Tynan O'Daly. My heart begins to race at the thought of him. Tall, even taller than Lady Carey, and built as if of solid rock, his breeches tight against his muscled thighs, his broad shoulders testing the seams of his shirt. He never once noticed me until I passed by in a new yellow dress, and then his blue-gray eyes widened, causing my cheeks to burn.

Of all the men garrisoned at Rathbarry—and there were eighty of them who might have raised an interest—none drew from me such a physical reaction, as if I'd bitten into a sweet that caused my mouth to tingle and my blood to surge. But worse so, for at the same time, my appetite left me like water squeezed from a rag, and thoughts of task and purpose thinned to vapor. I was always scheming for a chance encounter, inventing reason upon reason to go out into the castle yard. Failing that, I couldn't pass a door or window without being pulled as if by a rope around my neck to catch the tiniest glimpse of him. Tynan O'Daly, marshal of the horse. Tynan of oiled leather and polished silver. Ty, of dark musty corners under thin streams of pale sunlight. Of high ruddy cheeks bitten by the wind.

Came the day then—not the Epiphany but a few days after—when I was just a few steps from the stable door, peering inside as I casually passed, intending a timely rustle of my skirt. The curs that slept in huddles against the outer castle wall roused with sharp report. In minutes, a sentry shouted an alarm as four stout men approached the main castle gate. Already the men walked past the northeast gate posts: brick columns half-again as tall as a man and topped with white stone spheres.

Perhaps to atone for the sentry's tardiness, a porter ran to alert the servants in the great hall. Those most curious servants stopped their work and hurried to the courtyard. The four visitors continued steadily toward the great wooden inner gate: the main entrance with guards and locks. Though it was opened, one of the visitors banged upon it with his walking stick, the sharp whack drawing even more people from their tasks.

"We've come from Ross to see the commander-in-chief, Sir Arthur Freke and none other," said the largest of the men. All four looked familiar, though I knew only one of them, our Mr. Taverner, who mercilessly bored us for hours with every Sunday sermon.

Beside the line of plum trees that led toward the castle's keep, the men waited quietly for Sir Arthur, as most of us were permitted to call him, and in the meantime straightened their hats and dusted off their clothing.

I moved closer to make sure I'd overhear whatever was said, and soon realized by the scent of leather, horsehair and dung that Tynan and his stable helpers, Giles and young Collum, had arrived behind me. Giles was a thin, wiry man with equally wiry sand-colored hair. The Irish boy everyone called young Collum was about fifteen, lanky and constantly red-faced. I dared not turn to look at Tynan, but it was all I could do to maintain my stillness. My heart wouldn't heed my efforts at all and hammered against my breastbone. At last Sir Arthur's stern voice bested the troublesome thudding in my ears.

"Gentlemen. Welcome to Rathbarry Castle," he said, palms open at his sides in greeting. His face didn't offer a similar kindness, looking every bit as severe as his grandfather's portrait in the great hall. A meticulous groomer, he'd combed his thick black hair straight back into curls nearly reaching his shoulders. Thirty-eight years of age, and he showed only a few strands of gray. His brows were heavy over dark, penetrating eyes. His cheeks flat and broad like shields. His brown doublet buttoned to his chin, where he maintained a pointed Van Dyke beard. He seemed fierce to all who encountered him, but I had seen him sing a song with his young son Percy, and rub the belly of his favorite hound, Cal.

Mr. Taverner stepped forward, confident in his relationship to Sir Arthur, and introduced the others: Mr. Newman of Ross; Mr. Cleland, the chanter of Ross; and Mr. Boyle, a relation to the Earl of Cork who owned most of the land in the county.

The village of Ross was well known in the Carbery barony, just to the northwest of Rathbarry and a good two-hour walk on a clear day. In most cases, Sir Arthur would invite guests into his state room to have brandy before discussing business. On occasion, I had served it myself. But these men came uninvited and without notice, and so such pleasantries were at first withheld.

"What brings you such distance on a cold winter day?" Sir Arthur asked.

Mr. Newman took a half-step forward. "Kind sir, we've come to inform you of important and distressing news. I have received several letters of late, and they are most earnest as to cause me concern. You will have heard, as we all have, of a failed attempt by rebel Irish to take Dublin Castle in a bloodless coup."

Sir Arthur clicked his tongue with impatience. "I have, of course. A useless and foolish endeavor. Yes, yes. Go on."

Bristling with his sudden importance, Mr. Newman tugged his doublet firmly over his belly. "Since the coup failed, the far north has become a bloody battleground, and the rising has unfolded in skirmishes and takings in other parts of the land. English settlers have been driven naked from their homes, sir, and far worse. These shocking events have not been quelled. In fact, they do spread southward, and we of Munster province are at great risk. Proof comes within these letters, as I have direct warning from Mr. Teige O'Downe of the MacCarthy clan, that the Irish of Carbery soon will rise in rebellion. We fear not for ourselves, sir, but the townspeople are..."

"O'Downe, you say. If I recall, he styles himself a chieftain," Sir Arthur said. He ran his knuckles across his lower left jaw.

"We've come to ask, honorable sir," Mr. Newman said, "that the good English settlers of Ross, with all their families, their servants and neighbors, and with all of their goods and provisions, might be received into the Castle of Rathbarry, under the protection of yourself and His Majesty's garrison, until we have certainty that the danger has passed. The women and ch..."

Sir Arthur raised his palm, silencing Mr. Newman, who then bowed slightly, and held that stance until Sir Arthur spoke.

Sir Arthur delayed, and I examined the delicate changes on his face as his mind worked. His brow furrowed. Of course, he could not refuse them. Not with the garrison there for which he likely received monies. Everyone knew he was responsible for the protection of the local settlements. He frowned. Was he concerned about the work required to have so many people properly housed? Or that it might tax his resources to see them all well fed? He cocked his head to the left and then right, as if to ease a tightening in his neck. Perhaps he considered how bothersome it would be to fill his castle with strangers. He was not an unkind man, but had little use for socializing and held rather tightly to his coins. His upper lip twitched.

He vacillated between churlishness and pleasantry.

Of a sudden, one of his eyebrows arched and I could not suppress a smirk. I suspected Mr. Newman's words had penetrated Sir Arthur's thoughts. If these people brought their goods, provisions, and most likely all of their money, it could be of benefit to Rathbarry rather than burden, and the people would be indebted to him for his protection—something that might facilitate future business dealings. Sir Arthur straightened his stance and nodded to the four men. "To the succor and shelter of Rathbarry Castle, I gladly welcome the people of Ross. Our mighty garrison will see that they come to no harm. Let us repair to my state room to discuss the particulars of their coming."

He nodded to Jenkin, who threw wide the doors to the keep. Sir Arthur's wife Dorothy had not come out to welcome the guests, but appeared briefly at the solar's oriel window.

She'd have to hurry to the state room to ensure all was in order. The stable men hurried off as well, to my disappointment, but the hum of conversation was rising in the courtyard. Something was about to happen, and if Lady Carey had been bored in her apartment, she was soon to have more entertainment than she might have desired.

3

Murmuration

Rathbarry Castle and the
Forested Ridge

Construction began the very next dawn beneath a heavy gray mist. Even before the rooster, the men of the garrison shouted orders to and fro, started cook fires, banged and clanged kettle and pot. Soon the outer ward filled with smoke and dust, the smell and pop of frying sausages, the splash of emptied piss pots, the grunts and squeals of mules under harness. Men loaded carts with stone and wood and cursed the groaning wheels over bumps in the courtyard. Sir Arthur's goats bleated their indignation, and chickens shrieked. A brisk wind howled around the castle's outer walls, and before long my spine jolted with every strike of a feller's ax as he harvested usable trees. But no sound overcame the voice of Sir Arthur himself, who shouted so many orders it seemed no one should dare draw a breath without him first commanding it.

"Gather my goats to ye pens, as ye should have done before daybreak, and my chickens as well before they be crushed beneath the cart wheels, stupid creatures they are!" He shouted from the stone rail of the gallery beneath the brick arch that allowed an unobstructed view of the stables, the garrison quarters, and the entrance to the garden ward. "Make way, make way! Seventeen new houses to raise and ye'll thank me if it won't be more! And you, there. Take those canvases to my fig orchard, and pitch the tents amongst my trees."

Rathbarry Castle was divided into three sections. On the east side, the inner ward was closest to the gate. It surrounded the keep—the tower house where the Freke family lived—and included the well at the center of the courtyard. Servants' quarters and guest houses were constructed along the castle walls on either side of the gate and behind the keep. On the west side, the outer ward included the stables and garrison on the south, and the garden ward to the north.

The brick arch divided the stables from the court but it remained within shouting distance of the keep. Beyond the stables, the pikemen, musketeers, cavalry and officers of the garrison conducted their drills in the parade yard outside the west curtain wall. The snipers, all former huntsmen hired for their skill with long muskets, clicked and clattered to the towers, the largest of which was south of the main gate: a hexagonal bastion with three arched openings for heavy cannon.

For the people of Ross, the temporary houses would be situated in the garden ward, commanding the northwest section. Here the thriving orchard included apple, cherry, elder and hazel, and a dovecote nestled in the northwest corner. There were numerous geometrical fruit, vegetable, and herb beds defined by narrow pathways. On an afternoon stroll one might find thyme, sage, mint, basil, and fennel growing on the left, strawberries on the right, raspberries in yet another bed, and then cabbages, radishes, parsnips, garlic, and onion, as well as peas. Around the perimeters, raised beds surrounded by wattle fencing flourished with leafy mustard and squash. Sadly, some of these beds would have to give way to cot and mattress beds for the new occupants soon to arrive.

I was on the steps going down to the keep's understory, the arched cellar with a large kitchen, pantry, and larder, when the morning's commotion began. Just the idea of such an influx of people gave my blood a brisk stir, and yet I grieved a bit for my charming Castle Rathbarry. I recalled the great castles I'd seen in my Dutch homeland when I was just a child—their red stone and pointed rooftops enchanted me, but I'd never been inside their walls and so I didn't miss them. Rathbarry had become my only true home, two hundred years old and beautiful in her fine gray stone, her emerald ivy and crenellated crown. Like me, she'd outlived her original owner and was at the whim and mercy of someone new.

Here she stood, bound by her size to a rock foundation, accustomed to the tiptoe of sunrise over the strand, the soft breezes off the ocean on one side, the gentle bend and creak of the oaks, ash and alder along another. By day the freshening rains cooled her, the sunny afternoons warmed her, and by night the starry skies defined her edges, moonlight painted distinctive shadows, and bits of quartz sparkled in her stones. The daily bustle of humans and beasts rushed and flowed as her breath and blood.

She'd kept her silence as disturbances grew within her. First came the garrison, these rough and ill-mannered clodpates; and now the hammering, sawing, scraping and pounding that rattled her windows and shook her timbers. Next would come the villagers of all sorts that she must accommodate with all of their fuss and brawl. Trouble was coming, and what was to become of Rathbarry? If only she could escape like a nimble bee, small, quick, and carried aloft on the fragrance of flowers.

"No matter, Rathbarry," I whispered, "because you are forever, and they, only temporary."

If indeed trouble were coming and our yard would fill with townspeople, my opportunities for freedom could become as few as the castle's. In the cellar, I secreted myself within a cabinet just large enough to bump my elbows as I shed my skirts and donned a boy's breeks and hooded tunic. Once changed, I blended with shepherd boys guiding the sheep through the main gate, and I darted around the north wall blissfully unnoticed.

The smell of damp hay and fresh manure was swept away by cold mist billowing over the hill. The animals grazed the clumps of green amid the brownish field before me. A half-mile in the distance, a dozen small cottages dotted the stony ridge, simple but beautiful in their way, with whitewashed daub walls, plain wooden doors, a single small window in front, and graying thatch roofs. Intended for the herdsmen and their families or for temporary laborers, most were empty now. To the east, brown and yellow-gold leaves littered the wide fields where corn stacks had been. But the trees, filling the space beyond the ridge and as far as I could see—they were my destination.

Most of these giants were bare as skeletons, their thin, crooked branches reaching upward to the vast blue beyond the mist. Some remained dense and brown with leaves not fallen, and some had great trunks and limbs stained forever green by the moss. Within their realm the tiniest secrets and surprises awaited; and seated upon the strongest boughs, I would capture the vistas for which I'd been sent.

"Take this with you today, my dear." Lady Carey had pressed a small, leather-bound sketchbook into my hand. "I care not where you wander or for how long. Take the day, if you will, but see can you conjure a bit of your father's artistry, and bring me a pretty picture, won't you? A view of the seaside, or a nice landscape. Everyone knows the Dutch invented the art of landscape. Go on with you, but don't let anyone know."

Gladly did I go, and without a moment's delay. But this was something new. She had dropped her pretense of ignorance regarding my disappearances, and now wanted a result from them. Certainly, she'd not have me spend the entire day when the list of chores in the castle was endless, especially in preparation for the new guests. It was not for me to complain or argue, but something mysterious was afoot. Best I should produce something to her liking if I would maintain my freedom.

I'd sketched a few things alongside my father where he apprenticed in a master's work room, but I was just playing then, and Papa had grumbled all the while that he was not allowed to draw or paint as he himself wished, but only could fill in the backgrounds for the master. What if that was because my father lacked the talent? And if he was so gifted, what if no remnant of it was passed into my own fingertips? What if my labors displeased my lady? And turning that thought about, what if my work did please her? Would she then own my little outings by tagging each of them with her expectations? My suspicion settled into a tiny knot that made its home in my belly, and I turned to the task at hand.

A few steps into the trees and the ways narrowed, the tree trunks crowding closer and the brown winter vines guarding their roots. An ancient yew grew as wide as three stout men at its base, and reached as high as ten men standing upon each other's shoulders. The branches were solid and many, with a low division in the trunk where I might easily step—as if the tree waited especially for me, offering a natural ladder to its highest points.

I climbed—the effort wearying but not difficult in my boy's attire—loving the smoothness of the bark, the sweet, woody scent of it. Near the top, a fine formation of limbs cradled me so comfortably I could've sat there for hours like a high princess, gazing across my lands, waiting for my prince who traveled from far beyond the heathered hills. In his embrace I would journey to a castle finer than any had ever seen—its towers rising from a cresting hilltop, shining in the sunlight. If only the mist would clear, I'd see vast distances, even as far as the church spire rising to the heavens.

Just then a flutter of wings broke my reverie and I turned. Upon the highest branches of a birch tree just an arm's reach away, the starlings descended, each black bird claiming its own spindly branch, bright white in the sun's glare. I quickly counted twenty of them, in branches so high the mist fell away, defining their forms against a brilliant field of blue. Then I realized there were hundreds of them filling the treetops well beyond my sight. They appeared black in flight, but these birds wore a splendid rainbow of color, from the purple heather at their necks, sea green at their shoulders, to lapis blue on their bellies. Their beaks were golden, and they were speckled all over as if they wore a king's cloak of ermine. What glorious creatures they were!

Madly I sketched, knowing at any second they could all fly away. I started in the center, with the highest branch. Three birds there, two at the left, another immediately to the right, and then down to a secondary level, six birds close together, then seven more on the next level down. The scene was magnificent if only I could reveal it. If only I had pigments to capture the startling colors. Then, as suddenly as they'd arrived they were gone again, all save one—the straggler—perched to the right of the center branch and watching me with his curious bead eyes.

Mr. Taverner, who made everything Biblical, would have said a black bird signaled desire, meant to warn me that I must resist the Devil's temptation. But the wise women in the village, who listened to ancient spirits, would say instead the bird symbolized courage, unity, and strength in numbers. If it wasn't so, how could they gather in such great flocks and move as if they were a single creature?

"Which is it," I whispered, "desire, or courage?" He started at my voice and leapt into flight. Desire then. Certainly not courage.

For a moment there was silence, the peace absolute. My sketch was unfinished, but I'd improve it once I'd returned to the castle. Until then I would seek a fine pastoral landscape for Lady Carey. I turned in my cradle seat to face west, and knew at once my sketching time had ended. Along the path that connected Rathbarry to the village of Ross, the people were coming—by cart, by horse, and by foot in a caravan that must have spanned half a mile. They were not walking. They were *running*.

4

The Arrival

Rathbarry Castle

I climbed down from my perch and swung from a low branch into a pile of dead leaves, then scrambled toward the path from which I'd come. I rushed through the opening and right into a man coming the opposite direction. He stumbled backward and I fell face first to the ground. Strong hands lifted me from the shoulders and set me right again.

"Jaysus. Yer a fine lookin' lad, all right, but in the good light of the mornin' I'd much prefer the lass in the bonny yellow dress."

"Tynan! What are…" I looked down at my clothes, in disarray and covered with dirt and leaves. What a fool I must have appeared! I jerked the hood over my tangled hair and my heart began to thunder. "What are you doing here?"

"Your Lady Carey sent me after ye."

"But how did you find me here?"

"I spied ye goin' out, and then ye spooked the starlings. Sure ye weren't tryin' ta hide, were ye? Coom now, there's trouble cookin' and we must get ye back inside the castle."

"I could see the villagers from Ross. They're already on their way."

He nodded. "The lads in the tower saw them as well. Sir Arthur is informed. Coom."

He lifted me to his horse as if I were no more than a sack of oats, and swung himself up behind me. "Take a handful of mane if ye needs," he said. He wrapped an arm around my waist. With a kick we galloped over the rise, then slowed as we neared the castle. I came aware of his strong hand, the dark hairs on his forearm, the heat of it, and the rising fumes of human and horse. When he slowed to a walk, I pushed his arm away.

"What on earth have you been doing to raise such a smell on your-self?"

He laughed. "Don' be troubled, lass. I'm muckin' the stalls is all. Giles and Collum are hauling wood fer the structures." He flicked a finger against my hood. "You're not lookin' your finest either, ye know."

I must have looked like a dirty beggar. My cheeks flushed. I could barely breathe by the time he reined up at the castle gate. He handed me down to one of the guards. "Ye take care, now," he said, and trotted off to toward the stables.

I ran to Lady Carey's apartment, wanting only to bury myself in my bed, but Lady Carey sat in her best chair by the window, looking rather odd. She was humming and sorting through her jewelry box. She selected a silver brooch and pinned it to the shoulder of her dress.

"My lady, something is wrong. Something has happened that..."

"Yes, little one." Without looking up, she closed her jewelry box and patted it gently before setting it aside on a table. "Now then. What did you do today? Show me your sketches."

I stared at her. "My...my sketches?"

At last she looked at me. "Goodness, you look a sight! Where is your dress?"

"I must have left it in the kitchen. I'll go..."

"Wait. Before you go, show me what you've done, dear. Your little sketches."

I pulled the sketch book from my breeks and handed it to her. She unwrapped the leather strings and looked at my drawing of the starlings. She glanced at me, furrowed her brow and examined the drawing once more.

"It does show some talent, I suppose. But it isn't what I asked for. It is just a bunch of birds. Anyone could draw a bird. All that time and this is what you have?"

"I..." I what? What should I say?

"We will do much better next time. Go and change, Merel dear. You mustn't look like this when the visitors arrive. Please hurry."

I scrubbed my face and hands and changed into a fresh dress, all the time wondering. What was she about? What difference did it make, the picture I had drawn, when something important was happening? And why did she call them visitors, when to my eyes they were frightened and displaced fugitives? Lady Carey seemed to think we were preparing for a banquet.

There was no time to brush out my hair, so I bound it as best I could and tucked it well beneath a coif. By the time we walked into the courtyard, Sir Arthur stood before the open castle gate, and Mistress Dorothy a few paces behind him on the steps of the keep. She wore a gown the color of port wine, her hands clasped tightly at her waist. She always looked pale, with her fine white skin and long, coal-black hair, but the paleness was doubled by a white lace cap and her lips pressed into a thin line.

In a few moments, the villagers did not arrive so much as they gushed through the gate, some of them wearing only their smocks, and some nearly naked, covering their privates. A wailing young woman cast herself at Sir Arthur's feet, causing him to step back and catch his balance. Behind her came two men bearing a third who was badly wounded, his hands out before him showing several bleeding cuts, and his face and head battered. He could not walk or stand without help.

Sir Arthur shouted to Jenkin, "Collect my physician and have him at once to the cellar with this young man..."

"Nicholas!" the wailing woman cried.

An older woman stepped forward as Nicholas was carried toward the keep. She was thin with coarse gray hair poking out from beneath a felt hat. Her eyes were small and dark and her chin was as pointy as Sir Arthur's beard. Several children came forward and clung to her skirts while others ran to the crying woman, perhaps their mother. "He is Nicholas Cambridge, my son-in-law," the older woman said, "and I am Mistress Coale. He was wounded defending me and my daughter from those despicable Irish scoundrels. They took everything. Everything! And one of them came after me with a bat. I said...I said nothing and those cowards..."

Her daughter glared up at her. "Mother, you said such things that..."

Mistress Coale's eyes flashed and her daughter silenced. Several servants came up behind them and a maid took the old woman's arm to steady her.

"Dorothy, can you..." Sir Arthur gestured to his wife. Mistress Dorothy hurried down the steps, helped the young wife to stand, muttering softly to her, and then led the family into the keep. She paused at the door and called to the laundress. "Agnes, find our supplies of fustian, that these folk may fix something to cover themselves."

Behind them more families pushed through the gates and into the court, most of them carrying no belongings, a few showing injuries, some weeping, all of them looking distressed. The horses were few, the carts fewer, and within the carts more people, but nothing to sustain them; no provisions, no sheep or cattle, no chickens, no corn. I began to count as the people entered. Twenty, forty, seventy. And at last it was one hundred people who had suddenly doubled the occupancy within the castle.

Sir Arthur's face was reddened and puffed, his gaze darting about, from the villagers, to his servants rushing around the court, to the guards, and to the garrison quarters. "Guards! Bring them all inside, into the courtyard quickly, and secure the gate," he shouted. He turned to the people arriving. "Quiet, please! You are here and you are safe. You are all welcome at Rathbarry. I am Sir Arthur Freke, owner of this castle and Commander-in-Chief of His Majesty's garrison here. I and the men of the garrison will see you are housed and protected. Some of you will sleep in the hall tonight, as the new houses we're building for you are not yet ready. Some of you can move into the tents in the garden. Some will be in our servants' quarters; others placed with our residents. Everyone will be accommodated, I assure you. Everyone will have a meal and a place to sleep tonight. Everyone."

The weeping began anew, and some men shouted "Arrah!" Others fell to their knees in grateful prayer. Amid the smell of smoke, manure, sweat and fresh-cut wood, a strange scent filled Rathbarry's court, like sweat but stronger—something bitter and repulsive that invaded every ward— perhaps the scent of fear from the mass of terrified people.

Sir Arthur turned toward the keep where Dorothy waited. She nodded, but her eyes bulged with question. What must they have thought as so many people entered Rathbarry without belongings or provisions? What were they going to do?

"Sir Arthur!" A shout came from behind the crowd, and Thomas Millett, Sir Arthur's groundskeeper, pressed his way forward. Millett was thinner and shorter than Sir Arthur, with a balding pate. His beard was similar to Sir Arthur's, and he frequently placed himself in Sir Arthur's vicinity, making obvious efforts to mimic his master's behaviors. Millett never missed a chance to volunteer for new tasks, perhaps elevating his station by making himself necessary.

"Might I assist you here, sir? I believe, in such circumstance, a bit of military order is required. Shall I set up a register, list our guests by name, family and age, and take note of who will be placed in which establishment? I am perfectly aware of what is available within the castle and what is being constructed. With Mistress Freke's advice I'm certain we will see that all are situated appropriately to their station."

"It will be most appreciated, Mr. Millett. Jenkin!" Sir Arthur called out and gestured toward his house servant. In a few moments a table and chair were set before Millett and an accounts book opened to a clean page.

"Please approach the table," Mr. Millett called to the crowd, "one family at a time."

"And Millett, you will minimize your consultation with Mistress Dorothy. She quite has her hands full as we sort out the evening meal."

"Of course, Sir Arthur."

"Mr. O'Daly!" Sir Arthur shouted across the court toward the stables. I jerked up at the sound of his name, and watched for the sight of him. In seconds, Tynan came through the crowd.

"Aye, sir!"

"I expect it shall be a cold night, and the garden tents will offer little warmth. We will need additional woolens than what we have in store. Take Sarcen, my stallion. He is fastest and shall hasten you to my nearest neighbor, Thomas McMahony. See what comforts the gentleman might be able to spare."

I watched Tynan ride out of the castle on the big black horse and wished I could be with him. A part of me envied him for being of such station that he could ride free from the castle on Sir Arthur's stallion, and at the same time I feared for him, for there could be danger waiting. I bit my lip as the gate closed behind him.

Lady Carey called for me just then and sent me to the cellar kitchen to help wherever needed. Mistress Dorothy was there also, and her bespectacled brother-in-law Thomas just behind her. Instead of a mad scene of utter confusion, all was quiet. The head cook Elinor, the scullery maids, the kitchen boys and house servants strained to hear her trembling voice.

"As I have said, the men of the garrison are accustomed to taking care of themselves. The soldiers have wooden bowls and drinking cups as part of their kit. But our new guests from Ross have arrived without their belongings, and our castle is not well prepared to feed a gathering of this size." She stopped to take a breath. Had it been a happy occasion, well planned and arranged in advance, her cheeks would have glowed with excitement. She was far from panicking, but the strain showed in the grayness of her face, her eyes focusing only on the floor as her mind searched for solutions.

"What we have ready and available we will use to its fullest extent, and be mindful of the size of each portion, to stretch our supplies as they will go." That meant dividing whatever portions of beef that had already been butchered, and then dividing them again and again. Boiled snipe and pickled turkey could be stretched, and hard biscuits would fill in where the fresh bread ran short. Wine would be served to the highest ranking, good ale and cider to those in the great hall, and the cheapest oat brew to the garrison and servants in the courtyard.

"Sir Arthur and all of my family will be served in the dining hall," she continued, "joined by Lady Carey and Mistress Coale and their families. We will use the porcelain, but mind you do not break or chip a single piece of it, or my mother will have your heads. Others will be served in the great hall, and in the court. Use all of the pewter in the great hall, then the earthenware, then whatever trenchers we have stored away. If needs must, we will be washing plates after the first ones dine, and offering them to others. Let no one at any time see a breakdown in our service to them. We will not embarrass Sir Arthur this night."

The cook, Elinor, responded, "Yes, Mistress," but the rest of the kitchen remained silent until Mistress Dorothy and Mr. Thomas ascended the stairs to the great hall. Then the shouting started and I, as usual, was assigned for my size to go digging through the cabinets and storerooms for the trenchers and serving utensils that had long been tucked away.

By the end of the evening I'd completely forgotten to eat. In the courtyard, someone occupied every bench, chair, stump and portion of wall that could be used as seating. I found an uplifted root by one of the plum trees and sat there to wait for Tynan's return. It was long past dark, the torches flickering wildly, and Mr. Millett was still patting people's shoulders as he guided them to their quarters for the night.

A kitchen maid plopped down beside me in her brown homespun skirt and white apron. Long strands of copper hair had escaped from her cap and teased the light with each movement. "I've brought ye somethin'," she said, with a bright smile of good white teeth.

"I'm Jayne," she said. She was Irish, an O'Keeffe, and near my own age. If I had worked beside her, I hadn't noticed—my head ducked inside the cabinets most of the time—and I didn't recognize her face, but I was glad for her company. "I'm Merel," I said, and nothing more. It would be just a matter of time until she heard the whole story from Lady Carey anyway.

She pulled a handkerchief from her skirt pocket and carefully unfolded it. Inside were two chunks of honey cake.

I gaped at them. "Lekker," I whispered. It was a word Papa had used when he was most pleased. How strange that the welcome sight and scent should suddenly restore the word to me, and with it a tiny rush of pleasure.

"Liquor?" Jayne asked.

"Oh no, I mean, good. Thank you!" I took one of the cake pieces and popped it into my mouth. I closed my eyes for a second as the sweetness oozed from the soft spongy cake onto my tongue. How long since I had tasted such a delight?

"I am told to find Lady Carey. I'm to sleep on her floor this night," she said.

And I, with a mouth still full swallowed too quickly and nearly choked on the cake. She laughed, and then I laughed, too. "I live with Lady Carey."

"Oh! Then I say 'lekker' as well, because now I have a friend."

5

Seven Castles

Dunoure Castle, Carbery Barony

Tynan flipped off his cap and tucked it into his coat pocket. To ride out of Rathbarry's gates alone and on Sarcen, Sir Arthur's finest horse, was to know true freedom, if only for a few hours. The chill on his face awakened him. The wind lifting his hair made him feel feral and reckless. And inside, his heart raced and the blood rushed in his ears. He grasped the reins, cool and damp, and his thighs flexed to the thrill of commanding a powerful, gallant beast.

What if he should ride on for miles until the horse grew tired, rest a bit and then ride on to the horizon, never looking back? Never again being ordered about as if he were a dullard? Never again to view those curtain walls as if they were prison walls? Never having to watch the horses being abused by arrogant fools who knew nothing about them? And never having to hold his tongue about it?

He would do it—take this steed and run—except that he had many relations in West Cork who would suffer for his crimes. And Sir Arthur likely had friends and relatives across most of Ireland. He wouldn't get far until one of them, or even the English army, cut him down. He slowed as the way narrowed through a grove of naked birches and vine covered oaks. The salt of the ocean reached his nostrils, and the hiss and sigh of it suggested low tide and calm seas. Rosscarbery Bay was a fine secluded anchorage at times, good for supply ships. But at other times it was a fierce, tumultuous danger.

He put his cap back on as he ducked beneath the branches. Rathbarry did offer shelter and safety, and for a good while he'd known regular meals. He was skilled at his job. If he did go, there were a couple of lads he might miss. And then there was the girl, Merel. Something about her. A tiny lass, for sure, with an odd speech. Pretty, sometimes. Clever, mebbe. It could be worth learning more about her. Her presence certainly made castle life bearable, anaways. So then, he'd stay around, just for now. He'd not mind it so much, truly.

Thomas McMahony's castle was an hour's ride from Rathbarry at the east end of the long strand. Tynan followed a cow path that wound its way across the bluff. It was slow going in places. He was almost upon the castle when the stone tower jutted into view. He rode along the castle wall, past a few sheds and a kitchen garden. The keep was smaller than most, three stories instead of five. He turned in the saddle to look back. From the top of the keep you'd still have a clear view across the bay and be alerted to enemies looking for landfall. The keep must have seen heavy use at times, when seafaring adventurers sought easy plunder or when warring clans clashed over lands and cattle, but its sharp edges were dulled now, stones crumbling in places, and the grounds showing a distinct lack of order.

The gate was open and he rode right up to the big stone steps at the keep. Once, instead of steps there would have been a ladder that could be withdrawn when enemies approached. He dismounted, Sarcen snorting beside him, then climbed to the door and pounded on the thick wooden planks.

The door stuck, creaked, whined and budged, and at last gave way to a crack wide enough for the reddish nose of a young lad to poke through. "What is it?" the lad asked.

"I'll be up from Rathbarry, sent by Sir Arthur Freke himself."

"Oh, aye?"

"Ta see Thomas McMahony, lad."

"I'm Thomas."

Then came a grumble and a shout. The lad was off and the door jerked wide. In his place stood a middle-aged man, thick wild locks half black and half silver, face pale and puffy, knuckles gnarled and red—working man's hands.

"I'll be the Thomas yer after. What is it then?"

"Sir. The villagers of Ross have coom to Rathbarry Castle for shelter, chased from the township by the Irish assumin' ownership there. The folk coom with no belongings. Sir Arthur asks, might ye spare a blanket or two for the cold nights, as we've a hundred souls added to our lodgings."

The man's eyes grew larger, examining Tynan's face from part to part as if he was troubled to see how all the pieces should fit together in such a way. Finally, he shrugged. "Come in. The lad will see to yer horse." He gestured to the boy, who hurried to take Sarcen's reins.

"Careful wi' him, young Thomas, he's Sir Arthur's favorite." Tynan followed Thomas the elder into the wide hall where a warm fire blazed. A single candle burned on an old trestle table. Thomas pointed to a bench.

"Ye'll want to wet your throat while I t'ink this through, what I have and what Sir Arthur needs. Good man, Arthur, but I may be having guests o' my own ta consider afore long. Help yourself."

A fair distance from the candle was a bucket of ale and a few pewter tankards beside it. The bucket sloshed a bit on the table's surface, but Thomas waved it off as no matter. Fine ale, it was. After a few moments, the young lad returned and sat by the hearth to warm his back.

"Now, what is your name, fella?" the father asked.

"I'm Ty. O'Daly." He waited for it, that old reaction that always seemed to come even though it was five and twenty years since his kinsman had shamed the clan O'Daláigh. Once, men would have bowed to him, descending from a clan of beloved bards who sat at the elbow of chieftains, telling tales of Irish heroism in glorious songs and poetry. It took only one to forever damn the clan to hatred: one who took money from the English—and from George Carew, the most hated of all—to flatter their butchery while satirizing and condemning his own countrymen. He was murdered for his betrayal; but every O'Daly still livin' had to fight each day for respect.

McMahony studied Tynan silently, his head tilting slightly left, his eyes narrowed. "Of Aonghus O'Daláigh, would it be?"

Did McMahony yet see the dare in his eyes? He could bare his sharpened skean fast as any man alive. "My uncle, Aengus O'Daly, owns a fine ale house up Skebreen, on the River Ilen. He'll be the only Aengus I know."

McMahony eyed him thoughtfully. A silent moment passed, only the crackle of the fire to be heard. Then he dropped a shoulder, jutted his chin as if pointing toward Rathbarry. "What of the garrison?" he asked.

Tynan nodded. Wise choice. "Aye, sir. Eighty men. Well supplied at present, but little to spare for others. Sir Arthur will likely be orderin' more things to meet the needs of his guests. He'd only be borrowin' from you for a while, so."

"Mmm." McMahony scratched the thick stubble on his chin. "I wonder. This disturbance may take a wee bit longer to resolve than any are t'inkin'."

"Is it so?"

"A man must t'ink with careful deliberation. There is kindness, and there is duty. There is friendship, and there is honor. Do ye know who my guest is to be, man?"

"No, sir."

"Do ye know of the seven castles, then?"

"I know of many castles, sir, but of seven linked together in some way? I do not," Tynan said.

"It's because ye're young, and livin' among the English. But the Irish. They do not forget. Isn't that so, Thomas. Are ye listenin'?"

"Aye, Da."

"Good. Run out to the court and bring me a handful of pebbles. Go on, and ye'll hear the tale as soon as ye return." A sliver of daylight brightened the hall for a moment as the boy went outside. McMahony rose from his chair to stoke the fire and add another log, sending bright amber sparks into the chimney. He stopped to refill his own tankard, eyeing the spill of ale Tynan had left, and sat down.

"I'll tell ye who's comin', but first, ye must know the lay o' the land," McMahony began. "The lad must know it as well."

Thomas returned and emptied a fist full of pebbles and sand into his father's hand. "Aye, that's fine. Here now, come and sit." Thomas sat on the bench at Tynan's side. McMahony moved his chair closer to the ale bucket.

"Ireland has always been troubled by invaders, no?" McMahony said. "The Milesians. The Romans who had no stomach for it. The Normans. The English. And always, we've been plagued by pirates, mostly from Algeria. You know where that is lad?"

"Aye, Da."

"Ireland has only merchant ships, and a few pirate vessels mostly along the west coast. So, we make a fine target, and this has long been known. Many years ago, the O'Cowig family built a string of castles—'duns' we called them. Outposts with watch towers."

He placed a finger in the spilt ale, drawing it back toward himself in two places, until the puddle resembled a dog's head, lop-eared on the left, pointy-eared on the right. "Here is Rosscarbery Bay." He pointed to the center of the puddle, near the lopped ear. "And over here, Clonakilty Bay." He tapped his finger in the tall, pointy ear.

"See how the land closes in and the bay narrows, just like a funnel leading ships right into our core? 'Tis like an open door, isna?" he asked his son. "If we're not watching out, the Algerian could sail right up into our belly."

"Yes, sir." Young Thomas's eyes widened.

"So, the O'Cowigs built the first castle here." He placed a pebble at the right edge of the lopped ear. "This is Dunoure, where we sit today, to keep watch and send out alarums so the sorry buggars can't beach their boats and march inland, takin' our wealth and killin' bairns and such. The tower was built in a day, folk have said, and I believe it."

"Killing bairns?" Thomas asked.

His father nodded. "Like I told ye. Next is Dundeady, a larger, stronger castle jutting out into the sea on Galley Head. Together with Dunowen on the opposite shore, these two duns defend Dirk Bay, and Red Strand in its middle—another place for beachin' a boat. Then east and inside the great funnel of Clonakilty Bay," he moved his finger to the middle of the pointy ear, "ye have Dunnycove and Duneen castles on the western shore, Dungorley and Dunworley on the east side." He placed a pebble for each one, creating a crownlike crescent around the puddle of ale that reflected the firelight like a set of pearl beads. "How many is that, Thomas?"

"Seven."

"Again?"

"Seven," Thomas repeated.

"Exactly so. They are watchtowers, and when needs be, fire beacons. They didn't save the O'Cowigs, who were wiped out by the Normans, but they were the beginning of stronger defenses for this land. The castles passed to the O'Driscolls, then the O'Mahonys, and then the MacCarthys.

"But, if that's so, how come we're here, Da? And not the MacCarthys?"

Thomas asked.

"We pay tribute to the MacCarthys for the privilege. Since the Desmond wars, all the Irish of Munster have suffered. Castles were taken, sold, burned and rebuilt, or leased. Ye know it yerself, Ty. Even Rathbarry. The Earl of Barrymore, David Barry, who has squandered everything his murdering father ever gave him, sold it just a year ago to Sir Arthur, who has made a fine go of it."

"Aye, Sir Arthur's done well. 'Tis a good, working castle." Tynan said.

"So, comes the situation we face presently," McMahony continued, "while the English are at war with the Scots. The Lord Deputy Thomas Wentworth with his greed and his plantations, was sent home from Dublin and dispatched to hell by Parliament. Good riddance, I say, but it means the English hold on Ireland has slipped. It's time, some say, to take back our lands, support the king against the corrupt Puritan Parliament, and protect the Catholic Church."

McMahony paused and looked into the eyes of Tynan and then Thomas. "A rising spreads across the land. With armies behind them, clan chiefs from north to south are joining forces, coming for what's theirs by right and heritage. D'ye see?"

"I know of the rising," Tynan said. "It failed in Dublin, and that's a far piece from here. Some lads have taken the village of Ross. You say it's the MacCarthys. What do the seven castles have to do with it?"

McMahony turned his head to the right and gave a sly look from his widened left eye. "I told ye I had a guest comin'. Well it's none other than Teige-an-Duna MacCarthy. The English call him Teige O'Downe, for they can't be bothered to pronounce anathin' resembling Irish. These castles belong to 'im, and Rathbarry as well, I expect."

With a handful of sand remaining, he cast it across the puddle of ale and thumped his fist on the table. "He is comin', lad. He and his men, for a war to shake the land. Should you stand on a mountain top and face each direction, everything ye see, every hill, valley and lough that is Ireland—they mean to take it all."

Tynan's breath caught in his throat at the enormity of McMahony's statement. A few skirmishes here and there, that's all Tynan had expected, and all that had happened in recent years despite the cruelty toward Catholics, the land takings, the lies, swindles and displacements of Irish people. But this would mean a full-on war. It might be the first time ever the clans had come together in such a way. The English had succeeded in years past by pitting one clan against the other, promising rewards of wealth and land but seldom delivering. The expulsion of the English from Ross was only a small part of a vast whole. If what McMahony said was true, if the clans could fight as one, what a deadly force they'd make.

Tynan clenched his jaw as his mind worked. How can it be, when the evidence is before you—a hundred people stripped of their belongings and wailing in your ears—and yet you don't comprehend that each day will not be like every other, and life has changed in a profound way? Something stirred in his gut that hadn't been there before. "I see your dilemma, sir," he said. "A prince cooms, and his men wi' him. Ye must be clear. Your friend may be important to ye, but your fealty is immortal. It is well. I'll take nothing from you."

"On the contrary," McMahony said. "Take you plenty for Rathbarry. I'll sort it and our prince still will be well served. The Irish have known lack and hardship from the cradle. It only makes our kind stronger."

6

Humans and Beasts

Rathbarry Castle

As dusk darkened to night, I heaved a sigh of relief when the chains on the castle gate rattled and clanked. The guards released the lock, slowly swinging the broad doors wide. Ty returned, and the gates closed to seal him in safely. He rode into court like a champion knight on the black stallion, pulling behind him a litter with bundles strapped upon it. I patted Jayne's hand. "You do have a friend, and it also looks like you'll have a blanket. We'll fix you a pallet to sleep on."

"Merel, who was the fella on the horse?"

"Tynan O'Daly. Marshal of the stables." My gaze fixed on his back as he rode forward, dismounted, and waited for Sir Arthur to approach. Jayne poked me with an elbow and gave me a wide grin.

"Well?" I said. "Didje see him?"

"Oh, aye, I did, and I see as well a lass who's completely besotted."

"I'm not!" I said, but then I smiled. Of course, I was. "Come, let's get a little closer, see if we can hear what's said." We moved toward the castle steps as if we were returning to the kitchen.

"You've done well, O'Daly, though I'd have hoped you'd return a bit earlier. Some of the folk have already bedded down," Sir Arthur said.

"Aye, sir. Mr. McMahony was a bit of a storyteller, but generous. There's no' enough for everyone, but there's a good supply of blankets, canvas and such. There's even a barrel of fine ale."

Sir Arthur waved a hand and stable boys ran out to unhitch the stallion and start unstrapping the load. People in the court moved closer, hoping to get first pickings. "Millett!" he shouted. "See to the fair distribution of this, will you, and have the ale stored with my others." Millett started counting blankets. Sir Arthur took Tynan's elbow, led him away from the others and nearer to the keep and to where Jayne and I sat, hidden from view on the steps down to the cellar.

"Was there news, O'Daly? Did he tell you anything?" Sir Arthur had shown great composure and strength all afternoon as his servants slowly accommodated and fed all the villagers and their families. But his voice sounded tight, infused with anxiety.

"Aye, sir," Tynan said. "He's to be visited himself soon, by O'Downe and some of his men. He said O'Downe has a grand plan to take this castle and seven more besides."

"I thought as much. His clan once owned this barony, but that was many years ago. In such a plan, Rathbarry would be his greatest prize. He thinks he can overpower us and the army will send no relief, but he's a fool to try. I'll get word to Bandon. They'll send more troops and together we will crush him."

Sir Arthur ran up the castle steps, and when I peeked out, Ty was gone also. We asked Mr. Millett for a blanket, and then crossed the court to Lady Carey's apartment, which I was starting to appreciate for its proximity to the castle gate. Without appearing to do so, I could easily watch the comings and goings and overhear conversations. When we entered, the lady was at her card table, stacking and restacking her favorite gaming cards.

"My lady," I said, "we are visited by Jayne, one of the kitchen servants, who was assigned to sleep here with us tonight."

"Oh no," Jayne said. "I'm not a kitchen servant. I'm a chambermaid to Mistress Coale, but as she has no chamber at present, I was sent to work in the kitchen for today. And I'm sent to you, my lady, if you'll have me."

A kitchen maid would have been several positions below me. As a companion, I held the highest position to Lady Carey. I was her novelty and her pet as well as her servant. Since moving from the main castle to her apartment, I also gained the responsibilities of a lady's maid, helping her dress, carrying her messages, and so forth. Jayne being a chambermaid meant she was closer to my rank and more acceptable to Lady Carey who continued looking at her cards. "Who has made this assignment, dear?"

"Mr. Millett, my lady," I said.

"He did not consult with me. I shall speak to him on the morrow." She pushed her cards aside. "Let's have a look, then."

I gave Jayne a bit of a shove and she moved forward, offering a slight curtsey.

Lady Carey raised her brows and smiled. "Well, you're quite presentable, I should say, and a good bit taller than my Merel. I shall ask you to reach the boxes on top of my cupboard." A flicker of jealousy crossed my heart. Jayne was beautiful. She was tall. She could do things for Lady Carey that I could not, and she had probably learned things I'd failed to learn because I was always slipping away from my duties. What if Lady Carey should prefer her to me? If I lost my position with her, what would become of me? I watched Jayne as she started for the cupboard.

"Yes, right away, my lady," she said.

"No, not now, but when I need them. There is an old quilt in the bottom drawer that you may use for your pallet. You'll sleep next to Merel at the foot of my bed. How pleasant to have two maids tonight to prepare my gown and turn down my bed linens."

Jayne fixed her pallet, humming softly the entire time, even though she'd been displaced from her home and would have to sleep in her clothes. She unpinned her hair and it fell to her hips in long copper tresses, thick and silky like a horse's tail. She had no pillow, so she shrugged, wadded up her coif and tucked it beneath her cheek. How easily she adapted to wherever she fell.

"You are happy, Jayne?" I whispered.

She smiled. "I am safe, my belly full, I have a new friend, Mistress Coale is not screamin' in my ear, and...you'll keep a secret?"

"Of course, I will."

"I'm proud of me Irish lads, standin' up for themselves. My brother's with them."

I smiled and pressed a finger to my lips. We put our heads together and tried not to laugh out loud when Lady Carey snuffled and snorted, but before long Jayne was snoring as well. I didn't mind. Rather, it was comforting. My jealousy softened to an admiration. I wished I could be as happy and lovely as she, to be just as comfortable with a coif for a pillow, to welcome comforts but not expect them. I gently lifted her head and slipped my own soft pillow beneath it. I had never had a friend before. I swelled with something I'd not felt in many years. An empty ache often kept me awake when I lay my head to sleep, and I missed my mother. This night the emptiness filled with a soft, willowy sweetness. Sleep came easily, without ghosts.

The next few days hummed by in a dizzy spin, a disturbed beehive of frenzied construction and constant movement of men and materials, humans and beasts. Jayne returned to the kitchen where Elinor and her helpers struggled with the greatest challenge to the castle so far, of feeding the people with winter stores meant to last until spring, but for half as many mouths.

Sir Arthur invited Mistress Dorothy for a stroll through the garden, perhaps intending to calm his wife by showing her the progress being made to house the villagers. His sisters and Lady Carey joined them, and I followed behind. The workers were near the north wall, completing the makeshift houses one by one. As we viewed them from a distance, the houses resembled an attractive miniature village, though they were unpainted daub amid the strong scent of fresh cut wood.

We might have stopped where we were and turned back to avoid the clutter cast about where the men still labored, but Sir Arthur pushed on down the lane. Infants cried behind the walls we passed while children played in the dirt and mothers and nurses sat on scraped ground beside them, faces sagging with despair. They'd lost everything: clothing, kitchen utensils, furniture, swaddling clothes or toys for the children, and even the combs for their hair. And all of the houses were filling up, and all would not be enough. Sir Arthur's sisters Ann and Mary turned back toward the castle while the rest of us approached Mistress Coale, who required two houses: one for her family and another for her servants, and both were overcrowded.

Nicholas Cambridge stepped from one house, his hands still partly bandaged and cuts on his face darkly scabbed. Mistress Dorothy's shoulders rose and stiffened like a cat arching in alert.

"Sir Arthur!" Nicholas called in greeting. He bowed to Mistress Dorothy and Lady Carey. "Please forgive my appearance. I must thank you again for your sheltering us here, and for your physician's good attention to my injuries."

"You are well, I trust?" Sir Arthur asked.

"Healing swiftly, and grateful for a roof above our heads."

"We are grateful to God."

"Truly. Most truly, sir. But my family does struggle and suffer, lacking the most basic of things that were so much a part of our daily lives."

"May God comfort you," Mistress Dorothy said, her voice high and dismissive, as if to forestall any attempt to ask for more.

"Thank you, Mistress." Nicholas said. He offered her a slight bow and stepped closer to Sir Arthur. "Sir, if you will forgive me. Word is passing among the villagers here. I am not certain of the source, but we believe the Irish rebels have stored all of our goods in the Church of Ross...Sir."

I could see only Sir Arthur's back, but his shoulders lifted as Mistress Dorothy's had done. "You are certain?" he asked.

"I've no way to confirm it, sir, without going there myself, but I'd think it a good probability. Apart from the mill, the church is the only proper building in the village to allow the space, you see. Might there be a way to...somehow without being discovered, to..."

"There is considerable risk to what you are suggesting, Nicholas. We would not have you injured further. I will see what might be done. Be at peace with your family while I look into it, won't you? Leave it with me."

Instead of turning back toward the keep we continued on, picking through the sawdust until we reached the end of the lane where the soldiers hammered together a wooden frame. Mr. Millett was observing the quality of work. Sir Arthur called him near, pulled a square sealed letter from his doublet, and pressed it into Mr. Millett's palm.

"As soon as you can," he said in a tempered voice, "I want you to take this letter to our friend in Clonakilty. Have him send it by trusted messenger to Sir William Hull, at the militia headquarters at Bandon. Wait for a reply and return to me quickly. I have news of greater trouble brewing across the land, worse than what we have at Ross. At the same time, I've good reason to suspect the rebel rogues steal my sheep during the night. I shall soon have a count. I'll not have them feeding on my sheep while they terrorize our people. I'll not stand for it. We'll fight them if needs must. I'll require Hull's promise of relief from the Bandon garrison, should need arise."

Mr. Millett's bushy brows arched and then creased with concern. "I'll go at once, sir." He bowed to Sir Arthur, nodded to the ladies, and was off toward the stables without even a parting word to his workers.

We returned to the castle, Sir Arthur pointing out the garden plots that had been prepared for spring vegetables, as if nothing more had been said. But surely Mistress Dorothy and Lady Carey had heard everything, as I had. The fear and frailty showed in Mistress Dorothy's face, and Lady Carey's hands trembled. Why do men treat women as if they are horses, with large ears but little understanding?

A few days later I'd nearly forgotten about Mr. Millett, so busy were we with the needs within the castle. Then one evening when the court was full of people finishing their repast, a silvery dusk claimed the castle and violent shouting overtook the chatter in the yard. The guards called to each other and the gate was opened. Mr. Millett rode in, slid from his saddle and collapsed in the middle of the court.

7

Hellkite

Rathbarry Castle

Jayne and I got to him first, and sat him up. His head was bleeding. Sir Arthur was soon beside us, shouting for his physician, and Ty held the reins of the horse.

"What is it, Millett? What has happened," Sir Arthur asked.

Mr. Millett leaned upon us until he managed to get control of his feet. "Sir, I..." He winced with pain, squeezing his eyes shut for a few seconds, then continued. "I was returning from an errand, you know, and as I neared the castle I came upon two of those rogues driving four of your sheep. I chased after them. I had a half-pike with me, and I ran one of them through. I had to leave it with him, for I couldn't draw it out, sir. Then the other one, he..."

"The other one what?" Sir Arthur shouted.

"He hit me over the head sir, with a bat. If I'd fallen they'd have killed me, but I kicked the horse to run, and returned to Rathbarry posthaste. For help, sir. We must go after them."

Sir Arthur shook his head. "You'll be staying here. You've taken quite a blow." He started shouting names until six or seven garrison men reported, mounted, and rode out from the castle. Thomas and the physician helped Millett into the hall.

"Everyone, go on to your houses and your beds. Mr. Millett will be tended, and you may rest easy that our soldiers will dispose of any trouble. You are safe this night." He turned to Jayne and me. "Thank you for helping. Off with you, to your beds, and speak no more of it."

But we could speak of nothing else and could hardly stop talking at all. We helped Lady Carey to her bed, and the instant she began to snore we crawled to the door and let ourselves out into the court.

"Did you see Millett's face? He looked as bright as an overripe turnip!" I said.

"And a bloody one at that. Who'd have imagined the man could do such a thing? He's a clerk, hardly a soldier. Why didn't he come for help before he piked a man and got hisself clubbed?" Jayne said.

"I wonder if the fellow died?"

"Died? For drivin' off sheep? Jaysus! It's somethin' every lad in Ireland does to show he's brave and ta show he's come a man. He drives off a ram from one fella's land, and next time the other lad goes over and he's after bringin' it back. It's just a big game! Legally, I s'pose he could be whipped or fined. But not killed."

"Those gents riding out didn't look very playful. They looked fierce."

"No, you're right about that. It's turned, somehow."

"I wish we could see what is happening. They couldn't be far off."

The moon was nearly full and I was certain if we climbed to the north battlement, we'd be able to see clear across the land. The only way up was by the spiral stairs in each of the towers. "The closest tower in the northeast corner has two guards," I said. "The second, near the gate, has the cannon and at least three men there. We'll have to creep through the garden ward to the northwest tower. Maybe it will be unguarded, or maybe we'll find just one guard asleep and we can try to slip past him."

"Asleep? Are ye kiddin'? Every lad in the castle is wide awake."

We looked at each other with no question whether we were going, only how quickly could we get there. Slipping through the garden ward was easier than I expected, as folk were about their own business. It wasn't unusual to see a couple of maids in the garden, maybe collecting herbs for the morrow under the bright moon. We hurried to the tower stair.

"Keep watch while I see if anyone's at the top."

"Let me go first," Jayne said.

"No, I'm much smaller and can race up there like a stoat. Just wait."

Jayne started to giggle and I pressed my hand over her mouth. "Don't start or we won't be able to stop."

I crept slowly up. Moonlight reflected from the bottom and filtered down from the top to light most of the stairway, but a torch in the middle wasn't lit and I had to feel my way along. The last five steps were easy but, before I reached the top, the heavy boots of an infantry soldier passed before me as he paced, and a long musket leaned against the wall. I crept back down.

"It's no good, the guard is there, wide awake, and the next tower is behind the garrison camp, by the postern gate. We'll never get through there without being seen. "

Jayne turned in the direction of the garrison. A fire burned in a pit and several soldiers stood beside it or sat on stools, drinking their oat brew and looking like pale statues under the moonglow. "Ah, now, we won't be discouraged that easily, so. I know just what to do. Stay close behind me, as if ye were my shadow. Then, when I make myself as wide as I can and none can see past me, run for the gate."

"Jayne!"

"I'm no' kiddin'. Ye'll see! It will be fine, and they'll love it."

She walked toward their fire with a casual gait, as if she were just off for an evening stroll. I stayed close as she'd asked. Jayne was tall enough to hide me. She was thin, and not voluptuous by most measures, but her face was pretty and her smile enchanting. When we neared the soldiers they turned to stare and were, it seemed, either embarrassed or confused by her presence.

"Greetings, lads," Jayne said. "I see ye're warmin' yerselves and havin' a bit o' entertainment on this lovely night."

"Yes, ma'am," someone said, "and mebbe we'll be having a bit more!" Several of the men started laughing and Jayne spoke up.

"Well lads, I'm in the service of our dear Lady Coale, in a good house just 'round the bend. In gratitude for the speed and fine workmanship of the shelter ye built for us, I wondered would ye care for a song?"

Brilliant. The lustiest soldier among them wouldn't touch her now, knowing she was employed by nobility. He'd surely get hanged for it. A cheer came from some of the lads and she laughed her contagious cackle. She gave them a quick bow, but not so deep as to expose me.

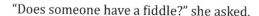

"Does someone have a fiddle?" she asked.

"No ma'am," one of them said, "'fraid not, we've just our hearty selves.

Ah, it's a pity, no fiddle. So then, ye hearty lads can clap out a beat wi' me. I'll begin, shall I? Don't be shy." She started clapping a steady beat until the men around the fire joined in and started elbowing each other. At last they achieved a bit of unity. She began to sing, her voice loud, low and clear.

I was told by my aunt,
I was told by my mother
That going to a weddin'
Is the makings of another.
And if this be so then
I'll go without a biddin',
Oh kind providence
Won't you send me to a weddin'
And it's oh dear me! How will it be,
If I die an old maid in the garret?

She lifted her skirt out wide to her right side, and leaned her face far to the left as if weeping on her forearm in despair, and that was my moment. From behind her skirt I darted around a tent that was nearest to the castle wall.

Now there's my sister Jean,
She's not handsome or good-lookin'
Scarcely sixteen
And a fella she was courtin'
Now she's twenty-four
With a son and a daughter,
Here am I at forty-four
And I've never had an offer!
And it's oh dear me! How will it be,
If I die an old maid in the garret?

Jayne finished the second verse and danced a twirl while the fellas clapped all the harder. I ran along the wall behind a row of tents and to the tower stair. The soldiers were singing with her on the chorus, and I climbed slowly up. I reached the top, fully exposed by the moonlight and as I'd hoped, the tower was unguarded because the bog behind the wall made it almost inaccessible. The worry for me remained, for how would Jayne escape the attention of those men, and then get to the tower? I peered over the battlement to see her cleverly dancing toward the opposite end of the fire pit. She'd find a way, and I'd never again doubt her.

I can cook and I can sew,
I can keep the house right tidy,
Rise up in the morning
And get the breakfast ready,
There's nothing in this wide world
That makes my heart so cheery
As a wee fat man to call me
His own dearie!
And it's oh dear me! How will it be,
If I die an old maid in the garret?

She finished the verse with a grand curtsey, the men clapping and stomping their boots, and shouting cheers. Another, another! They called as she stepped backward from the gathering.

"Ah, thank you gents! Wasn't it fun? Sorry, that's the only song I know!" She turned and ran. A couple of the lads half-heartedly chased after her. "I'll marry you! I will!" one of them shouted. But she disappeared into the shadows and they came tromping back to the fire amid jeers that they'd never catch a crippled old lady in the broad light of day, and so might have to marry each other.

I waited for her at the bottom step and she came, gasping for breath. We grasped each other for a moment, sure we would die of laughter if we held it in one more second. But then we climbed the tower, quick and eager as barn mice. We ran along the western wall and collapsed against it about halfway toward the north end, stopping there so as not to alert the pacing guard in the next tower.

The moon illuminated the entire field by the castle but no one moved, no one in any direction, until several minutes later when two horsemen came over the rise heading back toward the castle. We waited, hoping to see a chase or a capture. Even the sheep running from the men. But all had gone quiet. Not a call, not a cry, not the croak of a toad from the pond, nor even the hoot of an owl from the forest.

A bit disappointed, we crept back down the winding stair until we reached the opening and glanced out into the light. "Looks clear," I said, and stepped down to the court with Jayne right behind me. Then a strong hand grabbed my shoulder.

"And where would you ladies be off to?"

My heart leapt as if it would leave my body altogether, and Jayne stifled a yelp, but at once I knew it was Ty. I turned.

"What are you doing here?" I whispered, as low as I could under the heaving of my breath.

"Didje not see me there by the fire, drinkin' wi' the lads? I saw the whole show, and a fine one at that, but I'm not foolish enough ta t'ink ye weren't up ta something. And I was right, for here ye are."

"We were just trying to see the…" I started.

"Oh, aye, ye were just trying. Ye realize this is an English army garrison, aye? Have ye lost yer senses? Some o' these lads have no morals at all. Coom now, I'll get ye outa here before an officer spies ye. God only knows what Sir Arthur would do wi' ye, did he see. Get behind me now."

I grinned at Jayne and she clasped her hand over her mouth to keep from laughing. He led us through a back door of the stables, the air thick with the smell of hay, manure and piss, and then to the front door nearest the keep and the main gate. He stopped, barely creaking the hinges as he pushed it just wide enough to see out. "Wait a bit," he whispered. "someone's passin'." He looked down at me and smiled. A silver band of light crossed his forehead like a beacon and a rush of blood flushed my cheeks. I prayed in the darkness he could not see it. He tugged a lock of my hair. "Ye're a little hellkite, aren't ye?"

"What's that?" I asked.

He shook his head and peered out the door, and then pushed it wide. "Go, the both of ye, and hurry. I hear the riders coomin' toward the gate."

We ran across the courtyard to Lady Carey's apartment and ducked inside as quiet as spirits, but we kept the door ajar to hear what the men said when they arrived. Sure enough, in minutes the chains rattled and the big gates swung wide. The rest of the soldiers returned and Sir Arthur came out of the keep to meet them.

"We chased after them a good ways, sir," one of the lead soldiers said. "We fired on them. I think we might have hit one of them, but in truth we lost them. If we ride out again at daylight, take Mr. Millett along, I'm sure we'll track them down."

"All right," Sir Arthur replied. He stood with hands on hips as the men dismounted. He turned left. Then right. Then around to face the keep. Then back to watch the men as they led the horses to the stables, then he stared at the ground, shifting his weight from one leg to the other. "All right, then. All right." He stood until he was alone, and then slowly climbed the steps to the keep.

Before dawn the slam and clank of the gate awakened me. The men rode out and then the guards shouted from tower to tower as the riders passed. It would be midday before they returned, and then we'd hear words of a different tenor.

8

Messages

Rathbarry Castle

When the party of riders returned from the morning search, I had just come from an outing to the lake outside the western wall where I searched for sage leaves or rosemary. I'd found only a few sprouts, the season not yet ready to reveal its treasures, but a far more exciting discovery was a passage out of the castle I hadn't seen before.

I'd searched from the postern gate to the southeast tower, and just as was turning back I heard one of the guards step onto a flat limestone ledge I'd not noticed before—a small expanse between the castle wall and the edge of Sir Arthur's lake. He splashed his urine from one end of it to the other, straightened his breeks, then opened a small wooden shutter mostly hidden behind a patch of tall weeds. He disappeared into the tower. A sudden spark of joy pricked me and I ran for the ledge.

I parted the weeds, opened the shutter as the guard had done, and found a narrow stair spiraling up. A light just a few steps up suggested an opening. I climbed as quietly as I could so as not to draw the guard's attention, and came to the tower entrance to the court, the plum orchard right in front of me. I went back down to look at the shutter. It was large enough for crates, barrels or sacks to be passed, but it was not the full height of a door. What had this been used for? Facing the lake and the shore, had it once been a place where small boats delivered supplies from ships anchored in the bay? Perhaps over the centuries the shoreline had receded too far from the castle, leaving the small lake as its only remnant, and rendering the shutter useless.

A little triumphant thrill stirred my blood. I could find many uses for such an opening. Truly I would chafe until I could use the passage again. I'd discovered an extraordinary treasure, but no one could know. No one, except maybe Jayne.

Just then came the sound of the riders returning. I ran from the tower to wait by kitchen steps.

Mr. Millett was at their lead, their cheeks raw from the cold wind in their faces. The horses were lathered and some of them muddied. The court filled with their energy and the smell of earth, the rustle and creak of leather, the clop of hooves, and grunting as the men dismounted.

Mr. Millett stomped his boots on the stones, and then approached Sir Arthur. He bowed his head in greeting and offered him the half pike he'd mentioned the day before. "We rode most of the way to Ross, which must be their base camp, sir, but we found them. One man was down among the yellow furze, already dead from a musket ball. One of our men found his target last night."

Sir Arthur said nothing, his face paling. He took the half pike and examined it. "Blood?"

"Yes sir," Millett said. "We discovered the other lad a bit further on, in the bog closer to Ross. He was yet alive, and had managed to pull the pike from his wound. It must have taken all his strength, and painful at that. He was bad off, couldn't rise from the ground. We questioned him, as to why he was driving your sheep, where he was going, who had sent him, and who was his leader. But he had no words for us, sir."

"I see. And, where is he? Bring him in."

"Ah, no, sir. We did not bring him. He'd nothing to say, no information to offer. So we killed him where he lay."

"You killed him?"

"Over the head, sir." Millett made a striking motion. "With the half pike. He was nearly dead already. I'd be surprised if he'd have lasted the remainder of the day."

Sir Arthur threw the half pike to the ground. "And so, two men are dead."

Millett's confidence faded. "Sir, as I say, he was nearly dead. It may have been a mercy."

"And the bodies are left on the field."

"Yes, sir," Millett said. "Their own folk can bury them."

Sir Arthur seemed to sway, and I ran toward him. If I couldn't catch him, at least if he toppled I'd break his fall. But he shot me a harsh look and his face flashed from white to dark crimson. I backed away. His spine stiffened and his shoulders drew back.

"Hear me, all of you. On this search today, I expected you to take prisoners if you found them. I issued no order for killing. You have done a service this morning. You've sent a warning to others who might come for our sheep or cattle, of where their fate will lie. But you have also done is this: you have committed the first act of war in this conflict here in Carbery. Yes, it is part of a rising all across the land, but here in this barony, you have made the first killing. They will say that we, of Rathbarry Castle, have started this war." He paused, looking at each man in turn, and then at Millett. "Dismissed."

"I...ah...Sir Arthur, if you please."

"Millett."

"I do...I do have one more, ah..." He reached into his doublet to retrieve a folded, sealed letter. "In the midst of late events, I had forgotten to give you this message. From Sir William Hull of Bandon."

"Forgotten?" Sir Arthur opened the letter immediately, read it and nodded. "Take your rest this afternoon, Millett. Perhaps that is what's required to restore your memory. It's the message I've been waiting for, from Sir William Hull. On the morrow you will prepare. In two days' time we are to meet a Captain Beecher and his ensign, Hungerford, who will be leading a company of the Bandonian troops. Mr. O'Daly should accompany us and rig pack horses for the return. If our first message to these rogues has not been clear, the Irish at Ross are soon to receive another."

9

The Rumor

Town of Ross, Carbery Barony

Ty shifted in his saddle, not wanting any part of what was about to happen, nor could he decline or turn away without losing his position and his living. Never trained as a soldier, he'd be restricted to collecting what goods they hoped to find—goods that had belonged to the villagers at Rathbarry. Well be it, for their needs were great, but to take from one and give to another would always leave someone without. Whoever resided in Ross, and whatever their deeds, they were of his island, if not of his clan.

The two forces met at mid-morning by the bog just east of Ross. Sir Arthur shook hands with Captain Edward Beecher, leader of the Bandonian troops. Beecher was broad and solid, though not fat. He seemed a man of some wealth in his fine leather doublet and a wide-collared cape. Behind him came sixty mounted soldiers looking smart in broad brim hats, dark coats, and spurred boots. Sir Arthur's seven cavalrymen and eleven foot soldiers all wore high crown hats and dark green woolen doublets with badges sewn on by the household seamstresses to indicate Sir Arthur's garrison.

Tynan's own attire changed not a thread for the occasion: the same dingy brown doublet and breeks he wore one day to the next. He would blend with the dim surroundings, the skies as dull and dark as Ensign Hungerford's tarnished breastplate. The soldiers' movements were likewise dull and heavy. The horses twitched uneasily, already worked by the distance traveled from Clonakilty. Tynan maneuvered his mount close behind the ensign to hear Sir Arthur's direction, leaving behind him his two stable helpers, Giles and Collum, and pack horses carrying rope and other supplies.

Sir Arthur sat tall upon his stallion, commanding attention. "The peaceful village of Ross has been forcibly taken from its rightful owners, the English undertakers—the settlers to whom the king has granted the lands," Sir Arthur began. "Irish rogues have cruelly stripped these gentle people of their goods, clothing, stores and other material possessions. Our mission today is not revenge. This is not an act of war, it is not a battle, and we will settle the dispute of the village habitation according to the law, not according to the sword." He paused, perhaps allowing his words to sink into the minds of the soldiers whose hands already grasped their hilts and muskets.

"Today we've come to seek out all of those possessions, that we may restore them to their rightful owners. I've heard the rumor," he continued, "that the goods of which I speak are stored in the Church of Ross. The church backs up to the inlet, among a dense copse of trees. We shall find it on our right side as we approach the town square. With good fortune, we'll find the rumor true and take everything, everything, from the church back to Rathbarry.

"Should the rumor prove false, we shall proceed into the village. From the town square, the streets extend in all directions and up the hillside. We will divide into four companies in the most orderly manner, as you would on the parade field, and then each company will search a quadrant of the town and seize as needs must until we have recovered what we came for. Those rogues who resist will be imprisoned. Our purpose thereafter will be a show of force without bloodshed. Let us not strike the first blow, nor fire the first shot. Am I understood!"

A demand, not a question. "Understood, sir," Captain Beecher said on behalf of the troops. "We are ready."

"We proceed in silence to the church, not to alarm those who might guard it," Sir Arthur said. He turned his horse in the direction of the village, and moved out.

Far from silent, the troops created a rumble like distant thunder as they approached the church, the horses kicking up dirt and dung to mix with the northerly wind. Looking left and right and amongst the trees, Tynan searched for people observing their approach. Only when they neared the church entrance did he spy the first two bare-headed men in dark clothing standing beside a small outbuilding. They held no weapons, and made no attempt to hide, but openly watched in silence the troops that halted in the churchyard.

The building was narrow, but stretching long toward the inlet with the transept and chancel at the far end. The walls were gray stone, the roof of slate, and on the front entrance a wood framed shelter for members of the congregation to shake off the rain before entering the nave. It appeared quite ordinary and peaceful, but any birdsong that may have filled the trees had silenced, and tension grew all around them, some horses rearing their heads, and others groaning against their restraint.

The cavalry encircled the church while two infantrymen bounded up the steps to the entrance. Not bothering to test the latch, they used an iron bar to open the double doors and then shouldered them wide. Several more soldiers ran into the church. One stepped out and reported something, then Sir Arthur and Captain Beecher dismounted and followed him back inside. In a moment Beecher returned to his horse, and Sir Arthur descended the steps and signaled to Tynan.

"Aye, sir?"

"Sacks of barley and some malt, nothing more. Have your boys collect it. All of it."

Tynan bowed and returned to his horse.

Sir Arthur called out to the troops, "Six men are to guard while the goods from the church are secured. The rumor is false." He paused for a moment, the hue of his face slowly shifting from natural to blood red, either reacting in anger to the findings in the church, or preparing his countenance for the actions ahead. His fists clenched at his sides. "Now, battalion...to the village!"

Several more Irish watched as Sir Arthur and Beecher turned about, and the troops began to follow. To a man, their eyes glared and their jaws clenched. Tynan recognized some faces, but he knew not from where. More people, men and women, appeared along the church road as the troops entered the village square. Here on market days the open space would be filled with carts and caravans of goods to be sold or traded, and pens for sheep and goats. But it was vacant and eerily still. More people appeared from the houses that lined the square. They were warriors, their families and followers.

Sir Arthur rode to the center of the square while Captain Beecher shouted orders. In minutes the cavalry and infantrymen divided into four groups, one on each side of the square facing outward. What risk Sir Arthur was taking, when even the most disciplined soldiers craved violence, fed on the power of firing their weapons, and lusted always for plunder. Tynan waited by a tree on the church road, out of the way for whatever the soldiers were about to do, but in view of Sir Arthur. His blood raced, hands sweating on the reins.

All became still and quiet again, but for horses voicing anticipation. Sir Arthur spoke, and then Captain Beecher shouted. The soldiers exploded into action. Screams pierced the sky. Wooden doors splintered under prying, pounding, and battering. Children cried and infants wailed. Men shouted furious warnings and oaths, and any who resisted were beaten and taken prisoner. Soon people began to stumble from the side streets, falling, pleading, howling. Like water sluicing from a leaf they came down from the hillside. Tynan's horse fought against his reins, groaned, whinnied, stomped the earth, but Tynan held fast. If only he could turn the horse and run, but there was no escape. The bile burned in his throat.

Soon the soldiers began to emerge from the lanes, placing before Sir Arthur great sacks of belongings, foodstuffs, furniture. Some drove animals before them. Others pulled wooden carts piled high with sacks and wares.

House by house for hours the soldiers' work continued. Men who fought them from their doors had suffered for it, their heads and hands bleeding, and were forced to sit in the square with their arms bound and watch the plunder continue, while soldiers held them at musket point. Women wept in the streets, and some screamed curses, their faces seething red. And on and on the piles in the square grew larger.

Yet no musket shots broke the air. No one died. In time the north wind stalled, the leaves on the trees settled, and the wailing grew louder, carried unfiltered by the cold winter air. The soldiers returned to their starting positions, their work concluded, and waited for their fellows.

"O'Daly!" Sir Arthur's voice rang out.

Tynan jerked at the sound of his name. Sir Arthur signaled for him to bring the pack horses. He rode out to collect his helpers. A man by the church road hollered at him and spit on the ground. "O'Daly is it?" the man shouted. "Ye bloody traitor. Your soul to the Devil!"

Tynan pretended to ignore him and continued on, but the burn in his throat now became like a hot stone expanding there until it burst and shot molten waves across his shoulders, his face, and his legs. By what right did a dirty, thieving, ignorant bastard call him such? He should bash the man's face in. How fortunate they all were that this had not been a massacre, that the soldiers had not cut them all down. And he? Who had done none of the plundering? A traitor? Ty O'Daly owed no allegiance to the fools in that village, nor to any of them—the so-called rebels. What loyalty or kinship had any Irish showed the O'Dalys? None. Only scorn, poverty and ridicule. An entire peninsula in Kerry had belonged to them, and now they scraped for every blade of grass.

He'd no loyalty to the English either, the arrogant lying swine, the spurious, cock-licking pond scum. But at least he was paid for a day's work. Ty O'Daly was owned by no one, owed his life to no one, was a traitor to no one. Except perhaps to himself, for getting sucked into a petty, stinking bit of business such as this day had brought. Were he so fortunate to sit astride that black stallion again, he'd ride off forever, and somehow make sure he never would be caught.

10

Plunder

Rathbarry Castle

"Come along, Merel," Lady Carey said as she led the way to the castle solar. I sorted and handed her threads as she stitched a new pillow covering. The court was still and eerie. We spoke very little, and other ladies were quiet, all of us aware of what might be happening at Ross.

By eventide, the gates clanked open and Sir Arthur returned to Rathbarry with Captain Beecher and some of his cavalrymen. Lady Carey bid me to go and bring her news of their operation. I hurried to the courtyard. If the captain had more men at the village, he must have sent them back to Clonakilty or Bandon—a blessing if that was so, for Rathbarry could scarce feed scores of soldiers on top of the villagers and garrison we already had.

I watched from a bench by the well as the garrison men left behind to guard the castle greeted the returning soldiers. Captain Beecher accepted their welcome as if he were King Charles himself. Sir Arthur quietly dismounted on the keep steps. Mistress Dorothy took his hand as the rest of the men passed through the gate: more than a dozen cavalry, then the infantry in Rathbarry livery, then several wooden carts piled high with furniture and bulging brown sacks. Next came Giles and Collum leading pack horses strapped with large sacks of victuals.

Behind them two more infantrymen pulled ropes leading several dusty and bloody men with arms bound, most walking upright, all of them with faces dark and defiant.

Villagers arriving from the garden ward stared at the prisoners, at first with curiosity, and then with bald hatred. As the soldiers led them to the garrison ward, someone spit at them, another cursed them, and Mistress Coale's daughter wailed until she fainted.

Jayne joined me on the bench and twined her arm around mine. She said not a word but pressed tightly against me, alarm on her face as the Irish prisoners passed. They moved away quickly, pushed on by the soldiers, but I was unsure where they'd be held, for nearly every possible space already was used or occupied by the villagers. Even the castle's prison was filled to its ceiling with stores and supplies.

All attention shifted from the prisoners to the goods brought from Ross as they were set in the center of the court. A servant lit the torches in their sconces. The villagers moved in as hungry dogs toward a carcass, some sorting through the goods and taking things. As might have been predicted, in minutes a fight broke out between two women claiming the same clothing. Millett held off the villagers until a more organized distribution could be arranged. Each person was required to describe their belongings before they were allowed to claim them. It might take days until they would clear the piles, Millett warned, but it would be handled in a civilized manner according to Sir Arthur's expectations. A guard would watch the goods in the court until the morrow.

Sir Arthur and Mistress Dorothy returned to the keep without comment or gesture. The usher closed the door quietly behind them. And Jayne beside me began to quake.

"What is happening?" she asked me. "What will they do with those prisoners?"

I had no answer and couldn't blame her for her fear. Several castle servants were Irish. It was one thing to have skirmishes happening outside of Rathbarry, and quite another to see real people of your own kind imprisoned in what was your home.

"'Tis the MacCarthys who've taken Ross. The O'Keeffes, my own family, run thick wi' them and always have. At this moment my brother could be tied up and mebbe hurt. Some o' them were bleedin', didja not see?"

"I saw them. Don't worry," I said. "When Ty gets here, he'll tell us everything." But Ty did not come, though everyone else had returned, and the court grew quiet.

"I'm so cold, Merel. I can't stay here any longer. Let's go inside."

But I shook my head, still watching the gate.

"You must get some rest," she said. "And Lady Carey will be needing you. Please come."

Still I waited on the bench for Ty, my hands and feet numbed. Jayne squeezed my shoulder and left me for her bed. What could have happened to him? He must be coming, for the guards hadn't closed the gates, and no one else seemed concerned. But dusk had long passed, and the cold stillness of night settled in.

I waited until my lips couldn't move and my fingers ached, but at last came the slow and steady clop of horse's hooves. Ty rode in and the guards secured the gate behind him. His chin was to his chest as if he was sleeping. He held the reins loosely, hands resting on his thighs, allowing the horse to find his own way home. I stood, so eager to see him, yet worried that he might be hurt. My heart flapped like a frightened bird. "Ty," I said. It came out barely a whisper, yet he glanced at me. His chin lifted to defiance, his spine straightened and he jerked the rein to lift the horse's head, looking every bit the proud knight in a medieval painting, returning from battle with high honor and untouchable spirit. I started toward him, but he urged the horse to a trot.

FEBRUARY

11

The Prince of Dunmanway

Blarney Castle

Slanting rain tapped like needles against the narrow state room windows of Blarney Castle. Tadgh-an-Duna—Teige O'Downe as the English called him—sat in a finely upholstered armchair across from his old friend and relation, Donough MacCarthy, Lord Muskerry. The hearth fire was hot and the wine nicely warmed, but Donough's reception was as chilly as fresh snow on the Kerry mountains. He'd no wish to hear about the Irish rising in Munster province. He feared the whole business would tarnish his political standing in Dublin. But it was time he acknowledged the truth. A man in his position owed as much to his clan. If the job fell to Teige himself to open the man's eyes, so be it. Lord Muskerry commanded troops for his branch of the MacCarthy dynasty, and Teige needed his support for what he was about to do.

Teige smoothed back his shoulder-length hair, roughly tossed by the weather. Once as gold and full as a field of wheat, it had thinned and faded with the years. But sure it could be worse. Donough's long curls were hanging from a stand in his bedchamber, awaiting the next formal dinner or political meeting. His natural pate was bald but for a sparse silver fleece from his temples to his nape. He was corpulent as well, bulging around the jowls, and not the least bit conscious of it, whereas Teige was as fit and fierce with a sword as he'd been thirty years past.

Donough reared back in his chair, slapped his ample belly, and huffed at Teige scornfully.

"I've done what I can in support of the Catholic faith. I have done. I've protected my family whenever their properties or positions attracted someone's greedy eye. And yes, I've helped arrange passage for certain English folk through embittered territory, to keep them on our good side, or at least open to negotiation if needs must. But a rising, after the Desmonds' debacle?" He sniffed, belched softly and gulped a bit more wine.

"That's what I call it. A debacle," he talked on. "Those damned Geraldines drew us all into a bloody war over the plantations, so foolish even we MacCarthys fought against one another, and for what? Nine years. Everyone suffered for it, no one gained. I thought we'd all agreed that the English were an infestation we'd never be rid of, and best to play the game, get what we could out of them. Of course, some of us have been cheated, that's just the nature of them. At least we've been at the bargaining table. But this business, the foolishness O'Neill and O'More cooked up—and how they drew Maguire into it I'll never quite understand—just baffles me. I've met O'More a few times. Decent, smart fellow. Heard he had a map of Dublin Castle, that he might find a way to just shove the whole pile o' rocks into the River Liffey. But I s'pose he couldn't locate the weakness, and thought instead he'd convince Maguire and his lads to march in and take over. What kind of fool?"

Donough scowled. "And then, O'Connor. Of course there would be an O'Connor, a flaw in the weave that causes everything to unravel." He flipped his hand back over his head as if swatting a fly. "If not this one, then another. The man has worked so long in service to the English he flatters himself that he's one of them. Oh, how the sheriffs all celebrated the great storyteller while he drunkenly revealed O'More's secret plan. The cleverer it seemed, the more brilliant the sheriffs would appear when they exposed it. But O'Connor would see no credit for his treachery. They slapped his arse in prison—maybe someday he'll sober up enough to realize it. Meantime, his blubbering sent many good lads to the gallows. O'More would've been there as well, had he not managed to disappear into the mountains somewhere. Mayhap that's where he'll spend what's left of his days."

Teige sipped from his glass, a bit disappointed in his cousin. "You know that's not true. It's just a tale fabricated by those same sheriffs. They just can't admit O'More slipped through their snare. He's in County Offaly continuing the fight. Ye know O'More is driven not by folly, but by the burden of vengeance. How would you fare if the English massacred your entire clan as they sat down for a feast—180 O'Mores. Slaughtered, all."

Donough MacCarthy turned his face away. "So they say. But it's ancient history, isn't it?"

"If you call sixty-four years ago ancient—an' yourself being just a wee bairn at forty-seven." Donough preferred always to ignore facts that conflicted with his present entertainments. Teige would let him blather on until he'd wound down a bit. Patience would win out, but not just yet.

Donough shrugged and then took a quick breath as if to cast it all behind him. "God's truth, I was at a dinner party just a few months ago. Lord Cork was there, Broghill and Barrymore, several others, and their ladies present. I had them all in stitches at this story. The absurdity of it. And O'Neill in Ulster takes this blasted failure of a rising and spreads it across the entire island? I thought Lord Cork would fall out of his chair, he laughed so hard! And believe me, the man does not laugh unless he counts his own money."

"Cork has stolen more money and land from the Irish than any other, probably since the Normans arrived. He stole from his own church," Teige said.

"Aye, likely he stole from his own mother, but at least he'll not discriminate. He'll steal from anyone."

Donough must have intended humor, but Teige couldn't laugh. He shook his head at the truth of it. "And St. Leger, president of our fine province of Munster? He's just the same."

"Sir William? Yes, he's done well for himself, hasn't he, sucking up to the likes of our former Lord Deputy, Thomas Wentworth, who was more land-hungry than Lord Cork or I daresay God himself!"

Teige grew more serious. It was time to tighten down on Donough and make him see some realities. "The thing is, Wentworth's designs on the land, while voracious, were not for himself so much as in King Charles's interest. Now Wentworth is dead at the hands of the Puritan English Parliament. Wentworth was the king's last stronghold against them. How long do you think King Charles alone will be able to defend the rights of Catholics?"

"But the king has acknowledged our grievances. The...the Irish Parliament has..."

"...Has never obtained anything from the English Parliament unless it was in their own greedy interest."

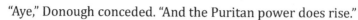

"Aye," Donough conceded. "And the Puritan power does rise."

Teige nodded, and leaned closer. "The king is facing civil war. It will keep Parliament engaged and their coffers drained for the next few years. Meanwhile, Wentworth left us the Irish army. Your friend St. Leger has tried desperately to send them to Spain because he knows if what might happen if the Irish clans take command of these troops, these Catholic Irish troops, trained, well-armed and ready." He paused long enough for that to sink into Donough's mind. At last he had the man's full attention.

"You call men like Cork your friends now, but in time they'll take your titles and property as swiftly as they took every inch of Desmond land," Teige said. "We have, only for a brief time, the chance to take that army and use it for Ireland, with every clan behind it. O'More saw the chance. Maguire saw it. O'Neill seized it. Unification of forces. The power of one vast iron mace to blast them all to the sea. Let this moment pass, and we'll not see such an opening again for a hundred years, I can promise you. The difference between us and the Desmonds is, with unification we will win this cause."

Donough shook his head. "My troops are for maintaining law and order. For protecting the Catholic Church."

It was Teige's turn to scoff. "Come now Donough! They have failed. St. Leger himself has dispensed with the law entirely, so rudely demonstrated by his trail of bloody murders, and yet he carries on."

"How do you mean?"

"Ah, it is as I thought. He keeps you ignorant of his darkest deeds. He's been murdering our people since December, when his brother-in-law complained of some horses stolen. He marched his soldiers to Clonmel and summarily executed three men. Then he marched on to Grange and executed three men more, who were only laboring in a field. He moved on to Ballymureen and killed six more, and then six more again in Galbertstown, and he burned half the houses there. At Ardmayle, he killed several men and women who just happened to be standing on their doorsteps as he passed."

"Surely there is some mistake." Donough winced. "If there's truth to it, I must discover who has kept this from me and why."

"I'm no' finished." Teige held up a steady hand. "Only a few weeks ago, St. Leger learned that Irish troops had pitched tents across the river in

County Waterford. They'd done nothing. Had not stolen the first sheep nor disturbed a single household. Yet, St. Leger sent his men over the ridge where they murdered six hundred Irishmen. Six hundred, by sword and by hanging. No battle, no rules of war, no warning, no mercy, no process of law. Six hundred, slaughtered. If that does not signal an intention to extinguish us all, what does?"

Donough's face turned bright pink and a sheen of sweat appeared on his forehead. "It is martial law, isn't it?"

"It is murder, and St. Leger knows it. He'll face charges if someone doesn't kill him first."

Donough's lips moved without sound, until after some clearing his voice blurted in an ugly grunt. He shouted for more wine, and downed what remained in his glass. "I trust you to bring me the truth. It is exactly why I avoid you."

Teige smirked. "Your English counterparts wouldn't bother to tell you. They wouldn't think it important, but St. Leger is responsible for all those deaths and even more. He's said publicly that he'll leave no weapon in the hands of men who are 'Romishly affected.' He defies the king who has promised tolerance, and plans to disarm us—to keep us weak and defenseless against their abuse and atrocities. Donough, it is extermination, as if we are vermin!"

"The king has issued a proclamation against Irish rebels."

"It was forced upon him by that Puritan Parliament, but Charles will repeal it when he sees our strength. He needs Irish supporters, for money if nothing else."

A maid tip-toed in with the wine, and the two men drank in silence for a while, until Donough began tapping his shoes on the polished floor. The rain had stopped, but the darkness in the room portended more storms coming.

"You'll stay for supper," he said.

"Aye. And mebbe breakfast as well. The night will be dark and poor for travel."

Donough nodded and shifted in his chair. "What of the MacCarthy Reagh? Has my brother-in-law Cormac declared for this? Does he inspire the clans to rise?"

Teige noted a hint of disdain for the younger kinsman. "Cormac is the

Prince of Carbery, is he not? He knows his duty. He stands as Commander of the Munster clans, and has named me his lieutenant. His troops train at Kilbrittain Castle."

"He is nearly more connected to the Englishmen than I," Donough said. "He is friends with many, drinks and hunts with them. How will he play this, I wonder? With what does he train? Have they weapons?"

"Cormac went to Kinalmeaky in Bandon, vowed he would fight for the English, and Kinalmeaky supplied him with muskets."

"God's wounds! They'll not be forgiving that treachery! Or will they? There are few more slippery than Cormac."

"He is deadly serious about this, Donough. He did what he had to do. We can't win every battle with ax handles and pikes. He had to give his men an even chance on the battlefield."

"All right. Fair play to him." Donough leaned back, thoughtfully examining the carved ceiling plaster. "Our MacCarthy Reagh is a man of vision."

"I would say so," Teige replied.

"Ah, then," Donough lowered his chin and met his gaze. "Would you also say he's a man of completion?"

He'd have to be careful. Donough wasn't always observant, but when he was, he could nail a man's hide to a tree and then hold him up by his balls to watch it bleeding. "Completion. Meaning, is he one to follow through on his plans? Let us say, thanks be to God, that if ever he should be such a man, may it be now. If instead ye mean, will he stand by his convictions, then I know he will, as sure as you or I."

Donough sighed and looked out the window, though there was only gray to be seen. "Tell me about this business of Ross. You drove the English from the village?"

"I did. It was ours before it was theirs. We've returned the favor, ye might say." Teige eyed his cousin for a moment. Donough had just crossed the line into the Irish camp. It was that bit about St. Leger that won him, and then the confidence in MacCarthy Reagh. Perhaps he's ready to hear what's to come. "It was a test," Teige said.

"A test! Well now, the villagers have gone, so how do we know if they passed or failed?"

"A different kind of test. When a wolf hunts his prey, he watches for signs of weakness, tendencies, vulnerability. He pushes a bit, to see would the stag run for the safety of the herd when frightened, or panic and separate. Or, does he keep his head and cause you to lose sight of him. The smart wolf won't waste energy chasin' after a stag he'll not likely catch. So then, we took the village, shedding ne'er a drop of blood, knowing they'd run for the castle, and they did. But we were not testing the villagers, ye see, we were testing Sir Arthur Freke."

"Oh, aye. Arthur. Yes, I know his father, quite well respected in Youghal. And how did young Sir Arthur fare?"

Teige settled his back more comfortably in the chair. "It was quite as I had hoped. He brought men from his garrison and a troop from Bandon. A show of force. They plundered the village most thoroughly. My lads were at ready in case something went wrong, but they were told to observe, not to fight unless the soldiers raised their weapons. Freke took a few prisoners, but fired no guns, and no one was seriously harmed. They took what they wanted and left."

Donough reared back, his eyes wide. "Is that so? Astonishing! What does this tell you?"

"What I hoped and suspected. Freke's a family man. His wife and child are within the castle. He is protective, a businessman who would not have his sheep slaughtered and his fields burned. He likes his power, but he hasna the taste for bloodshed. And that suits me passing well."

"You old rogue. Wait a moment, just one chary moment. I don't like your eyes when they squint like that. They're small and merry to begin with, but behind them is something sharp like the hawk's claw. Simplicity masking shrewdness. You've something planned."

"No less than would you, were ye settin' in my chair. I'll have my land back, and I'll have my men to work it wi' me. Not the blood-soaked field St. Leger would have. And, my son will have his birthright—of land, of position, and of all the wealth to which he's entitled."

"Ah yes. I see. Well I suppose there's no argument to that. What is your plan?"

There—at last he had Lord Muskerry's ear for what was to come. He stood, placing his hand on the mantel next to the fine plasterwork of the MacCarthy coat of arms: the proud red stag beneath a knight's helmet. Let the image seize Donough's heart.

"Should you choose to take your part in this," Teige said, "your battles will be on the highest level, engaging and defeating the Parliament dogs that oppose us. I will go about my part in the bogs and the meadows at our feet. The Barony of Carbery belongs to Cormac, legally granted to his father decades ago, and don't we both know what great hardships he suffered to secure it. But part of that barony is to be mine, including Ross, Clonakilty, and everything between them and down to the sea. I'll have my heritage and my rights, and my son after me will be prince over all of it.

"A thousand years we MacCarthys have lived on this land. Six hundred years the MacCarthy name has commanded great respect. Will it fall to us to let the whole of our legacy slip into the hands of the English who canna respect it? I was nearly resigned to that, and it ate at me like a cancer. Look at me. I'm not a young man. Death waits before me, and a bitter fate it will be if we let the English steal everything we've built and fought for. 'Tis my last chance to do something about it, and sure I'll use it, run it through to the hilt. Ye know my plan before ye ask, Donough. It's the seven castles, as always it has been."

His cousin nodded, his face darkened and serious. "And Rathbarry?"

"It sits on my land. It was built by the Barrys who owe me tribute. Dunmanway is secure, and my brother holds Togher Castle. Rathbarry will be mine. I will make it my residence and headquarters."

"And now that you've tested Sir Arthur, when will you start?"

"As soon as your hand clasps mine in unity, in commitment, and in unrelenting faith that we will prevail."

Donough stood to face him by the hearth. "I'll make my oath to you, but on one condition." He furrowed his brow and glared directly into Teige's eyes. "When the castles are yours, you'll come northward to join me in the fields against the Protestants."

Teige returned the penetrating stare. They were more brothers than cousins. Donough's eyes reflected his own. He extended his hand.

Without hesitation, Donough MacCarthy grasped his hand firmly and completed the oath. *"We will prevail."*

12

The Long Strand

Rathbarry Castle

With Lady Carey put to bed, I stepped out into the courtyard to watch the waxing moon rise. With it swelled a tide of anticipation that flooded throughout the castle. I climbed to the battlements to peer into the dark heavens, where the moon loomed like a white porcelain bowl tipped sideways. My mother once warned me it was a beautiful but dreaded omen: things beloved and familiar contained within it might at any moment come spilling down and down.

Every afternoon, Sir Arthur's younger brother Thomas Freke put on his spectacles and went to the kitchen to tally expenses with Elinor: check supplies of bread, butter and staples in the pantry, and list supplies received such as meat, fish and grain. The goods Sir Arthur had ordered from Kinsale hadn't arrived—either delayed, lost or stolen. Thomas insisted all meat should be cut in his presence, and portions counted as they were delivered to the cook. Supper portions were noticeably smaller as Elinor tried to stretch their provisions.

Sir Arthur's step grew heavy, his brow almost always furrowed. He required a daily count of his sheep, and each day the number returned was lower. Night by night the Irish claimed a few more. The curs at our perimeter barked and growled if anyone came near, but so far the guards had not spied men or movement among the sheep. The animals just seemed to disappear. "Those rogues have sharpened their skills for thievery," he said.

And then there was Ty. Since his return from Ross, he had not shown himself when supper was served at court. Though I knew he was within the stables, he didn't come out. How I longed to see him, to know what troubled him so. As time passed, my thoughts moved from concern to obsession. Why should I be this way? I had no claim on Ty. No words of love had been spoken between us.

Yet, each day I fell a little deeper into emptiness. It wasn't for lack of food, for I was allowed to eat what I wished within the keep. Nor was it illness, for I was well by all the usual standards: no fever, no vomiting nor bowel problems, and no visible sores or injury. Instead I was weighted by some internal stone. No distraction helped to lighten the weight. What a surprise then, to learn that my mind did not control my body, but in fact my body held full authority. I offered my bread to Collum if Jayne wouldn't take it. I breathed, at times with some labor, but not even the scents of wood or sea, nor the smell of bread baking could lift me up.

One evening in early February, Sir Arthur sent a night watch of riders out of the castle in each direction to scour the grounds. Listless, I waited on the steps after supper while Lady Carey was having her wine with the other ladies in the hall. After a time, the guards called to each other and then opened the gate. Into the courtyard came a horse without its rider.

People drew near out of curiosity. The guards summoned Sir Arthur, who hurried from the keep with brother Thomas close behind. After one glance at the horse, he ordered, "Get Ty O'Daly out here." My spine stiffened. A guard fetched him from the stables while Thomas examined the horse for injuries. He shook his head. Sir Arthur called up to the tower.

"Does anyone approach? Can you see anything amiss?"

"No, sir!" the soldier returned.

Ty took the horse by its bit, and studied it as Thomas had done. I clasped my hands at my waist to hide the tremble.

"Whose mount was this?" Sir Arthur asked.

"John Sellers, sir," Ty said, his voice calm. "He rode out with three others, who have returned. Sellers was riding the strand and may have fallen. The hocks and hooves are sandy, and the left flank as well."

"Perhaps Sellers took a fall and is walking home," Sir Arthur said. "But it's a dark night and I've an ill feeling."

"Shall I ride out after him, sir?" Ty asked.

"No. We must wait. If there are rebels beyond that gate, I'll not have them diminish us one by one. I'll question the other riders first. No one leaves the castle until we know what's become of Mr. Sellers, or what might be at hand."

Sir Arthur pressed Ty's shoulder and Ty followed him and Thomas to the garrison.

Jayne stepped in front of me and blocked my view of their passing. She took my chin in her hand. "What on earth ails you? Yer lookin' as if someone just drained the blood out o' ye."

She held a cloak over her head as a light drizzle of rain began to fall. "Come on, dear. Mebbe we should go inside, it's spittin' rain."

"Is it?"

"Oh dear, ye poor girl. Have ye lost sight of what's about?" She sat beside me and pulled the cloak over both our heads. "Tell me. What has happened?"

I began to shiver and could not stop though I wished so much to hide myself away.

"Here." She pulled the cloak lower, hiding our faces. "I'll wrap it close around us. It's our secret cloak and no one else can hear us except God and the angels, and they're far too busy to listen. Ye don't even know John Sellers, so I know it's not about 'im. Ye must tell me. What troubles ye so? Ty, is it?"

Of a sudden I was awash in my own foolishness. My throat closed in upon itself and my cheeks burned. I turned my face away as if to hide. "He's not spoken to me for some time. I may have offended somehow."

Jayne shook her head. "Oh, ye silly thing. He's a fella, ain't he? Fun and boyish one minute, then dark and cold the next, and all the while it hasn't a thing ta do wi' you. Something's afoot. We're all of us a bit troubled."

The words stung. "It may have nothing to do with me, but it's no remedy. I was fine, and now I am not. I was strong and sure, and of a sudden I am lost."

Jayne's breath caught in her throat. "Oh, sweet. What am I thinking? Of course it's no help to you. Go on. Tell me."

I sighed as if to speak was beyond my strength, but then I began. "I know what it is to lose people you love. The grief is hard. So hard. Parts of it never to go away. But it is quite another thing to begin to care, and then things fall away suddenly, leaving you nothing but longing in its place. As strange as she may be, Lady Carey lifted me up, and gave me a home. I am grateful, truly. But Ty *saw* me as a person again, not an orphan, not a servant, not a lost oddity picked up on the strand, nor a doll to be played with and then cast upon the shelf. I was more myself when I stood beside him. Now he turns away when he sees me, and it's a shaft of ice to my heart. I *ache*. And somehow, I am even smaller than before."

Jayne stroked my cheek with a knuckle. "Merel. Ye've fallen in love and you're only suffering for the want of it." She hugged my shoulders. "I know just how you feel. I loved a lad once, and thought I'd surely die."

"You did?"

"Aye. Of course. It's a great wonder and a terrible wound all at once. But comin' through that pain was a lesson for me, that one lad, be he good or awful, canna make me large or small, smart or foolish. He canna cast me down nor lift me up but that my own heart permits it. But listen. Ty is Irish. He sat his horse in Ross and watched this garrison strip those Irish families of everything. He knew they came from people of his own blood, and yet he had to cart their things away. Can ye understand the bitter conflict? He couldna help anyone, and he looked like a traitor to his kinsmen. You and I know the truth about Ty. He's caught in the middle, aye? As are we. None of us asked for it, but stuck we are."

Jayne shrugged her shoulders. "Don't ye worry. His troubles will pass. Some lads are a just little dull and ye have to bring them to their senses in ways they can understand. The next time ye see him, just let down your hair long in the back, and then let out a big NEE-hee-hee-hee-hee! He'll pay attention."

I jerked backward, surprised. How could I not laugh? "Jayne! What about our secret cloak? Shush!" We peered out from under the collar, but no one looked in our direction. Some had left the court to avoid the rain, and paid no heed to the maids on the steps.

"Good," Jayne said. "Ye can still laugh, and by my eyes, ye've grown no smaller. I'll teach ye somethin' important I learned a while back. When ye feel yer heart breakin' but ye ne'er want to let folks see ye cry, just pinch yourself here, in the fat between your thumb and pointin' finger. Pinch it hard as you need to, and ye'll straighten up. It always works for me. Along with that, the surest remedy for getting through such misery is to keep yourself busy. Shall we go collect Lady Carey?"

Before we could even stand, the sentinel shouted down to the court and the gate was opened. The guards rushed out and soon returned, one on either side of John Sellers to help him walk. He looked exhausted, his clothing soiled, but he bore no sign of bloody injury. They helped him to the bench by the well as Sir Arthur came from the garrison.

"Sellers! It is a great relief to see you. Your horse returned and we thought you surely killed." He touched Sellers' shoulder and examined his face. "Someone get our man some water! And a whisky!"

In a moment Sellers seemed to catch his breath, and fully swallowed both drinks. Sir Arthur stood before him, and others began inching closer, eager to hear the man's story.

"I set out to secure the strand, sir. The west strand, below the lake. I quickly came upon about 60 men, in two companies. I'm not sure what they were doing, but feared they could be preparing to attack Rathbarry. I fired my musket on them and..."

"Sellers! You fired on them? On 60 men, and you alone?" Sir Arthur asked.

"I..I did, yes sir. I didn't think they could see me. I situated myself behind a bluff, and I thought to scare them off, is all. I killed one of them, I'm fairly certain. I may have injured a few more. It seems I did scare them, because they fell over one another in their haste to get away. But then my horse lost his footing in the sand and went down, and I with him. The horse got up and bolted away. I feared the men would come after me, so I buried myself in the sand until I knew they'd gone and I could get back to the castle safely."

"And so you have. Well done, Sellers," Sir Arthur said. "But in the future, I'd have you return to the castle for more men before you go firing your weapon on full companies. You're lucky to be alive. We'll talk more about this when you've rested."

"Sir, I..." Sellers shook his head as if to shift his brain back into its proper position. "I do need help, sir. If I've killed a man, I cannot just leave his body lying out there. I must bury him properly. It is right and Christian that I do. And also, better that his mates do not find his body before we are prepared against them."

"You want to go back down there?"

"Yes, sir."

Sir Arthur stared at Sellers in disbelief, but then dropped his shoulders, put his hands on his hips. "Thomas, have the ensign assign four men to assist Sellers down to the strand. Make sure they are well armed. And send the snipers to the west wall to watch over them."

In a quarter hour the men rode out, carrying a single torch by which light they would bury the dead Irishman. Jayne and I looked after Lady Carey who knew nothing about what had happened to Mr. Sellers but babbled on about a card game in the solar. We put her to bed most comfortably. I banked the fire and we bedded down as always on our pallets.

But Jayne couldn't sleep. She was chilled and shivered beneath her quilt. "They killed that lad on the strand, and maybe others. That's what they said, isn't it? That's three Irish dead that we're sure of. We are in the midst of a war, aren't we?"

"I think so."

"I've tried to find where they are keeping those prisoners. I'm so afraid for them. Agnes, the laundress, told me today her brother was among them, and she thinks they are tied up somewhere in the garrison. Every day I fear I'll find me own brother among them. What will be done with them?"

"I don't know."

"Sir Arthur won't release them, for they could just rejoin their folk at Ross, or join those men on the strand, to fight him again. But he won't want to keep them here, either, will he?"

"I don't..."

"Merel. What if he decides to..."

"Don't say it. Don't even say it, Jayne."

She quieted, but still she trembled until at last her weariness overtook her. I lay awake for at least another hour, haunted not only by my own pain, but also by what could become of the prisoners who had been our neighbors only a few weeks past. Then the men returned from their grim errand. The gate clanked shut and soon the court was quiet but for the bitter screech of a ghost owl hunting mice.

13

At Sunrise

Rathbarry Castle

Before dawn the following morning, Lady Carey awakened me, her bare toes near my face as she stood in her nightgown, tapping my shoulder.

"Merel, dear. You must wake. Quickly. It's to be a lovely sunrise, I'm sure of it. Get dressed and find a place along the wall to make a nice picture. Or two, if you have time. If they are good, you can make some pigments and add a bit of color. Hurry, the time slips by."

I rubbed my eyes, a little embarrassed that my lady had risen before me, and yet Jayne didn't stir. I relieved myself in the chamber pot as Lady Carey paced before the window, and then I slipped into my dress. She even fastened the laces for me, so eager was she to have me off to my task.

"Not to worry, Jayne will assist me. You go now."

I stopped on the threshold, peering out into the lingering darkness, the sketch book in hand. "My lady, please tell me, what urges you so for these pictures?"

"Well, my goodness, who would not wish to own a picture by a Dutch painter?"

I must've frowned. Her shoulders sagged a bit and she pressed closer.

"I have no coin, you see. The ladies are at their games in the afternoons, and I do wish to play, but I dare not grow a debt that my son will have to settle for me when he returns. I shall sell some pictures, or place them on the table as my wager. I've seen it done. If I do well, I will buy you an easel."

While men are dying, people are made homeless, and we suffer the threat of war, she wishes to play her card games? Her face in the darkness allowed no insight to her mind. I suppressed a sigh—though an ea-sel might be nice—and hurried out the door toward the garrison and the south wall for the best east-facing view over the bay. The octagonal tower might have been better, but with three guards there I would either be sent away as a nuisance, or used for their pleasure.

As I found my position, a blood-red band already marked the horizon. I closed my eyes just long enough to let the sea wind cool my cheeks and brow, and breathe in the rich, salty essence. After my talk with Jayne, I was starting to feel myself again, and eager to try a new sketch. I imag-ined a gentle arc where the band separated sky from land and sea. I drew a curve from the bottom of my page up to the imaginary line, to repre-sent the shoreline from Rathbarry to Galley Head. Then, above the hori-zon I drew the faint outline the land's rise and fall, and of the tower of Dundeady Castle. Beyond that, the sketch would be a series of horizontal bands in varying widths and shapes, to show the rising sun, the clouds above, and the thundering sea below. How in the world did the lady ex-pect me to capture a sunrise without pigments?

It would take time, but I could make them myself, grinding vegetables, fruits or earth with ox gall. What colors would suit? Ochre of course, and indigo, but then also saffron, violet, vermillion, and russet. Late winter was a poor time to find sources for the bright colors, though, and Elinor would likely frown on my borrowing her mortar and pestle for such use. Still, the idea entertained me as I continued my work. Perhaps I'd learned more from my father than I'd realized.

The blood-red line soon turned to orange, casting upward a brighten-ing haze of gold and pale yellow. Above that a dark gray cloud line hung low like sacks weighted by stone. Below the bluffs, the ocean battered and teased the shore with relentless white paws. I gazed the horizon from left to right until a flutter of dark wings caught my eye. I followed it to my far right and then the bird disappeared beyond the lake, beyond the trees, and beyond the bog just after. A bright spark flashed, vanished and flashed again a little brighter. Then another like it, just a short distance away. The clouds climbed and billowed, allowing more of the palest light to spread beyond the bog. There, a faint outline of pointed shapes ap-peared that hadn't been there before, aligned and uniform, growing more distinct, like tents positioned shoulder to shoulder in low profile. Tents. A *camp*! Was it the Irish companies Mr. Sellers had encountered?

My breath stopped and in my belly the pins and needles began to spin and stab. I waited just a moment longer. Perhaps I was mistaken. But then came the unmistakable scent of smoke. Smoke from *a cookfire*. My shoulders rose toward my ears while my legs began to shake, eager to run. I must go to Sir Arthur immediately with the news. I tucked my sketchbook and instruments into my skirt pocket and peered over the wall into the garrison before I descended. But from there a deep groan found my ears, and not that of a sleeper rising, but of an agony endured. It stopped me cold, as if a great hand grabbed the scruff of my neck and forced my attention. The jaundiced light had reached the bottom edge of a tent just below me, where bloody fingers caked with dirt held the hem of the canvas and lifted it, exposing part of a face and the blatant terror in one cerulean eye.

In the courtyard, Sir Arthur was shouting before breakfast, waving his hands at Ensign Hungerford in front of everyone near. "You have failed. Six of my cattle are gone, secreted away in the night. How can this happen with snipers in my towers and guards in my fields? I want you to double the men on night watch. If you come upon these cattle drivers, take them prisoner, or shoot them if needs must."

Not wishing to approach him at all in his present mood, I knew I had to do so. At the moment he dismissed the ensign I summoned my courage. "Sir Arthur, if you please."

He turned to me. "Yes. What is it, child?"

"I am not..." a *child*, I wanted to say. But that is how he saw me, and there was no profit in my retort, nor would it convince him otherwise. "I am not positive of what I witnessed this morning, sir, but at dawn I saw from the west wall what appears to be a camp. Sir."

He threw his shoulders back and his face inflated, his eyes wide, his mouth parted. "What on...What on earth do you say? What were you doing up there? What did you see? Tell me."

I bowed my head quickly and began. "I saw sparks in two places, that may have been from morning fires..."

"Glow worms, surely."

"...and with the dawn's light I saw the pointed tops of tents."

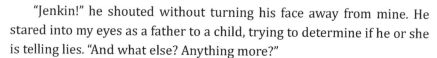

"Jenkin!" he shouted without turning his face away from mine. He stared into my eyes as a father to a child, trying to determine if he or she is telling lies. "And what else? Anything more?"

"Smoke, sir."

Jenkin ran out, his long legs gangly like a new colt, nearly tripping over his own shoes in the process. "Yes, Sir Arthur."

"Fetch my spyglass. Quickly."

Jenkin hesitated and seemed embarrassed. "Your what, sir?"

"By God! On my desk in the stateroom. My *spyglass*. Bring it now!"

Jenkin turned and ran. Sir Arthur glared back at me. "Where were you on the wall. Show me exactly."

I hurried to the stair by the postern gate with Sir Arthur at my heels. We were halfway to the top when Jenkin joined us. I led them to the position I'd chosen to make my drawing. "It was just there," I pointed, "on the far side of the bog, sir."

It was not even a half-mile distant, but between castle and camp there was considerable change in terrain, from rock to lake to forest to bog, and then to low hills covered in brush. Instead of becoming brighter with the dawn, the area was darkened beneath the gathering clouds. We watched for a moment but saw no movement or evidence of any man-made structure. Sir Arthur looked down on my head and scoffed as if at a frivolous, imaginative girl wasting his time.

"Give me that," he said to Jenkin. He took hold of a brass cylinder, lifted one end to his right eye, and pulled the far end out slowly. He squinted through it, pulled it away, peered through it again. "Damn that old sea captain, sold me a piece of...some poor invention that I...well, it...Oh, damn that antiquated rogue." He took a deep breath, held the instrument to his eye again, and braced his elbow on the wall. "Maybe I can... I think...wait, it's just...*God confound me!* I see a head, a billow of dust, and yes, what could only be the top of a tent." He straightened, the spyglass grasped in his fist. "Jenkin, get Captain Beecher up here!"

Jenkin threw himself down the stairway, arms and legs swinging until he clattered upon the gravel below and ran into the garrison. Sir Arthur turned to me.

"You've done well, Mistress Merel. I did indeed need to see this straight away."

Had he touched my shoulder just then, I would have fallen over like a long-dead oak. He knew my name? At least when it suited him to do so? And it suited him now, to acknowledge my act. I must have beamed. Captain Beecher was beside us in minutes, still tightening the belt of his breeks, and peered through Sir Arthur's spyglass. He lowered the glass and stepped back from the wall, staring toward the hills.

"Captain," Sir Arthur said. "How is it so, that here in my castle I house a fine garrison of eighty trained men, and yet this morning, not only have I six fewer cows than I had yesterday, but also it appears that a pack of Irish rogues has just pitched camp upon your arse?"

After a moment of painful silence, Captain Beecher recovered. "Sir, the troops shall ride out immediately and burn them out. This cannot be tolerated."

"You'll do no such thing," Sir Arthur said. "That is my land, my lake, my forest, my bog, and those are my hills. Set torch to them and I'll hang you myself. We shall wait. I expect I'll hear from this Teige O'Downe fellow by and by. When I do, we'll choose a course of action. But from this moment, let there not be any approach to this castle left unguarded, and I want to know precisely what goes on within a mile of it."

"Sir." Captain Beecher bowed his head and waited for Sir Arthur to descend the stairs. He turned to me with his round, hooded eyes, allowing a measure of disgust as if to a passing rodent. "A wicked and cunning little trollop you are. You think you've won his favor? He'll forget you before he reaches the keep. You should have come to the garrison, come to me before alerting Sir Arthur. You've done more harm than good, and you'll get your lesson soon enough. Lord, let it be sharp, for it's no more than you deserve." He returned to the garrison, his boots pounding.

A buzzing sound grew louder and louder in my ears, and then came the shouting and activity of the soldiers in the garrison, as if a hundred wasp nests had been plucked from their lodgings and smashed upon the stones. They swarmed my face and pierced my gut with their long daggers. I hoped I should never see Captain Beecher again. I ran for the keep and the safety of Lady Carey in the solar.

14

The Proposition

Rathbarry Castle

It had been late September 1641, when Sir Arthur arrived in Fermoy with his carriages to move Lady Carey and myself to Rathbarry Castle. He was full of boasts about his purchase just six months earlier of the castle and the vast lands surrounding it. "David Barry, Earl of Barrymore, inherited all of this from his grandfather, but he was eager instead for money to renovate his house at Castle Lyons. I paid him a fair sum for it, but still less than it was worth. I think it was a fine bargain."

He spoke of the many improvements he'd made to the grounds and structures and at great expense, including a stained-glass window for the chapel, and a garden area geometrically designed in the style of John Tradescant, the keeper of King Charles's gardens. Not the least of these refinements was a new garderobe set into the wall between the solar and state room. It was a privy intended primarily for the convenience of master and mistress and their guests, very modern with an arch overhead like a fireplace and an oak door similarly arched, with black iron hinges.

I knew quite surely it was *not* intended for servants, even those of my station. I glanced at it as I reached the top of the stair, realizing with a sudden pang that in my rush of events, I hadn't relieved myself since early morning. I dared not stop. Mistress Dorothy was speaking to the ladies in the solar about her project to make new clothing for the children from Ross. I'd arrived slightly late at Lady Carey's side, and tried to make up for it by quickly sorting her threads for color and quantity.

If Mistress Dorothy's feelings toward Lady Carey had not altered, she'd set them aside to gain her help along with Sir Arthur's mother, sisters, Mistress Coale, and a few other ladies from the garden ward. "All must contribute to this important, charitable endeavor," she told them, but I knew she'd relented because Lady Carey's needlework was quite superior.

For her part, Lady Carey thrived under purpose and the opportunity to chatter and tell her stories. The women gathered around a table beneath the room's single window, augmenting the light here and there with candles. Lady Carey began to converse about the merits of Dutch artists.

"Some of the newer works are the small landscapes, depicting rivers and dunes, often with horses or cows in them. The painting in my home in Fermoy—my son brought it to me from France, you know—shows a flowing river with tall birch trees along its banks, and beautiful clouds overhead. Oh yes, the painting of clouds is remarkable, isn't it? Such depth and fullness, as if you could reach out and touch them. And the seashore and dune paintings—my goodness, we *must* have them paint our dunes here by the bay, don't you agree, Mistress Dorothy?"

My physical discomfort had edged into pain. With everyone involved in conversation I could escape with hardly a notice. I borrowed a candlestick and bowed to excuse myself, but upon standing I realized I'd never make it outside to the servants' privy. I shouldn't use the mistress's privy, but wouldn't it be worse if I should shame myself within the keep? I chose the arched door, hoping to dispatch my need before anyone was the wiser.

I ducked inside the narrow enclosure and shut the door, but had only begun when male voices filled the stairway. I halted my waters and prayed those males did not seek the privy. They, Sir Arthur and Thomas, continued past but left open the stateroom door. If I came out of the privy I'd be seen. Even worse, if I continued my business I would be heard, I was certain, because I could easily hear the men talking. I clenched my fists as if that could help me withstand my pressing urgency.

"Hand me the letter, Thomas." Sir Arthur said. "I know you expect the worst, but McMahony writes often enough from Dunoure that he simply could be sending news. I don't expect he'll be the bearer of O'Downe's demands, but let's have a look."

Even the crack of the letter's wax seal penetrated the privy door. I was afraid to breathe too loudly, let alone make any move. How long could I hold on? I summoned my determination. If only I had upon me Jayne's secret cloak.

"He says the news has spread throughout the barony of the shootings on the strand. The man Sellers killed is noted, but others were shot who died later of their wounds." Sir Arthur continued.

"And so," Thomas replied, "the Irish invaded our lands with two companies of armed men, and we will be called the villains for killing to defend our property?"

"I suppose the judgments will depend upon whose ears are hearing, and whose lips are telling the tale."

"So right."

"Ah, you were correct. McMahony is pleading for O'Downe after all. He writes as if concerned for our safety and well-being. He's heard that the gentleman of Carbery—I assume he means O'Downe—will speedily besiege Castle Rathbarry unless we deliver it into the keeping of a certain gentleman, along with the remainder of my stock. He wishes for my own good, he says, I should deliver the castle to a Mr. McDirmond O'Shane, for Lord Barrymore's use. *Barrymore.* The same David Barry who sold it to me? Who was drowning beneath debts for his other properties, wants me to simply give Rathbarry back?"

The whump of a cushion and groan of wood suggested they had sat down in the chairs. I took a deep breath for strength, and prayed the letter was not long.

"And there is more, growing in absurdity with each line. If we deliver the castle thus, O'Shane, his son, his son's wife, and their servants will all move into the castle with us, will 'preserve' us here with service and safety, and restore the stock justly."

Thomas huffed. "More likely," he said, "they'll hang us one by one and toss our bodies into the sea without even a glance over their bloody shoulders."

"Quite. I should give my answer swiftly. But Thomas, with the Irish camp already at our walls, if we are so besieged, how long will we be able to manage? The castle wards are crowded already. Could we bring our stock within the walls for protection? And even if we do, how long could we withstand without receiving additional supplies?"

"It is difficult to predict, but I don't suppose a siege would last more than a month. With Clonakilty and Bandon less than a day's ride distant, they would send troops to relieve us, would they not?"

"In normal circumstance, yes, of course. But I fear O'Downe being so bold may suggest he knows something we may not. What if there are other things afoot that could distract the army from our distress? I'll dispatch a letter to Bandon this afternoon. In the interim, we must prepare for the worst. Our overwintering supplies dwindle, we are approaching the height of lambing season, and there is much work to be done on my lands outside the castle walls. Without the ability to work, to hunt, and with our sheep being stolen, we could quickly run short of food."

"O'Downe has timed this well, hasn't he?" Thomas said. "But remember, Arthur, you have much bargaining power. Not only are you well connected with the garrison in Bandon, but also Kinsale and Youghal. And, you have eleven prisoners the Irish will want returned to them. If yet they insist on a siege to starve us out, the prisoners must be the first to die. They cannot take food from the mouths of our own families. You'll have to hang them. And let the sight of their corpses hanging from the castle wall send a great and terrible message."

"I do not hope for such a day. In any case, there is only one possible reply to McMahony," Sir Arthur said. After a moment of silence came a rustle of paper and the shuffling of boots. "Come, Thomas. Captain Beecher rides out soon to survey our boundaries. We'll have him deliver this to Dunoure."

Their footsteps passed the privy door to the stairs and with great relief I let go my waters. I rose in such haste I nearly fell into Mistress Dorothy's skirts when she opened the door.

"Merel! What are *you*..." Such a deep crimson surged into her cheeks that it could only be surpassed by the searing heat in mine.

"Oh, mistress, please forgive me. I was in a wretched state and could not manage to go down the stairs. I beg your indulgence just this once."

She raised her chin and glared down at me. "As companion to Lady Carey you enjoy certain privileges. But you by far exceed your limits. I should have you whipped for it. Only because you assist in our charitable work today, and because I heard of your service to my husband this morning, will I overlook this disrespect. Let it never happen again. You will go and fetch the maid right now to give the privy a thorough scrubbing."

"Yes, mistress."

"And that will not be all you will do for me. Another task you shall owe, but I will decide what it is to be when I need it. Remember that. If you do not, you will suffer for it."

"Yes, mistress." I gave her a curtsy and dashed down the stairs. How can a woman who appears so gentle in visage be so harsh in her conduct? Escaping her presence was my primary concern, but by the time I reached the hall below, my thoughts returned to Thomas's words. *You'll have to hang them...Let the sight of their corpses...send a great and terrible message.*

15

Vision of Stone

Rathbarry Castle

Throughout the day, messengers arrived and departed from the castle, and Mistress Dorothy ascended and descended the stairs to consult with Sir Arthur. By mid-afternoon she came to the solar, her face pale and her gaze held downward. "You must all go now, and there shall be no gathering or sewing in the solar for at least a day or two," she announced, "until Sir Arthur has settled some household affairs."

I collected Lady Carey's sewing basket and walked her back to her apartment where she might rest before supper. Soon Jayne arrived. She tapped the back of my arm at the same instant she greeted Lady Carey with kind concern and wished her good rest. "Follow me," she whispered. "*Quickly.*"

She led me across the court to the laundry. In the back of the drying shed, Agnes Cahill was sorting and hanging bedclothes across thin ropes strung from the beams. I'd met her before in the kitchen, but didn't know her well. Her arms were thick and puffed around the wrists as if she had not lost her baby fat, yet her waist was small. Her visage was round and plain, with eyes as bright in hue as those I'd last seen peering from beneath the hem of a garrison tent.

"Here, Agnes," Jayne said. "Ye know Merel. Tell her everythin' ye just told me."

Agnes looked over our shoulders and then pulled us farther back into the shed, against the wooden slats of the back wall. We were alone, but the shed was open in front so that someone could enter at any moment.

"I'll keep a watch," Jayne said. "Tell her."

Agnes released a big breath of air. "It's me brother Duff. He's a prisoner in the garrison here."

I looked back toward Jayne. What was this all about? Why the urgency? But her back was to me. "You are sure of this, Agnes?" I asked.

"Aye. I only knew it because I was deliverin' to the captain's quarters, and I heard him. I'd know his sound anawheres for I'd lived wi' it most o' me life. I slowed as I passed the tent and said his name. He called me closer. Ags, he calls me. Wasn't anybody payin' me notice so I slipped around to the side where he was."

Jayne shook her head with impatience. "Hurry, Agnes!"

"He said a guard come just before, a-kickin' him and the others in the head or the ribs and laughin'. Told 'em they're to be hanged *tomorrow* for their thievery. They ought sleep well this night, he said, for 'tis their last."

"Tomorrow? But I just..." My words halted and my mind ran wild. Hadn't Mr. Thomas just said it *might* happen if a siege began? How could it come about so quickly? It couldn't be true. Sir Arthur would use them to bargain with the Irish leaders. He wouldn't just kill them. Surely a sheriff would come and collect them first, before they were just murdered? But Agnes dropped to the ground, sobbing.

"My poor Duffy! I'm the fortunate one, at least I have a meal each day, but he...and most o' those lads. Sure they moved into Ross when the English come out, 'cuz they've got nothin'. They'd been livin' in the forests, scruffin' every day for anathin' just to stay alive. They were cold and starvin' and no place ta go. They're doin' what they must. It shouldna mean he has to die."

"No! Of course not. It can't be true," I said.

"We were run outta our house, me and him, muskets pointing at our heads, the land taken over by an Englishman and new settlers to come and take our place. Our Da died, just straightaway died, and Ma with no hope, was soon ta follow. But my Duff, he's fightin' fer all of us. If mebbe the Lord Carbery could win the lands back, then mebbe Duff could mek a way for hisself again. But it's...too late, innit?"

"How many are in that tent?" I asked, my blood pulsing.

"Eleven, Duff said."

Jayne glared at me, a fire in her eyes like I'd not yet seen. "Could be my own brother there too, for all I know." She spat on the ground. "He'd never be far from the MacCarthys. I'm sure of it. Could be your own brother, too."

"If I had one," I said.

Jayne nodded. "Aye, if ye had one. What if it were Ty?"

A fierce heat surged into my throat and spread across my shoulders. Then came a pressure behind my eyes and I was not sure if I would scream or cry. "What do you expect me to do about it?"

"Ye know things others don't know," she said. "Ye go 'round the castle as no one else can. Ye get yerself in and out, so why not them?"

I stared at her and my belly seized as if she, my best friend, had just stabbed me in the gut. "They'd hang me, Jayne. They would hang all of us."

"They won't. You're the only one in Rathbarry who can do this, and do it well."

"To hell with that," I said, too loudly. I stomped out of the shed, passing Jayne with enough force I could have knocked her flat. Yet I knew she still watched me. I headed straight for the stables and Ty. He would have some sense about this. Surely, I could talk to him. But if he even knew about such talk he would be at equal risk. My pace slowed.

As I passed the guard by the main gate, he struggled to carry a black chest, the kind they used for ammunition. He dropped it against the wall, causing puffs of dust to rise around its edges, then he returned to the tower. I approached the chest as if I were just walking past, and silently lifted the lid. No wonder it was so heavy. Inside were stacks of thick coiled rope.

Words came in a flash of air as if Jayne breathed them into my ear— You must lead them out—but the sound was too great to be whispered. Had she shouted? The words repeated in my mind like the chorus of a song that will not quiet, and then the very same words appeared like a vision upon a flat, gray, rain-splattered stone.

My breath shortened to quick gasps as if the stone was upon my breast, the weight almost unbearable. I sank to my knees beside the chest of ropes. A shudder ran up my spine. The weight slowly lifted and when I breathed in fully I saw the stone again, its surface as clear as the face of Agnes, just inches from my own: not a flag stone, no, nor a rain stone. It was a *piss* stone.

And then it all came clear to me fast.

16

A Brave Thing

Rathbarry Castle

I ran back to the laundry shed, where Jayne and Agnes still waited. "To-night," I said. "Go on about your tasks, both of you. Have your supper. Wait until after dark, and after the night watch leaves the castle through the main gate. Once outside, they'll divide and go northeast and northwest minding the livestock. When the court is quiet and empty, meet me be-hind the plum trees under the southeast tower, the big one. Be quiet, do not be seen. Jayne, bring a dagger from the kitchen. Sharpest you can find."

"What are ye plannin'?" Jayne asked.

"I'll tell you everything tonight." I said. "For now, we should go."

Agnes sobbed again. And wiped her eyes with her apron.

"Agnes," I said. "If you can't act like nothing's amiss, take to your bed, claim a belly ache. Do nothing to draw attention. Can you manage?"

"I swear to it." Agnes straightened up, thrust back her shoulders and smoothed her skirt. "I can soldier up as well as anyone."

"Good. I'm depending on you."

Agnes returned to her work. Jayne headed toward the kitchen to help with the evening meal, and I returned to Lady Carey, to help her dress for supper. My belly fluttered. I struggled to eat my salted trout and thin bit of stew. But I ate, and though I'd never been much of one to do it, I prayed to God. *If you sent me that vision, then please shelter us in our task. Unless it be your will, those prisoners shall not hang on the morrow.*

The halfmoon was just waning, shedding more light than I'd have hoped with such a deed ahead of us, but it was not enough to stop me.

We'd all hang if they caught us, that was sure and true. But I could not think about such things.

The plum trees offered the best seclusion in summer, when their boughs were heavy with leaves and fruit, but even in February the thicket of branches and the shadow provided by the servants' quarters made for good cover. After Lady Carey was asleep, and after the night watch left the main gate, I watched from the window as the guard climbed to the tower. When he was gone, I slipped out the door and along the castle wall until I reached the plum orchard. Jayne met me in the darkest corner just a minute later. "Did you bring the dagger?" I asked.

"It's just here," Jayne said, drawing it from her skirt pocket. I gently tucked it into my own and we pressed together, silent and still as we could be, until Agnes joined us, quiet as a beetle creeping across the court. We waited for sounds of any others who might be stirring. The keep was closed up, its windows dark. The court was alive with shadows dancing about with every breath of wind, but the cold kept people indoors. There would be guards on each tower watching the outer walls, and a guard at the prisoners' tent.

"The shadows are our cloaks tonight," I whispered. "Stay always within them. Being small—it's how I have learned to get by, so follow close behind me. We must move quickly and make no sound." We crept against the edge of the servants' quarters and along the outer wall of the stable, which was closed and dark. To cross the open ground from the stables to the garrison tents, we had to rely on timing when the tower guard wasn't near, and on darkness and speed.

The prisoners were in the second tent past the postern gate. If only we could have used this gate to free the prisoners, close as it was to the tent, and to the Irish camp beyond. But it was heavily locked, and both sides of the gate too visible to the tower guard above it.

I wasn't concerned about passing the first tent, which held heavy barrels and crates stored within easy access to the gates. There'd be no one inside to overhear us. Next to it, the prisoners' tent was guarded in front by a single armed soldier who paced, and then sat a bit wobbly on a small wooden stool.

"Jayne," I said softly. "Can you distract him? I mean, without waking anyone?"

"Of course. I served him his beer after supper—wi' a few drops of the Elinor's valerian tincture. He ought be quite sleepy," she whispered. "I'll mind him."

"Good. Go then. Agnes, behind me."

When the tower guard walked toward the western wall, we crept silently behind the tents. I slid the dagger from my skirt. We couldn't afford the sound of ripping canvas to expose us, so I'd need the sharp blade to fray open the tent thread by thread, just enough for the men to slither out the bottom.

We couldn't have one of the prisoners groan or shout in surprise either. I motioned to Agnes to peek under the tent, get Duffy's attention, and press a finger to her lips for silence. Scuffling movements sounded like a dog circling before he flops to his bed. Agnes looked up and gave me a nod. She held her brother's hand beneath the tent's bottom edge.

I went to work, for there was no time to waste. I started at the hem where the canvas was doubled and sawed until a slit opened. How I wished I could grab each corner of it and rip the canvas apart. Instead I kept sawing, silently as possible. I'd cut about six inches when Jayne's distraction turned into a soft giggle, and her soldier was awake. I froze, as did Agnes beside me. The guard was at the wall just above. The tiniest movement and he might see us. He seemed to be waiting for another sound, and I was afraid even to breathe. Jayne must have somehow silenced her man, and the tower guard moved on. The knife cut so slowly on the canvas, for what in truth was only minutes but seemed like an hour until the opening was large enough for the prisoners to slip out.

One by one they came, as silently as possible, knowing their lives depended on it, but my heart jumped with every exhale, scrape against ground, or creak of leather, and I held my skirt against my nose for they stank of sweat and dirt and their own filth and waste, having been treated worse than the curs in the ditches. They followed Agnes against the wall beneath the shadows until they reached the stables. My heart thundered within my chest, amazed more than anyone that we'd managed so far.

I led them low and lithe as cats on the prowl to the side entrance Ty had used for bringing Jayne and me back to the castle the night she sang for the soldiers. Here was the weakest part of my plan, for I'd not seen Ty nor spoken to him. I knew Giles and Collum had gone to their lodgings for the night, for I'd watched them depart, but if Ty slept within he'd be surprised by our arrival. Most of the time he was reserved, dutiful. I assumed he'd not wish to see his countrymen hanged, but I had to take the gamble that he'd protect us, for there was no other way, and there'd be no better time.

The door creaked slightly when I pushed it open and peered into the darkness, the shadows all the darker for having the moonlight filtered out. In only a second I recognized the human figure standing right before my eyes. My heart leapt and my breath caught. It had to be Ty. I looked to his face but couldn't see his expression. He bent forward to look beyond me to Agnes and the men lined up behind her. He looked back at me, then quickly ran to the stable's front door. My belly twisted. He wouldn't betray us to the guards, would he? He opened the door but a sliver, and then closed it again. He nodded and pointed toward the opposite wall of the stable.

I ran in that direction, not knowing what I'd find, but trusting he had a reason to send me. I came upon a half door in the wall. It opened to a large hay bin, and on top of the bin, a canted lid. I crawled through the bin and slipped out the top like a lizard over a garden gate, and my followers came right behind me while I held open the lid. My blood flushed with relief, for we'd avoided crossing an open space nearest the keep where we most risked discovery. Yet, we had one more space to cross before the prisoners could be free. We had to pass in front of the servants' quarters to reach the plum tree orchard, and cross from there into the tower's lower stair. The shadows favored us, but the distance seemed so much greater when moving so many people.

Now, with the stealth and cunning of a mother fox and her kits we crept one behind the other until, *God be thanked*, we made it to dark haven beneath the plum branches. And then the distinctive clicks of a musket hefted to a shoulder froze us all in line.

"Halt! Who passes there?" One guard minded the hexagonal tower that night and somehow he'd been alerted. We were done for. None of us dared to breathe. My heart thudded wildly within my chest. A second passed. Two. Three. Four.

"Sorry! 'Tis only me, sir." Jayne popped out from under the trees to draw his attention, and held out her skirt as if to curtsy. When had she arrived? *And God bless her for it.* She stepped closer to the tower as he watched. Clever girl, for if she continued calling from the orchard, she'd surely awaken others. "I canna sleep," she said. "The moon keeps me awake. I'll come up for a chat, will I?"

"Sorry, I cannot...you're not supposed to..." the soldier started.

"Only for a moment or two?"

He hesitated. Jayne stepped slightly toward the stair and removed her cap, so that her hair fell about her shoulders. "Just a little while. I'm so lonely," she said.

"Arragh," the soldier consented, and Jayne ran for the winding stair to the tower.

The instant the soldier turned from the wall, I guided the first three men to the winding stair, down to the limestone ledge where the soldiers pissed, and it smelled so. The men crept across it and along the castle's outer wall until they could dart past the lake into the wood—thence to freedom. Three more went, and then three more. The last two were a skinny, hairy lad, and Agnes's taller but equally thin brother whose eyes it was too dark to see. Before I closed the shutter, Agnes hugged me.

"God love you for this, but I must go." She slipped out behind her brother, and then all were gone.

I secured the shutter and crept back to the shadows to wait for Jayne. The curs outside barked and yelped, but did not raise an alarm greater than that of a passing deer. I realized then, I had left another major detail unconsidered. The moon now reached its zenith, reducing the shadows to insufficient cover. The way across the courtyard to Lady Carey's apartment was now well-lit open space. I contemplated the desired door, and at the same time hoped Jayne was not having to sacrifice too much of her virtue before she could escape.

A slight rustle frightened me, but I caught the scent of horsehair, and knew it was Ty beside me. He must have guessed my concern. He whispered gently in my ear.

"Jayne will cross the court, fair enough. The guard already knows she's about. But you would stir questions, especially by morn when the deed is discovered. There's but one way to get you home. Should someone see, your reputation will be lost. Mebbe even your position, but it's better than losin' yer life." he said.

"What do you propose?"

"A walk with yer lover." He scooped an arm around my waist and held me so close as if to squeeze the breath from me, then he swept my feet from under me and carried me the rest of the way. When we reached Lady Carey's doorstep, he tilted me backward and landed a warm, lingering kiss upon my lips. My heart drummed in my ears and for a second nothing in the world existed anymore. Then he set me on my feet and kissed my hand as any good suitor would do. "A brave thing you are, for this. I wish I'd done it meself. Sleep well, hellkite."

17

Oaths and Promises

Rathbarry Castle

I slept not at all, alert for whatever might come. If there had been a storm of activity in the garrison that morning, and if Sir Arthur had shouted his fury, I did not hear it. I stayed within the apartment, as did Jayne, until Lady Carey was dressed and ready to go to the keep for her breakfast. Jayne and I didn't speak, and barely allowed our eyes to meet until she hurried out to the garden ward to attend Mistress Coale.

I followed Lady Carey up the steps, noticing the courtyard was oddly quiet. When we arrived at table, Mistress Dorothy was absent, and the other family members offered no greetings. They kept their eyes focused on their plates. My lady took her seat with a loud exhale of disappointment. Then a realization washed over me like a basin of water to my face. The Irish prisoners, I assumed, were safe. That their escape had been discovered, I'd no doubt, but the result wasn't the disturbed wasp nest I'd expected. Instead, the escape had provoked an eerie terror across the court.

All within Rathbarry had assumed they were protected by the castle's great walls and the armed garrison within. That safety had been breached, and danger was not over there at Clonakilty, or even at Ross. It was within and among us. Everyone's life was at risk, and I—the diminutive and unimportant—was responsible. Something about that thrilled me. I couldn't suppress the slight grin that curled my lips for the secret triumph that I could have such power. But then came regret for the result so completely unintended. My triumph was swallowed whole by the dark foreboding that I'd surely be discovered.

Though my emotions warred, I had to bury them deep inside for I could never speak of the escape nor even suggest I knew anything about what had happened, and couldn't allow any strange or fearful behavior to draw attention. I wasn't the same as I'd been the day before. I'd taken great risk. I'd been a leader. I had rescued and betrayed. I was both hero and villain. And now I carried the heavy burden of a most dangerous secret. Was this the lesson Captain Beecher had foretold? I would have to think on that. But in the meantime, there had been *that kiss*. Ty had called me Hellkite, and I was beginning to like it.

After breakfast, my lady retired to the solar, assuming Mistress Dorothy would be away and she could do as she pleased. She sent me back to the apartment for her sewing. I stopped at the well to replenish our water, and from behind me came unusual sounds of stones tumbling, loud scraping, and subdued male voices. I turned to see three workmen at the entrance to the southeast tower, where I had been just hours before. I walked over.

"Good morn, gentlemen. My goodness, such a rattle and clatter. What are you lads up to this fine day?"

Two of them ignored me, but the younger man spoke over his shoulder, "Walling up an opening here. Sir Arthur ordered it."

"Oh. Well then, I shouldn't disturb you." I gave a polite nod, fetched my herb basket and wandered toward the garden ward, by way of the stables and garrison. The stables were closed up as before, but sure enough more workmen labored to seal up the postern gate. Now there would be only one way in and out of the castle: by the main gate.

Sir Arthur was nearby, observing the work and engaging in what appeared to be a serious conversation with Captain Beecher. I moved closer.

"Sir, you are correct," Captain Beecher said. "We cannot know how it happened, but it was under my watch. I am the ranking officer for this garrison. I have failed, and should return to Bandon for reassignment."

Sir Arthur held out empty hands. "Captain, we were all a bit too comfortable in our remoteness, and none of us aware the Irish were capable of such stealth. My laundress is gone. *She* planned this, betrayed me and has escaped with the rogues. You did not foresee something like this, nor did I. If you go, I should go as well. As owner of this castle, I should have known its weaknesses and warned you of them long ago. I should have offered you a better place for the prisoners, and considered the loyalties of my Irish servants. Yes, there has been failure here. But if you return to Bandon, you leave me, my family and all these people even more exposed and vulnerable."

I turned into the garden ward. Exposed, Sir Arthur said. What a strange word. I had only meant to save some men from hanging. Must I now think of them as enemies? Would I be forced to choose a side between the English, my employers, and the Irish, my friends? Things had grown personal where before they'd been distant. If I'd said the word 'war' to Jayne, we could've agreed it was upon us, but not that it might actually touch us, much less *kill* us. And now it was possible—no, *likely*—that some of the men I had secreted to safety could come back upon us in hostility. I, in doing my good deed, had *exposed* to the Irish Rathbarry's weaknesses.

The idea produced a bit of nausea, and I searched the garden ward for Jayne but couldn't find her. Lady Carey would be vexed with me if I didn't return to her soon. I ran to exchange my herb basket for the sewing basket, and then back to the keep.

Sir Arthur and Mistress Dorothy were in the state room behind a closed door. I could hear them speaking quietly as I entered the solar, but couldn't recognize the words. How I longed to press my ear to that door, to know what they were thinking and planning. When had I become such an eavesdropper?

"My goodness. I thought you weren't coming back at all. What took you so long?" Lady Carey said. "Our Thomas Freke rode out on Sir Arthur's stallion while you were gone. Did you see him?"

"No, my lady. I'm sorry for my delay. I was looking for Jayne but couldn't find her."

"Mr. O'Daly was there, helping Thomas to his mount. Then Thomas rode out with two guards beside him. I wonder what that is all about? It seems there is quite a stir in the castle today, but no one wants to talk about it. Terribly irritating, if you ask me."

"Yes, my lady. Would you like a sherry?"

"Yes, dear." She picked at the items in her sewing basket and selected an infant's white gown. She sipped her sherry and smacked her lips, then turned to her project. We sat in silence while the voices in the state room eventually hushed as well. I paced the floor.

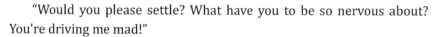

"Would you please settle? What have you to be so nervous about? You're driving me mad!"

"Yes, my lady, I'm sorry. I will sit," I said.

She sighed and handed her sewing to me to trim the loose threads. "That horse marshal. He is quite handsome, wouldn't you say?"

"Yes, he truly is, my lady."

"I wonder if Jayne is interested in him. That would be a clever match, wouldn't it, with both being Irish? They'd make a lovely couple. As I think of it, the stable has been quite sealed as of late. And today you couldn't find Jayne. How amusing if the two of them have already found each other behind those closed doors."

The back of my scalp lifted as if someone tugged my hair, and hot blood rushed to my cheeks. My emotions were not so under control as I'd hoped. Did she know of my attraction to Ty? Did she make such statements on purpose just to tease me? Or was she truly connecting the two of them in her mind? "I think Jayne would not like him," I said. "I've heard Mr. O'Daly has a violent temper, aside from the fact that he always stinks of manure."

"Dear me. A temper? Truly? I s'pose all men tend to be demanding, but I thought those who were good with animals were gentler with their wives and children."

"One can never be sure. After all, he uses a whip on the horses." My wickedness had cast off its restraints.

"My goodness. I must ponder this, certainly. Perhaps I'll ask..."

Loud voices reached us from the great hall, and then the clomp of heavy boots upon the stairs. Thomas reached the top stair and turned toward the state room. Behind him came three large men in dark cloaks, one who had a broad red sash across his chest. The others wore heavy woolens beneath brown leather jerkins. They were wet, perhaps from a light rain, and seemed to shed the dampness as they crossed the oak planks. Thomas pounded on the door. Lady Carey's head jerked up from her work. The hinges creaked.

"Gentlemen. Please come in," Sir Arthur said. They clomped forward. "This is my darling wife, Dorothy."

"Welcome, kind sirs," she said. "Please sit down and make yourselves comfortable. Will you have wine?"

"Och, aye, just to warm the blood a bit, shall we, lads?" One of the visitors said.

They didn't close the door, perhaps not realizing Lady Carey and I were nearby. My lady's eyes widened with surprise. She pressed a finger to her lips to signal we should not reveal our presence. If I were over-curious about other people's business, I realized the acquired trait had not traveled far—I'd picked it up quite naturally from my lady.

"Brother," Thomas said. "As you requested, I've escorted these gentlemen from Donoure Castle by the arrangement of Mr. McMahony. May I introduce Mr. John Oge Barry, his brother Edmund, and Sir Robert O'Shaughnessy, who has come on behalf of his father, Sir Roger, at Timoleague."

Sir Arthur cleared his throat so loudly it sounded like a growl. "Gentlemen. I understand you've come to discuss the proposition set forth yesterday in Mr. McMahony's letter," Sir Arthur said, not giving them an opportunity to speak. "It seems your Mr. O'Downe wants me to *give* him my castle. And all that is within it. And all my sheep and cattle, too. And this not only, for he wants his people to move in, presently, here among us. Where shall my family be allowed to sleep? In the hay bin?"

There came a sudden blustering of voices and a scraping of chair legs on the floor. Then the activity settled to a single voice, perhaps the one with the sash who displayed the most authority.

"Sir Arthur, we have come..."

"I believe you should call me Commander-in-Chief."

There was a silence. How I wished I could see the men's faces as Sir Arthur demanded respect. The speaker cleared his throat loudly and continued.

"Commander-in-Chief, then. Let it be known and understood that we speak for our leaders, the MacCarthy Reagh, Prince of Carbery, Commander of the Munster clans, and his second in command, Teige O'Downe, Lord of Glean-na-Croim, the vast valley and lands of Dunmanway. To these men and to these clans the great Barony of Carbery belongs, and has done for 400 years."

His voice was a bit high for a man, soft with his words as a kindly neighbor might be, but at the same time a sharpness seemed to flicker around its edges. Someone scoffed loudly, I guessed it might have been Thomas, or Sir Arthur, or both of them together.

"We, collectively," the man continued, "have great respect and affection for your father at Youghal, and for you, who have lived prosperously, provided employment for some, and shelter for others, in peace. We are obliged to you and your families and do swear by the precious ground of Carbery herself, that you should live safely and happily, and to that end we would never do anything that might cause harm to you or your family, and would so die in your very defense. But you must understand that, by legal right, custom, heritage, and under God, our Lord of Carbery must take possession of *that which is his.*

"Our hope is to conduct this peacefully and in harmony. And that is, as was stated in Mr. McMahony's letter, that ye shall deliver the castle to Mr. McDirmond O'Shane, and for Lord Barrymore's use. Only, if you so refuse, he shall besiege the castle forthwith and take all within."

"Just one moment. That which is *his*?" Sir Arthur said, his voice strong but shaking with rage. "This castle—and all its lands, sheep and cattle—belong to me. I paid a large and worthy sum for it and owe nothing to any man. I shall no more hand it over freely to your gentleman, than your Lord of the Barony—so to speak—would do for me. Land does not belong to any man just because you say it does, and your 400 years mean nothing to me, nor to any law in the land."

"So then," the man said, ignoring Sir Arthur's retort, "the Gentleman does provide that ye shall reside in safety and comfort within the castle, and may choose from among the residents those who should remain herewith. The Gentleman is prepared to take custody immediately."

A sound came forth, as if Sir Arthur had pounded upon his desk. "You come to us, behaving as friends, and you dare to praise and threaten my family in the same breath. *All lies.* Rathbarry belongs to me and this is our home. We'll want nothing from you and you'll get nothing from us."

The silence returned, but this time with a tension so palpable I could feel its sting on my own skin as if I'd met a patch of nettles. Lady Carey was seized with fear, she who had left her comfortable home in distant Fermoy for Rathbarry's presumed safety.

The chairs scraped much louder, sliding backward on the floor as, I assumed, the gentlemen guests rose to leave.

"Commander-in-Chief Freke, we have come to you in kindness, our wish only to prevent any discomfort or, perhaps, unpleasant confrontation. Ye should know—the town of Clonakilty has been taken, and the properties of your friend, the sovereign Linscombe, are confiscated. Ye will not be celebrating your Christmas with him next year. Ye shall only have this day to reconsider. The soldiers of our holy Catholic camp are prepared to take the castle by tomorrow nightfall," the visitor said.

"Good day, sirs," Sir Arthur said, "for under such a threat I cannot, *shall not* call you gentlemen."

A chill climbed my spine. I quickly closed the door to the solar, that none would see us there and question our presence. Lady Carey's face had lost all color and tears welled in her eyes.

"What shall we do, child? What in God's world shall we do?"

We waited in the solar until we were certain everyone had left the rooms, and then we hurried outside to get Lady Carey to her bed. The fear had taken her strength, and she sought comfort and seclusion. As we crossed the court, the wasp nest activity I'd wondered about before now came to be, as Sir Arthur and Thomas shouted orders from the center of the court.

"Mr. Sellers!" Sir Arthur shouted. "Bring some men to start gathering my sheep into the court and the garden ward. Make haste. We expect no good to come from our Irish neighbors. Mr. Beecher! Millett!"

Captain Beecher soon stood before him. "Sir Arthur."

"I understand Lord Kinalmeaky is in Bandon with his troops. Hasten to him with my letter. I am sending to his protection diverse members of my family and residents herein, that he may receive them to safety in Bandon, and escort them thence to Kinsale. Mr. Millett will see they are promptly packed and loaded into carriages for travel. Millett, make sure that they bring with them only essentials. They must leave Rathbarry quickly and arrive in Bandon before sundown. Mr. O'Daly!"

Ty must have been at ready; he appeared before Sir Arthur within a few seconds. "Aye, Sir Arthur."

"Prepare my best carriages with sturdy horses, and have them in the court within an hour."

18

Tethered

Rathbarry Castle

Six carriages creaked and swayed as the horses pulled them beside the castle steps. Jayne and I had scrambled madly for Lady Carey who wanted to take everything she owned, fearing all would be destroyed or stolen by the Irish. She sat on a bed stripped of its linens and coverings, and wept as she ordered us about. Mistress Coale already waited within the castle hall, having few belongings to pack since her arrival from Ross. She, her family and servants alone would fill nearly two carriages. I hoped not to ride in her carriage, for she would likely complain during the entire journey.

We waited while Ty double-checked the rigs and harnesses, and Mr. Millett checked his list of boxes to be loaded and arranged to ensure proper balance of weight. The largest of these held the household valuables that would be in the care of Sir Arthur's mother Ann. Giles and Collum brought up two wagons behind the carriages, to carry the boxes, trunks and cases of clothing and personal belongings for the passengers.

Garrison soldiers loaded the wagons and strapped down the cargo. When they had finished, Jenkin opened the keep's doors wide and the passengers waiting there stepped down to board the carriages. Sir Arthur's mother and sisters filled the first carriage, along with his son Percy, and his tutor. Ty helped Lady Carey and Mistress Coale into the second carriage. As her companion, I should have been seated beside Lady Carey, but I could see there was no room after Nicholas Cambridge, his wife with their children climbed in. Mr. Millett called other families and servants to board the next carriage, including John Sellers's wife and their children. Jayne paced back and forth as we awaited our turn, wringing her hands, distress drawing her face to a long, pale mask.

Ty brought Sarcen from the stable, saddled and ready. Thomas took the reins and mounted. Captain Beecher rode forward from the garrison with twenty soldiers riding behind him, making a great deal of noise as they crossed the court in their armor and weapons clattering at their sides. They filled the air with the musky scents of sweat and horse flesh.

"The men are well-armed, I trust," Sir Arthur said. He stood on the castle steps, Mistress Dorothy like a marble statue beside him.

"As you commanded, sir," Captain Beecher said. "Two armed guards for each carriage, and escorts in front and behind. We shall stay to the open road, stopping as little as possible if at all, to avoid ambush. After delivering our precious cargo to Bandon, we should return to Rathbarry in roughly eight hours."

"Thank you, Captain, and God be with you," Sir Arthur said, and nodded him forward. "Thomas, there won't be much time, I know, but do send the carriages back with any supplies you can acquire."

"I shall, Arthur. Be at ease," Thomas said.

Sir Arthur patted Sarcen's neck. "I shall miss you, brother, and I'll miss Sarcen nearly as much as my son. He's a fine horse. But you must keep him for the longer journey. When you arrive home, do give our father my respects."

Ty, on another of Sir Arthur's horses, rode up beside Thomas. He would mind the carriages for the return trip. I'd be glad to have him in our company, for I couldn't think yet about being separated from him. Perhaps he could even stay with us all the way to Kinsale.

With everything secured, the soldiers stepped away from the wagons, and helped the servants into the last carriage. I looked to Jayne, but she wept and seemed stiff and immovable, as if her shoes were nailed to the ground. Then came a slam, and the door to the last carriage was closed. Mr. Millett stepped back from it.

"Wait!" I stepped forward, and Lady Carey peered out her window at Jayne and me, left waiting outside. Her eyes rounded with question, and her lips trembled. Then I began to tremble. Mistress Dorothy came beside me and grabbed my wrist. I tried to pull away, but her icy fingers squeezed like a vice.

"Merel will stay to attend me, Lady Carey. I do hope you won't mind. She will be needed here, and I trust you can manage without her for a while," she said.

Panic rose to a boil beneath my skin. My eyes filled and my nose swelled until I could barely breathe. Was I *crying*?

"And I'll stay as well," Jayne said, stepping to my other side. Mistress Dorothy looked at Jayne with raised brows, and then nodded.

"Jayne!" Mistress Coale cried out, but she must have received a fierce look of warning from Mistress Dorothy, for she said nothing more.

Sir Arthur spoke from the castle steps, his voice firm as if for a formal announcement to be heard all across the court. "Bandon is a walled town, secure, well-fortified. It has walls nine feet thick, and fifty feet high, and it's defended by a strong, trained militia. You will be safe there, and well looked-after. It is my promise."

Lady Carey then nodded, but her face looked slack and pale. She glanced at me once more and then slowly slipped away from the carriage window and out of my view. Mistress Coale, not being one to let things lie, jammed her face into a vacant window frame and shouted, "Sir Arthur, we came to Rathbarry for a reason. It is well known those townsmen at Bandon charge rents to English refugees at thrice the normal rate. How are we supposed to pay?"

Sir Arthur's fists pressed to his hips. "We are talking about survival, Mistress Coale. We are all doing our best with what we have."

She shook her fist at him. "Robbed by the Irish, next we are to be robbed by the English, too! And you, Jayne, you will regret this."

I barely heard them, so crazed inside, filled with disbelief. Would my lady do nothing to keep me? Not even a word? After all these years, would she not want me beside her? Knowing not which way to turn, my arms and legs demanded to fly from my body but they were as tethered to me as I was to Mistress Dorothy. I couldn't scream, because I couldn't breathe, and yet I looked to Jayne who showed no sign of panic, but instead seemed to have calmed.

Captain Beecher caught my eye and smirked, then snapped the reins and was first to ride out, followed by Thomas and Ty, and then four men of the escort. My heart careened within my chest as Lady Carey's coach disappeared through the castle gate. My vision failed me and all I could see was a sheet of gray-blue water rising, covering me, choking the air from my lungs. My legs trembled as if to collapse beneath me but Mistress Dorothy yet held me in place, and then Jayne grasped my elbow and held me up.

"This was our agreement, Merel. Remember, you owed something to me. This is what I require," Mistress Dorothy said.

I gathered what breath I could. "Too much." The words came from my lips in little more than a whisper. Jayne held me tighter and I regained my legs. "It is far too great," I said with more strength, "for the use of a privy."

"Nevertheless," the mistress said.

I watched through welling tears, my teeth gritted together as if that could keep them from streaming down my face. As the last of the wagons left Rathbarry, followed by the rear guard, the gate clanked shut and the guards secured it behind them. Only then did Mistress Dorothy release my wrist.

"You will both move into the keep. Get your things, and see Jenkin for your new lodgings. Then report to me in the solar," she said, and returned to her husband's side.

Well I had *no* things, had I, since all had been packed with Lady Carey's. My dresses, my nightgown, even my precious, beautiful pearls. Gone, all gone. And my lady, my second mother. Gone and leaving me empty as if my belly had been ripped from my body. Was I to lose and lose and lose, and never be held close and loved by anyone? Was that God's plan for me?

I looked down at my pale pink gown made of twill, the stiff bodice tightly laced. I hadn't even worn my stomacher, so as not to be uncomfortable while traveling. Lady Carey would have been scandalized, had she noticed. It was my least-favorite gown in my least favorite color, so I worried not that it be muddied, wrinkled or torn during travel. And now it was my only gown. My skin shivered with frustration.

Jenkin led Jayne and me to the top floor of the keep, a garret, just like the one in Jayne's song—dim and cramped with a sloping roof, two cots, a small hinged chest, and a rug woven from rags. We'd get the heat from the hearths in the apartments below us, if there be wood to burn, and the cold from the wind and snow above us, of which I had more surety. It was quite a bitter change from the comfort and freedom we'd known at Lady Carey's courtside apartment.

I faced Jayne. *"And we'll die as old maids in the garret,"* I said.

19

Court and Castle

Rathbarry Castle

"It will be all right," Jayne said. "We have each other, and at least we'll eat well here in the castle, like family."

"But the family is gone," I said. "Who will live in those warmer apartments below us?"

"I don't know, but we'll see soon enough."

"Let's go down to the solar before Mistress Dorothy sends someone after us." I knew my voice sounded bitter, but so be it. The solar was two floors down, and when we arrived the room was nearly blue in the clouded afternoon light. Mistress Dorothy wasn't there, nor was she in the state room. We waited, assuming she was detained.

"Why did you stay, Jayne? You were not held. You could have gone with the others, even if you had to squeeze into that last crowded carriage. You could have escaped," I said.

She looked at her hands folded in her lap, and then out the window at the gray. "Do you remember, the night we let the...you know. I dare not say it."

"Yes. That night."

"I went up to the tower."

"You were so brave, Jayne. You saved us all."

"It seemed a natural thing to do. I had to make sure he heard nothing. It could have...we could all have been caught and..."

"Hanged," I said.

She turned her face away. "That soldier, David, from the tower. He and

the other lad, James, they were punished."

I was so tired, drained of all my strength so that I could hardly lift my hands from my lap, and it was not even noonday. Of the sorrows or difficulties of others, I hardly cared. Yet would I have to learn more painful truths. "How? What did they do to them?"

"They were flogged, no rations given, tied nearly naked to a post, and left out for a day and a long, cold night."

"Oh..." I recoiled as if someone punched me in the stomach. "I'm sorry, Jayne. Truly. So sorry. Did they..."

"They came through it all right, and neither of them told about me. If they had, it would have gone worse for them—beguiled by a woman. And James is married, so. But David is..."

"Is he ill?"

"No. He is healing. It's just that I spent a lot of time with him that night. And then after, I..." She stood and went to the window. "Remember what you told me about Ty, when we were under the cloak that night? About the way he made you feel?"

"Jayne! You've fallen in love with this soldier?"

She nodded. "David Hyrd." Tears filled her eyes. I stood up and hugged her. "So that's why you wanted to stay? You didn't want to leave him?"

"Him, yes, and my brother. I don't know when I'll see either of them again, but I fear if I go to Kinsale, I'll never be able to come back."

I stood beside her and we clasped hands. "I'm glad you stayed, for David, but also for me."

"We are better off here, maybe," Jayne said, "With Sir Arthur and the garrison. Sure all of this trouble will end soon."

I had my doubts. If Sir Arthur thought it would be over soon, would he have sent his family away? But we spoke no more and waited in uneasy silence for a while longer, the brooding skies deepening and shifting, allowing occasional shafts of light that then faded into a soft gray mist. More than an hour passed and Mistress Dorothy still did not come.

"I think I should go. I'll be needed in the kitchen," Jayne said.

"I'll go down with you. Our mistress is probably in the court. Something must be afoot."

When I reached the courtyard, it was as if we'd returned to the day the villagers had arrived from Ross. Mr. Millett and Mistress Dorothy were directing movements of families from the garden ward into the main court and the castle, while sheep and cattle were being brought in from the grazing fields to overnight within the castle walls. The movements of people allowed space for more animals, but Sir Arthur's flocks numbered in the thousands. There couldn't be room enough for all, and some still would have to remain in the fields.

The mistress waved me to her side. "Go to the garden ward and find the May family among the tents. Bring them up. They are to go to Lady Carey's apartment."

I found them ready, a husband and wife with sacks slung over their shoulders that held their meager belongings, and at their knees were six children of various ages.

"Please tell the mistress," Mr. May said. "We are grateful for the use of the tents and the shelter provided, but are so very eager to have walls about us again, and a proper roof above our heads."

"I will tell her truly, sir," I said. He didn't seem to realize, or perhaps didn't care that the true purpose of his move was not for his family's comfort, but to pen the animals in his place. And it would not necessarily mean greater shelter or safety for them, because our danger had increased.

After supper I waited in the court for Ty's return. If Mistress called for me, she would not find me. The evening light passed into darkness, and the stars were bright by the time the tower guards shouted. They had sighted Beecher's troops and the carriages behind them, returning to the castle. My lungs released a burst of air when the gates opened, he was among the first to enter, riding Sarcen and leading the other horse behind him. He gave me a nod unsmiling. Captain Beecher rode just ahead of him and stopped in the courtyard where Sir Arthur approached.

"Welcome back. You've kept to your promised time. Are all well?" Sir Arthur asked.

"Sir, all passengers delivered safely to Lord Kinalmeaky. He will see them to Kinsale within the fortnight."

"Excellent news. Are there any incidents to report? Any troubles along the road?"

"None, sir. Exceedingly quiet, which is perhaps more alarming."

Sir Arthur waved Beecher on to the garrison, and approached Ty.

"Why have you returned Sarcen? Thomas was to keep him."

"Aye, sir. Your brother insisted on a garrison horse to Kinsale, and that you had greater need of your favorite stallion than he."

Sir Arthur looked down at his boots for a moment, and then stroked Sarcen's mane. The horse snorted and pawed once at the ground. "I was rather hoping for his safety away from here."

"I'm sorry sir. I'll take him back then, shall I? 'Tis a quick ride."

"No. It is well. Another time. The carriages are in good state?"

"Quite fit, sir. Four were left with Lord Kinalmeaky."

"Yes, to go to Kinsale. I should have thought. We will retrieve them when...well...mayhap Thomas can have a care for them."

"Aye, sir."

Sir Arthur waved Ty on and turned toward the keep. Ty looked over his shoulder at me and tilted his head toward the stable. I looked about, but no one paid any attention to me. I waited while the rest of the rear guard passed and then crossed the courtyard to the stables.

The smell of hay, horse sweat and leather settled me, as if none of this disruption was happening and everything was still as it was. Ty removed his coat and doublet and unsaddled Sarcen. He bent down to retrieve a brush from a box and stood by in his loose shirt and breeks, the lantern light softening every edge, painting Sarcen's sweat-dampened flanks a deep indigo and liquid gold. Ty's eyes were nearly as dark as the night sky. His lips parted; his brow furrowed. He cast the brush down and reached for my shoulder.

"Are you well?" he asked gently.

The feel of his hand raised my blood. "Of course, I am fine. Why wouldn't I be?"

He looked into my eyes as if searching for something, then released my shoulder and picked up the brush again. "Well, let's see." He brushed Sarcen's neck for a few strokes, and then the shoulder. "Ye worked for your lady for a decade, and then worked your tail off to get her packed and ready for the carriage, aye? Ye stood by her and saw her safe to her place, and then waited your turn to board. But then the door was slammed in your face, aye? And Mistress Dorothy held ye back like an untrained pup. That had ta hurt a little. "

"I guess I was…"

"Then, your fine Lady Carey spoke not a word, made not a single gesture. She peeked out the window, and just gave you up."

"Well, she was afraid, and sh…"

"She wasn't that afraid. She gave you up. She said nothing. Not even a good-bye. After all the years you worked for her, she didn't fight for you."

Tears sprang to my eyes. I cursed myself, and suddenly my shoulders shook, my throat swelled. Had she just not loved me enough? That could be my only conclusion. I struggled for air, burying my face in my hands so that he'd not see my ugly, shattering countenance. How shameful that he should witness such weakness, and yet he'd laid open my heart as if parting the shell of a walnut.

He stopped working, wrapped his arms around me and held tight. "It's all right, go on, let it out. If ever in your life there was a time to cry, sure this is one of 'em." He held me so for several minutes until I quieted and stilled. Then he rested his chin on the top of my head.

"She didn't fight for you. She's a woman who flows through life like a leaf in a river, always doing nothing, always expecting to be carried along. She doesn't even know what she's lost. But I know. And were it me, I would fight hard for you. In fact, I will." He leaned back enough to look into my teary eyes. "It's my oath. I will always fight for you."

I took a deep, full breath and swallowed, though my mouth was dry and my heart thudded quick and hard like an ancient drummer summoning the spirits. What had he just said? He lifted my chin and gently kissed my lips, my eyes, my lips again, then kissed away the tears and brushed my cheeks softly with the sleeve of his shirt. It was almost more than I could bear.

"I'd better go," I said.

"Aye, someone will be lookin' fer ye." He turned me slowly by my shoulders to face the door, and kissed the back of my neck, the sensation tingling across my scalp and all the way down my spine.

20

The Warpipes

Rathbarry Castle

I awakened to the sound of the warpipes that morning when the Irish marched on Rathbarry. There came a long, low, and sorrowful note, as if a fiddler had chosen it to warm his instrument for some tragic ballad. The draft from the garret's roof swept easily through my blanket, the chill as good as a shake to drive my sleepiness away. The sound shifted to a lower note and I shot up. It was no fiddler playing. Far away, insistent, and stirring like the howl of a wolf, it was a piper's call to the soul.

"Jane!" I shook her shoulder. "Get up. Something's happening."

"No, no I can't," she said through a dream, but I tugged her hair this time as the piper stopped and restarted. She heard it and leapt from her cot, her eyes wide with fear. "It's the Irish army come. I know it."

I jerked the blanket from my bed. "Let's get our shoes on and go down. We can't see a thing from here."

Wearing only our night shifts, we ran to the court. We were not the first. Others headed toward the north and east towers, and Sir Arthur stood at the center of the curtain wall, peering through his spyglass with Captain Beecher beside him, and Ty.

Jayne dragged me up the tower steps, gripping my wrist so tightly it hurt. She knew from the sound what was happening, while I did not. When we reached the top, we hurled ourselves against the wall and pulled the blanket tight around us. "Look to the top o' the hill," she said.

Not still like an earthen feature should be, the hill writhed with movement. Men stood at intervals like giants in red sashes, their colors defying the swirling mists. The piper, wrapped in thick woolens, raised his tune from a doleful ballad to a high, demanding march. One man stepped forward, his sash billowing as if to signal the sun, and then indeed it shone on him, his figure godlike against the multitude of darkly clad soldiers heavy with weapons, surging forward behind him.

"They declare war on the castle," Jayne said. "They could overrun us in an instant."

I shuddered and we held each other tightly, but inside me something different than fear twitched and stabbed. Fear, yes, and confusion over why this should be occurring, and one thing more: resistance.

21

Eyes and Ears

Rathbarry Castle

The next morning, Jayne and I found Mistress Dorothy hunched against the closed door to the stateroom, the hushed voices of men coming through the door like the hum of swarming bees. She gestured urgently toward the solar, and we waited there for several moments. I took in the stale scents of smoke, polishing wax, and lavender, wondering if soon I'd be sent scrubbing to the laundering shed, smelling instead the lye soap, mildew and mud. She joined us and closed the door behind her.

Her skirt rustled as she sat in the largest chair. She raised her chin. "I make no apology for listening at the door," she said. "After the spectacle witnessed yesterday, it's clear these are frightening times and a woman does what she must."

"Of course," Jayne said immediately, but I withheld comment. Had altering my life completely also fallen into her category of things she *must*?

"It was good of you to stay with us, Jayne. I'm sure you have your reasons, and I do not need to know of them as long as you are sensible and maintain good service to the castle. I shall ask you to be present in the mornings when I rise, help me dress and arrange my hair. In the afternoons you will help in the kitchen. We must take over where Thomas left off, managing the inventory of our supplies, and making sure we economize that we might feed all of these people each day. I'm afraid there will have to be rationing. It is a painful task, and I'm sure I need not say so."

"Yes, mistress."

"Merel, I have something quite different in mind for you."

"I'll go then, shall I?" Jayne asked.

"No, stay. There may be times you'll be needed for this as well." She turned to face me directly, her forearms braced upon her knees as if she might be disciplining a small child or a house dog. "The day you told my husband about the Irish camp. You were first to discover it. What were you doing atop that wall so early in the morning?"

I sighed, rather resenting the question. "I was sketching. Lady Carey sent me there."

"Did she know about the camp?"

"No, not at all. She wanted pictures of the sunrise. To sell or to gamble with. She wanted to join the gaming tables."

The mistress raised her brows. "And yet you came away knowing more than any of us about what was to befall our castle."

"I only told what I witnessed, mistress."

"Lady Carey always seemed to know where I was, and where I was not, so that she could avoid me. I suspect you had something to do with that also?"

"It was purely coincidence. I didn't spy on you, if that's what you mean."

"I don't care if you did. What I do care about is your ability to go places, to know things, to appear and disappear as you please. Don't bother to deny it, I know it's true."

"I don't...I'm sorry, mistress, I haven't meant to..." I thought I was to be punished though I wasn't quite sure why, and I was growing anxious. Jayne rested her hand on my wrist.

"My husband has sent our son away," Mistress Dorothy said.

"Yes, mistress. For his safety. I'm so sorry. You must be quite sad."

At last she turned her piercing look from my face and gazed out the window. A tear slipped down her cheek. "He is a bold, selfish child. Mean, even. He hardly had a care for me, and when he did it was not the kind of attention that a mother would, well...I know it is awful for a mother to say, but I shall not miss him. The trouble is, I am afraid Arthur will send me away, too."

I hesitated, speechless for a moment that she should so confide in us, mere servants. "Sir Arthur depends so much upon you, mistress..."

"It's true," Jayne said.

"I had to beg him to let me stay, and finally he conceded so that I'd manage our provisions. But he'll forget all about that if he learns I'm with child."

Jayne gasped. My back stiffened. I just looked at her in disbelief.

"You show no sign, mistress," I said, though I knew I sounded the idiot as I spoke it. "Perhaps you are..."

"I'm not mistaken. It's been nine years since Percy was born, and after him I've hardly wanted another, but I do remember what it feels like. It is very early, yes, but I have no doubt of my condition."

"But, I...I have no experience in midwifery."

"Merel, please calm yourself and stop trying to guess what I want from you. I'm trying to tell you."

"Yes, mistress."

"The only reason Arthur will not send me away is if he needs me more than he fears for me. I must know what is going on everywhere in the castle. I need to know what Arthur knows. I need to be, not just needed by him, but *indispensable*. Sometimes he loves this castle more than he loves me. I don't ever want him to think he must choose between me and Rathbarry. I fear I would lose that battle, and if he sends me away one of us will die. I can't say why, but I know it as sure as if it was writ across the insides of my eyes. We *must* be together for the sake of this child."

"I'm to be your eyes and ears."

She nodded. "Can you pledge yourself to me, to help me in this way and keep my confidence always? Because if you can't I shall have to send you far away, and you'll not see Lady Carey, or your young fellow Tynan O'Daly again."

Jayne stiffened in her chair, her knuckles whitening against the carved wooden arms, waiting, I suspected, for what I might say. Perhaps it was becoming clear where our mistress's son had learned his behavior. I had my rebellious streak, that much was true, but I wasn't angry at her now. I'd discovered something about my new mistress. Now I'd found her tender spot, as she had found mine, and I no longer feared her. I took a deep breath.

"Mistress Dorothy, you need not threaten me. You've asked for my help, using skills that I bring forth readily. Your cause is right and noble, for the good of your child. I pledge to you, I'll do all that you ask, all that

I can, and freely. Only, you will owe *me* one favor, just one. I will decide what it is to be when I need it."

Mistress Dorothy pursed her lips, sucked in her breath and looked to her lap. "Done."

"All right then. How would you like me to begin?"

She opened a drawer in a side table, pulled something out and handed it to me: my sketchbook!

"You used this for Lady Carey, as an excuse to gain access to places you should not be. I expect the same service from you, and better."

22

Rare Bird

Rathbarry Castle

That night I left my bed in the garret to climb the towers and walk the castle walls. Disguised in a hooded robe, I chose my times and places carefully, haunting the darkest corners. It wasn't so much that I hoped to uncover secrets, but more because the assignment to do so released me—gave me the freedom I craved, even and especially as we were all confined within the castle. If I was caught and questioned, Mistress Dorothy would find a way to excuse my behavior.

As if to spite my little pleasure, the telltale sounds of barking dogs, bleating sheep, shouts of men and galloping horses shattered the night's quiet. It meant the night guard had encountered Irish rebels driving away sheep and cattle three and four at a time. I knew with each animal the Irish took, they robbed the food from our mouths. And yet I knew as well that their own mouths remained empty if they didn't.

In such times, with men at arms instead of at their plows, what other industry could feed them? The Irish made money from timber, cloth, corn, flesh, and other works by which they paid their rents and expenses. Now the English plantation settlers and the Englishmen rewarded with properties for their military service owned most of the productive lands. They'd surveyed all the richest meadows and arable pastures, and then claimed them. They'd even claimed sections of rivers, and all the salmon and trout that came from them.

Such a shift in ownership left many Irish families in debt and struggling. Was this the English way of keeping the Irish down? Under great burdens of debt and hunger? If so, then Sir Arthur himself was having a taste of such troubles. Because of this war, marketplaces were closed. Thoroughfares were perilous with ambush and treachery. Sir Arthur couldn't sell his wool, and so couldn't pay his garrison soldiers, who drank his beer at one turn and cursed him at another. His goal was the same as the Irish: to survive.

And so was mine, for everything was uncertain. Lady Carey had provided stability by our daily ritual, and through her I had some level of belonging among the English, but in truth I had more in common with the Irish. I was not of English blood nor necessarily of their religion. I owned no property. I was wholly dependent on others for my meals and every comfort. And, I was *different*—the proverbial rare bird: elusive, curious, not edible, unnecessary, mostly uncontrollable, but perhaps somehow useful.

With the dawn, the night watch returned and Sir Arthur met them at the gate to learn the numbers of cattle they had rescued. The previous night they had shot one man, or possibly two. This night they had killed *seven* men. No more did anyone speak of concern for proper Christian burials. The Irish would have to take care of their own.

My night's adventure was blighted. Those men killed—who had they been? Had they once led quiet lives in the village? Were any of them among those we'd helped to escape from the castle? What would become of their children and wives?

I gained no answers, though I used every excuse I could imagine that allowed me to linger near Sir Arthur while he was in the court. I wandered by the stables when he passed there, and leaned against the garden wall when he spoke to someone in the garrison. When he went inside the keep, I used the privy without fear of punishment, and Mistress Dorothy pretended not to see.

By mid-morning when a messenger called at the gate, I hastened to the stateroom to be ready with wine, sherry or beer. I could even remain there if I quietly served Sir Arthur's guests, so trifling and unremarkable was I. He arrived in minutes, followed by Captain Beecher and Ensign Hungerford. "Please be seated, gentlemen. Will you have wine?"

Both men agreed and I set about my task of slowly filling their glasses while Sir Arthur broke the seal on a letter and smoothed it upon his desk. I positioned myself behind the serving table, pressed against the cabinetry almost as if I were part of it. I had not been dismissed from the room, after all.

"It is news from McMahony," Sir Arthur said. "The Irish have taken Dundeady, the next castle along the coast after his Donoure. It couldn't have been much difficulty for them. Dundeady is owned by another branch of the Barry family. And, our troublesome John Oge Barry—along with some O'Heas, MacCarthys, O'Donovans, and other rebels who infest our barony—also besieges Dunowen Castle."

"They spare no time," Beecher said.

"They are starting, I suppose, with targets they think will be easy for them. Dunowen is probably better defended than the first two, but it is owned by Sir Roger O'Shaughnessy, who they themselves installed at Timoleague Castle. His son was among the three men who first came to parley with us when all of this began. There's some kind of strange dealing there. The next on their list would be Dunnycove, but it's not much more than an outpost, meant for lighting a signal fire if enemies approach by sea. What truly concerns me is that, should each of these castles fall into rebel hands, we will be cut off from any friends, and from supply and support. They will surge across this land like a wave and we'll be overcome."

"Yes, sir," Captain Beecher said. "Clonakilty is already in their control, and they could close the road to Bandon, our most likely source of relief. By sea, there is only Kinsale."

"At Bandon, Lord Kinalmeaky is well aware of our circumstances. I pray he'll act quickly, because I can't be sure my messages will continue to get through," Sir Arthur said, returning his gaze to the letter. "As we wait, McMahony goes on to assure me we are safe. These Irish gents would *never* attempt to cause us injury, he says, or to hurt us in *any way*. We should feel free to go about our normal plowing and sowing, and carry on our commerce." Sir Arthur smirked and shook his head. "What would truly would happen, should I open our gates to such business?"

The three men were silent for a few moments, and then all at once burst out laughing. It was no laugh of mirth. Even I could hear the difference. It a nervous laugh, the kind one has when he thinks he's got away with something, and yet senses a painful retribution waiting just around the corner.

23

Maulemartyr

An Irish Camp Near Bandon

Teige O'Downe led his wearied troops through a grove of ancient and brittle oaks, past scores of dripping tents pitched as if God had cast a bucket of rocks across a hollow. Stores, firewood, horses, cattle, wagons and carts were set haphazardly. The gray smoke of scattered pit fires rose in wisps and stutters as the rain continued. At the center of it all, the abandoned fortress of Maulemartyr looked little better than a ruin, with crumbling corners and a partial roof, but a thick billow of smoke above the fortress promised warmth. He found his cousin—Cormac MacCarthy Reagh, prince of the great Carbery barony—in the hall at a trestle table scared by decades of murderous use. The whole place stank of sweat, piss, and rotting timber.

Yet in his thirties, Cormac scowled like an old man and stabbed his skean into the table's surface, jerked it out, and stabbed it again. His thick black brows knitted together like an iron bar. No one joined him at the table. The few others in the hall chose instead the dark corners, a cold stone wall to lean against, or a worn step upon which to sit and absently carve the mud from his boots. Teige took a bench opposite his commander.

"I counted on you to join us in battle. You did not arrive as promised." Cormac, who had inherited his title of leadership rather than earning it in the ancient Irish tradition, was often defensive. His sound was hoarse.

"I warned you we'd require at least four days," Teige said. "I needed to make our strength known at Rathbarry. 'Twas a glorious spectacle, too. Ye should have seen it for yourself. The men were in perfect precision, the warpipes cutting through the air, the men marching forward. Fierce, they were. And from the English, not a sound, not a move. We'd terrified them, sure enough. I expect there will be resistance, but the garrison is weak and the castle will soon be ours."

Cormac said nothing and went on with his fuming.

"We marched from there to Dundeady where I divided my force," Teige continued. "A hundred of my men hold that castle, and two hundred more marched to take the next, Dunowen Castle. The rest of us marched directly to you, prepared to attack Bandon. This was the plan we agreed upon. We'd have arrived a day earlier but a flood tide at Timoleague cost us several hours before we could cross the Arigadeen river."

Cormac stabbed the table again. "Excuses. Have ye not had enough time to bring me better?"

Teige's breath caught in his throat. He was too old and tired to be barked at by a younger, even if Cormac outranked him. "Aye, and we're here exactly at the time promised. What is your own excuse? It was ye who marched a day ahead of when we said. Did ye expect I could read it in the clouds, and we'd hike up our breeks and pole vault ourselves across the river and into the battlefields? When *you* deviate from the plan, you're *buying* your own trouble."

Cormac grunted. "The men grew restless. I had to get them thinkin' about killin' some English before they started killin' each other, so. We marched straight through to Knockagarane, and piled into the ring fort ruins there, just outside the Bandon wall. I tasked the men with buildin' earthen barriers against the Bandonians. But the Hurleys were late as well, and in the meantime, we'd been discovered and measured by the Bandon militia. Lord Kinalmeaky set his soldiers upon us. They are all savages."

"I gathered it's no' just the rain that has ye men downtrodden."

"The story's to tell and bleak it is."

"I'll hear it, then. All of it."

Cormac kicked something under the table and a boy shot out from beneath, rubbing his eyes. "Find us some whisky, lad. Our man here is goin' ta need it." The boy ran off. Cormac set his skean aside and braced his hands on the table. "The Bandonians, bastards all, came upon us unseen, silent as the dead, breakin' through the morning mists and the men taken by surprise. Our brave warriors, instead o' cutting them down, panicked and scattered like a flock o' wee birds. Some were shot as they ran. A good number caught the tip of a pike. Good lads they were, but ill prepared in spite of all our drillin'. We fell back until the bastards stopped pursuit."

"Ye were wise to retreat and conserve your men for a planned assault. How many lost?"

"Yet I canna say. The Bandonians regrouped, and marched down river to Dermod's fortress, Carriganass. You know of it? I had a hundred men there. A well-fortified place, and Dermod suffers no shit from anyone. I hear his garrison fought mightily, but they were overpowered. Dermod signaled surrender, but when the Englishmen were crossing his moat to negotiate terms, he shot them down. The Bandonians must have pissed themselves. They armed their cannons and blew the fortress to hell. Pounded the battlements to rubble."

Teige's belly lurched as if he'd taken a boot to it. "Damn Dermod and his foul temper. Did any escape?" The boy returned and handed him a bowl half filled with whisky. He grabbed it, took a deep swallow and passed the bowl to Cormac.

"Enough to tell me the tale, but all are wounded and I don't know what's become of Dermod himself. Hanged, if he was lucky. If he was not, well, as I said the Bandonians are savages."

Teige held his tongue. It was only the beginning of their plans, and such a loss of fighting men and fortresses could put the whole of the rebellion at risk.

Cormac wiped the whisky from his chin. "The Bandon pigs took Dermod's gate down from the castle's entrance, and set it to burn there, knowing our men were hiding in the arch above. Those who stayed hidden were roasted. Those who came down were hanged."

Teige nearly overturned his bench as he stood, needing to pace out his fury back and forth across the stone floor. A swallow of whisky was hardly enough for this kind of news. The few men who remained in the hall bolted out to the field. Cormac picked up his skean.

"Those who escaped the English at Carriganass made their way south to my next castle along the river, Kilgobban. They told such a ghastly tale that every man abandoned his post, even before they should see the first sign of enemy approach," Cormac said.

"That's enough. I need hear no more."

"Oh, aye, ye said ye'd hear it all, and so ye will. Dundanier Castle was next, and fell to the English with hardly a fight at all."

Teige stopped his pacing and heaved out a deep sigh. "All right then." He paused for a moment, framing his words, and returned to Cormac's table. "Listen, now. We knew Lord Kinalmeaky would go after the castles along the Bandon River first. They're too close to the city, and with water access. Ye do realize, the most important thing to Kinalmeaky is not the castles themselves. It's that he can't risk his father's pet project, can he? The great walled city of Bandon? The famous English settlement built by the Earl of Cork himself, should be allowed to fall into the hands of the Irish? He'd impale himself first. We half expected this could happen. And so it has. It's early in the fight, no?"

"It's a major blow to the men. And the Bandon bastards are coming far too close to our other garrisons."

"Cormac. *Cormac.* We can't lose heart yet. Other troops are fighting in other fields." Teige reached for the bowl and took another draw of the whisky. Too large of a draw, it hurt and burned going down, but he suppressed a cough—a sign of weakness to men like Cormac. "Other places are falling to our favor. Our man Mountgarret beat the tar out of St. Leger's troops at Killmallock for the Catholic cause. St. Leger has tuck-tailed off to the English fortress at Youghal, out of our way for a while at least. Better still, he's left Cork exposed, and our Lord Muskerry has it under siege. If we take the City of Cork we've nearly won. Meantime, Mountgarret has marched on to Mallow. He's taken the Short Castle, and he'll have the main castle as well. It's just a matter of time."

Cormac was silent for a few moments, nodding slowly. He scratched thin lines on the table with his skean, instead of stabbing at it. "You're right. There's a bigger operation than what falls along Bandon River. And we'll yet have our victories."

"That's right. We've *had* them," Teige said. He held up his hand, pressing down one finger at a time as he spoke. "Ross is ours. Clonakilty is ours. Timoleague as well. We've taken Donoure, Dundeady." With each finger down, he held the fist over his head. "And, we have Rathbarry and Dunowen under siege. Both are soon to fall, and then we'll have a mighty hand across all of Carbery."

"Aye. We must keep the faith." Cormac rubbed his belly as if to soothe an old ache, and peered up at the open part of the roof, the rain still coming in splashes of light to puddle on the worn and pitted floor stones. He straightened his back. "Tonight we'll build a roaring fire in the camp, and tell of these victories to lift the men's spirits. We have greater victories ahead of us, by God who favors us."

"It is so." Teige held out his hand, and Cormac grasped it firmly. "Let no man doubt it."

As evening fell, the men of the camp took well to the idea of fire, and spent good effort collecting moss, faggots and logs to stand a good burn. But the earth was saturated where the pit was dug, and the wood was soaked through by the endless rain. The bit of cheer they had mustered seemed to fizzle with the staggering flames. Gangs of men set out in different directions hoping to find more incendiary fuel.

MARCH

24

Shrove Tuesday

Rathbarry Castle

One morning early in March, Mistress Dorothy insisted on walking through the garden ward. I couldn't be sure if this unusual interest was sparked by her physical condition, by concern over having enough fruits and vegetables for the kitchen, or simply by the onset of spring. With the mistress, I was always wary of her motive.

"Jayne, I want my light blue gown, and my hair pinned at the nape. Merel, fetch my straw hat with the ribbons, and gloves." Though she didn't ask for them, I also fetched her ankle boots. I knew she'd not walked there for some time, and would hardly recognize that place from what we'd seen in January.

While some of the garden ward's growing area had been sacrificed to provide housing for the villagers, still more was lost when Sir Arthur brought in the sheep and cows to keep them from being stolen. It didn't seem to matter so much in February, when the ground was still too cold or frozen to plant, and we'd not yet realized the intent of the Irish troops. When the first two-hundred sheep were driven into the ward, the trouble was clear. Arriving with their innocent white faces lifted to the sun, they quickly began to do what sheep naturally do. They nibbled to nothing the chervil just sprouting around the vegetable beds, and where one went, they all went—knocking over or completely trampling the woven fences and low hedges, bumping and breaking chicken pens, befouling the once-lovely pathways, and utterly confounding everyone.

The cattle, however, were far worse. The herdsmen tried to enclose them in a portion of the ward with hastily erected post-and-rail fences, but the men could not sustain them without constantly gathering grasses from outside the castle at great risk. Soon the curious creatures seemed not to notice the fences and pushed through them, leaving their cramped quarters to explore the wider spaces. They wandered from ward to court eating nearly every leafy thing along their path, until Jenkin had to shoo them from a shriveled grapevine at the keep steps.

After a brief examination of the damage done, the mistress declared her decision. "The garden ward must be closed off completely. I'll speak to Arthur about it. Instead, we shall have a new kitchen garden adjacent to the chapel. All the residents of the court will be expected to do their share of tasks, and all harvesting will be done under the direct supervision of myself or Elinor," she said. "The same soldiers who built the garden ward houses shall dig and construct new garden beds in every space about the court that is not paved with stones. If needs be, they shall take up the stones in places less traversed. Our vegetable beds must surely take precedence over convenient walking paths."

The mistress assigned the ladies from Ross to the sowing of endive, chervil, purslane, skirret, leeks, and turnips—starting with those who were unaccustomed to having their hands soiled. Considerable grumbling and fussing silenced only when the mistress was within range of hearing. She seemed not only aware of it but rather pleased by it, the corners of her lips curling upward. With that, she turned and walked straight back into the keep, dropping her hat and gloves behind her for Jayne to retrieve. It was a grand show of authority, and little more.

In half a day, the beds were framed and newly moulded. The strawberry beds, expected to produce fruit for years, were most disappointing. The plants were completely eaten and trampled, so Elinor provided what few seeds she had been able to save, and we could only hope for the best.

At supper that night we had leek soup, bread, sausages, and dried fruits. Afterwards, the sour smell of the leeks lingered in the air, reminding me of something from long ago. My mother making hachee, our favorite beef and onion stew, just a day or two before we were to board the ship for Cobh Harbor. In the low-ceiling kitchen, all of our meals had been cooked in the large open hearth. She must have been nearly as small as me, for she stood on her toes to brown chopped onions in a big soup pot hanging from a hook above the fire. Oh, the taste of her stew, the gravy rich and thick, the onions soft and bursting with butter. My mouth began to water even though I'd finished my meal, and something stirred that I had not, or perhaps would not attend to in the past. The place left empty by my mother yawned wide again with the loss of Lady Carey. But this time I remembered something else.

My father had been there that night while mother cooked. He was packing a large wooden crate with several of his paintings. Beautiful landscapes with rich greens and golds, and dreamy clouded skies. He wouldn't let me touch them as he covered them, for they were all too delicate and valuable. He'd sell them when we reached the Indies, and they had to be in perfect condition. Even after we'd boarded the ship, he wouldn't leave the heavy crate, protecting it from any possible damage.

How grand for Papa to have such paintings when he'd been so angry at his master for allowing him to paint only the backgrounds: the blue of sky, green of foliage, and brown of earth, plus a few featureless forms. He was kept from painting the lifelike detail and romantic scenes for which Dutch painters had become famous. Was it because he was untrained, or perhaps because he lacked the artist's gift? But he couldn't lack the gift, or we would not have the paintings. Was it possible they were not my father's own works, then? And if they were not, had they been given to him? Gifts for his voyage? Or...or, had he stolen them? If that could even be considered of Papa, it would explain his urgency to leave Harlingen, and his protectiveness over them—his refusal to abandon the crate even when facing mortal danger.

He would not leave the paintings, and my mother would not leave him. When the ship faltered and water poured in, she'd shoved me through the great hatch toward the deck, and then she'd fallen back as the water took me. There came the icy, dark gush that swept me away. My head bumped against things I couldn't see, my body tumbled until I popped to the surface like an apple, and then the iron fist of a sailor snatched me from the waves and hurled me into a small, tossing boat.

Of a sudden my interiors were as vaporous as air, and yet I couldn't inhale enough to fill my lungs. A fit of dizziness swirled through me. I struggled to right myself when Jenkin rang a bell for attention.

Sir Arthur took a stance on the castle steps, to speak to the people before they departed for their lodgings. I sucked in a good, cold breath and navigated through the crowd to where Ty stood outside the stables.

He smiled and pulled me closer. I steadied myself against him. Let him ask me nothing, for should he ask even the time of day my delicate composure might shatter into little pieces.

Sir Arthur wore his blue velvet doublet, red sash and sword. Mistress Dorothy stood dutifully behind his left shoulder, her hands clasped at her waist. Mr. Taverner, displaying his most pious smile, stood behind Sir Arthur's right shoulder. And behind them, Captain Beecher, Ensign Hungerford, and two other soldiers from the garrison. Silence settled quickly, for everyone wished to hear what would be done now that the Irish soldiers surrounded the castle.

Sir Arthur slid his right foot forward, his left hand resting firmly on his hilt. "Good people of Ross and Rathbarry, welcome," he began. "We are all aware of the clan soldiers who have approached our castle, and of the threatening demonstration they have made. Perhaps you fear, after the experience at the village, that we too are in a precarious situation. And that is exactly what they want. Your fear is their greatest weapon. But let me assure you, we are *not* in danger." He paused as a soft rumble seemed to pass among the crowd.

"I ask you all to summon your courage and do not let a single, theatrical display weaken your resolve. Rathbarry Castle is among the finest fortifications in Munster, and to defend us we have a brave and well-armed garrison that will not fail. We are blessed to be so well protected and supplied."

"Hear, hear!" Mr. Millett shouted from among the crowd. Mistress Dorothy nodded and the rumble among the people seemed to quiet.

"Our walls are constantly guarded by the garrison's snipers and musket men. These walls are eight feet thick. Our gates are secure. The tower guards and curs provide early alerts if anyone should approach. We can rest in safety within these walls. I expect our situation to resolve soon, but in the meantime, I beg of you all to remain here in the castle, keep close yourselves and your families, be alert, and be strong."

He paused again, took a deep breath and one step forward. "We will not surrender Rathbarry!" he shouted. To this, a great cheer rose from the crowd. Sir Arthur shouted above it. "We shall not be bullied, and we shall not be robbed of what is rightfully ours; we shall not suffer the rude and malicious, nor the treacherous. We shall stand for peace, good order, and the Laws of the King of England." Again, a cheer. "And should we have to fight, we will *bloody well do it.*"

At this, the shouts rose to the heavens, and women and children began to cry. Some children ran wild around the court, pretending to be warriors in battle—something they knew not of.

"And know ye that, should they try to overpower us—may God himself prevent it—our good Lord Kinalmeaky of Bandon and his great militia will come to relieve us in due time, never fear."

"In the meantime, my good folk," Sir Arthur reached for Dorothy and she stepped up beside him. "Merely as a precaution, should we be unable to receive supplies for a brief time, we will do all to be self-sufficient. My wife and I applaud the efforts to establish the new garden spaces. Soon they'll be bright with color and rich with fruits and vegetables for our table. However, we are wise to conserve, at least until we can see the end of our enclosure. Our Parliament in London has considered the same and, in December past, decided that during these unsettled times, a monthly fast was in order," —several among the crowd groaned— "to implore God's mercy and favor. The troubles from the Irish rebellion have caused Parliament to establish fasts on the fourth Wednesday of every month."

"Let them, the dozy pigs!" a woman shouted from the crowd. Laughter erupted, and then settled into a roar of murmurings that passed through the crowd like rolling thunder. "We're nearly starvin' already!" another shouted.

Sir Arthur waited calmly, and let it pass before continuing. "My wife and I ask you to join us in observing this very small sacrifice in view of the protections and safety we are provided. Together we may also pray that our humility before God brings us the favor we so truly need." Mr. Taverner stepped forward, his brow furrowed, one hand patting the air as if to quiet everyone with a gesture.

Sir Arthur continued, "You are all aware of this special day, Shrove Tuesday, when we must personally rouse our repentance and self-discipline in observance of Lent."

"And ye folk in the castle," someone shouted from the crowd, "what will ye be repentin'? Yer second glass o' sherry?"

A few people laughed, and murmurs rippled outward. Sir Arthur held out his hands as if to offer something. "Trust in me," he said, "that we will fast, and we will sacrifice, in the same ways. We ask nothing of you that we're not willing to do ourselves."

The murmurs slowly settled into silence, and then Sir Arthur—I had not before seen how masterful he could be in managing people—took one more step forward. "Those words having been said, tender people, I now have a surprise for you." He turned, and he and Mistress Dorothy clapped their hands. Up from the cellar stairs came kitchen maids two-by-two, carrying great platters, each piled high with pancakes: thin, pan-fried flour cakes rolled and lightly drizzled with honey—the traditional sweet to enjoy before Lent. And suddenly the sour smell in the court was replaced with the rich honey scent, and the delightful smell of something baked and buttered wafting as butterflies above our heads.

"Enjoy! All of you. And may we remember that this state of affairs affects each one of us, and together we will overcome it. Let us unite under God against this and any enemy who truly threatens."

Sir Arthur could say anything he wanted, for no one was listening, completely distracted by the trays of delicious pancakes. I reached for mine and Ty for his. We looked into each other's eyes as we bit into them at the same time, and shared the elation as the honey melted on our tongues. In seconds it seemed, the pancakes were gone and we were left licking our fingers. My dizzy emptiness departed, my secret tucked away again for no one to see, all crowded out of mind by the pleasure and the comfort of his nearness.

Ty glanced up at the people starting to drift away from the court, and then he grasped my elbow. "Look, just there, the two fellas by the north tower."

I turned. One of the men was tall and rather bulky with a low, bulging belly: Mr. Tantalus, who had been the barber at Ross. The other man was shorter and leaner: Mr. Rosgill, one of Sir Arthur's tenant farmers. They had separated from the crowd and talked privately, looking back on the rest of us with amusement and disdain.

"I'll take a wager with any man," Ty said, "that if there be trouble coming because of the fast, it'll start with these two."

APRIL

25

Before Dark

Rathbarry Castle, McShane's Farmhouse

The first of April arrived on a crisp wind, the sky so bright and cloudless one could hardly have a negative thought, though the troubles of Rathbarry did rankle. Tynan set Collum to muck, and Giles to rake the stalls, while his farrier checked the hooves of every horse for tending or shoeing. By late morning the man was three-quarters of the way through the stalls.

Tynan left him to his work and began grooming horses in the open air by the stable door. Here, he could breathe the sea wind and catch a whiff of something cooking in the kitchen, unless the west wind brought the odor of cow manure. He could look up to the castle windows and sometimes see Merel peering out. It cheered him. He must find a way to be alone with her and not just in passing, though it was getting harder now that she served Mistress Dorothy. He was never quite sure where she would be.

At mid-afternoon Sir Arthur came into the stables, unusually casual in his shirtsleeves. He smiled when he found Tynan brushing Sarcen. Even in filtered sunlight the stallion's fine coat shined like lacquer. He nickered his pleasure when Sir Arthur approached.

"Ah, there's my boy, looking smart," he said, palming Sarcen's nose and then rubbing him behind the ear. "How I would love to saddle you and go for a hearty gallop."

"Aye, he could use the exercise as well. Ye might tek him for a run when the watch goes out tonight," Tynan said.

"Nay, I dare not risk him. He'd be too a fine prize for the taking."

"Yea, that he would."

"The day I bought him at Cahirmee horse fair, I knew he was something special. Beautifully formed, without a doubt, but it's far more than that. His temperament, and his intelligence. He looked directly to my eyes. Some men want a fierce look in the horse's eye before they buy him. It's wise I suppose for a battle horse, but I wanted a trusted companion, that I might leap upon his back at any moment and ride like the wind, just for the pleasure of it. That's what I saw in him. Joy and readiness. If only he could he speak, we'd have quite the conversation."

"Does his name mean smart, then?" Tynan said.

Sir Arthur allowed a half-smile. "I suppose I should have named him for that. In truth, it means something of the opposite. It's the name of the village where I was born, and where sarcen stone is quarried for the construction of castles and fortresses, the same kind of sandstone used in the ancient circles you see in open fields."

"Ah, then he's named for strength." Sarcen flicked his tail as if to remind Tynan he'd not yet brushed it. "A horse ye can trust is a treasure, and there's no match for it. But he has to trust you first."

"Yes, I've learned that. It's the reason I hired you. Once you gain their trust, then you simply teach them. I abhor the beating, constraining and whipping that some men require. I s'pose it's necessary sometimes."

"Never in my experience, sir. Force only breeds fear and defiance, a waste of time."

Sir Arthur rested his hand on the horse's neck, his gaze focused on the ground. Tynan continued brushing and waited silently. It seemed the man wanted to tell him something, but was reluctant at the same time. After a few long moments Tynan prodded, "Sir?"

Sir Arthur looked up. "Yes," he said, "You must pardon my distraction. I'm...concerned about something. This morning, when some of the herdsmen left the castle to gather grasses for my cattle, two of the men from Ross went out to help: Mr. Tantalus, and Mr. Rosgill."

The hair stiffened at the back of Tynan's neck. "Yes, sir, I know them."

"They didn't return with the others. The afternoon sets and yet they've not been seen. Mistress Rosgill tells me they've often visited the house of our neighbor, Mr. McShane, to purchase tobacco. On a fasting day, it helps drive the hunger away."

"Aye, sir. And ye are wanting me to go after them?"

Sir Arthur nodded. "I'd not ask, it being a risk, but the lady is quite beside herself with worry. I thought it likely you would not be stopped this time of day, and being Irish..."

Tynan clenched his jaw. Being Irish would offer little protection if he's seen coming from an English castle under siege. But the house wasn't far, the two men had walked there, and he knew McShane. He supposed he could make short work of it and return without much of a stir. Still, there was something disturbing about it. He knew those two would cause trouble. He looked away toward the shadowed end of the stables. "I'll take one of the draught mares, sir."

McShane's house was to the north and east, a little less than halfway between Rathbarry and Dunoure Castle. The way was along a winding deer path that passed McShane's farmhouse, a whitewashed wattle and daub that was yellowing and stained, the thatch roof grayed and hanging loose in places. The path wandered past his crop fields and disappeared into a dense strip of woods by a dry riverbed known to flood with the spring rains.

He found McShane sitting on a stool outside his door, puffing tobacco from a small clay pipe. The man didn't move as he approached, nor speak in greeting, nor alter his countenance in any way. He sat still, the smoke drifting across his wiry gray brows and upward to the thatch. Between the house and barn, a lad raked up hay scattered in clumps and masses as if tossed by some kind of whirlwind. He didn't look up to acknowledge the new visitor.

Tynan dismounted and stood beside the mare. "Mr. McShane, sir. I believe we've met once or twice before. I'm Tynan O'Daly, come at the request of Sir Arthur Freke of Rathbarry. Within his castle lives Mistress Rosgill, who is concerned for the safety of her husband. She says he and Mr. Taverner may have visited you today, for a bit of tobacco."

McShane hacked and cleared his throat, then spit on the ground, just missing his own bare feet. "Aye."

"Aye, they were here, sir?" Tynan said.

McShane looked up with cloudy blue eyes, one side of his mouth curling upward to reveal few teeth. "Aye! It's naught ta do wi' me."

"But they were here. Mr. McShane, can you say where they might have gone?"

"Wha' do I care where the soddin' bastards ere!" He spat again, and leaned down far enough to grab a handful of dirt and cast it at Tynan's chest.

Tynan could have cuffed him right then, but he waited, allowing a silence for McShane to fill. The man said nothing. "I should look around for them, shall I?" He went for McShane's front door.

"Get thee away from here, ye bugger. Ye want ta know wher dey be? Find 'em yerself!"

After the spray of dirt—the sort of thing his younger brother might've done, and he'd toss him in a trough for it—Tynan was in no mood to waste time or tolerate obstruction. He grabbed McShane's arm, jerked him up and held him against the wall of the house, his feet dangling. The lad by the barn kept sweeping and didn't look up.

"God blast ye! Wat ye doin' ta me! Feck off!"

Tynan let go and McShane fell to the ground. "You're the one being troublesome. Where are they? And don't tell me you don't know."

McShane stayed silent. Tynan stood over him. "Ye turned on them, didn't ye? Two gents come to ye, just ta sit on yer step and have a smoke with ye. How much did they pay? It must be searing a hole in yer pocket now."

He paused, but still there was no response. "Did ye welcome the Irish camp behind yon wood, and try to buy favor by offering up yer customers? Yer friends? Ye sent yer lad down to the camp, didn't ye? To let them know there were English at yer door. Ye served 'em up like meat on a trencher."

McShane looked up at him with a sly eye and satisfied grin, confirming to Tynan that was exactly what had happened. He jerked McShane up again, but this time slammed him to the ground. "English or Irish, they'd ne'er have done *you* this way. Where are they!"

McShane sat up, coughed and wiped his mouth with the back of his hand. "By de river, das where, and as they belong." He waved a hand in the direction of the strip of woods Tynan had noticed before.

"Get up." Tynan helped him to his feet. McShane wobbled at first but then regained his balance. "Show me."

McShane led the way and Tynan followed, leading the mare behind him. The afternoon light was turning amber. Walking into the woods with this man was probably not the wisest thing to do. Irish warriors were particularly skilled at making themselves invisible in the forest, emerging as if from nowhere for a fierce attack, and then disappearing again like ghosts among the trees. He ought to know; he'd learned it himself when he was younger. Still, he should at least take a quick look. If the two men were yet alive they'd probably need help. If they weren't, what then?

McShane continued through an opening in the trees that led down to the riverbed. From there Tynan had a clear view along the bank to the left and right. He didn't have to look long. Only about twenty yards away, to a towering oak with great arching limbs: the black form of one man, large and low-bellied, hanging by a rope, and the form of another, nearly flattened, on the ground below.

He pushed McShane before him toward the bodies. From the largest limb hung Tantalus, his eyes and tongue bulging and discolored. And on the ground the body of Rosgill in a dark stain of blood that had soaked into the sand. He'd been piked through the chest. A blazing anger seared into Tynan's shoulders and neck. His skean was in his hand even before he knew it. His mouth filled with the most bitter taste of choler.

"Ye get 'em outa here, you!" McShane shouted behind him. "'S nothin' ta do wi' me! The lads come up for 'em. 'Tis no loss. Couple o' Protestant hogs is all dey be!"

Tynan swung toward McShane, his skean up, ready to slit the arsworm's neck. Instead, he marched up to the tree and quickly cut down Tantalus. The body fell like a sack of stones, but there was no way Tynan could prevent it. He pulled the blanket from beneath the mare's saddle, but it was too small to cover both men. He shoved McShane. "You get me some kind of shroud for them," he shouted. "I'll sooner leave the bodies to rot on your doorstep than carry them home to their wives in this state. You want them out of here, you owe them that, at least."

While Tynan wrapped Rosgill's body in the blanket, McShane went up to his house and soon brought back a threadbare and moth-eaten woolen. He threw it at Tynan amid a shower of curses. "Here ye are. An' ye best watch ye don't become one o' dem." He then returned to his house leaving Tynan to his work.

With great effort, rolling the weight from side to side, Tynan managed to wrap the body of Tantalus in McShane's blanket, then secured the two bodies as best he could. He used the mare's reins to fasten them behind her, knowing she had the strength to pull this much weight and far more, but he hadn't the time or the tools to fix a proper litter. The bodies could only be dragged. Urging the mare forward with his voice and his hands in her mane, he slowly returned down the path from which he'd come. If he could make it all the way to the castle before dark it would be a miracle.

26

A Hard Lesson

Rathbarry Castle

The snipers were first to see him, and sent the guards out to escort him back through the castle gates. Tynan rode in dragging his cargo. The blankets had torn in places, enough so that Mistress Rosgill could recognize her husband's body from several feet away. She screamed with such terror the people ran forth from all parts of the castle grounds, filling the court, and bringing on more screams, next from Mistress Tantalus, and then from other women from Ross who had known such terror before. Mistress Rosgill ran at Tynan and pounded upon his legs as if he were her husband's killer.

Sir Arthur arrived then, and Mr. Taverner, to try and settle her. Mistress Dorothy came forward with Merel and Jayne, and together they drew the women away from the sight of the bodies, and led them into the keep.

As Tynan dismounted, Mistress Tantalus pushed several children ahead of her toward the keep and turned to scream at him. "How dare you do this! Bring them here, for all to see! *My children.*"

Captain Beecher and some of the soldiers examined the bodies and unfastened them from the mare. Collum ran out to collect her.

"What was I to do?" Tynan said. "I couldn't leave them there."

"No, you were right to bring them." Sir Arthur squeezed Tynan's shoulder. "It's a terrible shock for anyone to see, but these men must have a proper burial." He gazed at the bodies for a moment, and released a sigh. "They knew what they were doing. They must have believed McShane to be trustworthy, but they knew they were taking a risk. They sidled away from the others this morning, as if we, or I, were the enemy. But in death, they are teaching all of us a hard lesson. We must accept that we are truly captive within the castle. To surrender is not safe, but to leave the castle is death."

Sir Arthur stepped back from Tynan, squared his shoulders and raised his voice for all who were near to hear. "We will *not* negotiate. We will *not* surrender. We will *fight*!"

Cheers burst forth like flames from the men, and piercing wails rose from some of the women.

"Mr. Taverner."

"Yes, Sir," the minister came to Sir Arthur's side.

"Arrange a funeral for these two men. They shall be buried with honor at the west end of the garden ward. Let their deaths stand for something. The love of their families—both had four children who now, all of them, will have to be under my care. Say something about their good works in the village, their reverence for God. And when you close, say they inspire the courage and conviction with which we will meet our enemies."

Tynan returned to the stables, his arms and legs heavy, his head aching. When had he been this tired before? He couldn't recall. He cast off his coat, went straight to Sarcen's stall, and collapsed against the wall beside him. The candle lantern on a hook just above him sent strange ghostly figures leaping about the stall, reflecting the disquiet that filled him.

"Today's work was not for you, friend. T'anks be to God, Sir Arthur didn't send you. I wish he'd not sent me, besides. And to hell with the fasting. I couldna care less for food right now." He sighed and let his shoulders settle. Then came a rustle and he lifted his head.

"Are you hurt?" Merel stood at the stable gate, her face dark with worry, her pink gown orange in the dim light.

He smiled and shook his head. "Coom and sit beside me."

She dropped to his side on the flagstones. "I was so frightened when I saw what had happened to those men, and knew you had been there."

"Aye. Bitter, it is." Tynan pulled her close and breathed in the wildflower scent of her hair. "But I am whole and unharmed. Though I must smell badly after all I've done."

"You smell like a sweaty horse, and I don't care." She wept a little, pushing away the unwanted tears with the heels of her hands.

"They didn't deserve to die. They weren't soldiers at war," Tynan said. "I've seen nothing like it before. I could no' stop to think, except that I had to get them back to the castle. I just did what needs must. But I hate McShane and those that did it. I hate Tantalus and Rosgill for goin' there in the first place. Didn't I tell ye they were trouble? And I hate the English for causin' Irish farm lads to turn killers. It was bloody disgustin' and I'm weary with it, not knowin' who to hate most, nor what to do about it. But it's not so bad now." He took her face into his hands and kissed her lips gently. She returned the kiss with greater passion, sending a surge of something sweet and syrupy into his veins, like a swallow of warmed brandy spreading through his arms, across his chest and through his body.

"Things won't always be like this, I know it," she said.

"If things could always be like this—like this very moment, I'd die in splendor." He put his arms around her waist and pulled her onto his lap, his body so tired, but his want of her surging into his thighs. He held her tightly and pressed against her until he could feel her heartbeat. She wrapped her arms around his neck and pressed her lips just below his ear. Ah, if only she had not done that. His loins burned, longing for more, aching to move upon her like an animal, but then she pulled back.

"*Wait,*" she said.

He released her. Even though his need intensified, this wasn't the place or time. His exhaustion had got the better of his conscience. When he loved her, it would be blissful and freeing, not tarnished by the day's horrors and murders. Not on the floor of horse stall.

"It's all right. I just...I just wanted to look at you." She tilted his chin toward the candle lantern above them. "Your eyes. I thought they were gray, but there was blue in them today. When you were angry about Mistress Tantalus, the color changed. And when you clenched your teeth and I realized your jawbone was quite strong with a perfect square chin." She drew her fingers from his cheek to the small place just below his lip. "I shall draw you one day."

She examined him, her deep brown eyes glowing amber, and her hands, small but not short, her fingers long boned as an artist's might be, smooth and clean like ivory. He reached out to touch the delicate skin from her neck to her collar bone, but remembered his calluses and pulled back.

She caught his hand and kissed his palm. "I don't mind if your hands are rough. They're warm, capable. They are…" she pressed her palm together with his… "hands that never sit and wait. They do. They go. They comfort horses. They solve problems." She turned his hand over to look at the back. "They are sculpted, purposeful hands."

He scoffed. "You humor me now."

"I might," she said, "but not about this, and not at such a moment."

He smoothed her hair back over her shoulder. "Remember the day I found you at the forest? We rode back to the castle together on Sarcen? Grand, wasn't it, for a wee precious time?"

"I wouldn't think you'd remember," Merel said.

"Every bit. I want more o' that," he said. "Much more. I want to know about you, and I want you near me whenever it can be so. We're locked up here in this castle, and of all the people, you're the only one I truly want to talk to."

"When?"

"When? What do you…"

"I mean when? How soon can we meet, where we can talk and no one will find us?"

He paused, surprised and pleased that she was serious about being alone with him. To his thinking, it would be no fleeting fancy, but a true change in the depth of their affection. There would be no backward step, not for him. "It's no' easy, lass, to find a spot where cunning eyes won't go. But leave it wi' me, and I promise I'll find it."

Merel smiled, the candlelight flickering in her eyes. "Once I dreamt of the two of us riding Sarcen and just galloping away, disappearing into the highest mountains."

"That," he said, his head becoming heavy with fatigue, "would be a mighty fine day, and I know just the mountain…" he trailed off.

"I'd better go," she said.

He watched her leave the stables and fell back onto a meager pile of hay, drifting into a dreamless sleep. When he awoke, the candle had burned out, the stables were dark and silent. Merel was long gone, but the scent of wildflowers yet lingered, if only in his mind.

The men were buried the following morning while a soft rain fell. Jayne and Merel took turns holding the umbrella over Mistress Dorothy, seated on the chair Jenkin had brought for her. Sir Arthur stood beside her in his tall hat and buttoned cloak. Mr. Taverner said his words and read the scripture while the two widows wept. The children sat on the wet ground before them, quiet, likely confused by what had happened to their fathers. Many of the townspeople stood by, offering condolence, but just as many stayed away, either blaming the men for the risk they had taken, or fearing that acknowledging these deaths allowed the tragedy to touch their own lives.

Afterwards, Mistress Rosgill returned to her house, leaving her children in the rain. She took to her bed, allowing no one to speak to her, no one to comfort her. She accepted no food nor drink, and demanded her solitude. Mistress Tantalus moved into the castle bringing her own and the Rosgill children with her.

The next day, Mistress Rosgill still would not be consoled. Her cottage having no locks, she'd piled stools and a table against her door so that no one could enter. She kept to her bed, and not even Mr. Taverner nor Sir Arthur could rouse her from this deep distraction.

27

Mistress Rosgill

Rathbarry Castle

I knew Mistress Rosgill only from the hours she'd spent sewing in the solar, next to Mistress Dorothy, while her children played on the stairs or out in the court. She'd always been kind to me, and I worried for her. Three days after the men were buried, I escaped Mistress Dorothy and ran to the garden ward to test Mistress Rosgill's door myself. It remained blocked and she gave no answer when I called to her. I crept around the side of the small cottage until I found her bedroom window, a small casement that swung outward.

She had lodged a blanket around the window frame to block the light, and also to make it difficult move. I managed to partially open it with a heavy stick for leverage, and peered into the dim room until I could see her on the bed uncovered, curled like a newborn kitten. I watched her for a few moments to see did she rest peacefully, or might she wake, or had she perhaps fallen into sickness.

I called to her but she did not rouse, and then it dawned upon me that I didn't see her breast rise and fall. I tugged open the window with all my might, the hinge screeching, and climbed through. Yet she didn't stir. Her face was without color, her hands cold and still. Her long, dark hair was dull and matted about her. Mistress Rosgill had died of her grief.

I stood back from her, frightened and horrified. The third death in as many days and I had disturbed her body. But before the fear set in, I grew angry. She'd chosen it, even forced herself to die, without regard for the children who still needed her. Just as Agnes's mother had done. We should have intruded on her grief. We should have beaten down her door.

If I had climbed through her window a day sooner, she might still be alive.

A dense, heavy weight formed in my stomach. Why would someone choose death? To abandon those she had birthed and nurtured? Was it not enough that her husband was murdered, that we all faced death every day in this crowded castle? Had she no love left? No anger, no vengeance to stir her blood? Or, had her husband left her destitute, in such low condition she had no hope for survival? Even if he had, how could she not wish to see the sun rise, the birds fly, the colors brighten and expand across the summer sky as the sun settled into the ocean? How could a mother not wish to hear the sound of her children's laughter?

I couldn't understand it, but there was nothing to be done. I went to inform Mistress Dorothy.

Upon waking, the mistress's first hour was given not to nausea like most pregnant women, but to tears, though never when Sir Arthur was present. Once the crying passed, she turned abruptly to anger at any error, tardiness, or inability to recognize her needs without her having to speak them. She took pleasure only in the tiny bits of gossip I could bring her that might somehow be useful. And she demanded to know immediately whenever Sir Arthur approached the keep, allowing her time to construct a sweet countenance. The news of Mistress Rosgill's death sent her into a rage.

"You go back there right now, Merel, and wake her up. Take Jenkin with you. She sleeps, that's all it is. She deceives us. We will not have this kind of foolery here. She owes us respect. She owes us money! Don't you *dare* let Sir Arthur know of this until she stands before me and apologizes for such a cruel trick."

Jenkin followed me back to Mistress Rosgill's cabin, bringing a kitchen boy along for assistance. The boy followed me through the window into her bedroom, and we went straight for the door to dismantle the barrier she'd created and let Jenkin in.

He sat on the edge of her bed, lifted her cold hand, touched her bare neck to search for a heartbeat. He stood. "Sir Arthur must know. My first responsibility is to him."

"No!" I said, perhaps too quickly. "You know how she is, Jenkin. If we don't go to her first, she'll torment us daily. Not you, but me and Jayne. Please, tell her what you saw, and then let her be the one to tell Sir Arthur.

It's little enough to ask, and he'll know within minutes, so nothing is lost."

Jenkin conceded, and after confirming the news to Mistress Dorothy, went in search of the minister, Mr. Taverner.

"Jayne, fetch a cool cloth for my face, and then tidy my hair. I wish to be in the dining hall when Sir Arthur arrives. Merel, go and find him, but reveal nothing. Do you hear me?"

I found Sir Arthur near the cattle enclosure, arguing with one of the herdsmen about the low quantity of grass they had collected before dawn. From there I followed him straight to the keep steps. Mistress Dorothy awaited him just inside the doors, her face bright, her hair perfectly smoothed, her gown without a wrinkle.

"My darling Arthur," she said in her most angelic voice. "I have very sad news. It is Mistress Rosgill. I checked on her myself this morning, hoping to lift her spirits, but it seems she has passed away in the night, the poor, sweet girl. She has died of a broken heart."

Mr. Taverner arrived then. Sir Arthur nodded without shock or surprise. "She must be buried beside her husband, and quickly. We cannot allow her despair to linger and poison the spirits of the other families who require every hope to survive. We must carry on."

"We will call on the good charity of the garden ward women to look after her poor little children, won't we, my love?" Mistress Dorothy said.

Soon after the burial, we celebrated Easter, the resurrection of Jesus Christ. Every child in the castle received a boiled egg, the symbol of rebirth. The sacrifices of Lent were behind us, and the green sprouts in the garden plots suggested spring renewal. Even so, these were not enough to lift the sadness. Death hovered as heavily inside the castle as it did outside our gates. My mind railed against it, against life confused by lack and hatred. If muskets were fired that day, or if children played in the court, I could not hear them.

28

Pistol and Sword

Irish camps outside of Cork City

Teige O'Downe tried not to question the wisdom of his leaders. His place was to advise, yes, but once the gentlemen in charge made their tactical decisions, he was bound to follow. On the heels of MacCarthy Reagh he'd led his men, one hundred in this detachment, to assist in the siege of Cork City.

Word was that the murdering coward William St. Leger had abandoned his own headquarters at Doneraile on a promise from Lord Mountgarret that the Irish army would not burn his estate. St. Leger had then marched his 700 foot soldiers and 200 cavalry straight to Cork City, where he took command of the existing troops—increasing his total force to 3,000. Even with such numbers, when he learned Teige's cousin Donough, Lord Muskerry, brought his Irish troops to besiege the city, St. Leger fled like a wharf rat to Youghal, taking most of his men with him and burning nearly everything along the thirty-four miles between.

Had he stayed, St. Leger would have realized Lord Muskerry's forces consisted of untrained peasantry scoured from the local area and armed only with skeans and pikes. But St. Leger was foolish. In his absence, Muskerry reinforced and re-armed his troops, and by the time St. Leger returned, the Irish were strong, confident, charged with purpose, and ready for battle.

Teige was certain the English wouldn't give up a valuable port city like Cork without a deadly fight. He suspected the officers in Kinsale were sending additional support by sea. Teige worried, were Lord Muskerry and General Barry truly aware of the bloody clash he saw coming?

In General Garet Barry's finely appointed military tent at Rochford-stown, about three miles from Cork City, Lord Muskerry—wearing his fine long wig for the occasion—rocked on his heels at the head of the table where a large map had been set. He rarely left his primary home and headquarters for something so dull as a military strategy meeting, but in this case he had the most to lose, with Blarney Castle just six miles north. More so, he did love theatre and the show was about to begin.

Lord Muskerry faced a great many clan leaders, fifteen of whom he'd brought with him, standing proudly around the tent in their coats and colors. Among them, the MacSweeneys, the O'Learys, and the O'Herlys, and more waiting outside.

Teige studied the men seated at the table. Aside from General Barry—a gentleman maybe a decade older and a head shorter than himself—there was Cormac, the MacCarthy Reagh; there was the broad-chested Barry Oge; then, Maurice Roche, representing the Lords of Fermoy. At the foot of the table was Finin MacCarthy—Captain Sugán, as he was called, an unofficial officer from County Kerry.

Among these men, Sugan held the lowest rank but was the most inspiring. His wild blond locks made him look more lion than man, and rightly so for he was notorious for his swordsmanship and tactical skirmishes. His troops idolized him, adopted his form and strategies, and followed him devotedly.

Teige would gladly stand beside any of these men in battle, but hoped this meeting would bring a decisive plan for victory, that he might return soon to his operation at Rathbarry.

The jokes and pleasantries having all been said and the drams of whisky passed, Donough rapped on the map's center with the head of his blackthorn walking stick. Then, having gained everyone's attention, he used the tip of his stick to draw an imaginary circle on the map. "You see before you, my good fellows, the City of Cork: an elongated rectangle punctuated by towers most unusual—nearly a dozen of them on the east side, and only four facing west. With gates on the north and south ends only, the walls enclose about thirty-five acres, densely populated. You'll notice two castles within, a main street running through the middle like a spine, with narrow lanes running from it east and west. The whole fortress—in truth, a fairly prosperous city—is built upon rock, you see. The

River Lee divides to encompass it, and between river and fortress there is only marsh. You cannot cross it, trench it, nor mine beneath it."

Donough paused and grinned. "A fine fortress it is, did you live in the fourteenth century. As it stands today, it bloody well floods every year, and it's prone to every pestilence one might imagine."

The men laughed, and Donough continued. "Its' principal value is in guarding the seaport, but at this it is quite efficient. Following a massive fire twenty years ago, many structures have been rebuilt, the walls fortified in a few places. But observe, the city fathers neglected its two greatest weaknesses. The first," —at this moment Donough held up a bejeweled index finger— "that its largest cannons are fixed, facing south against invaders from the sea, and we besiege it from the north. The second?" —up went his middle finger to create a V, and then he rapped his knuckles on the table— "The city relies entirely on a weekly market for food and supplies, and as I mentioned, it is overcrowded. With the market closed, and the city being two months blockaded, already they resort to horse flesh."

A few men laughed again, but most—those who had experienced such hunger firsthand—did not.

"Had we only a bit more time, we would do nothing and quite soon starve them out. But time doth work against us, as the English will send more men, arms, and powder. We must press hard for a quick result." Donough lifted his walking stick and placed it at his side. "I turn your attention to our good General Barry, to reveal our combined strategy."

Teige considered the graying hair and protruding belly on the general, very like a man grown accustomed to directing battles from afar, not the trim and muscular form of a warrior. Being a younger son who lacked an inheritance and turned to the military for his living, mostly with the Spanish army in Flanders, he'd earned a reputation for siege warfare that involved mining beneath fortress walls. He'd written a book about military discipline. Mayhap he'd grown too comfortable at his writing desk, for his talk was slow and lacked passion.

"St. Leger has raised support in Youghal. Unfortunate, yes. Yet our powers are great," General Barry said, a touch of phlegm catching his voice. "Besieging the city on the north side, we shall have Lord Muskerry, the McCarthy Reagh, Teige-an-Duna of Dunmanway, and all the men of the western districts. We'll use the abbey and Barry's Castle for shelter and supplies. Barry Oge will strike camp in Belgooly and pitch a new camp within view of the city's north gate.

"Besieging from the south near Abby Island, we have the forces of Tipperary: Lord Roche, Lord Ikerrin, Lord Dunboye, and the Baron of Loghmoe. In total, our forces exceed four thousand. Our objectives are unchanged. We confine the enemy in all respects. They must feel our presence in the extreme, know the sharp pain of famine, and demand of their officers for relief and capitulation.

"Is there no possibility of breach, then?" Cormac asked.

"Lacking cannon, and low on muskets and ammunition, an attack would be unwise.

There is too much marsh and water, and no adjacent houses to provide cover for our miners," the general said. "The losses would be unreasonable. Our best advantage is through time and terror."

"Fire then?"

"The most effective delivery of fire would be by catapult, which we do not have. One could be built, but there is no solid land within range upon which it could stand, nor have we the proper materials."

"Our soldiers are prepared to fight." Cormac's voice became edgy. Only weeks ago at Bandon he'd faced the similar issue of how to keep his men occupied, otherwise they'd fight amongst themselves or simply return to their homes. "What do you expect us to do? Play at cards?"

"Our sharpest weapon is fear. Sound the warpipes," the general said. "Build campfires. Build earthworks. Drill your men in great numbers and with great noise. We'll schedule assaults to raise terror at their most peaceful moments while conserving our own ammunition. Particularly, an irregular volley into the battlements, to pick off the sentries. We'll guard the walls mercilessly, that no one escapes. Simply said, we worry them on all sides, and I assure you, sir, we'll not have long to wait. "

Teige scratched the back of his head. What the general said was true, but it wasn't so simple. "General, if you will," Teige said. "With such a gathering of fighting men, delay creates its own set of problems. The issue of supply exists for us as well. Men will itch to pillage the nearby homes, if they haven't already been stripped by the camp followers."

"At present we are in good stead and hold the roads. We *are* supplied, and so problems are solved through work and discipline."

"General Barry, sir. Forgive me, please," Captain Sugán said. "The gates. What if we storm them, at night?"

"You are young and eager, captain, with a desire to prove your valor, but such an attack is suicide. The gates are heavily guarded, lit by torch fire, and accessed only by stone bridges across the rushing river. They are fully exposed under the guard towers." The general glared down on the subordinate, and took a deep breath. "Gentlemen, I have studied all angles and options. If it's a fight you wish for, fear not. If Cork doesn't soon surrender, there will be a battle most ferocious."

"General, can we take the port before their reinforcements arrive?" Cormac asked.

"The seaport is guarded by two watch towers with cannon, the south gate bastions, and the largest guns at the southeast corner of the curtain wall. We have no comparable artillery. They could cut us down within an hour. Victory lies in the art of intimidation."

Teige wondered if the man had become overcautious. Nevertheless, the camps were pitched, the fires lit with every scrap of wood that could be found. The pipers from Kerry played a fierce march just out of musket range. Drills upon drills gave the great show of force, and when the winds favored, the cooks roasted fresh meat to cause the enemies' bellies to suffer and want.

Teige set his men constructing earthworks at one-third mile from the north gate. He walked the trenches as soon as the men reached a proper depth, but quickly the water seeped in to fill their boots.

On the morning of April 13, he joined Cormac to ride up to high ground while squads of men conducted regular expeditions through the suburbs along the marsh. The morning was overcast and dreary, draining the landscape of color. He viewed the houses below, mostly thatched wooden cottages where some men were billeted. Where white sheep should have dotted the landscape, the hills were barren, all the stock likely stolen by their own troops or confined within the city walls.

Cormac said nothing, only grunting at the sky, when sharp, urgent shouts startled them. Before he could speak, the pop of musket shots came from below, a horse's scream, and the thunder of cavalry in hard gallop. They glanced at each other and dashed down the hill.

29

Captain Sugán

At the Front Line

Two Irish squads joined in pursuit of a party from Cork garrison, out foraging as if they thought the Irish army slept. They were quickly driven back, Irish troops chasing after them with pikes raised, caps and cloaks flapping with the wind. The English cavalry thundered back across the bridge as the north gate opened to receive them and the tower sentries fired down on the pursuing riders who then fell back out of range.

The commotion caused an explosion of energy on all sides. Eager soldiers leapt into action. The Irish infantry searched every house and business along the river. Snipers fired precious ammunition on the city towers. Cavalry checked and rechecked the roads, and set up ambush points for any approaching relief.

It was a brave show of force, a demonstration of commitment, order and responsiveness, the like of which Teige had not yet seen—stirring the enemy's fear faster and greater than even the general might have hoped. And it pinched the English, wounding their pride, igniting a fury.

Within the hour, the north gate of the fortress shrieked and cranked open, the sound traveling across the river even as thunderclouds rumbled overhead. The English poured forth, banners waving, leaders in breastplates and helmets. Then the musketeers sallied forth, and behind them four troops of horse. The English reinforcements already had arrived. And the Irish, uninformed, were unprepared. Had the advance party been just a trick, to rush the Irish out?

Officers shouted orders that blazed through the camp. Cormac sent a messenger galloping to warn Lord Muskerry at nearby Barry's Castle.

Teige split off to help maintain order as the English drove the Irish back toward the hills.

He recognized at once Lord Inchiquin, Murrough O'Brien. A traitor to the Irish cause, he was son-in-law to the coward St. Leger, but by his own bloodline far more courageous and ruthless. Behind him came another officer, the man called Colonel Vavasour. Teige knew little of him except that his presence gave greater strength to Inchiquin, and thus he was cause for concern. Their troops moved fast into Irish ground, their muskets and armor gleaming despite the clouds.

Teige's men fell back. A few of the officers fired flintlock pistols, but the infantry was armed only with pikes and bats. The pikemen, well-trained and disciplined, stood shoulder to shoulder, their pikes braced at their feet, gripped with both hands, angled precisely against cavalry and prepared to charge, but men from other companies broke ranks, sought refuge amidst the pikemen, causing disorder, imbalance. Musketeers shot into the lines and several men fell, creating a panic. The captains shouted, ordered return to formation, but some soldiers ran for cover. And yet the English pressed forward, the muskets reloaded, fired again. The main line of defense faltered.

Inchiquin's cavalry split into two lines, one pursuing the Irish west toward Kilcrea, the other thundering east, through the blockade on the Cork road toward Barry's Castle. Teige's face burned as he realized they would try to capture Lord Muskerry. He signaled to Cormac, who turned his troops to chase them down.

The rout was almost complete—the knot beneath Teige's heart dropped to a scourge within his belly. He sent his men through the marshy ground where the English cavalry could not follow. Then from behind him came raging shouts. He recognized the voice of the young Kerry officer, Captain Sugán, and turned to see the captain's company backed into a large garden, unfenced but defined by a wide ditch, and the English cavalry going at them as a mad hound corners a fox.

With pistol and sword, Sugán fought at the front line, his men at his sides and behind him with pikes and swords. They held the cavalry off with remarkable intensity, the captain at the fore shouting oaths as if by his own fury he repelled them.

Teige searched for a way to rescue the men, but they were hemmed in, surrounded, and he could not desert his own troops still under fire and retreating. Yet the captain fought on with great valor, his coat bright with blood. A few more men escaped, scrambling through the ditch before the English infantry poured in like an ocean wave, sweeping up and over the ditches to fight hand-to-hand on precious little ground. Those few Irish who remained behind Captain Sugán joined his chosen fate, and one by one they fell. Sugán fought with enviable grace, his mastery of weapons and his sheer power standing out above all others—until an enemy captain said something to him. Sugán stopped, drew back as if he was twice as tall as he'd been a moment before. He raised his sword with a great call to God Almighty, and charged his enemy with the fury of ten men. But he was outnumbered, the English captain and his cohorts fell upon Sugán and cut him down. They killed all the Kerry soldiers before Teige's eyes.

He had no choice then but to push his men to safety and restore order as quickly as possible. Yet he could not clear his head of the sound of Sugán's oaths, the fierceness of his charge, the passion and fearlessness of his face, and the great courage that would stain forever every man who watched him fall.

On the heels of Cormac, Teige led his troops eight miles north to Carrigveare, where Donough's younger brother Daniel had built a castle. In the courtyard they dismounted to greet him. He was not as large and jowly as his brother, but the resemblance in eyes and posture was clear. Daniel urged them to the castle to hear his news.

"Donough didn't stop here, but he sent me warning," he said, "that the English hold Cork. The siege has been broken. He had to retreat so quickly, the wagons carrying his personal belongings were left behind and are in English possession. He and General Barry are marching north to Limerick, which Barry claims will quickly fall, and deliver to them the great commercial port, and of course control over the River Shannon."

Cormac cursed the ground and spit. "It's where we should have begun. Of course Limerick will fall to us. The townspeople are mostly Catholic. The Protestants will run for the castle, and Barry will undermine it in a matter of days. It's what he knows. The man was baffled at Cork, with nowhere to fight but in the marshes. He was useless there."

Teige's hands tightened into fists. Abandoning them as he had, if cousin Donough was present he'd suffer mighty blows, and not just from

Cormac. Teige ached to pound someone to powder as well. What was to become of the vast army assembled to bring Cork down? After overcoming all the difficulties to align these the forces, what sense did it make to suddenly retreat and disburse them after the first challenge? What goal had changed? What of the men who died at Cork? What about the sacrifices of men like Captain Sugán?

Daniel shook his head. "I've little to offer in victuals for your soldiers, but I'll send out a bit of beer and they may camp here tonight," he said. "I've rooms enough for the two of you herein."

It would be a cold night, but the men were so tired they would hardly notice. Soldiers pitched camp on the ground, bedded down in the stables or slept beneath the stars. Teige joined Cormac and Daniel by his hearth. Each time his tankard was empty Daniel refilled it, and his temper calmed. He began to drift in a dream state, the day's events melding with the wood smoke swirling above their heads. There was comfort in having survived a bitter battle, and yet wistfulness for what might have—should have—been, if only they'd learned of the reinforcements in time, if only they'd had more guns, or more men like Captain Sugán.

Teige recounted the story of the valiant captain, Finin MacCarthy, and the hero's death he had witnessed. "Had I a thousand men, or a hundred men. Had I even ten men of Captain Sugán's caliber, t'would be the English expelled from Cork, and not the Irish," he said.

"Aye, 'tis a sad tale." Cormac nodded. "My men tell me he was offered a gentleman's surrender. He refused, and that is when he attacked the English captain. They cut him down, and then cut off his head and his hands, and hung them from the north gate. They captured his pipers, and forced them to play for their captain beneath his severed head. Then they executed all three of them."

Teige's breath stuck in his throat. "How I wish to burn them all to bloody hell."

"Listen, my friend. It's all well, isna, to shout and swagger and give a great show of courage, fine though it may be. But Sugán forgot the first rule of war."

Teige scoffed. "Sugán inspired men with his passion. They loved him, and would follow him anywhere. As for rules of war, from what I've witnessed the English have never imagined any."

"Well then, in the *MacCarthy Reagh's* rules of war, the first one is, *kill the enemy* and stay alive yerself. The dead see no reward for valor. Sugán's responsibility was to protect his men. He led them to a trap. He gained nothing while the English saw his great passion quickly snuffed. 'S true, he may ha been a legend one day. As it is, his life was too short to be memorable. Only his survival would ha been, to the English, the worthier insult."

"Ye may be right there, he should ha' survived," Teige said. "Men like Sugán are rare, but they should be the standard—lead others to arms and lift them to greater courage and commitment. Donough and his general can ride off as if this siege never happened, but the captain's life and death will have purpose. Be it God's will that I'm to survive this war, I'll see to it myself."

The fire crackled. An oak branch popped and broke into two halves as cinders burst upward. Daniel nodded sleepily in his heavy, carved armchair. Cormac stood, rested his hands and his tankard on the mantel before him and gazed into the flames. "Well now. We are not summoned to Lord Muskerry's side," he said. "General Barry is right that Limerick will be ours. It's as well, for he needs a victory badly before his reputation is lost. The castle at Limerick has a high wall, but it's too close to the keep, so instead of protecting the castle it gives the general perfect cover for his men to dig their mines and collapse the towers. He doesn't need us, and doesn't care to share the glory when he gets it. So. Where would you go from here?"

Teige pushed his tankard away and stood, meaning to find his place to rest. He allowed his shoulders to settle, his indignation over Captain Sugán lost upon the current company. "Rathbarry has weakened, but she hasna fallen. If my Lord MacCarthy Reagh does not need me straight away," he gave Cormac a questioning gaze but Cormac shook his head, "I will see an end to that siege better than what we've had here, and make the castle mine."

Cormac grinned. "When it's yours and well defended, come to me at Kilbrittain. Now that their reinforcements are coming through Youghal, I fear the English bastards will have an eye for it. My wife and children reside there. My mother as well, and all that I love. I must not lose it."

30

The Cabins

Rathbarry Castle

On the 25th of April, St. Mark's day, Mr. Taverner acknowledged the evangelist with one of his lengthier sermons. Mistress Dorothy had embroidered a winged lion, the symbol of St. Mark, upon a white banner. "Merel," she'd said, "see that the minister hangs it on the chapel door."

He did so, and called attention to it as he began. "Why the winged lion?" he asked those of us crowded into the small, dark chapel. To the silence he replied, "Because, of course, St. Mark described the voice of John the Baptist as 'the one who cries out in the wilderness.' Don't you see? Like the roar of the lion." Taverner delivered a self-satisfied nod to the mistress. The whole sermon dulled my senses along with the heat of too many bodies, and the smells of old wood, candle wax and human sweat. Sir Arthur himself nodded his chin to his chest.

When at last we were released, we shuffled like cattle toward the door. Sir Arthur asked Captain Beecher to attend him in the state room. Mistress Dorothy pinched my arm—her way of telling me I must go before them to prepare the room, and report to her their conversation.

I dusted and aired the room by the time they arrived, and glasses of sherry glistened on Sir Arthur's desk. He wasn't surprised to see me when he reached the top of the stairs. He surveyed the stateroom until Captain Beecher arrived, but he was starting to catch on to my presence. I would have to find a way to be even more stealthy. As it was, he said, "Merel, please close the door on your way out."

This proved no hindrance, for I was still able to hear most of what was said from my position at the top of the stair. I had the privy behind me and

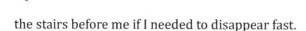

the stairs before me if I needed to disappear fast.

"Captain," Sir Arthur said.

"Sir," Beecher replied, and the glasses clinked together.

"We have much to discuss, but first I must know how the garrison fares. Are the men well?"

"As could be expected. They are hungry, growing tired of reduced rations, and they are discontented. They need something to do, other than guard the walls and gates. They itch for a fight and complain they could destroy the Irish camp in minutes if only they were released to do so."

"Ah, yes. The typical short-sightedness of infantrymen." Sir Arthur paused. "Do they forget the numbers of troops we saw on the hill that day in February? The camp below us, the troops at Ross to the west, the camp near McShane's to the east? The men at Dunowen Castle to the southeast, and to the north, the town of Clonakilty? We remain surrounded."

"Yes, sir. And worse, no means of communication."

"Why do the Irish wait?" Sir Arthur voiced a twinge of impatience. "They have the advantage of great numbers—certainly three to one, and probably even more. They could easily swarm over us."

Beecher grunted. "Our cannons are a big deterrent, sir. The Irish style of warfare favors ambush and skirmish. They lack artillery and the training to use it. Even more than that, my sense is that their leader, this Teige O'Downe, is a conservative man. He protects his men, and wants this castle intact. He wanted his people to move in, you recall."

"Do you advise firing the cannons, then, as a warning?"

"It would do no good unless they are attacking. We'd still be wise to conserve our ammunition. But there's something else we must do. We've talked of it before," Captain Beecher said, his voice turning grave.

"I know. My cabins. I ought to have burned them before now—it's just that they were costly, and useful to me at harvest time. You understand, I had little choice than to allow the herdsmen to take the cattle back out to the field. The men never once collected enough forage to feed the cows sufficiently within our walls. I decided that, if the Irish would steal cows by threes and fours, we were better off with that than to have the animals starve to death before our eyes. If only we had more salt to preserve meat, I'd slaughter them straight away, but we've little enough to season a cauldron of soup."

"The Irish steal far more than a few cows or sheep at a time. Your cabins give them a place to hide, a place to sleep, a place to sharpen their skeans...and they take at least a dozen cows every night."

I shuddered. Captain Beecher spoke of the little white cabins that lined the ridge, so charming to my eyes, so friendly and familiar. I'd hate to see them burned, but we couldn't allow them to harbor so easily those who would steal the cattle. Already the people complained for having so little meat in their bowls. Much less and we would truly suffer.

Sir Arthur allowed a heavy sigh. "I never intended to make it easy for those rogues. Burn them."

The shuffle of boots and screech of chair legs across the planks sent me cowering behind the door of the solar. Captain Beecher wasted no time but thundered down the stairs. I rushed to the window to see him bound out of the castle, shouting to Ty at the stables. Ty ran out, Giles and Collum behind him. I couldn't hear what the captain said, but everyone leapt into action, and Beecher ran for the garrison, shouting all the way for those he'd have serve him on the task.

I left the window, but I'd forgotten that Sir Arthur remained in the stateroom. I went to the door. "Sir Arthur, may I get you something?"

His shield-like cheeks were dark, his brows furrowed. "No. Nothing... No, wait...Go down and tell Jenkin to prepare my musket. He shall bring it to me at the northwest tower."

"Yes, sir." I ran down the stairs to find Jenkin, my heart pounding, my shoulders tingling with excitement. It was true that activity—any kind of activity, any kind of purpose—served to alleviate the boredom, hunger and constant fear that weighed upon all of us like a rain-soaked cloak.

Mistress Dorothy paced the floor of the great hall. She watched Jenkin run for the armory, and dragged me by the elbow into the buttery. "What is it? Why does Arthur want his musket?"

I told her everything, but she frowned. "Next time come to me first, not Jenkin." She released my elbow, which ached where she'd squeezed it. She left the buttery and followed Sir Arthur out to the courtyard.

I counted twenty horses being saddled and mounted until the guards drew open the big doors of the gate. Two of the men held unlit torches as the troops rode out, two others carried pikes, and the rest had muskets. How thrilling to hear the hooves hit the dirt, the shouts and huffs of man and horse, the creak of the leather reins. Something new was about to happen. We were taking action after so much confinement and waiting. And, we would have a rare spectacle.

The gates clanked shut and I ran to find Jayne. She was in Mistress Dorothy's bedchamber, stinking of lavender, airing our lady's gowns. "You're all red-faced. What is it?" Jayne asked.

"Sir Arthur's called for his gun. They're burning the cabins."

Her eyes popped wide, she stopped her work and we both ran for the stairs. "David!" she said, gasping. "Is he riding with them?"

"I don't know, let's hurry." We ran through the garden ward and climbed the tower until we were both quite breathless. Gray-tinged clouds scudded across the sky with the occasional yawn of blue, and gusts of wind out of the north huffed like a schoolmaster grown impatient. When we reached the wall, Sir Arthur was sending Mistress Dorothy away.

"The gun is just a precaution, my dear, they are only burning the cabins. But I'll not have you risk yourself in any way. Get back to the keep. *Please*, Dorothy. You may see us from the window in the stateroom."

Mistress Dorothy glared and grabbed my elbow again as she returned to the stairs. "Do not leave no matter what he says. I want to know *everything* when you come down."

Men from the garrison lined the wall next to Sir Arthur, so that he paid no attention to me and Jayne. We watched as the riders came two-by-two around the northeast tower and up into the meadow where the herdsmen had led the last few dozen of Sir Arthur's cattle. Then they crossed over the hill toward the ridge. How I longed to be there, riding among my beautiful trees waving and bending just beyond the ridge.

"I think I see him," Jayne said. "There, the third one on the left. He sits so tall in the saddle, it must be him."

The two soldiers holding torches dismounted while the others spread across the length of the ridge before the row of cabins, forming a barrier around them. The two men with pikes ran from cabin to cabin, kicking in the doors to make sure no one was inside. I hated to think what might have happened had they found someone. The men lit their torches with flint and steel and started, a man on each side of the first house, putting fire to the lowest ends of the reed-and-grass thatch. At first a white smoke rose straight up from between the reeds, then suddenly the flame burst up and quickly spread left and right, growing taller than wide in a bright, angry plume. The men cheered. Then a piece of flame separated and leapt to a higher place on the roof. In seconds a black spot appeared where it landed and expanded like a pool of ink. Then flames reached up between the reeds, came together to consume the dark circle, and spread across the whole top of the roof.

Jayne nudged my shoulder. "Look a' that," she said. "Gruesome, isna?" The men moved to the second house. By this time the burned husks of the reeds curled and twisted like great black spiders, and a blood-red glow climbed within the hollow stems to burn higher and higher. Parts of the blackened husks broke away in a sudden gust of wind, sending billows of smoke toward the castle.

The second house lit up in the same fashion as the first, and the men moved to the third. A portion of roof from the first house fell in, sending sparks and thick smoke gushing out the door. The men worked faster now, though I worried whether they could stay ahead of the fire as it spread. The men on horses moved back, likely feeling the heat of the flames. The thatch crackled and wood beams screamed, buckled, and crashed inside the burning structures. By the sixth house, the gray smoke formed into dense puffs like rolled wool that rose slowly above the houses, upward and outward, concealing the trees behind. Such a plume would be seen from most parts of the county, and still another six cabins to burn. A gust sent smoke toward the castle, clouding our view.

"I can't see David anymore. The smoke is so...how can they breathe?" Jayne couldn't stand still beside me, as if she might heave herself over the wall and run out to save him herself. She started to cough.

"He's a soldier. He'll be well. Just wait, they're nearly done and can back off from it," I said. But I worried. Were they far enough away? Could the fire jump to their clothing? Could the trees beyond the cabins catch and start a wildfire?

The north wind gusted again, pushing the dense, rolling smoke like a boundless veil from the trees to the castle, and then it descended—a blinding fog heavy enough to sink a ship, stinging our eyes and obscuring anything farther than a foot from our noses. We choked and coughed until a great rumble moved across the hill, and then came urgent shouts from the field and ridge. Jayne screamed.

"What is it! What is happening!" Sir Arthur shouted. And yet the smoke billowed, flames still flicking above the ridge. The shapes of the cabins and all of our men were impossible to see.

Then came the rumble again, like thunder. The veil lifted for just a moment. Men were running through the trees, from behind and between the cabins. The Irish, bare chested and nearly naked so that nothing could hinder their speed. They got behind some of the horses, causing them to scream and rear. They got between Captain Beecher's men and the cattle. Someone fired a gun. Then the gusts blew down upon us and pressed the smokey veil over us again. Were horses galloping?

More muskets fired, and the veil shifted to reveal a crowd of men on the field, eighty or more, fighting for the cattle, some already driving them away as other men tried to seize the horses. Three ran wildly without riders. Captain Beecher chased after them and managed to bring them back to the hill, even as the Irish still attacked from the sides. Captain Beecher shouted orders. The garrison men aligned and galloped through the maze. The snipers and Sir Arthur fired upon the Irish from the castle wall as the soldiers returned to the castle.

Jayne ran for the gate, fearing David could be one of the three men unhorsed. The rest of us waited on the wall while the worst of the smoke cleared. The cabins had burned to the ground in big black humps of smoldering wood, the timbers glowing an eerie bright red. The cattle were all gone, but no one had been killed.

Three men in the courtyard stood apart from the others of the garrison. "When the attack came," Captain Beecher told Sir Arthur, "these three abandoned their horses and ran back to the castle for safety."

Sir Arthur faced them. "You are cowards. How dare you leave your fellow men out there to do the fighting for you. How could you make such a shameful flight? You are maintained here under my command and Captain Beecher's. And as such you are expected to do your duty."

One of the men, Mr. Crood, replied, "Maintained under your command, you say? You maintain us not, Captain Freke. Therefore, we'll *not* be commanded by you."

MAY

31

In Tatters

Rathbarry Castle

Where the early days of spring should have delivered color and the glow of new life to Rathbarry, there remained shadow and sorrow, the people of the castle still grieving the dead though few would speak of it. Within the court, the women fussed over every sprout, that it might more quickly bear fruit, while beyond the castle walls the wildflowers romped unhindered over fields not plowed, grazed or reaped. No half-year rent could be collected; no men could seek work at hiring fairs. A cold east wind blew, signaling bad luck for the harvest, and the bees were slow to awaken.

I emerged from the dark cavern of our garret to find low-hanging clouds drifting sullenly toward the sea but offering no rain. Jayne and I went to the mistress's bedchamber at our appointed time to find the door firmly closed and Sir Arthur within, shouting.

"You've deceived me. How long have you known?"

Mistress Dorothy answered in a voice too high and breathless. "Arthur. It is a baby. An heir for you. You are angry at me instead of happy?"

He paced heavily, though it was clear he'd not yet pulled on his boots.

"You know the troubles we face, Dorothy. You should have been sent away with the others to Bandon where I'd know you were safe. The Irish are closing in on us, and I don't know how or when we'll get relief. There are too many children in this castle already that I must worry about feeding. Most of our meat is gone. Bread. Fruit. Cheese. And *milk*? How shall I get milk for an infant? I shall never know another night's sleep."

There was silence for a couple of minutes. I wanted to knock but Jayne stayed my hand.

"Why did you not tell me as soon as you knew?" he said.

"I didn't *mean* to hide anything from you. I knew you had much on your mind. The garrison, the killings of those men, and then the cattle. What could I do?"

"I shall send O'Daly out this morning, straight to Bandon to beg Lord Kinalmeaky to collect you. *No!* I shall send you there immediately, escorted by the entire garrison. There's nothing more important they could do."

Mistress Dorothy cried out then, her tears and her fear genuine. She did not want to leave Sir Arthur. "Please, *please* do not send me away, Arthur. I must be here with you. You need me here. Who will manage the servants? The kitchen? Who will see to the gardens? Who will look after you while you're looking after everyone else? I *must* be here with you. Please!"

She wept so hard, Jayne and I squeezed each other's hands as if we experienced her anguish. Then she coughed and wept even louder. Was *that* part genuine? I couldn't be sure.

"Dear Dorothy," he said after a few moments. "You must take care. Be calm. Your condition."

"Oh Arthur, I am not made of glass!" she screamed, and hurled some things against the door. In a moment Sir Arthur opened it, retrieved his boots from the floor. He only glanced at us and then stomped down the stairs in his stockings.

We waited until she quieted and then cautiously entered the bedchamber. Mistress Dorothy was sitting on her stool. She didn't even look up at us, but continued weeping. Jayne went to her and began gently brushing her hair. I straightened the bedclothes, picked out one of her favorite dresses and brought it to her. She touched the lace on the sleeve.

"It was my breasts," she said. "We'd just awakened. He watched me pulling on my smock. He gazed at me with a strange smile, and then he cupped my breasts in his hands. 'They've grown larger,' he said, and then it occurred to him what that meant."

I brought her a linen and she dabbed away her tears. "My waist has grown. I can't even wear that dress anymore." She sighed heavily and her shoulders shuddered.

"Oh, mistress. I shall let out the seams for you. You may still wear it," Jayne said.

Then our lady quieted, stood up from the stool and sniffed. "The both of you. Get down to the kitchen and bring me something to eat!"

That very afternoon, I sat at Mistress Dorothy's knee in the solar, reading poems to her while she embroidered a new pillow cover and Jayne altered her dress. Suddenly she nudged me with her ankle—in truth it was more of a kick.

"You shouldn't be here; you should be out doing things for me. Go and find Sir Arthur and see what he's about. Don't come back until you have news," she said.

She might have found a kinder way to ask, but certainly it was my preference to be away from her and free to roam about. I went straight to the stables because, why wouldn't I? The clouds still had not cleared, and the stable was dim and quiet. I peered about but could not see Ty, only Collum sweeping the floor.

"He's at the garrison," he said, with a smile and a nod.

There, several soldiers moved hastily to and fro while saddled horses stood ready, perhaps for some kind of drill, but there was no sign of Ty. How I wished I had my boy clothes on, for I tired of trying to be invisible in my insufferable pink dress. As a boy, I could simply stroll through the garrison with no one paying me any mind. I continued toward the garden wall when Sir Arthur and Mr. Millett rounded the corner.

"Merel, what are you doing here?" Sir Arthur asked.

"Sir, Mistress Dorothy sent me to ask if you might care for some biscuits and a sherry."

He shook his head and smirked with mild annoyance. "Tell her she is not to fuss over me. I'm quite busy, and need nothing at present. She should have some for herself."

He continued walking in the direction of the stables so I followed at a reasonable distance as if I returned to the keep.

"As I was saying, sir, the sheep do suffer for want of grass," Mr. Millett said. "We are doing what we can to keep them fed, but the herdsmen fear to go outside the wall, and when they do, they grab handfuls of whatever is before them and rush back in. It's mostly weed, not enough to sustain the herd, and yet the summer pasture is riotous with sweet rye. The sheep will want the tender shoots, but at this stage I do believe they'll eat the tall grass as well. They'll eat anything. If we take them out under heavy guard, perhaps we can protect them while they graze. So soon after the Irish have taken the cattle, might they be a little less hungry for mutton?"

"All right, all right," Sir Arthur said. "We shall test the ground. Take a small portion of the herd at a time, and see if the Irish come for them. Talk to Captain Beecher about what sort of guard and what troops he recommends. You'll go at dawn, and graze three hours but no longer. Have them back by noontide, and let not the herdsmen be idle. Have them fill sacks with more grass while they're there."

"Of course, sir. Excellent plan."

The saddled horses must have been intended for Mr. Millett, and he was getting Sir Arthur's permission after he'd already planned to go. Now that Sir Arthur had given him such detailed instruction, he would have to wait until morning.

I returned to the keep to deliver the news to Mistress Dorothy. The solar seemed strangely quiet, but someone was weeping, and it didn't sound like the mistress. When I entered the room, the lady stood in her smock, one hand on her hip, the other dangling a large pair of sewing shears. She pursed her lips so tightly the skin around them turned white. On the floor before her, Jayne wept, sifting through her fingers the remnants of our lady's favorite dress.

"She cannot fix it as she promised. It still doesn't fit." The mistress stamped her foot like a peevish child. "What am I expected to do? Stand around naked all day? What benefit do I know from having servants? Particularly, *Irish* servants. I shall have all Irish servants banished from the keep. They cannot be trusted."

Jayne looked up at me, tears streaming from her eyes and her hands filled with strips of fabric that could never again be assembled into a gown. I gently took the shears from Mistress Dorothy's hand and set them in the sewing basket. I helped her into her velvet robe and fetched her a very large glass of sherry from the state room cabinet. Then I pulled Jayne from the tangle of fabric, gathered up as much of it as I could, and led her down to the kitchen. There, I handed her an even larger glass of sherry.

"She is a tyrant," I said. "She is mad. You mustn't listen to a single word from her lips." I stood by until Jayne's tears ceased of their own accord. Finally, she heaved a great sigh.

"The gown did fit her. Truly it did. I let it out as far as the seams allowed, an inch on either side," Jayne said. "But it didn't look as it had before. It was obvious her shape had changed, and the drape of the fabric couldn't disguise it. 'Tis not the dress she despised."

"No, that much was clear."

"If she meant what she said about banning Irish from the castle, I shall be glad, the horrid witch. There's no Irish alive who deserves such treatment."

"Exactly so. In truth, I think she was casting upon you her anger at Sir Arthur. Had he been the least bit pleased about the child, she might have been softer. But to expel all the Irish servants? She cannot mean it."

"Well, I cannot go back there. Not with her like this."

"And *I* can't manage her without my friend beside me," I said. "What if we were to praise and congratulate Sir Arthur on the new baby, to swell his joy about it, perhaps then restoring him to the doting husband Mistress Dorothy needs? Surely this would lift her spirits enough to make her bearable. We must do *something*, for it isn't only you and me that she terrifies, but the entire kitchen and household staff—even Jenkin, who vanishes when she enters a room."

"I don't believe for a minute ye can change her, but she's lucky to have someone willin' to try. I'll give it one more go, but for you, never for her," Jayne said.

In the meantime, Jayne started altering another dress, working on a gathering technique that might help disguise the growing bulge of our mistress's belly. I took the strips of fabric from her shredded dress, and began braiding them into a new mat where Jayne could wipe her feet.

Over the next several days, Mr. Millett's experiment with the sheep proved successful, such that each day he was taking several sheep out of the castle, and bringing them all back fatted with grass. He urged Sir Arthur to allow grazing larger groups, being that there were 1,200 sheep remaining of the herd, requiring many days to feed them all in small groups, yet their exposure grew each time they left Rathbarry.

32

Shafts of Light

Rathbarry Castle

A few days later, Ty found me in the courtyard. He looked tired and rumpled, but his eyes sparkled with good cheer. "Will ye coom wi' me, Merel? There's somethin' I must show ye."

"Of course," I said, and tried not to appear too gleeful as I followed. I couldn't match his stride but made up for it with quickness, into the stables to a wide stall in the far corner. I could just see horse's dark head above the gate.

Ty patted a wooden tack box next to the enclosure. "Step up here, an' ye take a good look."

I climbed upon the box to see well inside the stall. The mare was sleek and long-legged, her black mane silky across her neck, a lumpy pile of hay at her feet. But then something moved, and I realized just beside her right flank stood a perfect new foal, with bright eyes, knobby knees and small hooves. Between its pointy ears, straight up and alert, was a tiny triangle with a swirl of white fur.

I gasped. "He is magnificent! It's a he, isn't it?"

"Aye, a fine guess. Born last night, had his first breakfast before dawn. He's as smart and fit as they come."

"May I touch him?"

"The mare's a bit protective just now, so we'll give 'er a day ta get used to 'im, then ye can coom back and pet him all ye want."

"I'll hardly be able to wait. Oh, thank you, he is so beautiful, and it brightens everything to see new life when we've had so much sadness."

He touched a finger to the rim of his cap, the look on his face surely the same as a proud new father.

"When did you first fall in love with horses?"

He chuckled. "I was a lad, naught but about nine years. My father needed a horse for haulin', and took me wi' him to a market at a crossroads near Tralee. It took all the day to walk there, and we slept on the ground that night. From then until dawn men and horses were arriving, horses of every size, color and temperament. There was clopping and stomping, whinnies and grunts, laughter and chatter and arguments and deals being made. Horses pissin' in the lanes and turning everything to muck. Drinkin' and swearin' and a fight or two, and then it grew raucous. 'Twas more excitement than ever I'd seen.

"My da was lookin' for a nice docile mare, and we strolled through the market, him stoppin' to speak with a fella or two. We coom upon a round enclosure, and a man wi' his horse chained by the neck against the fence, and he was beating it. The horse's eyes were wild and she was screaming. I didn't know what the man wanted her to do, and sure the mare had no idea. She was terrified. The man kept yellin' as if she should understand. I yelled at the man to stop. He yelled that I ought mind my own. I was holdin' back my tears when Da spoke to the man so softly I couldna even hear. The fella reared back, glared and said, "Ye can tek 'er, then. She's thick as a plank. I'll not 'ave 'er." Da passed him a few coins—a good bit less than he'd intended to spend that day—so we all went home happy.

"'Twas my job after to train her ta be a good working horse. An' what did I know of training a horse? Not the first thing. But I started by makin' friends with her. We called her Cara, which means friend. An' once she trusted me, knew I wasn't goin' to strike her and she was safe, she'd do anathin' we asked. She learned fast after that, our good Cara."

I stepped down from the box, standing close to Ty and lingering much longer than I should have. The smell of horse and hay overpowered any other scents, and I breathed it in as if it was honey. Maybe it was the new foal, along with Mistress Dorothy's condition, that filled me with a sense I'd not known for a long time. I entered another world, with no castle, no Mistress Dorothy, no siege, no hunger, no death. Only me, Ty, and the horses—as if he and I could simply admire them, and then walk out of the stables into our own sunny meadow. As if life would move on from this wretched time and we would never recall it. He touched my hand.

"I wanted to apologize to ye for bein' a bit far off. After that day at Ross, I was…well, it was no' my best time. So, I told ye I'd find a place. Where we could be alone together. If ye still want to, I have done, if it isna too strange."

"Strange? How could it be that?"

"It's in the chapel. A storage room where none would find us. After sermon."

I sucked in my breath. "The chapel? In a storeroom? But not in the nave. And not in the sanctuary. The vestry?"

"Next to the vestry."

"Show me? Now?" I asked.

His eyes widened, but he took my hand.

Our footfalls seemed to thunder across the vacant chapel's floor. Inside the storeroom were shelves stacked with prayer books, altar linens, candles and the like, and yet it smelled musty as church rooms seem to do. The only light angled through a narrow, stained-glass window that depicted John the Baptist in a pink robe not too far removed from my own pink gown. But he wore a halo and carried a holy cross, while I was contemplating my very first sin—if I didn't count lying. I'd done a good bit of lying already.

Within my breast my heart fluttered and of a sudden I was shy. What should I say? What was I meant to do? Ty sat on the floor, his back against the wall. He reached for me, and for a second I couldn't breathe. I sat beside him. He draped his arm around my shoulders and pulled me close against his ribs, his heart beating against my arm. My fear began to dissolve into tiny little parts.

Shafts of colored light filled the little room and tinted Ty's face in pale shades of ochre, rose and ash blue. I turned my face into his neck and breathed him in—he would always smell of horsehair, but there was something else today, perhaps wood smoke, but more earthy and alive, like the scent that rises from oak leaves crushed in your palm.

"Do you remember when you told me you'd like to ride off into the mountains on Sarcen?" he asked.

"I do." My voice sounded strange to my own ears.

"Aye, so. There's a place a bit west of here, across the county line into Kerry, called Kilsarkan. A small village, a crossing of sheep paths, more like. My uncles run a school there. 'Tis quite near the highest mountains in all of Ireland—*Na Cruacha Dubha*."

My anxiety was forgotten as I imagined a great mountain range just a short distance away. "What does that mean?" I asked.

"The Black Stacks—the mountains look like giant stacks o' hay, black against a blue sky. In truth they hold many colors: green moss and grass, purple heather, yellow furs, brown and gray rocks. The highest of all, *Corrán Tuathail*—Tuathal's Scythe—is named for an ancient high king, mighty in battle."

"Mighty in battle. It stirs wonder in me. Do you ever wish..." I started to ask but stopped myself. What if, instead of wonder, my question stirred a struggle within him?

He shrugged. "Aye, I know what ye meant to say. Do I wish I was a warrior like Tuathal, takin' part in the battle?"

"Yes."

"At times, though I'd ne'er want Sir Arthur to know. I've done well here. I doona wish to leave it for a war I t'ink we canna win, or to die for the same fellas who shoved me about like a beggar. And yet this rising is different. The clans have fought each other for centuries. Ye could ne'er put four of 'em in a room and them not come to blows. But now, they've forged a rare unity, crossing all provinces, an' it's the one thing pushin' me to question my loyalties."

I leaned forward to face him. "I'm sorry. It must be..." He touched a finger to my lips to silence me.

"Ne'er ye mind. The other thing that keeps me from hurlin' myself o'er the wall is settin' right beside me. I wait each day until I see your face peerin' down at me from the lady's window, to see ya scurry past on some errand or other. I'm wonderin' will she be in a fine dress today, or wrapped in an apron, or dressed as a peasant boy off to the fields? I wasna' looking for someone, content as I am wi' my work, but I canna stop t'inkin' about ye. An' so I'm to wonder, what am I doin' talkin' my fool head off when I have ye beside me. And am I right to hope that ye feel the same?" He pulled me forward and kissed me firmly on the lips, the warmth of it sending a blush to my cheeks and a sensation that seared through my body as butter across a heated pan.

"I feel…" I said, gasping for breath, "the same." I pulled at his doublet as eagerly as he pulled at the ties of my dress.

Though I had not yet experienced it, I'd dreamt of what lay ahead, imagining what it might feel like. Even such thoughts could send a warmth to my belly and between my thighs. There would be pain, yes, but what else? And even if I was a little scared, it only fueled the excitement. I was tired of being treated like a child, wasn't I, and here was a man who saw me as a woman; who wanted me as much as I wanted him.

I ran my fingers across his chest, the muscles firm, the hair not course but pleasing. His warm hands on my skin both calmed and thrilled me that I could rise straight into Heaven if there was nothing more. But there was something more, and slowly, gently, with kisses more sweet and thrilling than I could have known, I released all my tension, all my fear, all my resistance. I wrapped my arms so tightly about him we were like one being. When the moment of joining came I opened myself to him, and though he was gentle at first, there came the instant when he could not bear it and I met his thrust, the acute pain causing me to cry out, but bringing with it a flood of such intensity rising from my womb as if I was made entirely of molten wax. The flood kept rising, to my breast and throat, to my cheeks, until the top of my head could hardly contain it. And then like a summer storm it gradually receded, leaving my body burning and throbbing, and my mind awash with joy.

We slept, and when we awoke the light through the window had changed from white to amber. Soon people would be arriving in the courtyard for their supper, such as it would be. With silent kisses, we parted, and left the chapel before we would be seen. I wasn't certain what Sir Arthur might do, but if Mistress Dorothy knew what had just happened, she would somehow turn it against me. I glanced around the chapel quickly before I closed the door behind me. I would never look at it the same way again.

On Sunday morning, Jayne and I waited on a bench in the courtyard just before the chapel, while others checked on plants in the garden, pulled water from the well, or chased after the few remaining chickens.

Perhaps we were not wise to give the children their eggs at Easter instead of hatching every one. There came a great clatter of noise, not unusual for a morning in the court, but this sounded like muskets fired at some distance away. It continued for several minutes, then returned to silence.

Sir Arthur and several garrison men climbed the north tower to determine what had happened. They shouted and pointed to a turmoil in the distance. Yet, the courtyard filled, the chapel doors opened, Mr. Taverner began his laborious sermon. Sir Arthur still paced the wall, and most people waited in the court for news. Gossip passed about like a flooding tide. Mr. Millett had left the castle in the early hours of morn, along with the herdsmen and an escort of garrison soldiers. They took the sheep to the summer fields to graze.

With every person in the castle on edge, no one spoke except Mr. Taverner who continued droning in the chapel. Half an hour passed before the horses approached the castle gate, and Sir Arthur shouted to the guards to let them in at once. The chapel emptied, with the minister calling after us as if anything could be done to stop us.

Sir Arthur met them at the gate and walked alongside the riders as they approached the castle steps. The gate closed solidly behind them, but the herdsmen drove no sheep. "What has happened? Tell me quickly," he said to Mr. Millett.

Millet dismounted, handed his reins to a Giles, and stood before Sir Arthur. "Phillip O'Swellivant and his men out of Bantry. They set up an ambush for us, sir. About thirty musketeers in a bog ditch not far from the castle, and more of them in the ring fort just east of us, sir, and still more, hundreds of them, behind a hill. They concealed themselves until we were half a mile from the castle, and then they rose up all at once, to drive all the sheep away."

"All of them? All?" Sir Arthur asked.

"Yes, sir, and all of our colts as well, sir."

Hairs on the back of my neck bristled at the word *colts*. It couldn't be *our* new little colt. It could not be. He was too young for the pasture. But the others? I glanced around for Ty but couldn't see him anywhere. My stomach began to twist.

Sir Arthur turned his back on Millett and lurched forward as if to vomit, but he recovered himself quickly when Mistress Dorothy arrived beside him. He swung around. "How could this happen Millett? Why did you take *all* of them?"

Millett looked down at his shoes, gathered his breath, then raised his head to reply. "Sir, it being a feast day, we believed these popish folk would have to be with their priests and all, it being sinful that they should miss a single Kyrie or Sanctus. But they are devils, every one of them destined for hell."

"Spare me your preaching, Millett, and tell me the rest." Sir Arthur's face was dark red by now and I feared for his health, but his unsteadiness before had now solidified, and he stood before Millett like a tower of rock.

"As soon as the sheep were beyond the castle, the rebels rose out of the ring fort just east of us, to drive our sheep and colts toward the bog. Our men rode out to retrieve them, along with our best horses that were then in the bog. but the rebels started firing muskets. Those rogues had the ditch to shelter them, while our men were in the open field, but they charged forth anyway, wounding a good number of the enemy, sir. We made them quit the ditch and leave the horses, but they drove away all the sheep and the colts with such speed that we couldn't overtake them. Then about 200 men rose up from behind the hill and began firing on us. We took a few rounds, sir, but their numbers were too great and we had no choice but to retreat to the castle, so many of us being injured."

"How many?" Sir Arthur's voice was sharp and curt.

"Most were shot through the clothes, sir. Only Rafe Davis took serious injury, shot through the thigh."

"Bring him into the castle, now," Sir Arthur said.

I looked back to the stables, and Ty was there, his hands coiled to fists at his sides. His gaze met mine, and his eyes burned as if on fire—crimson rimmed, the whites shot with bright red, the gray iris turned to a searing, fierce, and luminous blue. Had he his skean, Millett's throat would already lay open.

Sir Arthur turned to his wife. "Our cattle and sheep being all gone, and our number of people increasing with refugees, we shall find ourselves in serious want, and no salt left to save any meat we still have. No milk for mother and child. Do you see why you belong at Bandon? Only now it is far too late."

33

Fire of Joy

Rathbarry Castle

Just before supper that evening, Mr. Millett came to the keep. Jayne and I were in the buttery. Having poured wine for Sir Arthur and Mistress Dorothy, we began filling pitchers with watered wine for the dinner service. Mr. Millett barged through the wooden door and stomped toward Sir Arthur at his table. He was bleeding from a gash on his lip. His left eye was swollen and purpling, his hair was disheveled, and his clothing was dirty and disordered. Sir Arthur jumped to his feet. "Millett, what has happened to you?"

"Nothing, sir. Kicked by a horse. Just an accident. Is your physician about?" Millett said.

"A rather well-placed kick, I'd say. I noticed earlier that our stableman Giles bears a similar injury." He smirked. "My physician's tending the wounded at the garrison."

"Thank you, sir." Millett wheeled toward the door, but before he could leave Mistress Dorothy rushed toward him and grabbed his arm.

"Tell me, Mr. Millett! It was the Irish, wasn't it? They've turned on you, all of them," she said.

Millett's mouth dropped open and yet he could not speak. Sir Arthur rose from his chair and took Dorothy by the elbow. "On your way, Millett. Dorothy, come with me."

Together they climbed the stairs, Sir Arthur never releasing her, and Mistress Dorothy's face as pale and stiff as white marble. As they climbed each step, it dawned on me who might have planted such blows on the fellow who had lost Rathbarry's colts, and on the fellow who had allowed him to take them.

The state room door slammed closed, but soon there was shouting and Mistress Dorothy started screaming, so that all the servants in the keep could hear.

"I won't have it, Arthur. They will cut our throats as we sleep. The Irish must all be turned out. I mean it. All of them must be expelled from Rathbarry, and tonight." Mistress Dorothy's voice was high and strained, and as loud as ever I'd heard. Jayne's face drained of color, her jaw tightened and her eyes looked dark and hollow. I grasped her hand.

"Dorothy, you're upset," Sir Arthur said. "Please sit and calm yourself. People can hear you and you'll frighten them"

"Them? You're concerned about them? I am your wife. I am frightened. I carry your child. Have you no care about me? About us? How dare you!"

"No, that's not what I meant. Please!"

Mistress Dorothy kept on bawling until he managed to calm her, and her sounds became horrid sobs, and then whimpers, until at last Sir Arthur spoke, his voice still loud but not angry. "You must understand, we depend on our Irish servants, we cannot send them away. Your Jayne, many of our kitchen workers, Mr. O'Daly in the stables. We cannot do without them, and even if we could, we cannot send them out where they might be executed as traitors. I'll not cast people to their deaths."

Then all became very quiet, not even a creak of the floor panels or a scrape of a chair leg. An hour passed before they came out of the room. Sir Arthur descended the stairs and spoke to Jenkin. Mistress Dorothy came as far as the bottom step, her face red and puffy. She gestured for me—not Jayne—to attend her. We went to her bedchamber and I brought her a cool, damp cloth to restore her complexion, comfortable slippers for her feet, and brushed her hair the way I'd seen Jayne do it. Her hands trembled, so I retrieved her wine from the dining table and urged her to sip. After about twenty minutes she'd resumed her normal countenance. "We'll go down to supper," she said.

She and Sir Arthur ate in silence. I looked for Jayne but she'd already left the keep. After supper Sir Arthur walked out to the steps and nodded to Jenkin, who rang a bell for attention—the call for the residents of Rathbarry to assemble in the court.

"Everyone," Sir Arthur began. "Most if not all of you are aware of the crisis that befell us this morning. Having previously lost all our cattle to the Irish rogues, we have now lost the remainder of our sheep, as well as the few colts born to our stable. This poses a crisis because we have no more meat. Our rations must be further reduced, and we must find other nourishment for ourselves and the horses until we are relieved by the Bandonians."

"Surrender with quarter!" a man in the crowd shouted. "Surrender, and let us all out of here!"

"No!" Sir Arthur said. "Surrender is not an option. I will not give up the castle that rightfully belongs to me. If you wish to leave, you are welcome to do so, but it's the fool who still believes he'll find safety and succor outside these walls. We have already seen what happens to those who leave. We can't expect enemies who offer quarter to be sincere in their promise. We will fight and resist until Lord Kinalmeaky comes."

"We will starve!" A woman cried.

"Not true," Sir Arthur said. "We'll work together to make the most of what we have. Our stores of beans, hazelnuts and walnuts, dried figs, dried fish, beer. Some grain and bits to make pottage. Our garden will produce more. We will survive if we work together." An angry grumble rolled through the crowd, many of the women weeping.

"We shall manage. You'll see," he said. "Now then, one thing more. From today forward, no Irish are permitted within the castle keep at any time. That is all. You are all dismissed to return to your lodgings. Good night."

His gaze downturned, Sir Arthur walked back inside the keep. Jenkin followed him in and closed the door.

The people in the court seemed spellbound, and I along with them. I looked to the stables for Ty, but he was not there. I found Jayne among the crowd, her face bright red, evident even in the fading light of dusk. Her body quaked. I pushed her to a bench where we could sit.

"Breathe, Jayne. He didn't mean it. He can't mean it. By morning it will change. You see that, don't you?"

She glared at me. "Ye've no idea, the treatment of Irish folk, as if we be not human. Here is more of it, and even from those I've trusted, have given my best for. Where are we supposed to go, then, those of us who live in the keep? Shall we live in the herd pen? Or in the stable where the colts were kept? Out in the dirt paddock where Tynan works them? And what's next? All Irish shall ha' no food? All Irish shall ha' no water?"

"If he wished to starve you, he'd just put you out of the castle. You can see, can't you, that this is not Sir Arthur, it's the mistress? She is frightened and lashing out. Sir Arthur made a compromise to keep peace with her. It won't last," I said.

"Bring me my things. I shall never enter that keep again, do ye hear? Never. If she's on her deathbed a-callin', she'll see no mercy from me. Cruel, selfish dragon that she is."

"But where will you go?"

"I know already. I'll move into Mistress Rosgill's house. Everyone's afraid her ghost is there and won't go near it, but I'll be darned if I'll let the mistress or the ghost get the better o' me. Get my things, and that's where ye'll find me."

I helped her clean the little house and sweep out the debris. Then I brought her few belongings: a seashell David had given her, a pair of stockings, an old hairbrush Mistress Dorothy had discarded, an embroidered nightgown Lady Carey had made for her, and the little mat I'd made for the floor. There was no furniture in the house, so I brought her bedding from the castle to make a pallet. We sat down beside it and I glanced at the window where I'd climbed in to check on Mistress Rosgill. And then we both cried. We couldn't be together as we had been, and we both felt the rift of separation. She brushed a tear from my chin.

"Ye need no' worry for me. There is no ghost here, Merel. I'd feel it if there was. I'll be safe enough, and no more worries about what mood the old witch will have from minute to minute. We'll still see each other."

"David can come and see you here, and I will be the lonely one, up in that dark garret without you. She will run me ragged."

"'fraid so, love."

That night as I went up to bed, an orange glow drew me to the stateroom window. A fire burned in the garden ward and the dark figures of people moved around it. A bonfire—a fire of joy. I ran back down the stairs and out to the ward to join them. There were dozens of people there, and not all of them Irish, who had torn down the herdsmen's pen and set the wood to burn. And around the fire they were singing. Singing. And on the opposite side of the fire from where I stood, Ty was drumming his fingers on an upturned feed bucket.

Jayne found me and gave me a vigorous hug. "I'm so glad you've come. If there is anythin' good from Mistress Dorothy's doing, it's that I've learned who the Irish are in Rathbarry, and who my friends are besides. And ye'll never guess! Your fella Tynan and I are cousins! His grandmother was an O'Keeffe from Duhallow, hardly a stone's throw from his home in Kilsarkan."

She took my hand and squeezed it. "I'm sorry to leave ye with the mistress as she is. She doesn't realize what she's done. She's made more enemies than ever she would've, and she's united them." She shook her head in despair. "We all suffer for what we cling to, by God's design, and she'll suffer for believing she's still the high lady of the castle. Her hunger's no different than ours. Don't give her the satisfaction o' makin' ye cry, aye? Remember, just pinch yerself to stop the tears."

Some of the men tossed a bit more wood to the fire, making sparks leap high into the darkness where they lingered just an instant like bright orange stars, and then vanished. "Jayne," someone hollered from among them. "Are ye willin'?" He started to clap his hands to a slow rhythm, and Ty soon matched it on his bucket.

"'Scuse me for a bit, Merel." She walked around the edge of the fire pit, each step falling with their beat. She set her hands on her hips and looked from left and right, as if acknowledging each person until she stopped and turned toward the fire. She drew her skirts wide as I'd seen her do before. I noticed then how thin she'd become. She gave a nod to Ty and began to sing, "I'm a girl from beside the River Suir," and then her speech turned to the Irish language and I could no longer understand her. I didn't care, but found a seat on the ground beside Ty and clapped my hands along with the others. Dear Jayne, only Jayne, who could always turn sorrow into merriment.

The next morning, there was screaming in the courtyard. I ran outside to see what was wrong. Two women were among the garden plots, fighting and pulling each other's hair, their coifs lying in the dirt. At their feet, the young, sprouting plants had been uprooted and torn apart. Just back from his walk, Sir Arthur was there to separate them. He demanded their explanations.

"This filthy cow has taken our food for herself," Mistress Hayes said.

"It was you, ye stinkin' pig! All our work for naught! Ye're a thief, ye've eaten it all yer ownself," said Mistress Grenham.

"I've not, ye lyin'..."

"Stop it now," Sir Arthur shouted. He gestured to the guards who came and pulled the two women apart, but then the courtyard began to fill with people from the surrounding lodgings, and a silence fell over the entire gathering as the truth of the matter came clear. Every plant in every section had been taken or uprooted, the dirt scattered in all directions.

The radishes, carrots and beets that were just beginning to sprout, gone, all of them gone.

Something dropped out of me then, as if a pike holding me up had just been removed. I fell to my knees. The terrible truth was that my world as I'd known it was gone. Our fortress, our safe haven, had become our prison. Enemies threatened us from the outside, and now within we were turning against each other.

I'd lost my Lady Carey, was separated from my only friend Jayne, and though I'd found love with Ty, I'd rarely see him for I was alone under the tyranny of a cruel and unstable mistress. All of my life I'd depended on others, and owed them my time and service. If I chanced one day to break free, to truly be independent, how would I live? I could rely instead on my art for a living. Or could I? My recent memory had put even that in question. Did my blood carry a gift of artistic talent yet to be expressed, or had Papa passed to me instead the gift of guile that was already too apparent? And in this new world, which gift would best for survival?

I climbed to my feet and brushed the sand from my skirt. One thing was certain. I wouldn't find myself quarreling over a sprout. If there would be any future at all for me, I'd have a say in it, and I'd not wait around for someone to come to my rescue.

JUNE

34

Kilbrittain

Arundel to Lisheenaleen Castle

Cormac's messenger arrived at noontide. He looked at Teige with the pleading eyes of a mongrel pup desperate for an open door. Cormac must have warned him not to stop for any reason, for he'd ridden five miles from Kilvarrig Wood to Arundel Castle without stopping to relieve himself. "Go on, then," Teige said, unfolding the sealed letter from the MacCarthy Reagh.

From the parapet, his view crossed the broad hillside sloping toward Inchydoney Island, and then across the wide, blue-water bay. His soldiers camped on the soft ground around the mill. They'd earned a few days' respite in the mild summer weather. For himself, the salt air relaxed him, and the peaceful setting could be quite diverting—if only he were not expecting unsettling news.

Word had arrived about the dismal failure in mid-April against the Earl of Ormonde. The battle at Kilrush had been an embarrassment. Combining the troops of O'More, Mountgarret, and O'Byrne of Wicklow, the Irish militia of 8,000 men was three times larger than Ormonde's royalist troops. How had the militia become so disorganized that the royalist cavalry broke their left wing on the first charge? Then the right wing retreated and broke soon after—the men running into the bog for safety. Ormonde was probably still gloating.

Arundel had taken that news with indifference, the battle being distant in both time and miles from his stately home. He gazed out to sea, his hand smoothing the surface of the tower's stone wall as a man might pet his dog. He'd fought his battle, hadn't he, confirming by way of a contentious inquisition his rightful ownership of castle and lands after his father's death, thereby maintaining the proud Arundel name. Yet he'd no interest in giving it up to the English again so soon, and stood firmly in the Catholic confederate cause. "What news comes from the MacCarthy Reagh?" he asked.

Cormac's scrawl was tight and jagged, the lettering style obviously his, but betraying agitation. His curt message explained well enough. "Coolemaine has fallen, twenty-ninth of May. We're to converge at Kilbrittain," Teige said.

Arundel's serene visage shattered, as well it might. Coolemaine was a small, rather unattractive castle but it was critical for guarding against attack by sea, and for transferring supplies from merchant ships to Kilbrittain less than three miles north. The two castles together were the beating heart of Munster's eastern flank. Without them, the barrier against the English evaporated, and supplies would have to come from West Cork—a logistical nightmare.

"We leave at dawn, then," Arundel said.

"No, we must leave at once." Teige said. "We march through Timoleague and gather at Lisheenaleen Castle, where we prepare for battle. The English have four companies in the area. Kilbrittain is their only probable target. If we start now, the men can pitch camp before nightfall, and the wagons can follow. Cormac needs us without delay."

Arundel nodded, though his reluctance was clear in the sagging of his jowls. Teige shouted down the hill to his nearest officers. "Strike camp! We shall face the English at Kilbrittain!" Shouts and cheers rose from the camp. Respite was fine, but could grow stale among fighting men who by far preferred battle to boredom.

The march was at first disorderly, men arguing over who should lead the companies. Should it not be Arundel's men? The troops departed from Arundel Castle and displayed Arundel colors. Or, should it be Teige-an-Duna's men? The answer was obvious, and he needed only to present himself for the men to recover their senses. He was second in command to Cormac, and a lord of a MacCarthy barony.

He rode in the lead, confident there would be no enemy confrontation on the way to Timoleage, for he and his men had cleared every hollow, every ditch, every cave and every meadow of anyone or anything that didn't belong to the Irish. Once they reached their destination, they'd be on high alert. After the fall of the castles along the River Bandon, rogue English infested the surrounding areas—including army deserters, greedy and callous camp followers, and desperate thieves who swore no religion or loyalty.

By dusk, Lisheenaleen's battlements rose above the grassy cliffs, proud like the short man who betters the tall one. A thin plume of white smoke twisted toward the sky and his heart quickened. Cormac had arrived, then, and they'd dine together to forge the battle plan. But a grim scene awaited them near the castle gate. In the oak grove beside the curtain wall, two bodies hung stiff from the ropes about their necks. Be they traitors, or thieves? Or English who crossed the wrong path? He reached out his right arm, sending his men to the opposite side of the castle to pitch camp.

Cormac waited on the flagstones before the castle door—unusual for the man who, like a king in his throne room, preferred to be waited upon. Yet here he stood in muddied boots, hands on hips, dark hair long and stringy about his shoulders, his countenance even darker. He grabbed Teige's shoulder as he approached.

"Ye've come swiftly and I'm glad fer it. Inside, we've a meal on the table. Your men can have what remains from our cook fires, and there is meat to be had from the supply wagon. Arundel, welcome." He shook the man's hand. "We need you, sir. Come and wet your throat."

"Who are the hanged outside of the wall, Cormac?" Teige asked.

"No one of consequence. An English witch and her greedy, lying Protestant husband. They cast spells among the men that caused them sickness, and my captain executed them by his own decision, before I arrived."

"He ought take them down lest the English come this way. It would only provoke."

"Let them be provoked, then. How many Irish have the English so executed? Besides, the men would not have them buried in Irish ground."

"So be it." Teige said. He didn't know the dead, and therefore had no great concern for them, but the back of his neck stiffened—it was a dangerous omen.

Inside the castle's keep, candlelight danced in a fury upon the long trestle table, and the alcoves reflected light down upon the bare heads of

Cormac's officers busy ravaging wooden trenchers piled high with meat and bread.

"Let them eat. Everyone, eat," Cormac said. "Tomorrow we tear the English bastards to pieces. We will never surrender Kilbrittain, for we'll never let them near it, aye?"

"Aye!" Every man at the table shouted and some stood, sloshing ale from their raised cups.

Cormac spread his hands on the table, looking well satisfied, then leaned back and gazed around the gathering as his boldness slowly reduced to a low simmer. He leaned toward Teige, and crooked a finger toward Arundel that he might listen in. "I've had news," he said, and swiped his fist across the bottom of his lip. "I sent a scout to have an eye for what's happened at Coolmaine. 'Tis a discouragement, so we'll no spread the story, aye? The English made sure, after murdering our men at Carriganass, to have the story told far and wide, ye see, so the soldiers would abandon their posts in fear, as they did at Kilgobban, and again at Dundanier.

"These are sad and treacherous tales I wished to put behind me. But stories have a life of their own, do they not, and carried all the way to Coolmaine. When the men there heard the tales, and learned the English at Bandon sent their man Captain Hooper to take the castle, so did they abandon Coolmaine. All but one, who secreted himself in a cave and came to tell me what had happened. Where has my garrison has gone? Probably home to their own hearths, and wise be they, for should one of those soldiers show his face here, he'll be hangin' from a tree beside the English."

Teige glanced at Arundel, who met his gaze briefly and then dropped his focus to the tabletop.

"Now," Cormac continued, "my scout counted eighteen men left by Captain Hooper to mind that castle. He'll be wanting to meet up with Lord Kinalmeaky's three other companies. I've scouts out lookin' for their whereabouts. By morning we'll have 4,000 troops to our side, while the English will number near 800. We'll have the high ground, and my men at Kilbrittain are steadfast. We'll slaughter them. They'll pay dearly for what they've done to my properties and my men."

"Aye, sir. 'Tis my honor to join you," Arundel said, his half smile betraying his doubt.

Cormac stood abruptly, jumped upon his chair and raised his tankard high. "Tomorrow's victory!" he shouted. "The Irish, for God and King!" And all the men at the table stood and joined him in cheers and joyful shouts, and pounded greasy fists upon the table.

The preparations for battle commenced. The bellows of officers, the clatter of arms and dismantling of tents overpowered the sounds of wind and ocean. The men would not sleep this night, for every wagon of supplies and artillery would be secured and ready for travel well before dawn.

Teige talked with Cormac and Arundel late into the night, considering tactical options and trying to predict the enemy's next move. "We travel in darkness to make sure we are first to the castle," Teige said. "The battle must be outside Kilbrittain's walls. We have the greater numbers to crush them on the field, but if we're within and besieged, their artillery could ruin the castle. And I don't suppose an offer of quarter would be forth-coming, nor worth the breath used to speak it."

"Aye, your words bear truth, an Duna, but the men need rest," Cormac said. "'Twas a long march today and much work besides. They've had a good meal and need time to get their minds right before facing battle. Besides, I've more men comin' from Ross. I agree, we must carry the field. We'll march two hours before dawn, that we have the castle at our backs before the English come. Will it be from the south? Or the north?"

"'Twill be both," Teige offered. "A pincer operation. 'Tis what I'd do. Captain Hooper comes north from Coolmaine, and the other troops south from Bandon. But, Hooper has already had time to march and join the other companies. If he'd a mind to do so, they'll come at us full force from the east."

"I'm thinking they remain divided," Cormac said. "The way from Cool-maine is marshy and then steep and rocky. It's no easy march, and if they use the main road my scouts would've seen them by now. Let's get some rest, give the other troops a bit more time to join us, and let the men sum-mon their warrior spirits, aye?"

Teige nodded. "By your command."

"By your command, my lord," Arundel said.

Rest they might have, albeit uneasy, and never any sleep. Teige tossed and turned amid the clang and clatter of pikes, the anxious murmurs of the horses, the trample of boots across the turf outside, and across the wooden planks inside. He lay awake considering all the details that had to be managed before going into battle. If he'd slipped into a restless doze, the pounding on the castle door in the morn's first hour made sure he was first to the hall in his breeks. Two guards opened the door to a messenger.

The hall was alive with shadows, only one torch still burning as Cormac stumbled down the stairs. He planted his legs wide like the piers of a bridge, waved the boy forward and took the message from him. "Light! I need light!" he shouted, and several men who slept on pallets in the hall scrambled to light candles at the banked hearth. Cormac made the boy wait as he spread the message on the trestle table beneath the flickering light. The script was delicate and flowing, the message brief. "It is from my mother." Cormac read out loud.

My Lord Prince and Dearest Son:

May God be with you in this troubled time.

At dusk yesterday, Lord Kinalmeaky's army arrived from Bandon under command of Lieutenant Colonel Brocket. There were three companies of infantry and one of cavalry, who approached Kilbrittain's gates with mounted guns.

On behalf of Lord Kinalmeaky, he proffered quarter to all within the castle, but this your officer in charge did then refuse. Whereupon, the army fired their guns upon the castle's curtain walls, and set their mynors to work to breach them. Their progress was quick, and your army's answer slow.

Today, by Vespers, your commanders cried for quarter and it was granted, the officers to walk away with their clothes, two horses, and three swords. I, your wife, and children, depart by carriage to seek refuge with Muskerry at Blarney Castle. Lieut. Col. Brocket now takes full possession of Kilbrittain, her furnishings, lands and provisions.

Our beloved home is lost. I beg you to join your family soon.

Your loving mother,

E.R.M.

Cormac stared at the page, his palms flat on the table, outstretched fingers curling upward. Teige reached out to brace Cormac's shoulder but Cormac shook him off. "There's nothing you could have done," Teige said. "There's no possibility we could have arrived before them," he said.

"I pray my scouts are dead at the hands of the fecking English, for if they come here I shall twist off their heads on sight."

Cormac's rage radiated with such power as to shove Teige and the messenger a foot away. He stood tall, glaring hate at all who remained in the hall, as if every single one of them had failed him. He stomped out of the castle like a giant of legend, trampling a small, defenseless village. Teige followed from a distance, long enough to see where he headed; Cormac marched far into the moonlight until he collapsed beneath an old, mangled oak. No one dared disturb him there, for the truth of what happened was clear. Cormac's pain would be unbearable, and there were no words of comfort to be found.

35

The Plum Orchard

Rathbarry Castle

I dreamt I wore a fine silk gown while eating warm salted eggs from a porcelain plate. The melted butter coated my lips and I licked it away, savoring the rich flavor. Somewhere near, bacon sizzled in a pan, its powerful scent lifting me from this precious fantasy into wakefulness. But it was only the corner of my bedsheet I tasted, and if any strong scent existed, it was only the mildew in the garret rafters where rain pattered instead of sizzled, giving me a chill. Real hunger tortured my belly, empty and cramping with want.

How long had it been since I'd tasted an egg? Easter. Six weeks past, perhaps not so long but it did seem like an unending interval. Our supply of eggs had dwindled steadily with chickens in want of their feed and a robust rooster. Some had weakened and died. Others just stopped producing eggs, and then they were destined for a pie or a roasting pan. Every soul in the castle craved meat, especially since the rations were reduced in May. A poultry dish would have delighted, but one freshly killed chicken would only provide meat for Sir Arthur's table.

Even Rathbarry seemed to be struggling with emptiness. Where had all the laughter gone that used to fill her hall? And the children who had taken their lessons, or the ladies who'd gossiped and sewed in her solar? Where was the chatter and activity that had coursed through her courtyard daily and filled her to the edges with life? Sometimes I would hear her sigh, high in my garret, slivers of light timidly piercing the gaps along the sides of the slate roof, the rain beckoning with a tap-tap-tap, and dampness seeping in like sorrow. Sometimes, though I may have dreamt it, Rathbarry would sway, rocking me back to sleep.

I forced myself from the bed to dress. Jayne had found some clothes for me from Mistress Rosgill's house. While I didn't cherish wearing the dead woman's clothes, nor could I bear much longer to wear my dreaded pink. And so I donned a crisp white shift, rolled the waist of a gray skirt until it touched my shoes instead of dragging the ground, and tightened the laces of a bodice the color of bluebells. I hurried outside to the well.

The rain had reduced to a sprinkle, but dark clouds formed over the sea in the southwest. We might have a storm by nightfall. I quickly drew the water for Mistress Dorothy's new morning ritual of soaking her swelling feet and ankles. She'd never wash her face with it, for she took enormous pride in her flawless ivory cheeks and believed water made the skin more sensitive to the sun. She soaked for exactly the time it took me to collect her breakfast. If I moved fast enough, I'd save myself a scolding and still could grab a bite of something that Elinor set out for me—usually nothing more than a hard biscuit or a piece of fruit, but I was grateful for it. Sometimes it was all I'd have until supper.

Though it was early yet, the court filled with guards, maids, soldiers and mothers walking their children to distract them from the hunger that marked every face. A panic lurked in the mothers' eyes who feared for the young ones who raised their arms to be held by women too weak to lift them. The children themselves looked old, their faces drawn, as if the lack of nourishment had robbed them of youth. Even Jayne was discouraged, her bright smile hidden behind thin lips, and her fair complexion cast with gray. Ty was more angry than discouraged. As he himself thinned so that the firm muscle of his thigh no longer tightened his breeks, he had to watch the horses under his care thinning, their ribs protruding, their backs sagging, heads down, and coats dull.

And yet, Ty's anger paled beside the men of the garrison, who demanded more meat to sustain them for the day's labor, and for their status as soldiers. Their eyes showed only hostility, aimed especially at Sir Arthur who they blamed for their suffering. "He's lord of the castle, arrah?" I heard one of them say. "Should beh his responsibility to feed a man what he needs. If the castle be under siege, it bloody well belongs ta Sir Arthur, an' he ought let us fight the thievin' bastards or get meat by some other means. He got no right ta starve us all ta death!"

Our saving grace was the plum orchard, safe within the castle walls and each tree bulging with green buds and dark ripening fruits. The sweet scent of them filled the court and gave me an instant of joy before my mouth began to water. Two kitchen boys had availed themselves of plums too early, and became sick in the process. Afterwards, Sir Arthur placed guards around the trees to ensure the fruits were picked only when ripe, and used only by the cook Elinor, so that everyone would get a fair share. How I wished we could fill a basket with eggs as well, that we might all have a plum pudding.

This morning Mistress Dorothy wept so loudly it reached my ears before I even started the last flight of stairs. With the heavy jug of water in my hands, I stopped outside her door and called to her. The weeping ceased, then something like a shoe or a hairbrush hit the door. I backed away until all was silent, then opened the door. "Mistress, are you well?"

She sat on a stool beside her bed, rocking forward and back with her arms crossed above her belly. "Don't be a fool. Of course I am not. I ache, I cannot sleep, and I hunger for things I cannot have. Hurry with that water. And then bring me something sweet from the kitchen. And milk. I need milk, and you should know that. Why am I always waiting?"

I hurried to the kitchen. "Here," Elinor put a few slices of plum in a bowl and sprinkled black raisins over them. "It's nothing so special, but different enough she might quiet. Don't forget her warmed wine."

"There is no milk? None?"

"I wish there were, dear. It can't be helped," she said. "Take her these small bits of cheese instead."

The mistress ate the dry, hard cheese first, and complained about the lack of milk. She picked over the plums and raisins, but finally ate every bite, and sipped her wine while I brushed her hair. She dressed in silence and then asked after Sir Arthur.

"He is taking his walk, mistress," I said. Each morning he rose at dawn, dressed, and walked the castle wards from end to end, corner to corner, and climbed every tower. It was his exercise, but also his way of minding the grounds, claiming them over and over each day, his boots on the soil, hand on the battlements, his presence filling every space. No one could question his devotion to Rathbarry, but did he question his own resolve to hold it, when the odds were increasingly against him?

Mistress Dorothy moved to her chair by the window in the solar. She called for her embroidery, and then for her prayer book, and then for her writing papers.

"I would write a letter to my mother," she said, her pen poised over the blank paper, "but how will she ever receive it? Those wild Irish will capture a messenger and tear my letters to shreds."

An impulse struck me, and the idea of it blossomed in my mind and lifted my chin. A chance perhaps for a brief taste of freedom. "Mistress, write your letter, and then let me take it to her."

She glanced at me as if I had belched and should ask excuse for my poor manners. "What a queer thing to say." She looked away.

"I am quite serious. I am small and quick. I know how to navigate the land and the wood. I would wear boy's clothing and hardly be noticed, but even if I was, I am so unimportant I'd never be suspected of anything."

"Oh, for pity's sake. Don't be absurd. She lives at Rathcogan, near Youghal. It's at least sixty miles from here, through lands crawling with our enemies who would either cut you to pieces or sell you to some disgusting miscreant. Even if we were to let you out of the castle, which we will not, you couldn't possibly travel that far on foot and alone."

I dropped my chin. She was right, it was perhaps a bit foolish to try and travel so far on my own. Even so, given the chance I would leap at it. The tears welled in my eyes. The mistress didn't notice but wept again for her own reasons and then left all her things as they lay and returned to her bed.

In the afternoon the southern sky grew darker and all around Rathbarry the wind tossed and gusted. The sky took on a pale shade of amber that deepened as the hours passed. The dark clouds I'd seen in the morning had shifted east, and gained size and menace, resembling an arm and fist with swollen knuckles dark as peat, moving steadily toward our strand. The thunder arrived first, booming and crackling, frightening everyone to their lodgings. When supper was served, meager as it was, they came out to collect their portions and hurried back to shelter.

After supper I met Ty in the orchard by the stables. The sea was sending up a terrible roar, and the wind howled impatience about our walls. Powerful gusts swept many a ripening fruit from its branch, every bit to be collected later for preserving or stewing. The wild air freshened, and fruity scents infused the night with enchantment. Ty had trimmed his beard, and his hair had grown long enough to brush his doublet's collar. He looked like a nobleman in one of the portraits in Sir Arthur's stateroom.

I pressed my lips to his jaw and breathed in the masculine scent of him. We held each other close, comforted in the darkness and the warmth of embrace. He kissed my forehead, my lips, my neck. And then we joined hands as if to join our beating hearts. A gust swept through the limbs, cool and fresh to make the skin tingle with liveliness, though it could not make us forget our confinement.

"Rathbarry grows smaller and smaller, the walls tightening around us like a belt," I said. "How I long for the days when I served Lady Carey. I didn't realize how good was my circumstance."

"She had her good bits, didn't she? Almost anythin' would surpass how we're livin' now, but in truth it could always get worse. An' I've no wish to t'ink about what that would be like. Let's just be at peace."

Another gust swept against the stable door and rattled the boards and the latch. Deep rumbles of thunder brought white flashes of lightning. Then the rains came in torrents, pounding upon the roof, pelting the walls and sweeping beneath the doors. We ran for shelter and watched through the stable door as deep puddles formed on the court. I rested my head beneath Ty's chin and told him of the conversation with Mistress Dorothy, and my offer to carry her letter to Rathcogan. He stopped breathing for a few seconds. Then he held my shoulders to look into my eyes. His were veiled in darkness, but his tension startled me. It was clear enough the warmth of a moment ago had turned into something else.

"Merel, what made ye think of such a thing? To go off by yerself? Why, it would take nearly a week's time! No water, no food, and what if ye were caught in a storm like this, or caught by..."

"I would not leave unprepared."

"D'ye realize it's a war going on out there? That folk who leave Rathbarry come back dead? My God, I can't, I couldn't...Merel, d'ye know what they'd do to ye out there?" His voice was urgent, his breath rapid.

"I'd dress like a boy, as I said, and no one would even notice me. I could just slip..." He was shaking his head. My blood began to race. Why was he so angry?

He turned toward the rain. "They're out there with scouts and snipers and night watchers, just as we have here—men just *looking* for somethin' or someone, and with a mind ta kill. They'd guess what ye are soon enough and...Merel, d'ye have any idea what they'd do? I've no need to say it, for you know what I speak of—and they'd do it, and I mean *every last one of 'em*, and it's nae matter whose side they're on." He started pacing, kicking up dirt and dead leaves that had blown across the stable floor. He slammed the side of his fist against the wall, alarming the horses. It seemed to offer some release and then he calmed again.

I waited until he could hear me. "I've evaded discovery before," I said, reminding him against his lack of confidence. "Anyway, she won't send me."

"Aye. I'm glad for it." He exhaled sharply and came to face me. "I can see why ye would want to do it, and I might ha' offered it myself, just for the chance to break free of these walls. But Merel, it's just too dangerous. If ye...if ye were ta do such a thing—sure I'd go out o' my feckin' mind."

I stared into his eyes, which told me he meant what he said, and deeply so. My desire for freedom from the castle was so strong, I refused to accept his warnings, certain I could evade or escape anything because of my size. I wouldn't want to hurt him. He had just told me he loved me without using the words, and in truth I wouldn't want to leave him. But, if the window was flung wide, wouldn't a bird most surely fly? Wouldn't Ty, if the opportunity was given? He would, and so why should he wish to stop me if Mistress Dorothy gave me permission to go? And if she did, would I ignore Ty and go anyway? Which love was strongest? For Ty, or for my freedom? I didn't want to choose. I wanted both.

After a few minutes the rain softened. A short time later a rustle and clatter disturbed us, and then shouting that came from outside the castle. The guards called to alert Sir Arthur. Someone pounded the gate and shouted until Sir Arthur ordered it opened.

The chains jangled and clanked and the gates slowly parted. Ty and I joined Sir Arthur and the others in the courtyard beneath sprinkling rain, as four men stumbled into the court. They were ragged, sandy and wet, and when they approached Sir Arthur they fell to their knees.

36

The Boatmen

Rathbarry Castle

Only one of the four men lifted his face that he might speak to Sir Arthur directly. His eyes showed such distress one could hardly refuse to help him.

"Kind sir," he began. "I am Peter Scurs, of Castlehaven."

I knew of the townland by name, but had never been there. By sea it was only about nine miles to the west. Sir Arthur allowed the man a nod. "Stand, if you are able, Mr. Scurs. I am Sir Arthur Freke, owner of Rathbarry Castle. Stand and state your business."

The man attempted to stand, but his knees gave way and he dropped back to the ground. He managed to rise again on one knee. "Please sir, we were coming by sea from Kinsale, bringing goods home to our folk, but the tempest turned violent and cast our boat upon the rocks near Ross Strand. We climbed to the strand for fear of drowning, but by God's grace there came a flash of lightning that revealed the camp above it, and then we feared being discovered and taken by the rebels. I knew of Rathbarry and have come to ye for shelter, sir. Will ye have us?"

Sir Arthur examined the state of the men. "You were wise to come, Scurs. Your men may be at ease. Jenkin! Bring them water," he shouted over his shoulder toward the keep. "Mr. Scurs, whereabouts is your boat?"

"It lies on the rocks between your Long Strand and Owenahincha. Her hull is pierced, though I think the rudder may be sound. We stashed our goods as best we could between the rocks."

"Some things may be recoverable then. What goods had you?"

"Wheat, mostly, some dried beans, wines and lard, a bit of cloth. In

Castlehaven, the Irish have taken everything and we were extreme in need of supply. I pray our goods remain, sir, if the storm surge has not risen much higher."

"Were you seen?"

"I think not, the weather being exceedingly foul."

"Well then, we do lament your troubles. You are welcome to rest here while we determine what to do. As long as none are injured, my most immediate concern is that our enemies shouldn't benefit from your boat or your goods. If I send men to help you, have you strength to guide them back to your wreckage, to retrieve what remains?

"With pleasure, sir, if I could but rest a short while."

"Of course, you must. Captain Beecher will organize his men to accompany you when you are able."

Beecher assembled a guard of eight armed men to escort Scurs back to the craggy rocks with orders to bring back everything useful.

Sir Arthur returned to the keep to await their return. In the meantime, word spread through Rathbarry, the people welcoming any diversion from hunger and boredom. I stood with Ty near the well, the bench there being too wet to sit. The court began to fill with people, even children who played and ran wild around the court, splashing through puddles and mud. Jayne joined us with David, and thereafter most of the people from the garden ward were there. We had no proper drum or fiddle to entertain us, only the continued howling of the wind pushing up and around the castle towers. An hour passed, and then two. At last, a tower guard spotted the men climbing the bluff toward Rathbarry.

They arrived at the gate to cheers and shouts from the people. Every man who had gone out came back, each carrying rundlets or rolling barrels. Two men delivered a barrel and then ran back down to the strand, returning later dragging the boat's anchor and rudder.

It was nearing midnight, but no one in the court was interested in sleep until they'd seen the contents of the barrels. Two men from the garden ward stomped forward with torches and an iron crow, meaning to break open the lids. Mr. Scurs tried to stop them but they pushed him out of their way. "We'll have a look now, back off," one of the men said.

Sir Arthur stepped in. "Stand back, all of you!" The guards who came to his side. "We'll examine these containers at first light, to be sure of what is here and whether its condition is worthy. Nothing is to be touched by any person here before then. These goods did not wash up on shore unattended, for anyone's taking. They were purchased by the people of Castlehaven. All containers shall be stored tonight and inspected tomorrow."

Ty placed a steadying hand on my arm. Sir Arthur was taking a big risk against an angry and hungry group of tenants and soldiers tired of the rationing, tired of the siege, and tired of confinement. The men bearing torches raised them high as if they were clubs. "By rights, these barrels have come upon this beach, and so they belong to all! We'll have what's in 'em, and we'll have it now!" They pushed forward.

Sir Arthur stepped into their path. Ty, David, and Captain Beecher moved behind him. "Touch them and I'll cast you into the field and let the rebels take you. I am master of this castle and all within it. Abide by my rules or take your chances outside. If you raise more trouble among us, I'll hang you as a traitor myself, and lose not a wink of sleep over it."

The guards glared at the men and leveled their muskets. A few trembling seconds passed, but Sir Arthur's stand held, and the two men slowly lowered their torches. Grumbling, they backed down from what could have been a disastrous event. The people, angry and disappointed, began to leave the court and return to their dwellings.

Ty returned to my side and squeezed my hand. "Do you see what goes on even within these walls? Hunger makes men into animals, without fear and without conscience. What you knew of the outside before has transformed into something none of us would recognize."

It was so, for an icy fear seared across my scalp, and my fingers trembled with cold. I was grateful for the solid ground beneath me and for Ty. Had I only appreciated Sir Arthur before, I now loved him for his courage.

In the morning, Mistress Dorothy stood by her husband's side, and I at hers, as Sir Arthur explained Rathbarry's situation to our four frightened and confused new residents who sat before him in the stateroom. They'd been given a tent by the garrison for the night. Each of them appeared calm compared to the night before, but Mr. Scurs still had the look

of desperation in his eyes.

"You must understand," Sir Arthur began, "we are besieged by the Irish under Teige O'Downe, since February. They've taken our crops, our sheep, our cattle, have sealed off all of our supply lines, and have killed some of our people," he said, though he made no mention of how many men the English had killed.

"O'Downe has taken every castle and fort along the coast between here and Clonakilty. He rules that town, and Timoleague, and Ross as well," he said. "To leave here on foot or horse is impossible. You'll have no protection and they will kill you."

"But we must get back to Castlehaven," Mr. Scurs said. "They need these supplies, and they will wonder what became of us. They'll presume we've drowned at sea. We all have families. Children. Can we not send word?"

"It's too dangerous by land, I'm afraid. Any messenger would be captured or killed."

"By sea, then."

"I have no ocean-going vessel to carry you. We sent word to Bandon of our distress. They will relieve us as soon as they can. But the Irish are in extraordinary number and strength, commanding every road and passage. Our only option is to wait for the Bandonians to break through," Sir Arthur said.

Fear and discouragement rose on the faces of the men, and Mistress Dorothy trembled so that I feared she might topple. To wait truly was no option. One could die trying to escape the siege, and die just as easily waiting for it to end.

Sir Arthur continued. "You understand we are all on half rations. The siege began when our supplies were at their lowest levels. If we are to sustain you here for an unknown period of time, we will have to make use of at least some of your goods."

The faces of the men darkened further. After the distance they'd traveled, and the dangers they'd confronted, what could be worse for them than to return home with nothing to help their township? But Sir Arthur was right, Rathbarry needed those supplies as well, and they were within the castle. "My advice is to decide what's most dear to you, and I'll set aside what I can. But there are angry people waiting outside. We must produce something or we'll face a violent revolt."

Inspection of the goods revealed grain, beer, lard, beans, and bolts of fustian cloth. Sir Arthur kept half of the wine, and set aside the honey and cloth, for there was not enough of either to cover the needs at Rathbarry. Every person in the court had a portion of beer for breakfast, and for supper, fresh bread and beans.

Even so, the men from the garden ward seethed. They carried their shoulders high, and walked with heavy purpose, as if daring anyone to stand in their way. They talked in small groups as they ate, brows furrowed, eyes furtive. Some of the women looked equally angry. Others looked weak and frightened.

I dined that night in the hall with Sir Arthur, Mistress Dorothy, and the others who lived within the castle. The thoughts from the morning returned to me as if a specter whispered in my ear. *To wait is no option.* The faces around the table all tilted down, and no one spoke. They ate as if the meal was truly stolen, and to enjoy it on this night could only leave them more bereaved the next. *Die trying to escape, die waiting for an end.* "To wait in hunger is a terrible torture," I muttered to myself. "To survive, one must do something. One must fight back."

All the faces around the table jerked up, and all eyes, including Sir Arthur's, focused on me. Had I spoken aloud? If so, then surely it was softly, meant for myself alone. I'd grown accustomed to talking aloud to myself in the garret. Had this behavior turned around to taunt me? "I'm terribly sorry. Please forgive me," I said. But Sir Arthur's face flushed such a crimson that must have burned nearly as hot as my own in shame and embarrassment. After a few moments he rose from his chair. "Quite right," he said, and left the hall.

Mr. Scurs and his men went down to the beach twice, hoping to salvage something more of their boat, or find a way to repair her, but each time they returned with discouraged faces. On the second trip, one of the men noticed Sir Arthur's fishing boat pulled up by the side of the lough. It had been used for gathering trout, but few fish remained in that water, and no one would spend the time required to catch them when they risked being captured or killed by the rebels. One morning, Scurs ask Sir Arthur's permission to borrow this boat, that they might try and venture home to Castlehaven.

"You may borrow it, but on conditions that you return it in good repair, along with some salt, some men, and some news of what is happening across Munster, for we've had no news since February."

A fortnight later, the men set off for home in the small boat, carrying as much of the remaining goods as it would hold.

A week later, another boat came into the bay, and two men knocked on the gate at Rathbarry. Sir Arthur received them on the steps to the keep. "We've come," one of them said, "wishing to collect the minister, Mr. Taverner. If he will have it, we beg of him to take up the benefice at Baltimore, for our own minister has passed away."

"We shouldn't wish to lose him," Sir Arthur said, "But if your need is great...of course it is Mr. Taverner's choice. Jenkin! Fetch Mr. Taverner."

Everyone in the court waited to see what the minister would do. In the meantime, Sir Arthur asked, had the gentlemen any news of the boat to Castlehaven. "Oh yes," one of them replied. "Mr. Scurs and his men arrived home safely to everyone's joy and relief."

Yet they had not returned the little boat, nor fulfilled any of the promises they had made before they left Rathbarry. Sir Arthur fumed. "If you will take our minister from us, or any other men, I cannot stop them from going. But I would ask that you deliver a letter to Mr. Salmon in Castlehaven. And you tell him, if he will take our men from us, then at least replace them with others, or otherwise fetch *all* of us away from here, rather than weaken us and leave us as easy prey for the enemy."

The two fellows looked embarrassed, but when Mr. Taverner arrived, he already carried his belongings and eagerly accepted the position, as it would take him far from the siege. When they were to leave in the boat for Baltimore carrying Sir Arthur's letter, other men ran down from the castle to go away with them.

More than a week passed with no response. And, as summer temperatures climbed, so grew the ill tempers of the people. That Sunday, with no minister to lead the services, Sir Arthur himself took to the pulpit, facing a hostile congregation. He began in silence, looking directly at each person until he had everyone's attention.

"Together we've persevered through a most difficult spring and the beginning of summer, and at times we've suffered terrible grief. Worse circumstances could not be imagined, and yet we've no relief, and no indication of anything soon coming." He paused to a nodding and somewhat tearful audience. Mistress Dorothy squeezed my hand until it hurt.

"We must join together if we are to survive—and we must—then we will need industry. Hard work and ideas divinely inspired. We must fight back!" He paused again. Had he actually used my words? My skin tingled with the surprise of it. I glanced around the chapel, and it seemed people listened intently, sitting taller in their seats.

"Firstly, I ask you, when you kneel for your prayers this evening, to ask the Father for his blessings to lead us out of this difficulty. Our combined prayers will send the loudest plea to the Almighty." He dipped his head, took a deep breath, and continued.

"We are given this guidance in Psalms: '*Let the favor of the Lord our God be upon us, and establish the work of our hands upon us; yes, establish the work of our hands!*'

"Quite regularly the ships in the bay passing us by. They know not our need, nor our dire circumstance. Would the men aboard those ships not, as good Christians, extend a hand of mercy if they knew?" Again, he paused to look at every face.

"My friends," he said with a powerful resonance, "the work of our hands shall build a boat."

Cheers rose up from the people in the pews, and children screamed and cried, but nearly everyone was standing, ready at once to begin on something. Anything.

"We shall use every bit of suitable material from within the castle, from all around it. Gentlemen, ladies, bring forth your skills. We build a boat for our salvation, and though it may not carry us all away, it will carry our message for the help we so desperately need. Good sirs, at sunrise tomorrow we meet at the center of the court closest to the stables, where we will find our tools.

"Our time of waiting and anticipating is done. Tomorrow we work."

JULY

37

Down to the Sea

Rathbarry, The Long Strand

Tynan rose before dawn and assembled from Sir Arthur's tools those he thought useful for boat building. A compass, a rule, a handsaw; hammer, clamp, mallet, chisel; a fore plane, a smoothing plane, a jointer, and a wimble for piercing.

From what he recalled of the fishing curraghs at Baltimore when he was a boy—and the one he'd fished in with his uncles—the best wood was oak or pine, as green as you could get, and hazel for the ribs. A curragh needed a good set of ribs made from wooden strips steamed and bent to give it sturdy shape, strong wicker to fill in the sides and floor, and fresh, untanned hides to cover the outsides and shrink tight as they dried. To his mind it was all a tricky business.

He put out the few scraps of wood that had been tossed behind the stable after the garden ward houses were built, and expected others would bring more from various parts of the castle. Sir Arthur arrived in the court and soon men started to trickle forth, one by one and then in groups of three or four. When all had assembled, Tynan counted sixty able men. Most identified themselves as farmers, shop keepers, and various kinds of craftsmen. Only two among them, Mr. Swanton and Mr. Kingston, claimed boat-building experience, and eight more had been house builders or cabinet makers.

Sir Arthur said, "These men before us having the most proper knowledge and skills, they will form the lead group, with Messrs. Swanton and Kingston in charge. The rest of you will divide into work groups to collect materials, assist in the labor and otherwise help the process until the boat is set afloat. We must make our work swift."

A few men walked away, but the others moved forward for instruction, and then set out to scour the castle for anything from bits of construction wood, garden wicker, and nails, to ropes, mattress slats, leather straps, and barrel staves.

Tynan stood by, minding the work area and materials as they were brought. Meanwhile, with a bit of chalk, Swanton drew a shape on the court stones representing the boat he intended to build: about ten feet long and three feet wide, with prow and stern but no keel.

"There, that should do it. Shouldn't require much wood or parts to get it together. We need only to get from shore to ship and back again. The sooner the better," he said.

"And how many lads are to board her?" Tynan asked.

"Four, I'd say. A navigator at the bow, steersman at the stern, and two strong rowers between," Mr. Swanton said.

"Might she need a bit more length? She'll be unstable wi' the weight. She'll sink from the head." It was meant as helpful advice, but Swanton looked Tynan up and down as if he was so much rubbish.

"S'pose knowin' a thing or two about horses meks you an expert on ever'thing? I know what I'm doing so you can keep your thoughts to yerself," he said.

"Aye, as ye wish," Tynan said, and stepped away. The chalk outline on the ground was brilliant, though. People walking past smiled when they saw it, and never tread upon it. They gave it the reverence of something that could very well save their lives.

Soon a mighty procession was underway, of men delivering piles of materials, Swanton and Kingston selecting the best, and arranging the pieces alongside Swanton's drawing on the stones. They set out wood for the upper and lower gunwales, then positioned the prow and stern pieces. Because the supply of barrel staves was greatest, they used them for the boat's bottom and sides. The process required to position and secure the barrel staves was laborious, and the vessel coming together would be heavy and forever lacking the sleekness to cut easily through the water.

When Swanton and Kingston were ready to test their vessel, they waited until dusk—just before it was too dark to see, so they'd not be discovered by the Irish camp. Ten men quietly carried the vessel down to Sir Arthur's lake. Tynan and several others climbed to the hexagonal tower to watch the test. Four men climbed into the boat as six held it in place, and then pushed it off from the bank. For a few moments it tottered slowly forward, a small white splash of water curling off the bow. The men in the tower resisted shouting a cheer. But a moment later, a man at the prow being heavier than the rowers turned and sent the boat into a violent rock, then the steersman's efforts to steady her were at odds with the oarsmen who struggled to balance their weight. The navigator dropped his oar, and when boat tipped starboard, he fell in after it. Then the bow dipped. In the time required for an otter to flip his tail, the boat took a mighty twist, cast the other men out, and plummeted to the lake's bottom.

For some time after, the men stood silent and still by the lake, perhaps shocked by what they'd seen. Sir Arthur met the wet and discouraged fellows as they returned through the castle gate. "Fine work, men, for a first try." He slapped Swanton and Kingston on the shoulders. "Tomorrow, begin again."

Before dawn the next morning, the men sent their best swimmer into the lake bottom to find the boat where it sank and secure a chain around her. Then they slowly dragged her back to the shore to salvage the pieces. The group decided, to Tynan's quiet satisfaction, that the boat frame was too short for proper stability, and that the barrel staves might not be the most suitable material. Tynan didn't so much as glance at Swanton, who might accuse him of gloating. It mattered little, for Swanton needed someone to blame.

"That boat was sturdy and sure. It was you what sabotaged her. She's stored in your stable until she's touched the water. What done you to her? Ye wrecked her somehow. Ye want us to fail. Ye want us all to die, ye bleedin', feckin' papist. What place have ye here amongst us? Ye're in league with them scoundrels in those tents, and with them filthy MacCarthys. It's treason, and Sir Arthur will hang ye for this. I'll see to it!"

Swanton marched up to the keep and banged on the door, calling for Sir Arthur while the others in the group stared at Tynan in fear and distrust—these same men he had dined with, worked with, talked with as neighbors and friends; the same men who had helped him with the bodies of Rosgill and Tantalus after he had risked his own life to bring them home. After several minutes Sir Arthur and Swanton emerged from the keep, both with expressions as hard as stone. Swanton returned to his work, his back to Sir Arthur who then spoke to the rest of the men.

"I will not any of you turning the one against the other. Look around you, and you will see we are all here together, trying to survive within these walls. The enemy is not within. The enemy waits outside. This task, this boat, was meant to unite us, not divide us. Mr. O'Daly has served me well, he is loyal and dependable, and he's an expert in his field of work. He deserves your respect. He shall not be treated with malice or mistrust, and should I hear more of it, those responsible will lose two days rations. Carry on."

Sir Arthur returned to the keep, but for Tynan this would not be the end of the troubles. The seed had been planted when Mistress Dorothy cast the Irish from the castle, and here it continued to grow.

38

Captain Brown's Ship

Rathbarry, The Long Strand

The second vessel was designed as it should have been from the start and began to resemble a proper Irish ocean-going curragh. Doubled in length and halved in weight, this one would have both keel and rudder—thanks to the one Scurs had left behind. The men had to venture outside of the castle under guard to cut more wood but all returned safely. Next, the wood for the ribs had to soak, and then a line of kettles generated the steam that heated the ribs enough to be bent into shape. While the ribs formed the skeleton of the boat, the wicker formed the meat on the bones. In this, everyone could lend a hand, even the children.

When Swanton declared it good, the boat was put to the test. Nearly everyone in the castle dared a peek over the curtain walls to see the result. This time, the vessel made a smooth pass across the lake, sleek and sure. The boat stood ready to serve as soon as the next ship was sighted.

It was no long wait, for within two nights a ship was seen, barely a mile offshore. The men set the boat in the waves at nightfall, and the rowers hunching forward and rearing back to approach the ship with haste. Upon return Mr. Kingston, gasping for his breath, reported to Sir Arthur. "Captain Browne's men nearly shot us, sir, thinking we were rebels come to take the ship. But when we called out to identify ourselves, we were admitted aboard. The captain is most concerned for our troubles, and offers to carry as many of us as the ship can hold, straight away to Kinsale. Then let our folk send help back to Rathbarry."

Before long, the people of Rathbarry had to silence their cheers lest they alert the Irish camp to the joyful sight, Captain Browne's ship out of

Castlehaven, easing nearer to the strand.

There was no time to waste, but the people had to be gathered and rowed to the ship through the night's darkness. "Jenkin!" Sir Arthur called. "Bring people out of the castle. Millett! Gather the families from the Garden Ward. O'Daly! The courtside apartments. It's to be women with children first, and old folk, as many as you can gather. Then the fathers. The garrison and any who are too sick to travel will stay behind, but we'll keep sending boatloads until Captain Browne says to stop."

"Aye, sir," Tynan said, but instead of running about the courtyard banging on doors, he ran straight into the castle hall. "Merel!" People started hurrying down the stairs into the hall, but she wasn't among them. He checked the buttery but no one was there. He ran down to the kitchen and right into Elinor.

"Elinor, where is Merel?" He was nearly out of breath. Elinor looked sad, and merely tipped her head toward the ceiling. Merel was with Mistress Dorothy. He bounded up two steps at a time. She was in the solar, stoking the fire at Mistress Dorothy's feet.

"Merel, you must..." he stopped himself, took a breath and lowered his voice. "Mistress Dorothy, forgive me. Merel, will ye coom, please?"

Mistress Dorothy turned her face away from him as Merel looked up, her countenance long and pale, her hair limp about her face, her eyes brightened only by the firelight. She shook her head slowly.

"Merel, there is a ship! Mistress Dorothy, will you not coom and be saved?" But then he heard the boots behind him, and turned to Sir Arthur.

"She will not come out, Ty, because my wife will not let her. My lady insists on remaining here with me, no matter how I have begged her to go and put herself and our growing babe in safety. She is as stubborn as a rock, and short of carrying her to the ship myself like a sack of cargo, which I will not do, she is immovable."

Tynan stared in disbelief. "But, why? Isna this what we've all been working for? Mistress Dorothy, do ye no' wish the proper care and nourishment for your bairn? And Merel, ye could be free. Safe, warm, fed. Isna that what you want? 'Tis but a short voyage away."

"I will stay until..." Merel halted. "Until the soldiers come to end the siege."

"That is not you speaking," Tynan said.

"Then it is not me," she said, though the rims of her eyes glistened. "It doesn't change anything. I will stay. Someone must care for mother and child. I and Elinor will remain in the keep."

She wanted to go. He was certain she did, and so why this? But then, what kind of person abandons a starving pregnant woman, hateful as she may be? And the woman would not budge. He looked at Mistress Dorothy with a malice he couldn't contain, but she never looked at his face.

"The ship sails tonight," Sir Arthur said. "They will soon get word to the garrison at Kinsale, and they'll send help. It shouldn't be long. We must take hope in that."

Tynan left the keep in a fury and banged his fist on every door in the court to alert those who would sail away. Most were already lining up by the gate in Millett's organized fashion. He paced and cursed and paced and cursed, watching the women crying in relief, the children crying in fear and confusion, and then the painful parting from husbands and fathers left behind, and others who watched from their doorways, too ill to travel. Garrison soldiers helped people down to the strand and into Sir Arthur's boat, while others watched the exodus, perhaps contemplating as he did their chances against the Irish, should an attack come before relief arrived. With the last group of people sent out, Captain Browne weighed anchor and the small boat did not return.

When there was nothing more he could do, Tynan went to Sarcen's stall, and sank to his knees. Sarcen nudged the top of his head. This splendid horse, once exceedingly strong, nimble and quick, and of such intelligence and spirit, slowly suffered in confinement and hunger. The things he loved, the open spaces and fields of grass, were blocked from view and untouchable. The joy of his legs beneath him expressing their power at full gallop was no longer unattainable. Things were not as they had been, nor as they should be, and he was powerless to change them.

The following morning, Sir Arthur came to the stables, looking for Millett. "He did not come to table for breakfast. Captain Beecher hasn't seen him. I thought he might have taken a horse out," Sir Arthur said.

"I've not seen him, sir. Perhaps he rests. We all had a busy, difficult night," Tynan said.

"He was helping load the boats, was he not? Keeping track in his book of who was boarding for Kinsale? He would have brought me the book, I should think."

"I could look for him, sir."

"No. I shall ask Captain Beecher."

"If I recall, Millett was helping people onboard the last load we sent out," Tynan said, "and the boat didn't return to us before Captain Browne sailed. Do you think Millett might have..."

Sir Arthur's face paled. "He would have wanted...I didn't...perhaps in my last talk with him...perhaps I was too stern in the way I..." He looked away. "Excuse me, O'Daly. I must speak with Captain Beecher."

39

Crows Calling

Rathbarry, The Long Strand

Two days later, Tynan spoke with a guard near the gate. A heavy mist had descended over the entire barony, dampening his face and hands. The stones of the keep dripped as if a night's rain had drenched it. He could smell nothing but the vague salt from a quiet ocean.

The guard complained. "The damp swells every thread of my clothes and chills me to the core, yet my watch from the tower was useless. I cannot see beyond the walls or my own hand before my face." The crows were calling, and then a runner approached along the outer wall. Tynan stood by while every guard on the wall lifted his musket. No one was sure whether the Irish even knew of Captain Browne's arrival or the people rescued, but the soldiers were highly alert, expecting the Irish to attack now that Rathbarry was weakened.

A boy called out in his alto voice. "A message for Sir Arthur! A message for Sir Arthur!" The master was at his breakfast, so the guard unlocked the gate and took the letter. The boy's shoes crunched the gravel as he ran away.

"Give it to me," Tynan said. "I'll take it to Sir Arthur." He carried the small missive, folded and damp, up the steps to the keep and inside to where Sir Arthur sat alone at the head of the table. A fire burned low in the hearth, and two servants moved about him. Had it been since January that the man had known such solitude?

Sir Arthur looked up. Tynan held up the message. Sir Arthur frowned and waved Tynan to the table. "Sit with me."

There was no scent of the hearty sausage and eggs Sir Arthur liked for his breakfast. Tynan pulled out the chair before him and sat down. A servant quickly offered him a plate of hard biscuit with a spoonful of plum jam.

Sir Arthur unfolded the note and spread it flat on the table beside his crumb-scattered plate. "Ah, it's been some time since I've heard from my old friend Thomas McMahony. I can guess what news he has for us."

Tynan waited as he read the letter. Sir Arthur shook his head.

"He says the Irish general, Garet Barry, led a siege against King John's Castle in Limerick. On the 18the of May, 600 people within the castle refused what he calls 'the most honorable quarter'. After much fighting, the people surrendered on June 23. Everyone within was taken by carriage to lodgings in Dublin, and they were allowed to keep their belongings. Sadly, 280 people perished."

"My God," Tynan said.

"I've visited that castle. They have no internal source of water as we do, and wouldn't have had food stores as we do either, because they rely on ships coming through every day. General Barry just held off the ships and cut their supply. The people would have started dying within days. Then he undermined— dug tunnels beneath the castle walls, working inside houses built right up against them. They couldn't do that here. There is no cover against our walls. We could just shoot down upon them."

"Aye. It is so. Still, so many deaths."

"Yes. And it would have been the weakest. The elderly and the very young. The governor must have expected relief from the royalist army that never appeared. Mistress Dorothy need not know of this."

"It remains between us, sir."

"The rest of his letter is as expected. McMahony says the MacCarthys can wait no longer to take Rathbarry. They've given us every courtesy, every opportunity to depart, and far more than the English would have allowed the Irish, so he says. We have one last chance to surrender. If we leave at dawn tomorrow, we will be escorted to Clonakilty, where we will be held as prisoners until the war is won. But should we decline this 'mercy,' they will march upon us with full and mighty force, no quarter given."

Sir Arthur looked up. "It tests my belief that Limerick's refugees were granted a fine carriage ride to Dublin. Even if it's true, they're not offering us the same." He rubbed the back of his neck and then hit the arm of his chair with the heel of his fist. "Jenkin," he said, without raising his voice. In mere seconds Jenkin stood beside him.

"Fetch Captain Beecher to me. I will address the garrison at nine o'clock this morning."

"Yes, sir." Jenkin ran out the great door, slamming it behind him.

Sir Arthur sipped his wine. "I am sorry, Ty," he said. "About your lady. About Merel. I know you feel for her. Everyone at Rathbarry knows. There's no point in trying to conceal it any longer. I'm not sure there ever was such a need. Many things do not matter anymore. You wanted her to safety. I did so want the same for Dorothy." He took a second sip and then gazed into the slow-burning fire. "We're told from a young age that men are masters of their houses. That women serve and obey, and deliver to you the heir to your kingdom. Someone to carry on. Once that person arrives and matures, then you yourself don't matter anymore." He scoffed. "But women are so much more. They are willful. They are secretive. Demanding. Manipulating. And in the end, it is the tenderness that conquers us. We are unguarded in the face of their beauty and affections.

"I wish...wish I had realized...No one ever warned me marriage would be a series of negotiations, at times seasoned with enmity; and other times with ecstasy that borders on madness. It is difficult though seldom dull. My father once said I was not born for this century because of my deference toward my mother, and then my mother said she wished she'd been born to whatever century I was intended, because when women know kindness, it will be a better world for everyone. I am wishing, right now, that women would recognize kindness when it's given. There may well come a point at which we cannot protect them. My only hope is to die first, that I won't have to witness what becomes of them."

He sighed, and looked Tynan in the eye. "I meant what I said, to the men building the boat. I trust you implicitly. I've seen you work, and how you are with children. I've seen your patience, your honest nature, and your passion for discipline without brutality. I've seen your passion for Merel, also. God help you there." He smiled. "You honor commitments, unswayed by anyone else's dogma. That is to be admired."

He stood, pushing his chair back with his legs. He placed a firm hand on Tynan's shoulder. "I'll see you at nine."

Tynan sat still for a moment. Never in his life had anyone said such things to him. With such a man, what does it matter his religion, his lineage, or anything else about him, if he is true and honorable and good? Tynan wanted to straighten his spine, hold his head high; and then the gnawing guilt in his belly returned. Could he stand beside Sir Arthur, and fight to the death his countrymen?

When Sir Arthur arrived in the court, the mist swirled at his feet as if he emerged from a cloud. Word had quickly spread that something was about. The men of the garrison awaited him, but the gathering crowd was much diminished from what it had been before. Tynan counted only twenty men and women who remained as tenants in the garden ward and courtside apartments, and a few kitchen and house servants. Merel sat with Jayne on the bench by the well, their hands clasped. How thin and small they both looked. Merel wore a white cap, her cheeks pink, her eyes wide and dark; but Jayne's head was uncovered, her hair damp, hanging to her waist in wet ringlets the color of oxblood.

A year ago at this time, the court would have been alive with sound: birdsong from the forest, hens cackling and scratching about, children shouting and laughing, carts rattling—the general hum of daily chores and activity. The garden would have burst forth with fruits and vegetables of all sorts, and the meadows around them brilliant with colorful wildflowers and crops swaying in the breeze. But now even the ocean was quiet. The mist pressed a hush upon everything, and extinguished any light but the dull gray screen of fog.

Sir Arthur wore his sword at his hip, his insignia pinned at his breast. He touched it and gave a quick nod. "Good morning to all. Today is a day of great importance. We see clearly, by looking around the court, how exceedingly our numbers have fallen. I am grateful for it, being certain that many of our loved ones are awakening this morning in safety. I thank all of you who worked so diligently to escort them to the ship for a quick and safe departure.

"We might have had a well-deserved rest after this, to reassess our supplies, housing and rations. But today the moment of crisis is upon us. I've received word. The MacCarthys are coming—demanding our surrender and evacuation of Rathbarry by dawn tomorrow. They would transport us hence to Clonakilty, and there imprison us and treat us worse than curs until such time as this rising comes to an end. Upon surrender, they will take our food and our horses, and some of us will surely be executed, as was my good friend Linscombe, sovereign of Clonakilty, who believed he was a friend of the Irish. They hanged him, along with his wife and sister, from the lintel of his own doorway."

He paused, and Tynan could see the reality of the situation dawn across the crowd as faces tightened, eyes widened, brows furrowed, and hands curled into fists.

"Our enemy must know that many of our families have escaped. They will also know the garrison in Kinsale is alerted to our predicament. Relief *will* come. The king's army will not forsake us, but first they must cut through Irish defenses at Clonakilty. I have no doubt they will do so as if it were seafoam. We may have only days to wait. The Irish must act fast to force us out, to eliminate us as their obstacle, to take control of Rathbarry Castle before they are overpowered."

Sir Arthur widened his stance and grasped the hilt of his sword. "We have before us two options. Surrender is one, and it will be as I have described unless they should decide to murder us all where we stand. The other option is to rise up ourselves, make the best use of this worthy fortress—build up defense works as best we can, prepare every weapon at hand, and until help arrives—*fight like bloody hell.* What say you?"

He rang his sword from the hilt and held it high, as shouts erupted up from both men and women on all sides of him. The choice was made. Sir Arthur had his answer: "We will fight!" "Fight!" "We must never surrender!"

"Yes! With such spirit we cannot be defeated. First let us ensure the security of our gates and walls. We must be impregnable at every point. Then check and prepare your weapons, that they are functional, loaded and ready. As soon as the mist clears, we will double the guard along the walls, to convince the enemy we are far greater in numbers than we are. And, we will set up shooting stations at every vantage point. Everyone will have a job to do. Captain Beecher and I will organize our plan and then we will all get to work."

40

Lord Forbes

Rathbarry Castle and Clonakilty

The next morning, July 17, Tynan climbed the octagonal tower before dawn to study the horizon in each direction. The mist hadn't cleared. If anything it had worsened with no wind coming off the bay to break it apart. It remained so thick that if the Irish were coming no one would see them before they were at the castle walls. Men were taking their stations with muskets ready, and a few who could handle bow and arrow took positions on the rooftop above the garret.

Tynan had prepared the most able horses by which Sir Arthur and Captain Beecher could move quickly from point to point within the castle. He'd lodged his own pistol securely in his belt. In the court below him the women fed fires and heated cauldrons. Should there be any attempts to scale the curtain walls, Rathbarry could ill afford to pour boiling oil down upon encroachers, but she had an endless supply of something equally deadly when very hot: sand.

Defenses were fully at ready, awaiting the dawn assault. The sky brightened. The sun breached the horizon in a flash of orange just below the mist. But no action began. No message came to the gate. No guns fired, no soldiers shouted, no sounds erupted from beyond the wall. The fateful hour passed, and then two more hours as well. Sir Arthur ordered everyone except the sentries to stand down.

The fear born of waiting spread like a dark and woolly mold tainting everything it touched. The unused energy turned bravery to bitterness, speculations of doom. By late morning the guards reported sounds of approach. A sentry in the north tower signaled a sighting to Ensign Hungerford, who alerted Sir Arthur and Captain Beecher. Sir Arthur peered through his spyglass but shook his head in frustration, for the mist still prohibited any but the most indistinct view. At the sound of cavalry approaching, Sir Arthur signaled for every soldier to be ready.

Tension rippled through the castle as all took up their weapons and work stations, expecting the bloodshed to begin. Then came a trumpet sound. Was it Irish, or English? Sir Arthur held up his hand, to halt. The sound came again but clearer this time.

"An English trumpet! Open the gate!" Sir Arthur called. He mounted his horse and rode out with Beecher and Hungerford beside him.

The chatter and excitement soared through the court. *Rathbarry would be saved! At last we will have food and warmth! We'll be protected! We will survive!* Tynan watched and waited, his instinct wary.

After several minutes Sir Arthur returned with an English officer riding tall beside him. "Ladies and gentlemen of Rathbarry Castle," Sir Arthur called out. "May God be praised for the relief he has sent us. With abundant joy, may we welcome Lord Alexander Forbes and his troops from Kinsale and Bandon. Your prayers have been heard and we are truly blessed!"

Amid shouts and cheers from the people in court, the two men rode toward the castle steps. In contrast to Sir Arthur's simple brown doublet, Lord Forbes was a shock to the eyes in his cobalt blue doublet and gleaming silver breastplate. A black ostrich plume fluttered on his broad black hat. Tufts of wooly, flax-colored hair poked out from beneath its rim. He dismounted at the steps and turned, then Tynan got his first clear view of the man's face. So prominent as to be alarming was his long, straight nose, protruding like the top of an axe blade, with no indentation between the eyes.

Behind Lord Forbes came his subordinate officers. One in particular with hawkish eyes and a red silk scarf about his neck was introduced as lieutenant-colonel, The Reverend Hugh Peters. Following him was Lord Forbes' supply officer, introduced simply as Mr. Parr. Then about four hundred cavalry and foot soldiers came forth, a number of them placed as guards around the castle, and the rest quickly filling the court to bursting point.

"Mr. O'Daly," Sir Arthur said. "See to the care of my lord's horse, and those of Lieutenant- Colonel Peters and Mr. Parr."

"Aye, sir," he said, and whistled for Collum, who came swiftly to lead two of the horses to the water trough. Lord Forbes and his men took a moment to direct their troops. Captain Beecher dismounted beside Tynan.

"Sir Arthur," Beecher said. "A caution. I've heard of this Lord Forbes. A Scot by birth, his nobility is bestowed by Parliament, and never approved by the king. He trained in Swedish service and takes advice only from his 'reverend' Peters. At best he is a freebooter, profit his only goal. You might mind the larder and your purse, sir."

Sir Arthur nodded, a dark cast rising to his face. "Thank you, Captain. Without alternatives, we must make the best of what we are given."

Tynan led Lord Forbes's horse to the stables as Beecher and Sir Arthur gathered Lord Forbes, Peters, Parr, and a few others. Forbes selected to take a brief refreshment in the hall, and then begin a tour of the garrison camp. At the stable doors where Tynan was directing his helpers, Sir Arthur spoke respectfully.

"Lord Forbes, I hope you'll find Rathbarry a fine fortress worth saving," Sir Arthur said. "If the Irish want it so badly, certainly that must tell you something of its value. As you can see even from the main court, there is ample room for a good, strong garrison, with water and feed grounds aplenty. The keep is in good form for habitation, and we have access to ships for supply. I might also note there are rich properties in our vicinity. Should you see fit to leave a garrison here, I would continue to defend this castle with my life and my fortune."

Lord Forbes clasped his hands behind his back. "Quite respectable. Braw, she is, your castle. And rich properties, say you?"

"It is so, my lord, to the north of us. If you should think a garrison not advisable, then I would ask that you fetch us all, with whatever goods we have left, and take us to Kinsale or Bandon. We cannot much longer survive in our current state, and my wife is with child, in need of proper nourishment. We have wool in store also, that we could not take to market, and so perhaps your Mr. Parr might assist in that regard, to our mutual benefit. We can make all ready to be taken by ship if you so think fit."

"Well, sir, there's much to consider here. I quite commend you on your efforts," Lord Forbes said.

"I'll take you through the garrison, then the garden ward, and we will return to the keep for dinner. Our cook prepares a modest repast."

Men bowed and women curtseyed as the soldiers passed through the court. All were uplifted by the surety that at last Rathbarry would be liberated, the siege would be ended and they could return to good health and prosperity. How quickly dreams and hopes take hold to mask grief and disaster. Lord Forbes nodded to each person as if he were the Pope himself, bestowing a blessing.

When they returned to the court, Tynan watched them enter the keep for a dinner in the hall, while Lord Forbes's garrison men received hard biscuits and beer. The meal would surely reduce whatever food supply Elinor had remaining in her larder, and deplete to nothing their meager supply of beer. Merel came to the castle door and looked to him from across the courtyard. Her eyes conveyed astonishment and fear. He nodded in sympathy. She must also suspect this was not the answer they'd been seeking.

Before the men had finished their meal, an English soldier arrived on a fast horse, to deliver a message to Lord Forbes, who joined Sir Arthur on the castle steps to receive it. Perhaps he expected a report of some kind of victory, for he smiled as he opened the message, and then his smile fell, and his face surged red.

"O mo chreach," he said. Tynan recognized the Scots Gaelic oath, but was probably the only one who had. "I left three companies of men in Clonakilty to mind our cattle and sheep, and they have been attacked by the Irish army, numbering in the thousands! I must go at once to relieve them."

Sir Arthur grabbed his arm. "But Lord Forbes, we expected you to stay, at least the night, to defend us and help..."

"It is not possible, d'ye not see? I cannot abandon my men to these rogues, nor the cattle that are rightfully ours. We are needed in Clonakilty post haste." He called for his horse and began shouting orders to his left and right.

"Lord Forbes, our provisions are exhausted feeding your men. We thought to be rescued, not to suffer in greater extremity. I must beg you," Sir Arthur said.

"Sir, in Kinsale they say you're a man of much courage and resolution. I've no doubt you will survive. Peters! Parr! Form the men for the march.

We must go immediately!" Forbes shouted. Sections of men lined up as the gate was slowly drawn open for them, and they marched a quick pace forward. Sir Arthur stared in disbelief, and then begged and prayed again but Forbes paid no attention. More men passed through the gate as Lord Forbes mounted his horse.

"My Lord," Sir Arthur's voice was stressed and pleading. "The men of my own garrison are leaving with your regiment. Even Ensign Hungerford, on whom I and Captain Beecher have very much depended. Please, I must forbid it. Will you not stop them? If you can do nothing else, I beg you to leave me some men to guard and protect the castle, even if they are sick and weary. You cannot in good conscience leave us so endangered."

"As you wish, Captain Freke," Lord Forbes said, using Sir Arthur's lesser military rank as if to demean him. "We must in haste depart."

"But you will return, my lord?"

Lord Forbes donned his plumed hat and rode out of the castle, leaving behind nineteen milk cows and a bull, more likely for his own haste and convenience than for Sir Arthur's succor. He also left sixteen of the most unhealthy, unfit, and factious men Tynan had ever seen. Without so much as a nod to Sir Arthur, these men trudged back to the garrison and disappeared into the tents. Sir Arthur seemed to be balancing on the edge of a terrible panic, his face flushed, his hands trembling. Relief so close, and then ripped away. The gate closed with a deep, hollow sound, and the mist filled the empty spaces within the silenced court.

Someone tapped upon his shoulder. Tynan turned to find David standing beside him. "Sure you're among the last of the original garrison," Tynan said. "Most of the others have gone."

"And it's good riddance to them, for I'd have it no other way. I've no interest in joining up wi' that swarm of locusts, with no allegiance and no mercy. It's not what I learnt a soldier to be. I'll stay here with my Jayne, and together we'll take our chances."

"Then it's glad I'll be ta stand beside ye," Tynan said.

41

Force of a Thousand

Streets of Clonakilty

Teige stood on the parapet at Arundel Castle, bracing against the wind and trying to remember the contours of his wife's face. *Honoria.* She was far more beautiful than his first wife, whose strong MacSweeny jaw and ice blue eyes evinced her Scottish heritage. Had she lived after their second son was born, she'd have seen those traits confirmed in their sons. He'd forever cherish the woman's memory, though theirs was not a love match.

Honoria captured his heart from the moment he met her. She was of the earth, dark haired, brown eyed, ruddy cheeked—always looking as if she'd just come from a wild run through a forest glade, and smelling of sweet herbs and heather.

Too many months he'd spent away from her. Too many delays, disorder, and failures had compromised the larger plan, giving the English too much time to build strength against them. He'd spread his own forces too thin, trying to cover the seven castles in Carbery while supporting Cormac's operations and then assuaging his wounds. The loss of Kilbrittain was so ruinous his cousin might never recover.

They couldn't retake Kilbrittain until they'd significantly weakened the English, and especially the brutes out of Bandon. We shall retake it, he'd promised Cormac, but it would take time. For now, he needed to focus on Rathbarry, to expel those people once and for all and move forward.

In the fields below, Teige's and Arundel's men worked together on much-needed firearms training and drills before they'd begin the four-day march north to swell General Barry's considerable forces. Some troops practiced ambush tactics just beyond the tree line surrounding the castle. The mists had thinned overnight, but the winds were pushing a dense new layer upon them.

"How go the maneuvers?" Lord Arundel asked as he joined him at the wall.

Teige clapped his friend on the shoulder. "Well. You can see them just there," he pointed, "but it won't be long before the mist blots them out. Did you rest? We've much to do today."

"I'm rested and ready. Our troops mesh easily enough. God help us if they don't make better work of it than they did at Cork. Of late, General Barry has given them courage."

"The general's victory at Limerick lifted their spirits after the Bandon River losses. He is helped by the artillery he captured. That battering piece—I'm told it weighs more than six thousand pounds and requires twenty-five yoke of oxen to pull it. He made a great show of the confiscated cannon as well. The monster is eight feet long and fires a thirty-two-pound ball. No wonder every Protestant settlement in Limerick surrendered upon sight of it."

"I admit, I had my doubts about Barry," Arundel said, "but Limerick gives us control over the port and the River Shannon. We won't have to worry about supply lines now. I'm glad for the advantage because we cannot afford more losses. We must succeed."

His sound was both urgent and anxious. Teige gave him a sidelong glance.

"That scoundrel Lord Cork must be stopped. I've no doubt he's funding the army against us, and with Irish money, too. He's swindled every Catholic he could find out of properties and fortune. It's common knowledge he bought his title by robbing the Irish and then loaning the money to the king at usurious rates. In the same fashion, he bought a knighthood for his thieving pirate cohort, William Hull. I refuse to call that criminal 'sir.' Hull is everything knighthood was meant to destroy. The word chivalry is unknown to him, and if the Bandon militia is savage, he's at the root of it.

"Cork and Hull together weave a spider's web so thick no sword can part it. Hull marries Cork's widowed sister-in-law. Hull's son marries

Cork's daughter, and then his daughter marries Cork's nephew. They all collude in business to own every bit of profitable land, control or pilfer from every business, and raise rents until they drive every honest proprietor—especially if he's Catholic—to his knees. Hull just built a house in Clonakilty—a huge, garish thing, lording over the whole township. The blasted thing cost £800. Where did such money come from? Cork, of course! It disgusts me. We must sweep these criminals into the sea." Arundel's pale face flushed dark red with anger.

"Aye, Cork's tendrils reach too far, and his greed only worsens with every new acquisition. He and his precious Bandon and Lismore are surely targeted, but for now the general's eyes are set on Liscarrol Castle. It ought to be a win, but it won't be easy," Teige said. "With five defensive towers and curtain walls thirty feet high, we'll have quite a go of it. Our general itches for this victory. The castle was built by his kinsmen in the thirteenth century, so why wouldn't he go after it? But the true and tactical reason is that the castle's owner, Lord Perceval, left it in the charge of a young sergeant and garrison of only thirty men. Our man Barry is a predatory cat set to pounce on an unsuspecting mouse."

A disturbance alerted him, and he glanced across the tree line below, searching for the cause. Sounds carried across the water. Something was happening in Clon. A scream. More screams. Then the boom of musket fire. Arundel looked as shocked as he, and together they ran down to the hall to alert all officers. Outside the castle, the sounds continued, the screams sharper, sending a jolt like lightning searing up Teige's spine. He grabbed Arundel's spyglass and ran for the northwest tower.

Smoke spiraled above some kind of commotion. He cursed the mist that hindered his view into the town's main street. On the lanes there came movement, troops marching forth like a violent whirlwind: things calm and tidy before them, and after them battered, broken, burning, destroyed.

"We've had a messenger," Arundel said, joining him at the tower. "English troops killing everyone they pass, mostly women sweeping their doorsteps. Butchers! They're taking all the cattle. We have no troops in Clon, only a few guards who are like to be dead."

"We've no time to respond. We're at tremendous disadvantage," Teige said. "Where was our intelligence, that a force this size could simply walk over us? If we try to attack, they'll burn the entire town. My gut says we wait. Let them take the cattle. We'll get them back when the time is right." Teige took a deep breath and looked across the bay. In a few moments it was clear what to do.

"Today, Rathbarry is to surrender," he said. "I have troops at the hill in Ardofoyle, set to move in. Instead, let them march toward Cloheen Strand. Send the messenger by boat to Muckruss, to run from there to the leader, Barry Oge O'Hea. He'll know what to do. Meantime, the English will come for the sheep. Send your troops by boat to Inchydoney Island, and there to form a barrier to push them back. For the townspeople who are trapped in the church, I'll try to rescue them by marching south from the Gullane road. We'll assemble quietly, surround the troops, close in and then crush them."

The march to Gullane road required just over an hour. Teige halt-ed at the outskirts of town, climbed upon a schoolhouse roof for a view through Arundel's spyglass. The mists still hovered, but the English had indeed gone after the sheep on Inchydoney, where Arundel's thirty horse and sixty foot soldiers attacked. Shouts and musket fire splintered the air, and in minutes English soldiers fell back, flooded into the village. Some hid in the churchyard. Teige set his soldiers upon them, but most ran for cover in an old Danish ring fort west of town. With the enemy behind breastworks nine feet wide, Teige's troops were in for a much longer bat-tle of musket fire and hurled rocks.

Then came a shattering noise from behind them, another cannon from a different direction. His gut seized. How *foolish* he'd been not to guess why the English troops had come, and it wasn't to attack Clon. They'd come to relieve Rathbarry. They took the livestock as booty, and divided their own forces, leaving a detachment to mind it. Now, the forces reunited. Teige's men faced a force of a thousand well-armed and well-trained men.

A powerful cannon fired, dispersing his troops from their formation around the ring fort. He pulled them back toward the village as a bar-rier to keep Arundel's men from being trapped. Then Teige rode south to Cloheen. From there, he saw what he'd feared. English troops had engaged Barry Oge's at Granagoleen, the ridge on the western edge of Cloheen Strand. The cavalry swung around Oge's left flank, forcing his men eastward toward the strand. Then the men from the ring fort poured over the breastworks like rats escaping a flood, and made for Oge's right flank. Oge's only options were to charge through the vale between two ridges—a certain death trap—or plunge through the inlet at the end of the strand. Teige stood helpless as the English pressed Oge's men toward the water. The strand was gray and dark, the low-hanging mist provided good cover, but the English kept firing. Some men fell, others sought cover under water. At mid-tide, most could stand on the sandy bottom and still have head and shoulders above water, but many stayed under to avoid the guns. The best swimmers reached Inchydoney beach in minutes, hardly stopping to breathe. But Teige could only stand and watch while others were slaughtered or drowned.

He sent boats to rescue Barry Oge and his men. They joined Arundel's troops at Youghal's Point below the village and withdrew across the bay to Arundel Castle. The bloody English looted the defenseless village and then marched northeast toward Bandon. Had they abandoned Rathbarry, or left it in ruins?

"They came upon the Ross road in great numbers," Oge said, "and my men withdrew. If these troops would evacuate the castle, our work was done an' no blood lost fer it. But I'm no sure he'd time for more'n a brush of hands wi' Sir Arthur, afor' he was away again."

Between Teige, Arundel and Barry Oge, none knew of this general with the knife-sharp face and the black plumed hat.

"I've heard talk of a Scottish privateer who calls himself Lord Forbes," Arundel said. "A disciple of Gustavus Adolphus of Sweden. I cannot think why he'd come here, unless he was promised rich plunder."

"A sizable force like that, and not a single man or woman came to report it," Teige said. "If what I suspect is true, Forbes ordered his soldiers to murder everyone they saw. Considering the number of pillagers following them, we'll find a trail of stripped and mutilated bodies, not only in the village but strewn along the entire road to Rathbarry."

He faced his two compatriots. "We're not beaten. We're injured and weakened. We lost mebbe sixteen men to the sea at Inchydony, at least as many to musket fire at Cloheen. But our losses in total are only five percent. It could have been far worse. We saved most of our sheep, kept them from burning the town, and we live to fight again. It is no failure, but a formidable response to a surprise action. Come, let us speak to the men."

Outside of the castle, small fires burned at irregular intervals where the soldiers camped. Teige walked among them, not above them. "We have had losses. We've lost friends, neighbors, brothers, cousins, but also you have protected the town and saved many, many lives. Tonight, we acknowledge this and lick our wounds. Tomorrow let us rise with the dawn knowing that each of them died fighting for our cause—our true religion and our king who protects it. For our ancient traditions. For our families and their future. For our livelihoods and our beloved way of life.

"They who have fallen would want—no, they would *demand*—that we carry on, and be as willing as they to fight to our last breath. It is far better to die quickly, fighting with passion, than to die slowly of starvation and humiliation as the English would have it. Death shall never stop our momentum toward victory. We persist with all the more purpose. The English show their savagery. If we must, we can and shall return it in equal measure.

"Care for your comrades, heal your wounds, regain your strength. Those who would, ye may return to your families. But, report to me here in five days. We will take Rathbarry Castle. We will march to Timoleague, where I'm certain they will next send Lord Forbes. We will see that he gains no ground. Then, we join our general in the north, for even greater victories."

Men clapped the shoulders of friends, and cemented oaths with drink. In the morning, Teige sent a messenger north to General Barry, confirming that his troops soon would come to his side.

Below the castle, bodies had washed up on the strand overnight, and he knew there would be more wherever Forbes' soldiers had passed. These were an army's first priority. Men of honor bury their dead.

AUGUST

42

Chaos and Ruin

Rathbarry Castle

By early August, the days were mostly sunny compared to the mists and rains of July, but no one cared about the weather anymore. I and everyone else in Rathbarry sought tasks both laborious and trifling tasks, anything to distract from the hunger and the constant, relentless dread. The Irish hadn't returned after their demand for surrender, and we feared at any time they would set upon us with deadly musket fire, or something even worse.

We had meat again, and milk, because of the cattle left by Lord Forbes, but the garrison claimed most of it. And something about the heat of the summer days, the long afternoons, the endless confinement, turned us all into something akin to wild forest dwellers. Scavenging, quarreling, spiteful and untamed. But even forest dwellers had more freedom than we.

"Merel, it is simple," Jayne advised. "Sing a hymn, a nursery song. Or better yet, something bawdy. You cannot think of discontent while singing something fun. Just try." But I wasn't much for songs. I couldn't remember the words. The best escape for me was to climb the steps to the curtain walls and peer at the distant trees, the shorebirds along the pond's edge, or the seagulls over the strand. I'd make myself one of them and imagine the wind lifting my wings in circles toward the heavens.

One morning Mistress Dorothy was awake and wrapped in her sapphire velvet robe by the time I reached the bedchamber. "Good. I thought you should never arrive," she said. "This morning you must move all of Sir Arthur's night things into his own bedchamber. He'll sleep there until after the baby comes. I tire of his tossing and turning in the night, and when he does sleep I do not wish to disturb him with my own troubles. He shall not know of, nor hear of such goings on as the baby presses against my bowels; and *for Heaven's sake* I do not wish to hear him advise me on what I should be doing and how I should behave. You will sleep here, on the trundle, from now until I decide something different."

I should've been excited by such an elevation of station and trust, to sleep in the mistress's bedchamber and assist her at her most intimate moments. Usually it was considered a high honor indeed. But I'd grown comfortable in my garret, cold as it was. It offered quiet solitude, time to think, to dream, and to do what I wanted instead of what I was told, even if it was nothing. I'd have to give that up and serve her all night as well as all day.

I s'pose I was being selfish instead of charitable. A woman six months into her maternity, no mother or sisters about her, no midwife to assure her, little food, few comforts, and a hostile army at her door—she deserves compassion. And so? I am trapped yet again. I may not even feel sorry for myself without having to feel much greater pity for her.

Still, she owed me something, from our bargain early on. It offered me hope, like the tiny crumb of cheese tucked into a corner of a mouse's den. I could call in that debt at any time, but not for this. Instead, I'd straighten up, take the days one at a time, and wait for a more worthy demand when she would have to concede. Not something trivial like privacy. No one really had privacy. I'd ask for something that would truly set me free, spring the lock on the cage and let me fly away.

On the afternoon of August 6th, I was waiting on her in the solar when a tower guard shouted an alert that someone approached Rathbarry. Several moments later came a pound upon the castle gate, and voices shouting and crying.

"Hurry down and see what is going on, but don't make me wait too long for an answer," the mistress said.

I ran—filled with glee for a reason to go outside—down the stairs, through the open front door and out to the steps. Sir Arthur was there, hands on his hips, shirt sleeves rolled to his elbows.

"Please, Sir Arthur," a man called from outside the wall, "we have come from Dundeady. We beg of you for shelter!"

The English accent was clear, and so perhaps confident this was no treachery, Sir Arthur ordered the gate opened wide that they might enter. In came eighteen poor and ragged English, mostly men but also several women.

"Oh, Sir Arthur, thank the Heavenly Father for thee!" the Englishman said. "For some months we've been prisoners in the hold at Dundeady Castle. A ship, yea, some ship sent by merciful angels, fired upon the castle twice. The Irish had no guns to return fire, and feared a full attack. They abandoned the castle, and with some last drop of charity within them, they set us free. We've walked from the headland across the long strand to find you. We've men among us good with muskets. Our women are gentle, skilled, and useful. Will you take us in, kind sir?"

Sir Arthur obliged them at once. He certainly had lodgings in abundance after the departure of those who sailed with Captain Browne. They carried no goods, and brought our numbers within the castle to eighty. But the unruly soldiers left by Lord Forbes were "utterly unexpert" with firearms, Sir Arthur told them, and he welcomed their help in the defense of Rathbarry.

I climbed the stairs reluctantly, and crouched beside the mistress's chair to tell her the news. She scowled toward the window. "Additional mouths to feed will soon tax us all to starvation, yet Arthur does not refuse them. They'd be much better off at Castlehaven," she said.

"If only they had a boat to take them there," I said.

She frowned and mocked me in a high, squeaky voice: *"If only they had a boat to take them there."*

I couldn't help it. I laughed out loud. She glared at me for a second, but then burst out laughing, too. It was the first laugh we had ever shared. The lid of the cook pot had lifted to release a puff of steam. I hoped that crack would remain.

A few days later, Sir Arthur called the mistress into the stateroom. I helped her to her chair. "I've received letters, delivered by boat from Sir Samuel Crooke of Baltimore. There is one from Lord Forbes," he told her, "and one from Mr. Parr. Shall we see what they have to say?"

"Yes, of course. I thought they had forgotten us," she said. I stood behind her at first, but she pointed to a stool where I should sit.

"Ah, you'll like this," Sir Arthur began. "Lord Forbes says he ordered twenty musketeers to be sent from Kinsale, but the governor suffered not to send them. Perhaps the governor prefers not to be ordered about by such a man as Forbes?"

"Better still, might we send back to Kinsale those frightful men Forbes left with us?"

Sir Arthur grinned and nodded. "If Mister Parr is coming to collect our wool, we'll do exactly that. We'll send those shirkers back with him." He returned to the letter. "Forbes says it was he who fired those two shots at Dundeady. He set some provisions ashore for us, but they were spoiled by the wet weather, and then the sea grew foul so they could not stay. He promises to visit often and try to provision us."

"Oh, Arthur. God help us if such a man is our only hope of survival. What about Mr. Parr? Will he sell our wool for us?"

Sir Arthur set Lord Forbes's letter aside and peeled open Mr. Parr's. He shook his head and scoffed. "Mr. Parr offers to come and collect our wool, but wants us to know we will have to pay for the thirty men they left here with us, and for the services of saving so many poor English."

"Thirty men! It was sixteen, wasn't it? And men so violent and unruly none of our servants will go near them, in fear for their lives. And what English have they saved? Certainly none among us at Rathbarry. As if it is not bad enough to be under siege by an enemy, but we must also have our own people—criminals, they are—terrorizing us. Why won't our own kind endeavor to save us?"

"Exactly so, my dear. I'm sorry, I should not have shared these with you and upset you. I had hoped for good news, and meant only to distract you for a few moments. I'm confident enough friends know of our predicament that true and honest help will come soon. Trust me, my love, all will be well. Perhaps it's best if you go and rest. Merel will fetch me Captain Beecher so we can discuss what to do. Won't you, Merel?"

"Yes, Sir Arthur," I said, but Mistress Dorothy was rising from her chair, and I helped her back to the solar first. She gripped my shoulder to steady her gait.

"He tells me all of this to amuse me, then dismisses me and seeks Captain Beecher for what's to be done. He thinks I'm as frail and thoughtless as a butterfly."

"To his peril," I said, and then bit my tongue. How thoughtless was I? How insolent, three tiny words. Would she see it as a criticism of Sir

Arthur or a judgment of herself? Would she slap me? Throw me out of the keep and have me sleep with those refugees? But she said nothing as I helped her to her chair, covered her knees with a blanket, and placed her book of James Day poetry on her lap. I hurried toward the door.

To my back, she said, "Don't think I didn't hear that. I'd be angry if it weren't true."

I led Captain Beecher up the stairs to the stateroom where Sir Arthur waited.

"Merel," Sir Arthur said, "bring us a whisky before you go, will you? It's at the far back of my map cabinet, on the right."

As I bent to my hands and knees to look for it, Beecher began. "Sir, I have some disturbing news for you, about Forbes's men."

"Well then, it is bad news indeed. Let us have it."

"Forbes brought in some prisoners he'd collected on his way from Clon. With so many men surging into the court, we didn't see them. The soldiers chained them up in one of the far garrison tents."

"They are still there?"

"Yes, sir. They are weak and ill. I don't know if anyone's even been feeding them. Two were released, I'm told. One of them was Philip McShane." Beecher said.

I found Sir Arthur's whisky but nearly dropped it at the name. I quickly righted it and stood to fill the glasses.

"McShane! I had no idea that scoundrel was among us. Had I known I'd have run all of them out."

"Two of Forbes's men released him when he promised them tobacco, and promised John Sellers an answer to his letters from his wife in Kinsale," Beecher said. "Why they believed him I've got to wonder, but Sellers has been so desperate for word since his wife sailed with Captain Brown. And then last night, these same two soldiers raided the kitchen."

"Our kitchen? In the keep? A breach of my own household? Why haven't I been told of this? Merel, please hurry up," Sir Arthur said. I did try, but my hands were shaking, and I needed to hear what was said.

"Sir, we thought not to wake you, for there was nothing to be done. They ran through the kitchens like animals, grabbing everything they saw and shoving poor Elinor into a cupboard. She's a bit bruised, but lucky they didn't kill her. At the same time, one fellow got free of his bindings and leapt over the curtain wall."

"My God! A fall of thirty feet? Is he dead?"

"Sir, he's escaped. Must have landed on soft ground."

"It seems Rathbarry is going to chaos and ruin beneath our very feet. Please, Captain Beecher, with such goings on, I *must* be informed immediately, at *any* hour."

"Yes, sir. My apologies, sir."

"So then, between those two—McShane and the second fellow—the Irish will have been informed of our weaknesses, our reduced numbers, everything we have, and all that we lack," Sir Arthur said. Beecher remained silent, letting his news be fully absorbed. I gave them their drinks, replaced the bottle and slowly left the room, leaving the door open behind me.

"And your news, sir?" Beecher asked while I was still in the hall.

"It is all rather pointless now."

Forgetting Mistress Dorothy for a moment, I ran down the stairs to the kitchen to find Elinor sitting at the work table. The kitchen was deserted except for one boy who crouched by the door and watched her, his own eyes sunken with hunger and fear, and Jayne, who looked up at me with sad eyes and drooping mouth as she gently stroked Elinor's back. Elinor glanced up at me and tried to smile, but then looked back at the table as if it caused her pain even to move her eyes. Her hair hung about her face. Her eyes were blackened from a blow to her head, and her hands were scraped and bruised. She held them against her chest, slowly rocking her body back and forth, back and forth between the table and the back of her creaky wooden chair. I ached for her. Dear Elinor deserved nothing but kindness.

"They knocked me 'cross the head with a bat. I fell, hurt my shoulder. They cared not, and kicked me in the ribs. I tried to fight them but ended up curled into a ball, and then one o' them dragged me by my skirt and shoved me into the cupboard. They took all the biscuit, plum preserves, cheese. The meat was gone already, so they started throwin' pots and breakin' the mistress's cups."

"I brewed her some willow bark," Jayne said, "and swept out most o' the mess they left about. Those brutes are sent from the Devil himself, to pile trouble on top o' trouble. "Sir Arthur ought to hang them by their heels."

"Tell Sir Arthur we must butcher some of the milk cows if we are to eat. I'll be blessed should I find even a sack of dried peas." Elinor said.

A chill spread across my shoulders. We were grateful to have the milk cows except that only a few were still giving milk, and even that was declining. All the milk we collected had to be rationed among the soldiers, the children and the sick. We didn't know how long it would last, which cows had been bred, which had recently given birth, and which were past breeding and could provide us meat again. What we did know was that we couldn't bring enough food into the castle to manage them anymore, and all had to be grazed outside at high risk.

Later that week, I stopped by the stables to bring Ty a bit of water from the well. We'd had no rain and I was forced to go rather deep to draw it. He looked tired and thin, but brightened when he saw me. He drank the water in one good gulp, and then kissed me with cool, wet lips until I giggled and pushed him away. The tower guards shouted alarm and our moment ended; there was more commotion at the castle gate. They opened it without even waiting for Sir Arthur, for it was only one lone horse, saddled but without its rider.

43

Pangs of Sheol

Rathbarry Castle

"O'Daly!" Sir Arthur shouted.

"Sir!" Ty ran toward the gate to examine the horse. I followed just behind him.

"That's my mare. What's this all about?" Sir Arthur demanded.

"Mister Sellers and two other men came to me early this morning, sir. Mister Sellers feared the MacCarthys or O'Donovans were after takin' the stones from his mill at Ross. They meant to ride out, come straight back, sir. Two o' them returned hours ago. This was Sellers' mount."

"Damned fool. He promised me he'd not ride out alone again without my permission. Take her back to her stall and give her a good going over, that she doesn't have an injury. Maybe she stumbled and threw him." He shook his head as if to clear it, yet his cheeks flushed a dark red. He shouted, "From now on, no one is to leave the castle without my permission. No officers or soldiers, no herdsmen, no townsmen, no one. No one! It is for everyone's safety."

"Shall I have a look for Sellers, sir?" Ty asked. A shard of ice shot through my breast at the very words. I could understand why he grew so cross when I wished to leave the castle. I never worried for my own risk of life, but deeply feared for his.

"No. The enemy is out there, and close. Lord Forbes stirred them to a fury, and we're the ones to suffer for it. I'll not make it easy by serving up my men to them one by one. Who were the other riders? I'll speak to them now."

Tynan whistled for Collum to collect the mare. "They were not of the garrison, but from Dundeady. I'll bring 'em to ye."

Sir Arthur fumed and paced in front of the stables until Ty returned with the two men, who introduced themselves as brothers, Joseph and Peter Hendley. "Our deepest regrets if we caused you trouble, Sir Arthur," Joseph said. "We are grateful to be at Rathbarry. We thought it served you to assist Mr. Sellers. He said the Irish at Ross were about dismantling his mill. He was most anxious about it."

"And you found no sign of trouble?"

"No sir. We saw no one along our way, and no sign of tampering with his mill stones. So we turned 'round and came back."

"You're most fortunate. It's not safe to do what you've done. Men who have gone from the castle have been ambushed and murdered. Never leave unless you speak to me, and certainly you shall not take my horses." Sir Arthur was still fuming, but he calmed after learning Sellers had misled the brothers and they meant no harm. "Where did Mister Sellers go, then?"

"Well, sir," Joseph said, "he spoke of going to a place he called Crones. Said he needed to look for a good grassy place for grazin' near to the castle, so I s'pose that's what he done. But he kept complaining 'bout a letter from his wife. Said someone promised to bring him a letter."

"McShane."

"Yes, sir! That's 'im. Sellers went on about it, sent us back, an' he'd follow in a short while."

Sir Arthur's color changed from crimson to ashen. He must have realized, as Ty and I both did, that Mr. Sellers had gone to McShane's house. I doubted McShane had done anything to contact Mrs. Sellers, and Mr. Sellers may well have met the same fate as Messrs. Tantalus and Rosgill. My skin tightened and tingled, and in the pit of my belly there grew something hard and spiny.

Nothing could be done but to focus on the tasks before us. We couldn't fret over a man outside the castle who might already be dead, when there were eighty within the castle just a whisper from starvation. While Mistress Dorothy dozed in her blanketed chair, Jayne and I helped Elinor make supper—a thin soup of powdered meat, bits of cabbage, and a few dried peas.

The next day, the shrill sound of Irish warpipes broke the mid-morning quiet. All the able-bodied within Rathbarry rushed to the towers and curtain walls to see what was about. The troops marched forward like an ocean wave to flood the top of the hill, just as they'd done months before.

Ty stood close beside me as people crowded on the north wall. "There are half as many men as what came to us in February," he said, his lips close to my ear, "but no less intimidatin' when ye consider we're half as many, as well. 'Tis not the Prince of Carbery at the head, either, but John Oge Barry, a man of thirty years, and fierce."

The army stood by while the warpipes played, and then a boy rode forth on a pony, bringing a written message for Sir Arthur. He dropped it outside the gate and rode swiftly to the hill again.

Sir Arthur ordered the gates opened. Most who stood on the walls kept their attention at the far hill and did not see what Ty and I saw by the gates. A terrible message awaited Sir Arthur. The boy had cast the letter, folded and sealed, upon the blood-stained shroud covering a body within. Sir Arthur stood still as a stone. He spoke not a word, but waved one hand for the guards to drag the shroud inside the gates. They struggled to heave it, and with it came the flies that hovered about. I knew before the shroud was opened whose body it held. We all knew.

Sir Arthur opened the message and read it aloud. "The letter is signed by Mr. Barry. It says we are to keep the new soldiers inside the castle. They have killed some, and disturbed others, and have carried away our hay and corn.'"

Sir Arthur scoffed. "New soldiers. They must mean Forbes's men. And they mean my hay and corn." He gestured to Captain Beecher, who knelt by the shroud and cut it open far enough that even I could see the battered and bloody face of John Sellers. It sent a sharp chill up my spine. Captain Beecher looked up. "He must have fought valiantly to defend himself. They have hewed him to pieces."

Sir Arthur's shoulders dropped. His arms fell forward as if to reach for the man, but stopped short. After a moment he took a deep breath and stiffened his back. "Captain. Tell me plainly. Have Lord Forbes's men been leaving Rathbarry at night?"

Beecher's face darkened. He inclined his head. "I believe so, sir. Yes."

Sir Arthur sighed once more. "Then, a good and honest man has paid a dear price for it."

He looked around the court at all who had gathered. What was he looking for? I followed his gaze toward the hunched and weary men and women who stood before him and their few children in filthy rags, like the cave dwellers who had once been hunters and now were prey. They were all reduced to skin and bone, their hands skeletal, faces dirt-smeared and blemished with sores, and their eyes either bright beams of desperation or blackened holes of despair.

"Captain Beecher. Send seven of Lord Forbes's men to the garden ward to dig a grave. My garden ward, which never was meant to be a burial ground." He paused and swallowed hard. "Stand an equal number of armed guards over them until the work is done to my satisfaction. As soon as it is, we will bury Mr. Sellers. Bring forth a litter on which his body can be carried to the site. In the meantime, assign your most trusted men to guard the gate and the front of the castle. Let David Hyrst be among them. I believe he can be trusted. You will then compose a letter for both of our signatures to Mrs. Sellers in Kinsale."

He raised his voice. "I have said this before and I want everyone to hear: no one, and I mean no one, shall leave or enter this castle without my direct permission." Sir Arthur started to go back into the keep, but four of the women from Dundeady approached him.

"Sir?" one of them called. Sir Arthur turned. "Please allow us to wash Mr. Sellers' body before the burial. It is a small thing we might do, for your kind favor of taking us in."

"Good ladies, I'm afraid the body is in such a condition that I could not..."

"Sir," the lady interrupted. "We are not new to the horrors of war. Cleansing the body is an act of respect, for the deceased as well as for God. This man does not deserve to meet his creator as those monsters have left him. He has no family about to perform this task, so let us be his family, that he may ascend to the afterlife a purified being."

Sir Arthur looked to the ground, his jaw clenched. "It would be a merciful task, a true and generous kindness," he said. He nodded and returned to the keep.

By the soft light of dusk, a summer wind swirling above us and the smell of turned soil in the air, every resident of Rathbarry—even Mistress Dorothy—gathered for Mr. Sellers' burial. Sir Arthur spoke over the grave.

The pains of death surrounded me,
And the pangs of Sheol laid hold of me;
I found trouble and sorrow.
Then I called upon the name of the Lord:
"O Lord, I implore You, deliver my soul!"
Gracious is the Lord, and righteous;

On the last day of August, the herdsmen left the castle hours before dawn to graze the milk cows and the bull. At first light, everyone in the castle heard the commotion. The Irish army had laid in ambush in ditches around the castle, to take from us all the livestock Lord Forbes had left us—all we had to sustain us. But Captain Beecher was not to be humiliated again, not so closely on the heels of our last misfortune. He shot out of the castle gate with garrison men behind him. Then came blasts of gunfire, the thunder of hooves across the field, men shouting, and horses screaming.

By the time the dawn spread across the land, Beecher returned with his men, and all our saddle horses that had been taken from us, as well as some of the Irish army horses. There were shouts of victory among the soldiers in the court, and gleeful cries from the people who knew how close we had come to disaster. Ty ran from the stable with laughter erupting across his face, the first time I'd seen him show such joy for months. And it was a fine thing, wasn't it, a gift for Ty's birthday.

Sir Arthur ran from the keep to congratulate Beecher, grab others at the shoulder for a hearty welcome, and shake hands with a few more soldiers in gratitude. I ran before them to prepare seating and drinks in the state room where Sir Arthur would bring Captain Beecher and his officers to hear the full story of the morning's glory.

But it was not to last. Within two hours, the Irish army of at least three hundred men surrounded the castle. Caption Beecher was first to see them from the state room window, and fired upon them, killing or wounding at least three men. They fell to the ground before Sir Arthur realized I was there and sent me to secure Mistress Dorothy. He and the others bounded downstairs and spread throughout the castle court, raising a mighty defense from all corners. Gunfire and cannon fire split the air with a terrifying thunder, but the Irish had created their own cover by digging ditches and shoring up the rocky hills.

We'd reached the point of an all-out fight to the death. The castle was filled with people and horses. Every person who could fire a gun was armed and engaged. And now as every living being within did thirst and suffer, for when our need for water was most severe, our ever-dependable well ran dry.

44

The Sharpest Thorn

Liscarroll Castle

Despite all of Teige's planning and pressure, the hoped-for surrender at Rathbarry had failed. Everything worked against him, from foul weather, to the timing of the ship that took away half of the residents, to the fluke arrival of a devil like Forbes.

There were benefits however, in that his troops' hatred toward the English army heightened. Fueled with fury, the men yearned for battle. They demanded revenge. The other benefit was fewer people in Rathbarry, weakening their defenses and their resolve.

In late August he left John Oge Barry to finish the Rathbarry siege, while he marched the majority of his troops through marsh, bog, rocky hills and the wooded lands between the English-held towns of Enniskeane and Bandon. They camped for the night among the ridges of Bealnablath. From there he led them north through Muskerry lands to ford the River Lee at its narrowest point. The men surged into Mullinhassig Wood, where they'd rest invisible beneath the mighty trees. On the last day they scaled a steep mountain pass heading due north to Duhallow. By noontide on August 29, his men marched in good formation to General Barry, just a mile from Castle Liscarroll.

His troops pitched camp while the general updated him on the siege plans and his assignments. How foolish and arrogant the English had been, to leave such a castle with weak defense, as if they believed the Irish Army posed no threat. They would soon learn differently.

"Liscarroll is formidable, beyond a doubt," the general told him. "There's no beauty in its appearance, but in structure it's as intimidating as the finest fortress ought to be, and it commands a major crossroads for the region. But the sharpest thorn in the English side is that once we control the castle, our men will bring in the harvest from its fields. The English will have to move out or starve."

"'Tis the pearl of targets in my estimation, General. What's our strategy then?" Teige asked.

"Fire power and intimidation, my lord. Especially intimidation. The castle sits on limestone rock with curtain walls thirty feet high and a good two hundred feet on the longest side. Defensive towers at each corner. But there's no stone keep to assault, just wooden buildings that abut the walls within. First, we shall set those afire, and then hit their water supply in the south tower with the 32-pounder.

"The lad in charge, Sergeant Raymond, is young and circumspect. He'll spread his men from tower to tower and concentrate his guns on the north gate. This will be useless because our focus will be on the south: an arched entrance sixty feet high, with heavy doors and portcullis. The passage is well pierced with murdering holes which also will be useless to them because we'll set the battering ram before it. We'll otherwise have the entire fortress surrounded. He'll surrender soon enough, but if yet he resists, we'll avoid the gates altogether and breach the south walls. The sergeant will soon give way," he said with a confident grin.

Sure it would be a victory of eminent satisfaction for the general to retake Liscarroll under his family name. Sir Percival, the greedy, heartless bastard, had wrested the castle and nearby fortresses from Old John Barry through years of loans and mortgages all designed for Percival's advantage and foreclosed at his convenience, until poor old John owned nothing, was deeply in debt, and hardly knew what had happened.

Teige's troops joined with General Barry's men—already assembled from among the Roches, the MacCarthys, the O'Callaghans, O'Keeffes and Magners—to form a siege force of seven thousand men, including five hundred horse, and the heavy artillery taken from Limerick.

At dawn on August 30, the forces surrounded Liscarroll, and General Barry delivered his demands to the sergeant. They were, as expected, refused. And so, the musket fire commenced, filling the damp morning air with clamor, smoke, the sour smell of gunpowder, and the shattering, jolting sound of every shot. Teige whispered his prayer that each explosion should be terrifying to the garrison within, and empowering to the men without. Should they use such incitements to advantage, General Barry would have his victory in an hour.

But it would not be quite so easy. On and on the pounding continued through the day, and the garrison returned gunfire. Several of the tower snipers fell. Pikemen showered fireballs upon the wooden structures inside the walls and the flames jumped and danced, sending their black smoke spirals to the sky. By evening Liscarroll's garrison quieted and seemed to simply take cover. Teige sent his men to restore their ammunition from the general's well-manned supplies behind an elevated rock formation. They easily maintained pressure on the fortress through the night, that no one inside should sleep.

By dawn the second day, the general set his great cannon on a rocky hill within musket shot of the south tower. Throughout the day, Raymond shouted over the walls that he would not surrender. "Our relief arrives with Lord Inchiquin in twenty-four hours," Raymond said. "You Irish will be wise to run for your lives."

But General Barry maintained the firing while the pikemen hurled rocks over the walls, inflicting both damage and injury. By dusk the following day, Sergeant Raymond capitulated. The general took possession immediately, his men to keep Raymond and his garrison under guard while he and his officers filled the hall to plan his next move.

Something nagged at the back of Teige's neck. He gnawed on a piece of bread as General Barry addressed his leaders. He was a venerable general, but often slow when the men's energy ran high. He might, after such a victory, congratulate them, but his inflated chest suggested he was taking full credit.

"Gentlemen," he began, "our scouts set out at dawn to survey the land. I had thought to turn our guns against Doneraile next, but our man Sergeant Raymond says the good Lord Inchiquin arrives soon for Liscarroll's relief. The earl is a bit too late, aye?"

Some of the men laughed, but with caution—not the robust roar he'd expected from a well-earned win.

"Lord Inchiquin brings 2,000 foot and 400 horse soldiers," General Barry said. "He is a vicious opponent, make no mistake, but we can wreck him. They know not that we've taken Liscarroll, for we've seen no scouts and allowed no messages from Raymond. We have the advantage. Preparation shall start immediately. We'll establish the main body of our forces on high ground at the east hill. Inchiquin will have the sun in his eyes, and when his vision clears, he'll find 3,000 soldiers bearing down on him.

"Then, on the left, another force rises, 2,000 musketeers and pikemen. On the right, an equal force of muskets and pikes. Our cavalry will drive our enemy back straight away. And, should he push on, remember clearly who this enemy is, what the English have done to our lives and our families. The murders committed at Cork, Clonakilty, Mallow, Kilbrittain.

"When he comes tomorrow morning, we'll be waiting for him—our muskets *fixed at his balls.*"

SEPTEMBER

45

Seven Hours

Liscarroll Castle

"Lord Inchiquin comes," General Barry shouted to the troops taking their positions. "And with him with the likes of Barrymore, Dungarvan, Kinalmeaky and Broghill—sons of the hated Earl of Cork, the greedy robber of all our lands, murderer of innocents, friend to the foreign bloodthirsty pirates, and he himself a bloodsucker of the church.

"We are 7,000 strong," he said. "We are men of power, of honor, men with fire in our blood, and a centuries-old right to this land. Let Inchiquin send his army forward. We shall squeeze the blood from them like oil from a fish, and then—we will pound the bloody bastards all to dust."

The shouts exploded from the troops. With a bit of spittle on his chin, at last General Barry had hit the mark. The officers took their places to direct their soldiers now ready in formations.

Teige's men set up a series of huts the general devised as cover for musketeers to block an attack from the southwest. Here an open meadow narrowed as it drew near the castle. They concealed the huts among the dense hedges and trees on either side. He'd ride behind them to maintain order while his cavalry repelled an advance. The English would be trapped to their doom.

By the first light of September 3, the Irish scouts sighted Inchiquin's advance party. As the sun started to ascend, the main body of the English forces approached the bracing Irish. The Irish cavalry charged and almost cut off the advance party, and a massive hail of shot from the castle let Inchiquin know Liscarroll had been taken.

Teige watched from high ground as the Irish horse and musketeers forced Inchiquin's cavalry to retreat. But the English were stubborn, slowing and turning to fight at intervals, then falling back, allowing time for the main body of the army to move westward.

The Irish pursued them, forcing further retreat with heavy fire, and then came an Irish officer's joyous cry, "Kinalmeaky is down! Death to the Puritans!"

Disorder mangled the English troops as someone tried but failed to retrieve Kinalmeaky's body. Teige's heart thrilled as the Irish took command, the musketeers combing through ditches and brush while the horse followed behind them in perfect time. The English scattered, retreated westward, their order lost. Was the battle fought and won?

But no, it was the Irish breaking apart, discipline failing. Some men dismounting to plunder houses as they passed. Teige instinctively reached for the ax on his saddle, as if he might crack the heads of those who broke order. Inchiquin drew at least sixty musketeers to high ground and fired down upon the Irish, who then retreated to fortifications near the castle.

It was just the first sally. Had they maintained order, the Irish could have had it all—could have crushed them without even engaging the entire force. Now they'd face a full pitched battle for which the English were prepared, and many more men would die.

The Irish restored their original formation with left, right and center. Soon the English approached, their men dividing into three forces directly opposing the Irish: pikemen to pikemen, musketeers to musketeers, and cavalry facing cavalry.

The Irish had the hill, and the English a wide, flat valley. Inchiquin led the onslaught, aided by his friends, Captain William Jephson, and that one Teige had seen before at Cork, Charles Vavasour. Four companies charged up the hill, a fifth company under Barrymore bringing the rear. Teige set his men at ready. The English rode into his trap.

His musketeers fired two volleys, but the huts did not serve. Sixty English horse charged the huts, and his men—Teige's good, dependable, well-trained men—ran for their lives. There was no choice then but to retreat back to the army's main body.

Oliver Stevenson, captain of the Irish horse, fought gallantly, holding back the English almost single handedly, his men at his heels. A musketeer injured Lord Inchiquin and the English leader went down. The Irish pikemen raised their weapons for the kill. Victory was at hand! But suddenly Stevenson halted, dismounted. He stopped the kill. Good God—how could Teige have forgotten that Inchiquin was Stevenson's cousin? Stevenson was trying to save the bloody bastard! But Inchiquin had neither loyalty nor mercy. He raised his pistol and shot Stevenson between the eyes.

Teige's gut nearly tore open at the sight, but there was no time to stop, for the field had turned to chaos, the Irish cavalry scattered in small groups, the English chasing after them to further divide them. And without cavalry to back them, the Irish infantry broke apart. The English surged forward, cutting a bloody swath through the soldiers until they reached General Barry's supply. The Irish guard held out until the cavalry deserted them. They fled to the castle, the English horse chasing after them, slicing swords through the air and cutting men down as they ran.

Seven hours the battle went on, until Teige realized the English were distracting Irish troops with small skirmishes while they systematically filled the woodland to the west of the castle, surrounding Liscarroll for a murderous end.

He sent word to General Barry, who promptly ordered his army into full retreat to northwest, toward Glenfield.

Liscarroll was lost.

It was a tremendous blow. Hundreds of men killed. Coming on the heels of the deaths at Clonakilty, it would wreck the army's morale for some time. For General Barry to lose an easy target to a far lesser force, primarily because of poor discipline among the soldiers—he'd lose the respect not only of his officers but of the politicians who'd appointed him. None would wish to stand in his boots, and no men of Carbery would thereafter serve him. Teige would see to it.

Burying the dead would take days. The camp followers already moved in to strip and loot the bodies. Teige longed to leave. To gallop to Dunmanway and see his wife and youngest son. To reassure himself that they were safe; to remind himself what he was fighting for. After so many crucial losses, could they yet turn the course of this war? Had Rathbarry yet surrendered?

46

Trenches

Rathbarry Castle

I picked weeds for my basket alongside the chapel where I could hear Sir Arthur, several men from the garrison, and a few of the villagers who gathered around the well to decide how to repair it. The late summer wind dashed around the court, tossing my skirt and sweeping sand and debris across the court. Men held their hats and allowed their hair to tussle.

Already they'd agreed there was but one option, if it could be repaired at all, and that was through difficult, back-breaking labor. They'd have to dig and dig until the water began to seep in again. But who would go down, how should the dirt removal be handled, and how would they shore up the sides of the well as they worked?

They began within an hour. Everyone in the castle who could lift a bucket helped. The youngest and lightest men dug at the well's bottom, one at a time. As a man was hoisted up, another went down, and the same with the buckets. As one was drawn up full of soil and rock, an empty bucket was lowered. Women and children emptied the buckets in the garden ward, and hurried back to trade empty for full. Sir Arthur made sure someone minded the windlass; if it broke the repair would be impossible.

For two solid days the men dug, sometimes sending down curbings to support the sides of the well as they went deeper. A lookout shooed people from the well's rim to prevent anything from falling into the well that could injure or even kill the man below.

No one knew how long it would take to reach water again, and so at the same time Jayne and I formed the first team of women to risk our lives, running outside the castle to collect water while under fire from our besiegers. Though it was frightening and daring work, still it would help to do something useful that might mean our survival.

"I'll go first," Jayne said. The guard opened the gate just enough for her to slip through. She carried two skins beneath one arm and hiked up her skirts so she could crawl quickly on her knees. The space between the gate and the tall grass was short but fully exposed. She scrambled like a sheep to his supper and, once under cover, paused for a deep slow breath. She crawled from there to the pond's edge, causing the grasses to wave and shiver as she went. All was still and quiet while she filled the skins. When she returned to the grasses a shot rang out. She stilled and I thought for a second she'd been hit, but then, dragging the heavy skins, she ran like a hare and burst through the gate gasping, the skins sloshing.

"I don't think," she paused, took a breath, and grinned at me. "I don't think they're about killin', but just mean to frighten us. The shot was miles above my head."

We emptied her skins into a barrel, and now it was my turn. I peered out of the gate. Jayne had made a path through the grass, so it would be easier for me, and I'd make a smaller target. With the skins in place, I crept through the gate slowly and then burst across the open space to the grass, as Jayne had done. I could see why she'd stopped to breathe. I was suddenly light-headed and for a second confused, not sure which way to go. But then the path came clear again and I hurried through to the pond. Just as I reached the edge, another shot rang out, slicing through the air above me.

It must have been close, *terribly* close. I dropped to my belly like a lizard, dragging the filled skins behind me. I reached the tall grass as a musket ball cut through the yellow blades just above me. They had switched to a better marksman, for this fellow was not playing about. I rolled on my side to be as small as I could, causing the least disturbance to the grass. It worked well, but I stalled upon reaching the open span to the gate, sweat popping up on my forehead and in my armpits. Jayne peered at me from the gate, her eyes bright with fear. Somehow her compassion restored my courage. I blasted from the grass to the gate, another shot fired and hit the castle wall just behind me. I fell through the entrance and the guard shoved it closed.

Jayne swung me into her arms. I whispered against her ear. "Not about killin', you say?" We giggled in silly relief, unable to stop until we lost our breath. Then we became most serious, knowing our danger was as real as any the men faced. We needed to choose our timing more carefully. Only the smallest and fastest among us would make the run, the risk being lessened. How I wished Sir Arthur hadn't walled up the passage under the southeast tower, for it was closer to the pond, reducing or even eliminating our exposure.

Thunderous shouts soon issued from the well and all those around it when the water began to seep in again. The last man to climb out fell to his knees in the court, his face and hands smeared black with mud. "The bottom is exceedingly deep, though she does fill," he said. "We've touched the lid of hell, and I pray the Devil himself doesn't discover it until the last of us has found our place in Heaven." If that raised any fears of hellfire, they were overtaken by the welcome consolation of having water again, and Sir Arthur cheerfully proclaimed the following day to be a day of rest.

But there would be no rest.

During the night, the curs barked and growled. The tower guards noticed activity around the castle perimeter and alerted Sir Arthur. His footsteps rumbled down to the court, but in only a few minutes he clomped back up the stairs to his bed, stopping to assure Dorothy there was nothing to see and she should go back to sleep. When the morning light allowed more distant views, I followed him to the northeast tower. He joined the guard there, and lifted his spyglass in the direction the man was pointing. He lowered the glass, then lowered his head.

"Merel," he said, already knowing I was hiding on the tower stairs behind him. "Run to the garrison and bring me Captain Beecher."

Beecher needed only to see my face and he burst from his lodgings, ran past me and bolted up to the tower battlement. I hurried behind him as best I could, but I'd already been up there once and the poor rations of late had weakened my legs.

"The Irish have dug a long trench during the night," Sir Arthur said, handing Beecher the spyglass. "I'd say it's about half the musket range, putting our tower guards especially at risk. Thank the good Lord our well has been restored, for any who venture outside the castle shouldn't expect to survive."

I peered over the edge of the wall. Something dark, a line like a wide deer path crossed the dead grass field. Then something moved, a human head, and the scale of it all became clear. I'd focused on the dirt piled along the curving path that at first concealed what lay behind it: a trench long enough, deep enough, and wide enough to shelter a hundred men. It paralleled the eastern curtain wall, stopping several paces short of the tall outer gate posts.

Beecher shook his head. "They've made our cannon useless, being so close that if we fired it, the ball would fly over their heads. They're planning to pound us. Hyrst!" he called, and David came running from halfway down the curtain wall.

"Sir!" he said, bowing to Sir Arthur and glancing quickly at me.

"See that every guard wears his helmet and breastplate.," Beecher said. "And see that all of our arms are at ready, and every soldier has his powder. It is going to get rough."

"Sir." David gave a sharp nod and bolted down the stairs.

Beecher pointed over the wall. "They've literally drawn a line in front of the gate, sir, from which to shoot it full of holes. It will be dangerous even to guard it if the gunfire is quite hot."

"Yes. I agree. My greatest concern," Sir Arthur said, "is if the gunfire is hot enough to set the gate afire, they'll soon breach the castle and we're done for. I'd have the mason wall it up, but it takes time and would put his life at risk even as he works."

Beecher stood in silence for a few moments, his gaze studying the ditch from end to end. "I have an idea, sir. Not a solution, truly, but it could give us more time."

"Yes, speak it."

"Have we something, a piece of roofing perhaps, or a plank wall from the stables, to let down over the gate?"

"Ah! A shield to slow them down. Let me think. Nothing too fancy, just nails in it or hooks so that we can lower over the gate with ropes."

"Exactly."

"O'Daly!" Sir Arthur shouted down from the wall, and within seconds Ty was in the court. My heart lifted at the sight of him—a sudden, involuntary response that never seemed to alter. He bounded up the steps.

"Suppose we were to lower a shield over the gate, to protect it from gunfire. Have you anything in the stable that might serve?" Sir Arthur asked.

Instinct must have made him glance over the wall to see the trench that troubled Sir Arthur and Captain Beecher. He cocked his head. "Why not a door to cover a door?"

"Of course! Thank you, Ty. The stable doors should be a perfect fit. Beecher, could you send your men to..."

"I'll unhinge it myself, sir, if the garrison men can manage the placement," Ty said.

"We'll get to it immediately, Sir Arthur," Beecher said, and hurried down the stairs and across the court.

Sir Arthur lifted the spyglass. Ty took my hand and pulled me halfway down the stairs before he grabbed me around the waist and planted a firm kiss on my lips. "Try not to get yerself shot at again, aye?"

I touched my hand to my tingling mouth and he smiled. "Come see me when ye want a bit more." How was it that he could say such things, light and playful, even when it seemed death had drawn its line before us? It calmed me, as if nothing could disturb what lay between us, not even this. If only I could make the feeling last.

I'd been away from Mistress Dorothy far too long. She could forgive me a short time away if I brought her useful information, but as the child within her grew, so grew her impatience, discomfort, and melancholy. She'd been three weeks without milk, and within another week the cheese would run out, too. I'd hidden the bit of wine that remained, to ease her in the afternoon when she grew restless. She'd be waiting for me quite keenly now.

Though I did have information for her, what was I to say? That the Irish had dug a trench, and doors that would be lowered to shield the gate against fire? That Sir Arthur would have the entrance sealed so that we'd all be trapped within? Would that lift her sorrow? Would that lift anyone's woe? I dared not fully embrace the idea myself or I might run screaming through the castle.

I ran to Elinor first. A sweet, some confection, even the tiniest bit of marmalade would raise a dimple on my mistress's cheek before I had to deliver any news.

Elinor had recovered from her injuries, but not from the haunting memory of the attack or her fear of a recurrence. Sir Arthur gave her Cal, his favorite old hunting hound, for a kitchen companion to alert her to anyone coming. He bayed weakly as I approached. The poor thing was skin and ribs, but he did his duty and Elinor welcomed me with a hearty hug. I told her of my need. Her delicious honey cakes were things of the distant past, but she thought for a moment, then hunted through drawers and cabinets for anything that might have been missed before. She came upon a jar at the far back of a cabinet that produced no more than a thimbleful of honey. It would satisfy for today. But what would I do tomorrow?

"Fool! Where have you been?" Mistress Dorothy said when I reached her bedchamber. She was in her night shift, sitting on her mattress with one hand grasping the carved oak post.

"Look what I found for you." I offered her the honey in a small silver spoon. She knocked it from my hand and the spoon clattered all the way across the plank floor to land in a dusty corner. My shoulders fell, and my tiny whisp of joy with them. My empty stomach cramped and ached. I could not even look at her. She whimpered and began to cry, uttering curses at me, at Sir Arthur, at the Irish, at the lazy and useless people in the castle, and even at God.

"My mother. I miss my mother. Why are we stuck in this strange outpost when I am in such a way?" she cried. "If only she could be here, hold me and tell me we are all right. Always she was there when I needed her. Always she was kind. I'll never see her again."

I sank to the floor and waited for her to become quiet. After several minutes, she looked up at me, her face red and swollen. She was miserable, and now I was miserable. I told her, slowly, everything I had learned. How could it make things worse?

"But," she said, "if the gate is walled, how will anyone get in who comes to save us?"

I shrugged. "I s'pose they'll just have to wait."

She said nothing, but when Elinor brought her warm cup of broth, she drank it, and returned to her bed. When her breathing grew soft and steady with sleep, I went to the corner to pick up the silver spoon. I licked it clean, though there was barely anything upon it. Then a beam of morning light fell on a tiny drop of the golden honey, bright as a jewel on the floor. I dropped like a cat and licked it up, dust and all. It might be the last taste of anything sweet that I would ever have. I went to my trundle, curled up and went to sleep.

A short time later I awakened to a thunder so terrible the very walls of Rathbarry seemed to be exploding around us. Mistress Dorothy sat upright in her bed, her eyes wide with terror.

"Go. Hurry," she said.

47

Under Fire

Rathbarry Castle

I ran downstairs, but Jenkin blocked the door so that I couldn't get to the court. "The Irish army fires upon us from all sides, especially the gate." He spoke so quickly I barely understood him, and his eyes were as wide as Mistress Dorothy's. "It's dangerous. Sir Arthur ordered me to keep you and the mistress within." He rocked side to side on his feet, so frightened he couldn't stand still, as if he might run in either direction at any time.

I pushed him backward and ran to the kitchen. A guard was at that entrance also but I ducked around him. I had to see what was happening. And where was Ty? Was he safe?

The gunfire pierced my ears once I reached the court. A dark cloud of pungent smoke rose up over the gate and climbed the towers north and south. Sir Arthur had been right. The Irish army intended to set the gate on fire with heavy musket shot, and was doing a fair job of it. The stable doors lay on the ground near the gate. The soldiers had no time to hang them before the gunfire commenced.

After several minutes the firing stopped, and left in my ears a high-pitched ringing. No one was in the court, all had taken cover. I took a few steps toward the stable and then, as quickly as it had stopped, the firing resumed its intensity. I ran back into the keep and up the stairs. What should I tell Mistress Dorothy? But I needn't have worried. Sir Arthur was with her. I dropped on the top stair to catch my breath.

She wept upon her husband's shoulder. He spoke softly. Gently. He took both of her hands in his and kissed them. Then he kissed her hair, and her lips. I slid myself down a few more steps where I couldn't intrude on the intimate moment. A sweet, consoling moment. A tender acknowledgment of love, being made should the opportunity not come again. I backed down the stairs to the hollow hall.

Jenkin had left his post, probably seeking the comfort of his bed as I had done. I crept to the door and let myself out, pausing as the guns blasted, and when another lull came, I ran to find Ty where I thought I would, on the floor in Sarcen's stall. I plopped down beside him and he pulled me close. Poor Sarcen trembled against the stable wall, his ribs clearly showing beneath his once lustrous coat, his head low and a high, soft whine issuing from his throat.

"He doesn't know what goes on around him. Mebbe it's best not to know, but it seems he's consumed wi' fear anaways. S'pose there is no easy way through a t'ing such as this—for man or animal," Ty said.

"If we were birds, though, we could just fly away."

"Right ye are. Next time we'll be askin' the good Lord for wings."

"As long as we're askin', why not our Sarcen, too? He'd be just like Pegasus."

"Aye, wouldn't ye love that, boy."

The pounding and thundering began again in a raucous flurry, so loud it was useless to try to talk. We held each other tightly until it passed like a violent storm.

"Could we," I asked, "I mean, if we were to escape this, could we somehow take Sarcen with us?"

Ty shook his head. "I've no stomach for leavin' him, but ye see how weak he is, an' with no food to give 'im, he'd no' get far. Best would ha' been if we could turn him out and let his instinct take over, find his own food and shelter, or mebbe someone who could take him in. I fear if the army gets hold o' him they might kill him just to spite Sir Arthur."

There was no way out, for any of us. Was this dull, heavy pain in my gut what my parents felt as the ship began to sink, the heavy crate crushed against them and no one to help? They must have watched their last bits of breath bubble to the surface, out of reach. I began to tremble. My eyes filled. He brushed away the tears with his fingertips. "I'm sorry," I said. "I mean to be strong, to be brave and take care of things. But in truth I'm just as scared and as tearful as Mistress Dorothy."

He scoffed and kissed my forehead. "Lass, ye hardly know yerself.

Who saved those Irish prisoners from hangin' so many months ago? Was that a brave woman, or just a frightened girl? And who was first to warn us all of the army camp outside the castle? Who ran through gunfire to bring us water? Who has taken care of a bitter and conniving pregnant woman every day, in the midst of war and starvation? Ye're stronger and braver than most o' the lads in the garrison."

He hugged me tightly, but then stiffened, jerked his head up and looked about. A lull in the shooting had lasting at least twice as long as the others. "Has it stopped?" he asked softly, more of himself than of me. And if it had, would that mean the shooting was over? Had the gate caught fire? Had the army retreated? He pulled me up by the hand and we ran into the courtyard. The black cloud still hung over us, but he was right, the shooting had truly stopped.

"Mebbe they're out o' powder and ha' gone for more. I don't know, but I'll go for Cap'n Beecher. We may have a chance to lower tha' cover o'er the gate."

The men had nailed together the stable doors to make one wide shield, and quickly lowered it over the castle gate using thick hemp ropes. It provided enough protection that the stone mason could begin walling up the opening. By mid-afternoon his work was mostly done. No sooner had he laid the last stone, than the Irish commenced their next tactic. The smoke had cleared so that the guards could see a fair distance. Sir Arthur was summoned. From the top of the curtain wall, we could see men setting the frameworks for seven small cabins being erected behind a rocky hill near the trench. Once these cabins were completed, the Irish musketeers would have dependable cover so they could fire on Rathbarry with even greater intensity.

Sir Arthur was furious, pacing back and forth across the courtyard, grumbling and shouting. "These rogues use *my* own wood from *my* own land, to build crude shelters from which to hide like cowards while they fire upon innocent people in *my* castle."

Curious residents filled the court. The more Sir Arthur ranted, the more people arrived: men in ragged and filthy clothes, women looking only slightly better in dirty and faded cloaks and mantles, and all of them looking diminished and desperate.

"I'll not give in to them. Let them fire all they might. Let them promise what they will," Sir Arthur said. "They *deceive*. To give in is to die, to suffer a slaughter as John Sellers did, or to be hanged like Tantalus and Linscombe. Our relief does come, I know it, or they wouldn't attack us so hotly."

He paced and paced, his boots pounding the dirty flagstones, his long pointy locks wild about his head, lifting in the wind like the feathers of a hawk ascending. "Let God confound them as they build their detestable cabins. The Devil take them! Will they use these shelters to fire their guns upon us? Then we shall build up battlements to fire down upon them!"

Shouts from the men in the court joined Sir Arthur's, and Captain Beecher stepped forward. "We can do it, sir. We have plenty of hands. We'll need to find a source of wood, or things that can be taken from one place and given new purpose in another."

Sir Arthur wheeled around. "Some of the apartments are empty. Take the stairs as a piece from one or two of them. Dismantle some of the tenant cabins. Tenants can be doubled up if need be. Some things in the keep can be taken. We must work fast, as fast or faster than they. Who is ready?"

Nearly every man came forward with a shout. "Better to work than to wait," one man said.

Without Mr. Millet to organize things, activity in the court rose like a violent and unbridled windstorm, twisting and hurling things and people in every possible direction. After so many weeks of men and women trudging around without strength or energy, I could hardly believe what occurred. Every house was opened and plundered for potentially useful items: every table and every door that could provide a standing platform, every stair and step, every post and rail, and then floor planks, bed frames, cattle yokes, laundry carts, and the wooden bench by the well. All would be transformed into supports, shields and platforms on the battlements that would elevate musketeers to a killing advantage, shooting down upon the trenches and cabins.

Sir Arthur hailed Captain Beecher. In minutes they sketched a plan for how the platforms could be constructed. The plundering turned to sawing and hammering, creating so much noise the Irish must have wondered what was underway. Upstairs in her bed, clinging to the only bed-posts not sacrificed, Mistress Dorothy groaned and shrieked, her eyes puffy, her nose swollen.

"I cannot bear it. I cannot! The shooting, the banging, the stink of smoke, and the hammering, sawing, shouting. And when they are done, more shooting. More banging. Can we not ever again know peace?" She wadded and squeezed one of her bed pillows to her breast, and then threw it across the room, stirring the fetid air. "I need silence, but if that cannot be, give me distraction. Read to me."

I picked up the poetry book on her bedside table. She had moved on from James Day to John Donne. I opened the book to a random page.

"The Ecstasy. *Where, like a pillow on a bed, A pregnant bank swell'd up to rest...*"

"No! No, not that one. For Heaven's sake, do we not have enough of pregnancy here? Find another!" she said.

I thumbed through the book. "The Flea." Surely this would be humorous and light. I began. *"Mark but this flea, and mark in this, How little that which thou deniest me is; It sucked me first, and now sucks thee..."*

"Merel!" she shouted. "What on earth? Do you think I must hear of bloodsucking? This child sucks away most of my remaining life, and me no nourishment to give it. And now you so console me? Put the book down. Come and rub my legs. They ache and they feel like useless tree stumps."

"I'll rub your legs, but first let's get you up to walk. If they feel like stumps it's because that's what they are unless you move them." With her arm around my shoulder we walked around the room and then turned to walk the opposite direction. She tired quickly.

"I am so hungry. I could eat my own shift. Is there not a portion of bread? A bowl of fruit? Those blasted cabbages make me flatulent, but I could even eat those. How is an infant to grow with no food? I tire of this, and my back hurts. Take me back to my bed."

"Lie on your side," I said. "I'll rub your back with oil of rosemary."

"No. It will only spark my hunger, and I *shall* eat my shift, and my mattress as well."

The now-familiar heat rose into my chest, then my neck, and then my cheeks and ears. I was crying. I hated it, but my emotions were raw as if my skin had been scraped away and the slightest brush could ignite them.

"I'm sorry, mistress. I'm trying to help you. Elinor could fix you a willow bark drink, and I could make you an ointment of groundsel for your back. Beyond that I know not what to do."

"None of that will help. No one can do anything," she snapped. "Now. *Out with you.* You're no good to me here. Make yourself useful, but far from my sight! Tell Elinor to bring me the willow bark. Anything except that tasteless broth."

I'd meant to lift her spirits, but failing that, at least I'd gained a little freedom. I fled downstairs, matching my steps to the furious banging of the hammers. My mood was heavier than it had been for days, and then I realized I'd not seen Jayne since the well had been repaired. I knew she'd learned some remedies from her mother. She'd be able to tell me what to do for the mistress. But truly I wanted the solace just of being with Jayne in her house. She always made me feel bright. I headed for the garden ward, and hoped the men had not pulled down her house about her head.

The sounds were no quieter in the ward, and debris lay everywhere in the lanes, to be stepped over or kicked away. Two posts and the door were missing from Jayne's house, a blanket tacked up in its place.

"Jayne?" I tapped on the door frame. How fortunate that it, at least, had survived the wild scavenging for wood. She didn't answer. "Jayne?" I called a little louder. Then came a reply, but not much stronger than the mewing of a kitten. It was dark inside, the one window shrouded as Mistress Rosgill had done. The very thought of it made me shiver. *"Jayne!"* I ran to her mattress, her thin form barely lifting the wool military blanket that covered her.

"What's this? Has someone hurt you?"

She lay on her side, and raised her head a little. I jumped up and pulled the covering from the window to light the room. Her hair was dark with sweat, her face pale as a lamb, her eyes sunken and dark.

"They think the spirit in this house tortures me, but it's not. It just be an ague. Fever comes and goes. I shiver, then I sweat." Jayne's voice was weak and gravelly.

"Where is David?"

"Gone to build the battlements. He'll come back."

"Not soon enough. I'll get you water."

"Ye needn't..."

"Hush, Jayne." I ran back to the castle and to my trundle, pulled off all the bedclothes and rolled them up. Then I ran to Elinor, who was brewing the bark for the mistress.

"What will work for fever? It's for Jayne, she's taken ill," I said.

Elinor looked stricken. "Oh dear, not Jayne. You'll need to cool her down. Fill a bucket with water and cover her with cool rags. When she chills and wants heat, don't let her get too warm again. I'll fix her willow bark water as soon as I finish Mistress Dorothy's."

I sat in the dark house and held Jayne's hand for the next few hours as she sweated through fever and trembled through chills. At last David arrived with hard biscuits. I had not seen those for weeks either, but he'd taken them from the garrison's supply. "How is she?" he asked.

"Better," Jayne said.

"She's not, she's very ill. She needs someone beside her," I said.

"I cannot stay. I must return to the battlements. One of the women from Dundeady will sit with her, just at the next cabin."

"I don't need..."

"Hush, Jayne. You do," I said. "We must get you well, or else there's just no point to anything anymore."

"I'll confirm that," David said. "Rest, love. I'll return when I'm able."

Before sundown, the Irish musketeers in the trenches resumed in earnest, pounding the castle walls and the gate, only this time our soldiers were shooting back—from several feet higher than the original battlements, with wood instead of stone as their shield. The gunfire roared to life, the terrifying noise even more ferocious than before, the smoke and stench devouring the breathable air. The ground and sky seemed to tremble as if the two might collapse together, crushing all life between them. Jayne trembled as if her body would shatter. I held her close, but I couldn't ease her tremor, nor stop it from shaking my own weakened body as a giant might shake his fist.

48

Velvet

Rathbarry Castle

By some sweet mercy we fell asleep together, and when I woke, darkness had fallen and the guns had silenced, leaving me in eerie apprehension. Jayne's fever had passed. She slept with clear, even breathing, like a dreaming child. Soon David arrived with an oil lamp and more water.

"How many killed?" I whispered.

"None," he said, "but several injured. They were not so fortunate in the Irish trench."

"Why? What happened?"

"We're high enough that there's no advantage to the trench anymore. We can see over the piles of earth, and fire into it. They've lost their cover and it's costing them."

"Ty?" I asked.

"He is well. He's in the stables."

I nodded, relieved. "I'll come back in the morning."

He set the lamp on the floor, where it flickered lightly and colored their faces a tawny gold. He settled down beside her. Something tightened in my throat; I could not swallow. The second I was out of the house, I ran as fast as my legs would allow—to the stables.

Ty stood at the opening where the doors had been, pale moonlight defining his strong jaw, his parted lips, the lines of his furrowed brow. I ran to him and he swept me into his arms, carrying me to his small, lonely cot by the empty hay bin.

We held each other and kissed, his lips so warm and firm and moist, and I could not get enough of them, hungry for the taste of him. The kisses were as necessary as breathing and I could not stop, for none were sufficient. I could not get close enough to him. I tugged at his doublet and he stopped just long enough to yank it from his shoulders and wrap me in his arms again. I pulled up his shirt and pressed my face and hands against his bare chest, the soft hairs of it, the smell of his skin and his sweat a forcible intoxicant that still was not enough. I pulled at his breeks and he at my skirt, both of us stopping only seconds to remove what impeded us. When the bare of his chest pressed against my own, and the heat of his naked thighs touched mine, my body surged with want in every quarter and nothing was enough, nothing could reach or satisfy my need until we joined, struggled to get closer and closer still, until something ignited and burned, and then everything expanded. After a moment it slowly melted away like butter on the tongue, and yet lingered and spread across my shoulders and down through my body the way a shot of whisky will, but far more potent and lasting.

He stroked the lengths of my hair across his chest. "I could not find you at the keep," he said.

"I went to Jayne. She has taken ill with a fever."

He shook his head. "She canna stay in this place. She'll die if this does no' end soon. Mebbe we all will."

"Don't say that, Ty. Please."

"Forgive me. I struggle for hope wi' what's happening here. They'll be coomin' tomorrow for some horses."

"Who will?"

"Men from the garrison. They'll want to kill them for the meat. The castle rations cannot sustain them anymore. The soldiers will take the best parts, sayin' they be entitled as the ones doin' the labor and takin' the musket fire. They'd send some o' the meat to the castle, no' much but some, and throw parts o'er the wall for the curs. He kissed my brow. "I doona guess I can stop them. Let the garrison bastards kill 'em, for I'll no' do it."

"So the fighting isn't over."

"Just beginnin'. The Irish soldiers will be back, and will keep comin' until they shoot us dead, until we run out of powder, or until we starve. If the English are bringin' relief, they sure be tekin' the longest route."

At dawn the next morning I jerked awake. The shooting resumed. Ty had left me in his cot to water the horses. How would he feed them, now that we had no access to grasses? When I left the stables I had my answer, for Giles was on a ladder pulling thatch from the roof of an older dwelling.

I found Jayne sitting up on her mattress, her back against the wall, sipping water from a cup. Her room smelled of sweat and smoke from the oil lamp.

"Are you better, Jayne?"

"Well, I'm no' dead, am I? If that's what ye're wondrin.'" She grinned.

"Thank God in his Heaven and all the little creatures. I'm off to check on the mistress then, but I'll find you something to eat and don't worry. I'll come back as soon as I can."

"I'm well enough. Don' fuss so."

In the courtyard, Sir Arthur paced and shook his head angrily, muttering to himself. I rushed into the keep and found Mistress Dorothy fully dressed in her loose dressing gown. She glowered at me but said nothing until I'd finished tying her laces.

"Jenkin tells me Jayne is not well. Is this true?"

"Yes, mistress. She is better this morning, but thinks she has an ague, so the fever may well return over the next several days."

She nodded. "You must take this to her. I cannot close it over my belly now." She pointed to the bed where her treasure, the sapphire velvet robe, lay neatly folded and tied. My breath caught in my throat. I looked to her, but she would not meet my eyes. "Just take it. Before you go, I need you to fix my hair. I want to wear it long today. And then fetch Sir Arthur to me."

"Yes, mistress," I said. Oh, what was she planning and what would this day bring? Sir Arthur still paced by the time I found him in the court.

"I've no time to be running in and out of the keep or to hear Dorothy's latest complaint," Sir Arthur said. "I know she's frightened. I know she's unhappy and does not have what she needs. We're all starved and wretched, but we are fighting for our lives here, do you see?" He glared down on me, his voice harsh. I waited, and after a minute his eyes softened. He touched my shoulder, a slight tap that carried with it so much meaning— of sadness, apology and kindness. "All right. Let's see what she has to say."

We climbed the stairs in silence. At the entrance to Mistress Dorothy's bedchamber, we stood in astonishment. She sat in a straight-backed chair in the center of the room where the sunlight fell across her hair and turned it from dark brown to spun gold. Her eyes were bright, her lips the deep red of wildwood cherries. She was at once a dangerous siren, a queen of state, and the blessed virgin. Her pale face showed not the troubled, sickly and spiteful woman I'd been seen only a little while before. She had transformed herself for this one moment with Arthur. She was beauty, serenity, and wisdom, calling him to her presence in a perfumed chamber.

Sir Arthur was instantly beguiled. He dropped to one knee before her and kissed her thin, fragile hand. "My darling, you are as captivating as you were on the first day I saw you. With all that we've been through, it seems a century ago, and yet you haven't aged a day since then. You unfold to me like the bud of a rose, every petal revealing greater beauty than the last. I am yours."

She smiled sweetly. "My dearest, gallant Arthur. My husband and my life. Merel, please bring him a stool that he may sit."

I ran for the cushioned, embroidered stool at her dressing table, and then tried to make myself invisible again. Sir Arthur sat with his knees against hers, her hands resting in his. "What is it, my love?" he asked.

"You and I, Arthur. We were meant to live here at Rathbarry. You and I, and our children. I believe that. But we were not meant to die here. Of that I am equally certain. You are the strongest, most courageous and honorable of knights. Descended from generations of honorable men who served King Henry, Queen Elizabeth, King James. You are your father's son. You are a proud father meant to instill in your children all the virtues you possess, and all that will create a lasting future. It is time, my darling, to focus on that."

He started to speak, but she leaned forward with some difficulty over her protruding belly, and pressed a finger to his lips. "I know you have much to say, Arthur, and of course you are more educated and experienced than I. But let me finish what I must say before you begin."

He clasped his hands between his knees as she continued.

"Six months have passed. Six months of bloodshed and decline. It is time to stop playing the game."

"Game!" he blurted, unable to remain silent.

"Yes, Arthur, my love. It is a game. The Irish take something, then we take something back. They shoot at us, we shoot back at them. They kill one of us, we kill one of them. Back and forth over the tennis net. Do you truly believe shooting at each other over a wall will end this?"

"Dorothy, please. The men are doing well. We are succeeding."

"I know, Arthur. But we are few and they are many. We will run out of ammunition while they have an endless supply. We will starve and our infant child will die within my womb while they feast on our cattle and sheep."

Sir Arthur's back stiffened. "Darling, we are at war. What else would you have me do?"

She shook her head gently. "We cannot outfight them. You see that, don't you? And so, we must outsmart them. Look at what you have done already. You built a boat, you saved many people, you sent for help. It is not your fault that the vast minds at Kinsale sent you Lord Forbes. Try again. Call on your friends. Your guns will not deliver us, but by your wit we will soon be saved."

He looked into her eyes for what seemed a very long time. "Thank you, my love, both beautiful and wise." He turned his face toward the window. "We fight because we must, you know. But I've heard you, and will look for alternative solutions. You must trust me now, and think no more of it."

"Merel, leave us, and do close the door behind you," she said.

I picked up the robe, closed the latch quietly, and hurried from the keep to Jayne's house. Jayne was awake and shivering, her neighbor dozing on a stool beside her. "Merel, my friend. What news have you?"

I untied the robe, opened it out and draped it around her shoulders. "A gift," I said, "from a suddenly generous Mistress Dorothy."

"You're jokin'!" She sniffed the velvet and started to pull it from her shoulder. "Take it away or she'll have my head!"

I laughed. "I'm not joking. She heard you are ill and she wants you to have it. By God's grace, I swear she is not the same person she was when she threw you out. Not today, anyway."

"But what if I sweat in the thing and she wants it back?"

"She won't want it back. She wants you to get well. We all want you to

get well. How do you feel?"

"Elinor brought me a lovely broth, and it has fixed me up, though my legs are a bit weak."

The neighbor started to awaken. "Oh dear, was I sleeping? I'm so sorry I…"

"Merel, this is Joan Pygot, and Joan, this is my friend from the keep, Merel," Jayne said. We both nodded in greeting.

"What a magnificent robe! You shall stay warm in that, I'll wager!" Joan stroked the soft velvet. "Lovely."

"I'm feeling weary of a sudden. Forgive me," Jayne said. "I must sleep."

"I'll stay with her," Joan said.

I knew there was work to be done at the keep, and I should hurry back to help Elinor in the kitchen, but I'd not roamed Rathbarry's corners since Lady Carey had left the castle. How I missed my tasks of sketching pictures for her. How I missed such pleasant daily life without fear or threat. I needed a few minutes, instead of rushing back to the keep, to walk through the garden ward, to feel clean air in my lungs, to smell the earth, to gaze at the open sky. When I reached the west wall, all the shooting coming from the northeast seemed distant. I'd be out of range if I climbed to the top of the west curtain wall from my daily routes. I climbed the tower at the wall's midpoint, hearing each footfall within the cold, dark spiral.

Near the top, I discovered a resting room for the sentries, with a fire grate. There must have been a table and chairs, but they would have been taken for the new battlement. Not far from the grate was a garderobe—a place for the men to relieve themselves without being exposed to musket shot. I sat on the cold stones with my back against its door. Had I known of this place I might have spent time here, or brought my mattress up the steps to live here, away from Mistress Dorothy. The guns ceased, and I closed my eyes to let the silence envelope me. I allowed my shoulders to slump, my belly to relax, my hands to uncoil.

What if this was the last part of my life? What if illness or hunger should claim me soon, or a stray musket ball should find me, and this would be the last time I'd climb a stair, or feel the smooth stones beneath me? Today I could take my very last breath, and if so, what had my life been for? I would simply cease, plucked off the flock like the slowest bird, gone. I'd done nothing to honor my parents, and had no children to carry on. I'd be so much dust, whisked into the wind, sure to be forgotten. Mistress Dorothy would miss me only until she replaced me. Ty would miss me, and Jayne. I would miss them, and I'd miss Rathbarry, too—her beauty, the trees, the life of all kinds that surrounded her. Beyond that, I could die without much notice, to float like a dandelion seed, land in some completely different place and start again. If I might soon die, I may as well feel the wind in my face and see the sway of the trees one last time.

I climbed to the top to peer over the curtain wall. The sky was a cold and dull blue-gray. To the west was the open field, muddy and barren, and beyond it the forest that grew between the castle and the inlet at Ross. Most of the leaves had fallen, making the forest appear as barren as the field. Not a single bird fluttered nor made its sound. The gunfire had made sure of that. Its smell lingered and mixed with the faint wisps of sea salt. The tumbling waves reflected the gray sky and then broke to sugar-white foam. I peered down to the bottom of the curtain wall, thirty feet or more to the rocky surface on which Rathbarry'd stood for centuries, covered here and there with dirt and moss, the curs curled beside the jutting shaft of the garderobe. She would survive, dear Rathbarry, even if all within her perished. She'd stand forever and we would be part of her everlasting story.

I barely slept that night, my mind alive with thoughts, images, memories, and questions. In the morning, after settling a surly Mistress Dorothy to her scant breakfast, I sought Sir Arthur.

49

Intent

Rathbarry Castle

Perhaps no one could hear them arguing, not with the musket fire exploding about the castle, but Tynan's shouts matched Captain Beecher's in volume and intensity surely to rival the firearms.

Beecher came to the stables alone but in uniform, his chest puffed out with authority. "I come on requisition, to obtain four horses from the stable, O'Daly, and as soon as possible. Choose them yourself if you wish, but we need them promptly."

"Aye, and what for?" Tynan asked, even though he knew.

"For the slaughter. The men need meat. And lots of it. We're fighting for our lives on those battlements, and fighting for your life as well, and everyone here. The horses must be sacrificed that our men maintain their strength. The garrison will see to the butchering."

"Aye, meat is in short supply, but there's other food to be had and as long as that's so, ye'll no be gettin' it here."

"We shall. Now stand aside and I'll choose them myself. You know as well as I there is no other meat in the castle, unless you'd have us eating our own dead."

Tynan winced at the thought of such a thing, but stood firm and blocked Beecher's path. "My duty is to care for and protect these horses. I'll no be givin' them up to you, and I'll cut yer throat to save 'em if ye try ta force me."

Beecher's face swelled. "The men need meat! Sir Arthur has permitted it, and so you cannot stop me. To do so is *treason*."

Tynan jutted his chin, clenched his teeth, set his shoulders wide and his fist at his sheath. "Then let it be *treason*," he said slowly, meaning every bit of menace he could summon. Beecher's eyes faltered and he slowly reared back. Captain Beecher was an accomplished cavalryman, but on the ground the odds were with him, Tynan, a skirmisher deadly with a skean.

He smirked as Beecher leapt up the steps of the keep. Let him run, the tattling bastard. Sure, he'd overstepped his authority and the incident only marked the beginning of the conflict. They'd keep coming, day after day, the men from the garrison; lusting for flesh from the same fleet animals that had been their companions, their work mates, their means of defense and attack, their recreation, and for him, his life's work. Human survival would always come first, yes, but these horses would be redefined as food supply only when nothing else remained. He'd fight it to the death. He'd said as much, and Beecher—and Sir Arthur, too— knew it was no boast.

And so, it was not much of a surprise that morning to see Sir Arthur heading toward him, looking pale and dour, his frame nearly lost within the folds of his clothes. Tynan continued working, the brisk September wind having returned to the stables the debris he'd swept away the night before.

"Mister O'Daly," Sir Arthur said.

"Aye, good morning to ye, Sir Arthur," Tynan answered.

Sir Arthur blanched. "Such a pleasantry seems foreign to me now. We've not had a good morning for some several days."

Tynan allowed a sardonic grin, and waited.

"I never imagined I should come to you with any request beyond pleasure or business, Ty. I never foresaw such a cold destruction to the happy life at Rathbarry."

"Nor I, sir."

"I've come to thank you for delivering the horses to the garrison. We had no choice, truly, and must keep our soldiers well or we will be finished. They must have the best of the meat, as is their right."

"Sir..."

"I need not trouble you with details, but our situation becomes dire, for ourselves and the other tenants. My wife is quite needful in her state, many of the refugees have taken ill, and some of our servants as well. Our cook is in tears this morn', for her larder is bare. I shan't explain further, I..."

"Sir Arthur, I must stop ye. I delivered no such thing to Captain Beecher. I assumed he'd ha' told ye by now. Not while there's breath within me, I won't. My job is ta care for the horses, sir, not to offer 'em up on a platter for the butcher."

Sir Arthur stepped back. "O'Daly! I authorized this yesterday. It was no easy consideration, but we can't have starving men on the scaffolds wielding guns."

Tynan shook his head. "Not to defy you or your authorization, sir, but we need the horses as much as the men. Beecher himself has used them when he seized back some of your livestock. Beside that, the garrison's need seems a might inflated. Except for a few of Forbes' men—who were sick when they got here—the soldiers are at least as fit as you or I. It's harvest time and we still have apples and pears in the orchard. Some broth in our pots. The trout will be of size and we ought devise a way to net them out. But the horses? Are we giving up? Sacrificing what we're meant to protect?"

Sir Arthur heaved a deep, weary sigh and rubbed his hand against his forehead. Tynan waited for his reply, standing firm before him. Sir Arthur had purchased most of the horses himself. He knew each one. Sure it was hard enough for him to have made such a decision, but Tynan meant to make it much harder. He tapped Sir Arthur's shoulder. "Ye must see Sarcen, sir."

When they stood at the opening to his stall, Sarcen turned a wide circle and bowed his head in greeting. He stepped toward Sir Arthur and pressed his muzzle into his owner's hand. Sir Arthur could not suppress a smile, and stroked Sarcen's forelock. "He's looking for a carrot, and I've none to give. Is he well?"

"Well, like the rest," Tynan said. "He's hungry, sir, and more than a bit confused. But he's far from the likes of a cow. These horses are smart. They've been finely trained. They'll look ye in the eye, isna that so? It's too large an investment to turn a horse to chuck and flank."

"Sir Arthur?" Merel stepped up behind him and they both turned to look at her. Her hair was wind-blown and her visage somewhat ruddy and bright with purpose.

"In a moment, Merel." Sir Arthur faced Tynan. "His legs. Do they retain their strength?"

"He is as the others. He needs more exercise, and he contemplates eating the walls of his stall. If we could just..."

"Sir. Ty. I beg forgiveness, but I must tell Sir Arthur that..."

Sir Arthur stiffened. "Merel! Truly? Do you not see I'm in conversation with my horse marshal? Wait by the keep and I'll be there presently," Sir Arthur said.

She started to step back but instead set herself between him and Sir Arthur. "I've found a way out. I could get a message out," she blurted.

That drew the attention of both men. Tynan stepped back to look at her. She was as serious as ever he'd seen her, eyes flashing with intent.

"What...what are you talking about?" Sir Arthur asked, impatience clear in his strained voice.

"A way out, sir. It is small, but so am I. There is a garderobe shaft in the west tower. It has space enough, if you lower me down by a rope, I could run to the next castle to get help."

Tynan was taken aback. She must be off her head. She's talking nonsense, and it was a dangerous thing for Sir Arthur to hear. He'd think she was ill, losing her mind.

"Don't be silly, Merel. I would never entertain such a thing, to send you directly into danger, and by way of a garderobe, certainly not. Return to Mistress Dorothy, she quite likely needs your attention." He turned further away from her as if to block her out, but she pressed herself between them again.

"Sir, I'm quite serious. I've looked at the shaft. It's two feet wide, maybe half as much deep. I can get through it with ease, and I know I can get out. It is far from the trenches where the army is concentrated. I'll dress in dark clothing, keep to the woods, run to the next castle and never be discovered. I know I can do it. You'll know it, too, when you see the shaft. There is light at the bottom..."

Sir Arthur paused and sucked in a deep breath. "This is madness. We have all gone mad."

"Please! If you'll just come and look. I wouldn't dare to insist if I wasn't sure." Merel said.

His shoulders dropped. "All right, if it will satisfy you, then let's have a look. Quickly."

"Sir Arthur, you couldn't possibly...she couldn't..." Tynan said.

"West tower? Come along, Ty, if only to convince Merel of her folly," Sir Arthur said.

Ty walked in silence behind them. Merel led the way in a determined march. At the tower, they ascended the steep stairway to the guard room. Sir Arthur looked from wall to wall. "It's been some time since I've been up here. Fortified for an attack from the west, and we are hounded from the east. I'd forgotten it had a garderobe."

"Yes, sir." Merel opened the narrow door to reveal the wooden seat with the hole cut for eliminations. "It doesn't get much use, so it seems," she said.

Sir Arthur lifted the wooden panel. "No," he agreed. "The size is as you described it, and there is a sliver of light at the bottom. There may be some stones in front of it, or other..."

"Forgive me, Sir Arthur, but you can't possibly be thinking of sending her down that shaft. What if she fell? What if she got stuck? And even if she's to survive the shaft, she's to crawl through excrement at the bottom, and mayhap be attacked by the curs, shot at by the army, hunted by wolves." Tynan's face turned darker red with each word he said, and Sir Arthur's brows furrowed.

"...or other debris blocking the way, as I was about to say," Sir Arthur said, his voice growing harsh.

"Come up to the wall, and you can see where the shaft lets out, and the grounds to the west," Merel said, ignoring Tynan.

They climbed the last several steps to the castle wall and looked down. "It seems there's nothing large blocking the shaft's opening." Sir Arthur scratched the back of his neck and nodded.

"And look, sir. It's a short run across the field to the wood. I know my way about there, and could move quickly."

"Merel, I know you're proficient at going unnoticed. And I know you're fond of the forests and fields. But it is some distance between here and the next castle that isn't under Irish control. It's more than ten miles to Glandore, the next castle after Ross, and that's in a straight line, but you'd have to cross through hedge and ditch and bog, and get around Rosscarbery Bay, all without being discovered. It is impossible."

"Sir, I know how to do it, the route I would take and…"

"It's impossible, Merel. Besides, Mistress Dorothy needs you now, in her condition."

"I'll do it, sir. I'll go," Tynan said, actually surprising himself, blurting the offer without any thought.

Sir Arthur looked as if he'd been physically shoved backward. Merel's jaw dropped open, and as she closed it her eyes darkened along with her cheeks. She glared at Tynan as if he'd committed the severest betrayal.

"I will, sir. I'm Irish, which has obvious advantages, but also I know these lands like I know my own stables. I can make my way swiftly. I'd sheltered and helped by the native folk. I could get to Glandore faster than Merel, and if I have to fight for my life, I damned well know how to do it. If you send a woman and she is captured, you know what would become of her."

Sir Arthur nodded. "It is a sad truth."

"But Sir Arthur, my size," Merel insisted. "Quick and shadowy movement is the one advantage to being small. And, I'm neither Irish nor English, I'm no one's enemy and would be welcomed anywhere. This is the one thing I can do for Rathbarry that could save her."

Sir Arthur looked down on her like a father to a misguided child. "You're a clever woman, to have found the shaft, and to have brought me the idea. We will test it first, and see if the shaft is sound. It is quite honorable that you so wish to do this thing, but I must go with Ty on this, Merel. He is right. It is not a woman's journey."

Merel's face paled. She barely breathed and would not meet Tynan's eyes, but instead turned her head toward the distant trees and gazed into the clouds above them. She pinched the skin between her thumb and pointing finger.

"Now then, do we have enough rope left for this?"

"Yes, sir. In the stables. I'll fetch it," Tynan said.

"We could do a test this afternoon. And if it works, you could leave tonight. Who should care for the horses while you're gone?" Sir Arthur asked.

"Certainly not Beecher, but David Hyrst. He's a good lad."

"And if the horses need protection again?"

"I can only hope that will come from you, sir. I'll be gone but a few days, and then we'll have hope of relief. The horses need no' be sacrificed if we can bear up a wee bit longer."

Sir Arthur nodded, a sad half-smirk upon his lips. "I need to speak with the guard at the corner tower. I'll meet you back here at, shall we say, two o'clock to test the shaft."

"Yes, sir." Tynan said. He descended the tower with Merel just before him. They walked together in silence until they reached the arch leading into the garrison ward, then he turned toward the stables. "It's for the best, you know, Merel. I did it for your safety. If anything happened to you, I honestly could not bear it..."

"And the same for me, should something happen to you, Ty. We both must take our risks. But it was my discovery, my idea, my plan, intended for me, not you," she said.

"You only want to escape the castle, to escape the siege."

"That's right. I want to escape. And at the same time, do something useful rather than fetch this and that for a pregnant shrew."

"Could be I've saved ye from horrors ye cannot imagine. I hate to even speak it, but ye could be raped, beaten, imprisoned, even killed. The thought of you injured, or dying alone out there..."

"Ty, I am dying in here. I thought you understood, but you don't. The only thing that restores me is being out there. And now you've robbed me of it."

He fell silent, staring at the ground, at the jagged rivulets where rainwater had stripped away the soft sand. His cheeks grew hot, and likely staining as they did when he was angry, like bruises tinged with crimson. He shook his head. Nay matter what she said, he couldna stand by and watch her drop from a rope into—and call it what it was—shit. And only the worse to encounter once she crawled her way out of it. "In any case, I'll only be gone a few days."

"Oh? And how shall you get back into the castle when you return? Will you kill all your kinsmen and then dance the Courante through the main gate, and be welcomed as Rathbarry's hero?"

Tynan reared back, as if he'd taken a mighty slap. "I wonder, ha' your hours with Mistress Dorothy been a bit too instructive."

Her eyes narrowed. "And I wonder, have you noticed, sir, that I have a mind of my own?" Merel hurried up the steps into the keep. Jenkin closed the door.

50

The Shaft

Rathbarry Castle

At two o'clock, Tynan climbed to the west tower guard room, a sack slung over his shoulder holding a thick, heavy rope. Merel was there ahead of him. Sir Arthur was late, leaving them alone together in a cold tension. He dropped the sack to the floor, forcing a sizeable puff of dust upward. He watched it settle back again to the floor.

"Are ye all right?" Tynan finally asked. She shrugged at him and peered out the arrow slits that allowed a dim gray light. So this was how it would be, eh? She'll no longer speak, nor have anathin' to do wi' him. Here was he, riskin' his life to protect her, so as not to lose her, and he was to lose her anaways because he'd made her angry. Well, it was too late to change what was planned. He'd no mind to change it even if he could. He might only hope she'd have joy for him when he returned, and forgive what he'd done, see the reason in it.

Sir Arthur arrived, bringing with him two strong men he'd selected from the garrison. The four of them set to examining the garderobe shaft, while Merel watched from the opposite wall, her face grim.

"We'll just secure the rope at his waist, and down he goes," one of the soldiers said.

"Maybe we ought send the rope down first, see if it's long enough or if it could snag on something," said the other.

"Yes, I agree. Quite." Sir Arthur said. "Proceed."

Tynan dumped the rope from the sack to the slate floor, disturbing more dust, and the soldiers hefted it toward the shaft. "Tie it off up here first, just in case it should be dropped. If we lose this rope we don't have another," he said.

They tied it around a support post at the center of the room and cast the rope down. It fluffed and fluttered and scraped as it went, but landed quickly being of such weight, giving a considerable jerk to the post. They all flinched at the solid snap when it reached the bottom. Merel smiled with haughty satisfaction.

"There seems to be more than enough rope to get you all the way down," Sir Arthur said. "I suggest we tie you about the waist first, and then fix a harness at your shoulders to keep you upright."

"Aye, sir. Shall we?"

The men wrapped the rope about Tynan's waist, then up around his shoulders, knotting it to an inverted 'v' above his head. "Now the sack," Tynan said. "I'll have it between me knees."

"What is in it?" Sir Arthur asked.

"Hammer and chisel, sir, should I find the opening too small at the bottom."

"Of course. Carry on."

Tynan climbed into the shaft, facing out so that he wouldn't have to turn around in the narrow space. The soldiers let the rope out slowly at first. The stench was not bad, but worsened as he descended. The enclosure seemed tighter than expected, and too coffin-like for his comfort. He shook off the anxiety, held his sleeve over his nose and mouth and called up to the men. "Faster." They reeled out the rope more quickly as his weight drew toward the earth. He was eager to make acquaintance with the rectangle of light at the bottom.

Here the stench was diminished, exposed to the open air, but the filth and scum had accumulated in heavy layers. Had he piled up horse manure in a corner for more than a decade, it would be no worse. The opening, as he'd feared, was not intended for egress of a man's body. It was plenty wide, but the lower shaft angled outward and then dropped about two feet to the ground. He chiseled away years of refuse narrowing the passage. With that done, Merel was right, she'd have had an easier time of it. He'd get through well enough, but he'd have to strip naked to do it, then pull his clothes through behind him.

He gave a sharp tug on the rope and the soldiers heaved him up the shaft again, with greater difficulty. They were nearly out of breath when he climbed from the shaft, and so was he, having held his breath for most of the way. Once in the light again, it was clear how badly he was soiled and stinking. Sir Arthur nodded grimly, and Merel's eyes widened, then she smirked and turned away.

"It can be done, sir. Tonight. Merel deserves the honor for finding the shaft and bringing her idea to you."

"That she does, Ty. I'll write letters for you to present. We'll want to secure them inside your doublet. You'll go straight to Glandore. The two castles before her are Irish owned and unlikely to help me. Clean up and see Elinor about something to take with you. We'll meet again at dusk, so that we don't need torches."

Merel hurried down the steps ahead of the others, and disappeared into the garden ward. In the state he was in, he could hardly chase after her. He went to the stables and used sand and a horse brush to clean his clothes. It was less than efficient but better than nothing. He found the cleanest and darkest horse blanket to take with him, for as luck would have it the weather was turning cold. Elinor fed him hot broth and gave him a bladder of water and some dried apples to carry. He could make it last a day, at least.

They all met at the appointed time. The soldiers secured the rope around him again while Sir Arthur offered advice, gave him coins and letters, told him what to say when he reached Glandore, and chattered nervously about the various people he might encounter. Merel arrived late, just before he was to climb into the shaft. The light was quickly fading. The soldiers wished him Godspeed.

"Good luck to you," Sir Arthur shook his hand. "and God protect you. Come home to us safely."

"Aye, sir." Tynan put his sack between his knees and took one last look at Merel. She stood distant from him, her hair hanging long in unwashed strings, her skirt and apron dingy and stained, her face streaked with tears, and never before had she looked more beautiful. Though she wept, he couldn't be sure whether she was sad to see him go, or sad because she was not in his place. He nodded farewell. What he did was good and right: he'd get help and the people in the castle would be delivered; Merel would be safe. He turned his back to the room and dropped into the darkness.

When he reached bottom, he had just enough light to map in his mind the shortest route to the woods, the distance of the Irish camp, the distance to the bog, and the direction to the short strand and the sea beyond. The darkness soon overtook him. He started, suddenly wondering why the curs didn't come for him. Sir Arthur must have found a way to distract them to another part of the curtain wall. He'd be wise to move out as quickly as possible. In as much silence as he could manage, he crept toward the bog where he'd find a better view of his surroundings.

He was rewarded almost immediately. A small flash told him where a sentry was stationed, as the soldier struck a match to light his tobacco. The first one to the southeast, guarding any approach to the camp; the second to the southwest, at the edge of the forest, and then finally a third to the northwest, directly across the open field from the west tower, where the old cabins once stood. His shortest and clearest path to the wood was a straight line west.

He waited until his gut told him the time was right, and then crawled on his belly across the field. The forest itself was equally dangerous, for only God knew what woodkernes might be hiding there. He pushed through the thick of it, over and under as the situation called, his skean in hand, and when he came to a clearing, the Owenahinchy river lay before him. He could wade across, but make himself an easy target by doing so. He found a crossing with the most cover, and crouched low to cross. From there, wet and sandy as he was, he kept to the shoreline and the darkest bluffs to the Ross inlet. The narrowest crossing point here was well known. He crossed instead at the strand where he was favored by a low tide.

On the peninsula at Droumgunna he found a small cave in which to rest. He closed his eyes but for a few moments, and must have fallen asleep. He hadn't realized how tiring the effort had been. Had the cold surge of the incoming tide not awakened him, he might have drowned there. He climbed to the top of the bluff, wet from the waist down, still with two miles between him and Glandore. He made his way to the standing stones at Drombeg, mostly avoided by the Irish who believed it bad luck to disturb them. He rested again and prayed the stones might protect him just this one night, for his mission was honorable. Even so, he left a coin atop the altar stone, and crossed the last hilly mile to Glandore.

51

Quite a Predicament

Glandore and Castlehaven

Tynan hid in a thicket as the first bits of morning light outlined the keep's twin towers and the square guard towers with battlements. A chill seized the back of his neck as his surroundings came into focus. Not far to the southwest the smoke of campfires rose into the mist. No livestock roamed the castle yard; no bustle of activity emitted from the gates. It was as if he faced Rathbarry just before the musket firing began and all of the people were sealed within its walls. Glandore wouldn't be able to offer the relief he sought. Still, he must get to the castle and deliver Sir Arthur's message.

He waited the better part of the morning until a group of boys ran out to collect grasses near the castle gate. He caught their attention, waved his letters to show he was a messenger, and they rushed him inside the walls. They escorted him to a hall where several Englishmen were arguing. None answered to the name on the letter Sir Arthur had given him.

He interrupted their heated discourse which made little sense to him. "Sirs, if ye please. Sir Arthur Freke has sent me ta ask your help. 'Tis clear ye face troubles of your own, but..."

"You are Irish! I hear it. Who let you into the castle? Who are you?" An agitated man questioned. Alarm was building in the room until he wondered would he find more safety in the field.

"Sirs! I come on behalf of Sir Arthur Freke. I have a letter. Please read it. The situation of Rathbarry is dire. Without relief our people all will die." Two men held Tynan by his arms as a third man, perhaps the oldest in the room and the least troubled by his arrival, sat down and read the letter. "I'm acquainted with Sir Arthur. I believe you're who you say you are, and I'm sorry for your difficulties. The sad truth is as you have witnessed. We've naught to give you, son, and no relief to send. Our supplies are dwindling and our danger vast. We await relief from Lord Inchiquin. Should he not arrive soon we shall fall to the same circumstance as Rathbarry. Have you any coin on you?"

"Only a bit, sir," Tynan said, wary of the question.

The man nodded. "If you have coin, my boy will take you through the souterrain and down to the bay. There is a cottage by the shore, and a couple of fellows there who'll take you to Castlehaven. You would see Mr. Salmon, the sovereign there, and he might be able to help. We can rest you here with a bit of gruel and beer, but as soon as darkness comes, I suggest you go from here as fast as you've come."

He welcomed the food and drink. Small though it be, it gave him strength to continue his journey by night. At dusk the boy led him into the dark souterrain. Tynan held his skean in his hand as they moved through the narrow corridor. At any time someone could cut his throat in the pitch-darkness, seize what little he had, and dump his body into the sea. His heart thudded in his chest with each step they descended. But the boy was true, and the souterrain opened into a cave by the ocean, the moonlight flashing on a wave beyond. A small fishing boat rested on the sand. A teenage boy sat beside it, and in front of an old plank fishing shack a man dozed under a tarpaulin.

"Name o' Buck," the elder said. "This here, Rowan," he gestured toward the lad.

Tynan had four shillings left. Buck shook his head. Wouldn't budge for one, and showed little more interest for two. It required all that he had, plus begging and then threats until the man agreed to make the journey. Tynan insisted on leaving immediately, and pushed the boat off the strand even as Buck and Rowan were gathering up the oars.

The darkness set in soon after. Passage was slow against the surf, but the current seemed to favor them once they entered the bay. The sea wind lifted his hair and filled his lungs, fortifying his courage and feeding his sense of purpose. The waning moon allowed him to keep the coastline in view, and this was critical, for they had three great headlands to pass, all with jagged, rocky edges. At the last turn into Castlehaven's inlet, the west wind picked up and threatened to push the boat against a tiny rock island. Buck was tired, his strength failing, and Rowan couldn't keep the boat from veering without his father's counterbalance. Tynan grabbed the older man's oar though Buck grumbled resistance like a sore old dog.

"Ye old bastard," Tynan scowled. "I paid ye a fortune and ha' to do the work meself?"

He helped the boy power the little craft around the bend until the winds were blocked by the bluff and the way came easier. The castle's black battlements came into view against the deep blue sky. There was no strand, but a small mud cove where supply boats might land. Buck took his oar again and heaved until the small bow scraped bottom. The three of them beached the boat for the night, and Tynan bid them goodbye as he climbed the bluff, clinging to the shadows as neared the castle gate.

A scrape and splash sounded. Buck and Rowan shoved off into the channel again. His back seized as if a bucket of cold water had been dashed against it. The cowards! Where were they going in the night? Voices just ahead of him passed back and forth. He dropped to the damp ground and crawled until he could hide behind a rock. Two men were talking, looking for something or someone. The rock was not enough cover. He moved a little further into the brush and came upon a larger rock, lower and wider. He flattened himself behind it, and found a depression in the earth, perhaps a den started by a rabbit or a stoat. He began to widen it, digging as quickly and silently as possible, grateful that the rush and roar of wind and ocean drowned out most sounds, and hoping he'd not discover a badger within.

The voices passed, going down to the cove where the boat had been. He dug furiously into the hole, squeezing himself beneath the rock inch-by-inch. If he were Merel's size, he'd already have been covered. He scratched and dug and pushed himself until at last he could curl like an infant beneath it.

The voices returned. An argument. The men stepped close to the first rock. Had he stayed there he'd have been discovered. He held his breath. The men stopped talking, and one of them said, "Bloody hell."

"Let's get back," the other said. And they walked on, but Tynan remained in his hole, unsure of who the men were, who or what they were looking for, and whether friend or foe. He'd have to wait until dawn for any answers.

He slept in fits, owing to his discomfort and vigilance. By first light, the voices returned. He moved from his nest just enough to see over the edge of the rock. Two men of the watch dressed in Castlehaven livery walked the grounds. Tynan called to them as they approached, and they came at him, muskets aimed.

"I'm sent by Sir Arthur Freke of Rathbarry Castle. I have letters for Lord Castlehaven or Mr. Salmon."

They rushed toward him. One of them jerked him to his feet. "Let's see the letters, then."

Tynan produced them, surprised they were in as good of shape as they were. Wrapped in fabric and concealed in his doublet, they were perhaps beaten about the edges, but not covered in dirt and mud as he was. The men each grabbed one of his arms and escorted him—or rather, heaved him into the castle hall and shoved him to the floor beside Mr. Salmon. The sovereign was eating a breakfast of fish, fruit and wine. Tynan's mouth watered and his stomach cramped.

"Who are you, and what's your business here," Salmon said.

"I'm Tynan O'Daly, horse marshal to Sir Arthur Freke of Rathbarry Castle. He sent me to Glandore, and the men of Glandore sent me to you. Rathbarry is under siege, in sore need for relief, or eighty men and women will starve to death."

"Horse marshal? And yet you come on your knees through the dirt?"

"Aye, sir. The castle is sealed, and under musket fire all day, every day, from the rebel army. It canna hold out much longer."

"You're Irish yourself, what the devil are you doing here? You're lucky we didn't hang you on sight." Salmon wiped his chin.

"I do my duty, sir. I've seen the people of Rathbarry in torment. Men, women, little children. I've no wish to see them die. Can you help us?"

"Well, hardly. It's quite a predicament we're in, isn't it? My Lord Castlehaven does not support the Irish rebellion, but he has committed himself to the Catholic Confederacy, on behalf of King Charles against Parliament. All our resources must be devoted to his needs, and I'm quite sure Sir Arthur and his father are Parliament men."

Tynan shook his head. "Begging your pardon, Mr. Salmon, but no. Sir Arthur is Protestant, not Puritan. He calls upon the kindness of his neighbors for succor. His only interest is the protection of the people within

Rathbarry. Our rations have failed. Few men of the garrison remain to protect us. And Mistress Freke is with child, sir."

"Oh Good God. What a cauldron of fury does stir!" He was silent for several moments, then he looked Tynan over from ragged hair to muddy boot. "At least get him drink, before he collapses upon the flags."

One of the watchmen gestured to a maid who brought him a plate of bread and a small cup of ale. He ate and drank with unconcealed need. Salmon watched, thoughtful.

"I am sorry for your troubles, Mr. O'Daly, but I cannot do anything counter to my lord's wishes. Though you say Sir Arthur is not for Parliament, I'm not so sure. We have little to offer anyway. Rathbarry needs military relief. The best I can do is get you to Kinsale."

"'Tis kind of ye, sir, an' may ye not think I'm ungrateful for it, but we've sent word to Kinsale before, an' the relief they provided left us worse than they found us."

Mr. Salmon frowned. "Ah, yes. I heard about Lord Forbes' visit. He sailed into Castlehaven as well. But he's gone off to help the poor wretches at Galway, and I should think we'll not see more of him in Munster. Give the commanders at Kinsale another try. A ship sails on the outgoing tide this morning. Have you any money?"

"No, sir. I spent my last coin on the boat from Glandore."

"I'll cover your passage, then. That much I can do. My men will escort you to the ship. Fare thee well, young man."

52

Mercy nor Honesty

Rathbarry Castle

I couldn't make Mistress Dorothy rise from her bed. Her arms were skin and bone, and to lift them required strength she refused to muster. Her face was pale, her hair dull and tangled. Her lips had lost the soft pink of health until they were nearly gray. Yet somehow the babe continued to grow, extending the mistress's belly slightly more as the days of September passed—and her seventh month. "I am the vase of water," she said, "and my growing little weed sucks me dry."

Each day Sir Arthur sacrificed part of his rations for her, and she had stopped refusing it. But one morning, as he walked the castle walls just before the musket firing began, Sir Arthur's legs collapsed beneath him. Captain Beecher brought him back to his feet and walked him to the keep. I'd just come into the hall to fetch the mistress's breakfast.

"I'll not be taken to bed," Sir Arthur said. Jenkin and I helped him into a chair at the hall table and stood by while Elinor forced him to drink a cup of cold, thin broth.

"You sacrifice your own strength for others," Captain Beecher said, sitting down beside him. "It is wrong thinking. We all need you. Without you we might as well give ourselves up to the slaughter this very day. You are the lifeblood for Rathbarry. Our backbone. Do not desert us now."

"It seems I said similar words to you not so long ago."

"That you did, and here I remain. You were right. I was needed. But never so much as you."

Sir Arthur dropped his chin to his chest. "Dorothy begs for milk," he said. "Such a small request, and I cannot give it. Not one drop. She wastes away before me. Only God knows what is happening to the baby. I fear it could be stillborn." His eyes glistened with tears he couldn't restrain. "Walk me to the battlements. I must prostrate myself to John Oge Barry."

"We are surrendering?" Beecher asked. "You can't mean that. We still have..."

"No, no! I will not surrender. But Barry has a wife; he must be a father. He should have mercy on a mother and child. I will try to bargain with him, appeal to his charity."

"Charity!" Beecher said.

"You finish every drop of that broth, Sir Arthur. I won't have folk around the castle say I didn't look after ye!" Elinor said.

"My bargain with you, Elinor, is that I'll swallow this if you'll bring me something stronger."

"Wait! I know where it is," I said, and bounded up to the stateroom to fetch his hidden bottle.

Elinor poured a shot and handed it to him with a wink. "There's yer strength back, sir."

Sir Arthur drank and looked to me. "Not a word to Dorothy. Do I have your promise?"

"You do. I promise."

Captain Beecher stood. "All right now." He helped Sir Arthur to his feet and steadied him until the square of his shoulders returned.

"Come," Sir Arthur said. He referred to Captain Beecher, but Jenkin, Elinor and I followed as well, to watch Sir Arthur slowly mount the steep and wobbly stairs of the wooden battlements and call down to the Irish trench.

"John Oge Barry," he shouted—and to my ears, with a lion's strength.

A few moments passed without movement or sound, and then came a return. "I am here, Captain Freke. What say you? Will ye now surrender?" He stepped from one of the shooting houses near the trench, looking every bit as worn as Sir Arthur.

"Ah, Mr. Barry. Good morn to you. Before the day grows older, there is one thing I beg of you. Just one thing. My wife has taken ill, and she being with child is in dire need of milk. I beg you for her sake and the babe, just one pint of milk."

There came no response at all. Only silence. Others came out of the shooting house to stand beside Barry.

"Mister Barry," Sir Arthur called out. "You are a father who must have compassion for an unborn child. I will pay for this milk with money or goods. Name your price, sir."

Several minutes of silence followed, and then Barry returned. "Your goods are mine already, ye've nothin' to offer."

"Then I shall forgive your debt to my father, that has lingered over your head this past fourteen years," Sir Arthur said. "Fourteen years since, in your necessity, my father in London generously filled your pocket. Do you recall? Twenty-three pounds, it was. The debt will be wiped away, for a mere pint of milk."

Again there was only silence for several minutes, until a last a man's voice carried over the walls. "Ye shall receive nothin' from the Irish, ye rogues! Ye devils! Ye Parliament dogs! Not a single drop, an' it's more than ye've ever done for me."

Sir Arthur stood on the battlement for a few more minutes, as still and stiff as one of the boards used to build it, until the clear rattle meant muskets were taken up, then came the rumble of movement and officers shouting in the trench. He climbed down to the courtyard again, his face ashen, his shoulders once again sagging but even worse than before.

"Sir, for that we'll give them a pounding today—the likes they have never seen," Captain Beecher said.

"Thank you. For that he shall deserve it. May God send down a lightning bolt to pierce his putrid heart."

Two days later, the sentries shouted with such urgency, all who could hear rushed to the courtyard. One of the men reported to Sir Arthur. "On the hill, sir. The Irish. Hundreds of 'em, with colors flying. They're comin' for us!"

Sir Arthur ran to the tower and mounted the battlement, Captain Beecher close behind him with the spyglass. The sentries remained still and ready.

Every person who could still walk crowded into the court. We huddled near each other and waited anxiously. None could hear the words that passed on that high wall. We had to wait for Sir Arthur to speak, and we dreaded it.

"They're come for us," a woman in the court cried. "They'll overrun us. And no quarter. Didn't they say? Didn't they warn us? *No quarter!* They'll kill us, all. The children, too!"

Behind her, other women screamed, and some—women and men—fell to their knees begging God's forgiveness and deliverance. Then came the banging on the gate. A messenger with a letter.

"Tell him to drop it and go," Sir Arthur shouted to the gatekeeper. "We'll not open the gate to him."

The sentry brought the message to Sir Arthur who started into the keep to read it, but then returned to the steps. He stood wide-legged before the crowd. "Good people of Rathbarry, you may as well hear the contents of this letter while we are all together, for we are in this fight together. Stand firm, and keep clear and foremost in your head that we cannot expect kindness, mercy nor honesty from this enemy." He peeled open the folded paper.

"It is from the Irish leader, John Oge Barry. Mr. Barry seems to think we are in our extremity. Because I asked for milk a few days ago—the smallest request for my poor wife and unborn child, which he then cruelly refused—he assumes we are ready and willing to surrender our home and our lives to him. More so, he writes that we must deliver Rathbarry to his army now, else it will ruin us. His soldiers are on the east, north and west of us, and on the south we are bounded by the lough. He says he will ruin the entire barony if we allow an English garrison to remain here any longer, and if we do not swiftly answer.

"I beg you to hear me now. What mercies have our enemies shown? Who among you has not been shot at, starved or terrorized by this army of rogues? How many have we buried here who knew no mercy?"

There was only silence from the people, many of their faces streaming with tears.

"How then, shall we answer Mr. Barry?"

The woman who had spoken out days earlier whimpered, but she quickly silenced, and no other sound came but the rattle and clap of muskets being mounted against shoulders. "By gunfire," Captain Beecher called out. "We answer by gunfire! Lead us, Sir Arthur!"

Sir Arthur drew his gaze from one side of the court to the other. "Positions," he said.

The men raced up to the battlements, and the women behind them bringing powder and shot. The children in the court were set to hauling water. Jayne, who had recovered enough to leave her bed, joined me to help some of the women set up a nursing station, with drinking water and bandages from torn sheets and blankets.

On Sir Arthur's word, the men fired into the trench and into the cottages, and fired into the distance toward the line of soldiers. They sent a thunderous shot from the cannon into the field. Men poured from the trench and ran for distance from the guns. They wailed and cried out that we should never have quarter.

No one expected it. The level of fear within the castle climbed to a higher rung, but it was used to fuel our resolve. Women divided into small groups and set a rotation so that no hour would pass without fervent prayer in the chapel. The days progressed as they had before with gunfire all day long, and there being no end to it but in death or in hope—small as it might be—that relief would finally come.

In the meantime, we still had to eat. Elinor managed whatever she could from the fruits, roots, and edible weeds people scavenged within the castle. We brought the horses whatever thatch remained on our rooftops, and then bed mats made of straw. Yet some of them were so starved as to eat their own dung.

53

Light that Fell

Rathbarry Castle

Michaelmas brought a chill to late September. In the intervals between gunfire, Jayne and I wrapped ourselves in blankets and scoured the castle walls for any new growth or old dead stalks on which the horses could feed. We'd walked the west wall, the garden ward, and worked eastward around the stables. We discovered sprouts behind the plum orchard. We dug and pulled and dropped them into buckets, and yet they seemed only a mouthful for a starving horse.

We labored painfully, Jane weakened by her disease, and I by frequent nightmares. Weeks had passed without word from Ty, nor anything from Glandore Castle.

"I don't believe he's killed, Jayne. He's a survivor," I said, and I meant it, "but every night I see him dying alone in a ditch, chained and suffering in some castle prison, or hanging from a tree. I am frightened for him, and can think of little else. Why is there no message, and still no relief? Why doesn't he come back? If another day passes, those garrison soldiers will slaughter every last horse. Sometimes I nearly want to kill one myself, my hunger is so great."

"He mus' be stranded somewhere. We can't know, but one thing I'm sure of, Merel. He'll do anathing to come back for you."

I tried to smile. What if I never should see him again? I shook the idea from my head. I couldn't think of such things or I'd break apart. "I'm still mad at him."

"Of course ye are."

We worked our way to the southeast tower. The thick branches of the plum trees crossed over us like a large woven net. Jayne spied a patch of ground elder sprouting against the doorway to the tower. "Merel! Look here." She pointed inside the tower to a speck of light that fell on a lower step descending to the old delivery shutter, the one Sir Arthur had sealed after the escape of the Irish prisoners.

We looked at each other, set down our buckets, and followed the steps down. Near the level of my knee, a sliver light shone through a rather untidy application of mortar, in the very passage we'd used that night.

I whispered. "The mason made a mistake. The mortar is weak, and he missed a spot. Do you think we might try..."

"Wait here." Jayne ran up the steps with an energy I'd not have expected, and returned after a few minutes with her hands in her pockets. She pulled out two hoof picks taken from the stables. I grabbed one and scraped at the sliver to see if I could widen it. In no time at all, one inch became two.

"Jayne!" I gasped and moistened my lips. "If...if we could open this enough, I could creep out at night to dig up those cabbages and get more grass and maybe even haul up some trout and..."

"I know what yer thinking, and stop it. Stay with the food. It's what we need, and ye must help Mistress Dorothy."

"I know."

"Ye must watch over her."

"It's true."

"And there's the baby."

"Yes. The baby." I tilted my head toward the opening. "Help me work on this and we'll see how much we can cut away. We can take turns until it's just wide enough that I can squeeze through. I promise I won't leave Rathbarry, Jayne. Not yet."

Jayne returned a half-smile.

"We need a hammer, a mallet, a chisel, or failing that a screwdriver," I said. "Something to crumble this mortar faster than a hoof pick, without alerting anyone until we see if it will work. It must be kept secret or it will cause a stir. People might try to get out, and the army could discover it. Agreed?"

"Yes, of course. Don' I always keep yer secrets? An' you with a few o' mine?" Jayne said. "I'll go look in the stable again. Those fellas left a mess of things after buildin' up the battlements. Fer the use o' my door, ye'd think they owe me a chisel."

She stood to go, but then her face suddenly paled. She sat down on a step, the perspiration glistening on her forehead.

"Oh Jayne, you are still not well. Let me get you back to your bed."

"No. Just let me be. This will pass, and I'll work on the gap. You go search in the stable."

I picked up my bucket and ran out of the tower doorway as soon as the courtyard was clear. The stable smelled not of sweet, fresh hay, but of mildew, horse dung, old rotting wood, and musk. Collum's head bobbed in a stall at the opposite end. I went first to Sarcen. He stood in the shadowy corner of his stall, his head hanging down and his ears not perked as they usually were, but pushed back like those of a beaten dog. I hugged him around the neck and gave him the contents of my basket. "Not much longer, my friend. I promise. You and I will survive, won't we? And I'll look after you." He allowed a soft puff from his nostrils, and I left him to search for the tools, which I found scattered haphazardly across a mud-caked bench. I grabbed two chisels and two hammers and tucked them into my bucket. I hurried toward the court and ran straight into David Hyrst's chest, rattling the tools.

"What's wrong?" he asked. "Why such a hurry? Is Jayne not well?"

"She is well. She is waiting for me." I tried to push past him, but he blocked me.

"Where is she? What is going on?"

"Nothing. She's fine. She's in the court and we are pulling up weeds."

He glanced into my bucket. "And for that you need a hammer? Merel. Your cheeks are bright red. What is it? Let me help."

"It's nothing. I can't, I..."

"I'll follow you anyway. You'd better give over."

I sighed and slumped. "It is a very big secret. Do you promise?"

"Do you truly need to ask?"

"All right then, follow me. But no matter your thoughts, you won't be able to stop it."

"Stop what?"

"Just…just wait."

He followed me across the court to the tower, and down the steps until we met Jayne. She looked frightened at first, but then her face softened and she gave a wide smile. "Another conspirator!" she whispered.

We needed no words, only to show him what we had done so far. His eyes widened. He looked at both of us with alarm. His lips parted as if to speak but then he halted, and nodded slightly. "I'll get the adze."

OCTOBER

54

Tangles

Rathbarry Castle

We worked by turns, each of us managing to widen the opening more and more by inches, from the size of a rat hole, to a rabbit hole, and then so much so that I had to find some scrub rags to stuff into it so the light coming through would not attract anyone else. I worked on when Jayne grew tired and David walked her back to her house. David worked while I attended Mistress Dorothy for her supper. By nightfall we had carved out three of the bricks. I could get my head through and more, but then the castle grew quiet. We couldn't continue working because of the noise.

When everyone else retired for the night, I couldn't sleep nor rest. I crept to the tower through the darkness and began again with the hoof picks, quietly scraping and nicking away at the sand-and-lime mortar around the brick edges until my hands were cramping, my back ached, and the tiny bits of moonlight streaming through the opening were not enough to aid my tired eyes. I crept back to my bed.

At dawn I awakened, wanting only to rush down the stairs and back to my work, but Mistress Dorothy had awakened, as well. She groaned with discomfort. She rubbed her swollen belly and began to cry, the tears streaming down her cheeks. "I'll get your dressing gown," I said.

She raised her hands to scratch her head. "No. I want my hair washed today. Go down and get the tub."

It was one of the worst things she could have asked me to do. It would take hours of time and require much water. "Mistress, are you sure? It will be quite hard on you, to lean over the tub, and would use much water from the well. The shooting will begin again in moments, and the men will need the water and buckets on the battlement."

"Oh. Yes, I hadn't thought about that." She paused and I hoped she'd next send me down for her breakfast. "Well then," she said, "you'll have to figure out a way to do it differently. You'll wash my hair today or I'll have Jenkin lock you in the garret until sundown. And don't let me hear you sigh, either."

I ran down the stairs to ask Elinor to take our mistress's breakfast to her, and then out the kitchen door to the laundry, or what was left of it. The thatched roof and trusses had all been stripped away, and all the ropes for hanging sheets and clothing, leaving only piles of debris, scrub brushes, a few broken earthenware bowls, ash and sand that had been dumped from buckets needed elsewhere. I found a large soaking basin, wide but not deep, and Elinor could fill a couple of pitchers with warmed water. But soap! Once there were shelves in the laundry jammed with large chunks of dried or drying lye soap, but now it was all gone, and no way to make it or substitute for it. Elinor gave me a few shreds of apple peel. If nothing else it would scent the water. I dropped them into the pitchers and hoped for the best. I hurried up stairs struggling not to spill.

"Where have you been? I've been waiting, and this room is cold."

"Forgive me, mistress, we must hunt about for supplies these days, but I am ready. Elinor has warmed the water for you. Here, I'll put the basin on the stool. You may sit in your chair and just lean over it."

She lumbered to the chair, sat down with a groan. "I can't lean over it with this belly. I must lean back."

I searched around the room frantically and settled on a bedside table for the basin, and she could lean back against it. I moved her stool and helped her toward it, then put a pillow behind her back. She swatted my hand when I tried to gather the lengths of her hair. "I'll get it," she said, and grasped her locks into a single rope and pulled it behind her head. She covered her face with a linen. "There. I am ready. Hurry up."

I placed a towel around her neck, drizzled the water over her pate, and as the basin began to fill, the ends of her hair floated on the surface. I massaged the water into her scalp and along the sides by her ears. "Your fingers are cold," she said, "but...the water is warm. More." I worked for several minutes until the water began to cool, then wrapped her hair in the towel and we moved her stool close to the fire grate. Then came the arduous combing, inch by inch, lock by lock, to release all the tangles and separate the hair so it could dry.

"My neck is cold."

I put aside her damp towel and rubbed the back of her neck, and then her shoulders tight with anxiety. Soon they began to soften, and I helped her into the dressing gown. The ends of her hair began to dry like silk ribbons, into soft, loose curls. She reached up and pressed my hand against her shoulder.

"You won't try to leave me, will you Merel? You'll stay, won't you, at least until after the baby is born? I can't do it by myself. I need someone I can trust. I'm not afraid to give birth, I've told you that before, but I *am* afraid of helplessness, and of being alone. If something should happen, I mean."

The bile surged into my throat. How could she ask such a thing? Did she somehow know? I *was* going to leave her, and as soon as possible, but I could no more tell her that than I could lift Castle Rathbarry up from her stone foundation and hurl her into the sea. And though I longed for my moment of escape, this woman had cast her golden net about me—a net of false tenderness and guilt—so that even as I ran free from my position and my circumstance, she would still be able to taunt me. My chest tightened until I could barely breathe.

"Of course not," I lied. "Just rest a while, and I'll fix your hair after it dries."

Puddles of water glistened across the wooden planks, and the apple scent seemed sour as I mopped it up with the towel, but the mistress seemed contented, and soon dozed off. That the Irish army was firing at our gate again escaped her notice. It shouldn't matter to her, should it? It was someone else's responsibility.

By the time I returned to the southeast tower, half the day was gone. I hurried down the steps, seeing far more light than had been there before. Jayne was there with David beside her, both of them grinning, but I was disturbed. "David? Won't someone notice you are missing? I'm afraid we might be discovered before we are ready. Sir Arthur should be the first to know of this."

"Yes, I agree," David said, "but we've little time, and I had an idea that could help."

"He widened the hole, sure enough," Jayne said, "and ye can conceal it after a body goes through. I'll show ye."

She pulled on a brick that it was still attached to the one next to it, and also the two bricks below it, and then those were attached to two more below. They had dug out the mortar all around them so that a panel of six bricks could be pulled out as one to make a larger opening, and then could be pressed back in to close it up.

"Brilliant!" I said. "Absolutely brilliant! No one would see it if they didn't already know it was there. We can fill in the gaps with rags and cover all with a blanket. Once it gets dark, well...I could leave tonight."

Jayne frowned at me. "Ye could go out tonight to collect cabbages and grass, so. But not leave."

"Yes, of course, Jayne. That's what I meant. As soon as it gets dark."

Something scraped and rustled at the top of the steps. "Hey-o, any be about here?" Collum called from the top steps. David rushed up to stop him.

"Nothin' at all here, boy. What do you need?" David said.

"Cap'n Beecher came lookin' fer ye, is all." He tried to peer around David's shoulder but David pushed him back.

"Let's go then, see what the captain needs."

Jayne and I froze in place, unable to breathe for several seconds. We'd nearly been discovered. Jayne looked stricken with fear.

"If he tells anyone, we'll look like traitors," she said.

"We must show Sir Arthur immediately. I'll find him."

55

To Endless Night

Rathbarry Castle

Sir Arthur was at the north tower below the battlements, talking with Captain Beecher. Smoke made the air thicker and heavier as I ascended the steps. I coughed, but they only glanced at me, and Sir Arthur held up his hand, apparently aware that I'd come for a purpose but halting me just the same.

"It is nearly a month he's been gone. We were in desperate condition then, and far worse now. How long can we hold out?"

I knew immediately they were talking about Ty. I'd counted the days since he'd been dropped down that filthy shaft.

"In terms of ammunition, we can continue for several more days, even weeks if we conserve," Captain Beecher said. "We ought fire the cannon again to set them back. It won't do much damage, but it does cause disorder. The larger and more immediate issue is that the men are tired, hungry and weak. I see them struggle even to lift their muskets."

Sir Arthur nodded. "God love them for their perseverance. It seems a torture to me, to have them continue without proper sustenance. I agree, we can't hold out longer. How many would you require? Could...could it be from among those confiscated from the Irish?"

"The Irish horses are smaller and thinner, and so I'd say three or four. But it might be one if we could choose the largest mare."

A chill ran up my spine. Again the garrison wanted to kill horses for meat. Where was Ty to stop them? David was subordinate to Captain Beecher, and though he didn't mind stating his opposition, he'd not be able to prevent it if he was given an order.

"Sir Arthur. Please, I have…"

"Merel, you *must* stop interrupting me. Captain Beecher and I have critical business here." Sir Arthur was irritated, but surely he knew by now that when I came to him it was because I had useful information. He examined my face. "What is it?"

"I have a way to get food."

He turned to Captain Beecher, who shrugged.

"Show us," Sir Arthur said.

They followed in silence down the tower stairs and across the court to the southeast tower. David stood outside and doffed his hat in respect as the men approached. They followed me down the steps to where Jayne was still waiting. She pulled away the blanket covering, and she and I together slid the bricks from their places, exposing a sizeable hole in the wall, even larger than I'd anticipated.

"There is width enough that I can crawl through, sir, and get to the lake for cabbages and such. It can't be seen from the trench," I said.

Sir Arthur inclined his forehead, his eyes dark and serious, then his face brightened. "How long have you been working on this?"

"A day and a half, sir," Jayne said. "We noticed a gap in the mortar."

Captain Beecher nodded. "It will be a significant help. But it still may not be enough."

I stood beside him though I still barely reached his shoulder. "I can get more than food, Sir Arthur. Something's gone wrong that Ty hasn't returned. I can go for help as I had offered to do before."

Sir Arthur shook his head. "The same obstacles apply as before, Merel. I cannot send a young woman into such danger and violence. It is worse now, for soldiers block the way to Glandore."

"Sir, I wouldn't go to Glandore. I'd go straight to Bandon, the nearest garrison."

Captain Beecher scoffed. "That's quite a distance for anyone on foot. You'd be discovered and likely killed before you reached Clon, nay even before you passed over the hill."

"Forgive me, Captain Beecher, but I would avoid the hill. I know my route, and I'd pass like a deer in the night. I know I can do this. Sir Arthur, please, you *must* let me. People are starving here and there is no sign of help coming."

Sir Arthur looked into my eyes, searching for something. I only hoped he could see the strength and determination I knew would carry me through. He took a small step back. "Let's try a test, then. Merel, when the shooting starts, we'll do what we can to distract the enemy, and you'll go out and gather that food. You risk your life to do so, of this I'm well aware, but we are all backed against the wall."

"Thank you, sir. I'll change my clothing, and be ready in minutes." I ran to the kitchen and found the boy's clothing I'd hidden there long ago. Elinor questioned me, but I had no time to stop. I tucked my skirt, bodice, shift, coif and lady's boots well into the same hiding place, and tucked my hair into a dingy gray cap.

Sir Arthur, Captain Beecher, and David climbed to the battlements. I waited by the opening with Jayne. Minutes passed, the two of us staring into the light outside of the opening, expecting some kind of signal. My boastfulness began to fade, and my unwavering courage to flutter like a leaf in the wind.

"Jayne, what if I'm seen?"

"Well, ye won't be, that's all."

"But I was shot at the last time. They nearly hit me."

"Aye, because we had to go out the main gate. They canna see you here. For Heaven's sake, ye'd have to jump up and down and wave at them. Stay low, fill yer sack, and come back in. Now is not the time to lose yer courage."

I inhaled deeply, exhaled slowly. "You're right, it will be easy."

"Of course it..."

At that moment the musket fire resumed from the trench. The smell of smoke reached us in seconds and the noise jarred us to utter alertness. We grasped each other's hands, both of us with fingers cold and bloodless. I crouched low and moved toward the opening. Just then an explosion overwhelmed our ears and shook the very tower above us. They'd fired the cannon, so close it seemed as if we ourselves were exploding.

"Go!" Jayne said.

I leapt out the opening and across the piss stone, then flattened to the ground, creeping through the tall grasses as we had done before. I quickly found the cabbages along the lakeside. They had grown wild and plentiful because we'd not been able to dig at them for weeks. "It's no one's favorite food," Elinor would say, "but it will keep you alive."

The firing ceased for a few moments but the shouting seemed nearly as loud. I could imagine men running from the cannon blast, seeking distance, seeking shelter, and their officers trying to maintain order. I dared not raise my head to look, but continued stuffing my sack with cabbages, roots, grass, weeds, and even acorns that could be eaten if boiled. Soon the sack was nearly as large and as heavy as myself. I dragged it behind me as I crawled. When I reached the wall Jayne helped me through and I jerked the sack in behind me. She hugged me tightly.

"Can you get this to Elinor?" I asked.

She tried to lift the bulging sack, but her strength failed. "I'll get Collum, will I?"

"Yes, and see if he might have another sack." I went out three more times, and filled four sacks. Sir Arthur returned from the battlement to pat my shoulder and congratulate me on what I had done.

"I am joyful, Merel, truly joyful for the food you've brought. We'll not go hungry this night. And you've come home safely each time. It's hope to every soul in the castle. God certainly has his angels watching over you."

"Thank you, sir. I am glad to do it." I swelled with pride, and whatever fear and anxiety had claimed me before lifted like a mist, replaced by the fiery warmth of my boldness. "I hope this convinces you I could get through to Bandon."

Sir Arthur held both of my shoulders. "Child,"—and there it was, that reference I so despised—"you've done enough for today. I shall send Giles and Collum out to collect grasses for the horses, and then let's close this up for tonight. We'll talk about Bandon tomorrow."

I couldn't breathe. I couldn't speak. Jayne's mouth opened but nothing came out. I looked at Sir Arthur: thin, weakening, tired, overwhelmed, and shrinking beneath the weight of his responsibility. He was making a poor choice, unable to see the rightness of what I had offered. Only an overtired and overburdened mind would send out two fools from the stables who could very well expose the opening, and with it the opportunity I, Jayne and David had created for him. "But, Sir Arthur..." I finally squeaked out from my cramping throat.

"I've decided, Merel. Say no more. Return to the keep. Mistress Dorothy has been alone for hours and needs care. Go, and do not argue with me. That is your primary duty, and you are well aware."

"But the hole was made for me. They are too big to go through, too clumsy and stout." I was on the edge of tears. To spill them would only confirm his image of me. I pinched my hand.

"Merel," he said, his tone angry and threatening. "I'll hear no more from you. Go."

I turned, ran into the keep and threw myself to the floor in the buttery. My hand had turned sore and bright red but couldn't stop the tears. I was acting like an infant, wasn't I, pouting and crying, angry for not getting what I wanted. And yet, did I not have good reason? We were starving, Ty was gone, men were trying to kill us, and yet I was kept helpless within, restrained from doing the one thing I knew in my heart could save us. I rocked myself back and forth, just letting all the tears bleed out of me until I gasped for breath and fell flat upon the floor, exhausted.

Regaining my composure and countenance, I put on my dress and climbed the stairs to find Mistress Dorothy. She wanted to sit in the solar while I read from her book of poetry. We sat by the window, where occasional blooms of sunshine glared on the page and then slipped away. Mostly the light was gray. I could barely sit still, glancing out the window between stanzas. Once I peered out to see Collum dragging a sack into the stables. And so he had done it, then.

"Give me the book. I don't know where you are today, drifting off with the clouds, but you should be paying more attention to me right here. I shall read to *you* this time," the mistress said. In reading, she had the ability to make her voice gentle and kind, almost like a cooling balm, as it was when she spoke to Sir Arthur—not the sharp and thorny voice she usually reserved for me.

She took a deep breath and began.

I am a little world made cunningly
Of elements, and an angelic spright,
But black sin hath betrayed to endless night
My worlds both parts, and oh! both parts must die.
You, which beyond that heaven which was most high
Have found new spheres and of new lands can write,

Pour new seas in mine eyes, that so I might
Drown my world with my weeping earnestly,
Or wash it, if it must be drowned no more:
But oh! it must be burnt; alas the fire
Of lust and envy burnt it heretofore,
And made it fouler; Let their flames retire,
And burn me, O Lord, with a fiery zeal
Of thee and thy house, which doth in eating heal.

Then she grinned at me, the most haughty and arrogant grin I had yet observed. Who was she to read to me of sin and lust and envy? What could she know of what I'd felt and what I'd done? I wished upon wish that I could slap the grin from her face, and yet I realized in her presence I had no veil in which to hide, no shelter from her piercing eyes.

"Get us some wine," she said.

"Mistress, we have no wine."

"In my armoire, among my summer gowns. Get it. And two glasses. You will drink with me."

The wine was dark and heavy compared to others I had poured, and my experience with them had always been pouring, never drinking. My first taste burned my lips. Mistress Dorothy laughed. "It's Portugal wine. Very expensive, and very strong."

I sipped once more. She watched me closely. This was no drink in celebration, nor a relaxation between friends, nor a drink in mourning or farewell. It was not a drink for fun or laughter. It was a sharing of blood, an unholy pact, a sealing of something dark and secret, but only she seemed to hold the mystery's key. Then it occurred to me. She believed she owned me now, and was closing her trap on my dull and simple senses.

I pushed the glass an inch or so away, and peered out the window. The days were growing shorter. The sunlight gone, the gray clouds moved in, and dusk was claiming the shadows and sharp edges. "I must go, mistress, and see about your supper," I said.

"You needn't..." she said, but shouts roared from the trenches.

"Something's happening." I ran from the solar, out into the court-yard where many people were gathering. The shouts were not threats, but cheers. Before long, from up on the hilltop, came the wail of the Irish warpipes. Sir Arthur headed toward the north tower with his spyglass, and I darted up behind him. We met Captain Beecher there.

"They are certainly celebrating something, sir. I cannot imagine what," Captain Beecher said.

Sir Arthur moved the spyglass from left to right, and suddenly stilled, his huffs of breath from the vigorous stair climb halted. Then he spit on the stones at our feet. "Confound me! Confound us all, and *damn those men to hell* for all eternity!" he shouted. We stared at him in shock and confusion.

"It is Giles, and Collum beside him. They are standing on top of the trench. I can only assume they have defected to the Irish camp. Collum is Irish, but not Giles. I'm surprised they haven't killed him."

He released a deep guttural growl like a wounded wolf. "I never would have believed it. I never saw any such indication from them. I tell you, if I had a musket in hand I would shoot them both between the eyes. My father took them in from the time they could walk. He taught them and fed them and cared for them, spent time with them that might have been spent with me. On feast days they dined at our table. To them he was jovial, to me always stern, and at times I did wish them ill. But they have always been like family to us, have always had work and food in their bellies. How dare they betray my father's kindness. How dare they betray me, in this most despicable, detestable way."

"They have gone over to the Irish...and that means," Captain Beecher said. "That means our enemies are aware of the worst of our circumstances, and how they might exploit our weakness. They'll likely also know of both the garderobe shaft, and the opening by the lake. They'll be able to breach Rathbarry, sir."

"And Sir Arthur," I said, with more purpose than I'd ever had before. "That means I must go tonight, while they are celebrating, while they are gloating, while they are distracted, and before they can get to the castle. I must leave for Bandon tonight. Otherwise, we are done for."

Captain Beecher squeezed Sir Arthur's shoulder. "Sir, I thought I should never say such a thing, but I do in fact agree. Merel should go straight away."

Tears sprang to Sir Arthur's eyes and he steadied himself against the curtain wall. "It is insanity. It is boorishness and cowardice, as if I *myself* betray my father. It is unseemly and barbaric to send a young woman out on such a mission."

Captain Beecher nodded, his hooded eyes dark and drooping. "Yes, Arthur, it is all that. And, that is precisely why it is going to work."

56

In the Dark

Rathbarry to Bandon

Had I undervalued or misunderstood Captain Beecher all this time, or was I simply grateful for his agreement? In any case, he was kind to me while Sir Arthur penned the letter to the Bandon commander.

"You must be especially careful when you approach Clonakilty. It was held by the Irish, then fired and looted by Lord Forbes and his men," Captain Beecher said. "I cannot say what state it is in presently, but there may be enemy scouts, and certainly rogues who would kill you for your dirty old cap. Embrace the darkness and silence, stick to dense cover, and avoid any dwelling where curs might raise alarm. And take this."

He handed me a folding knife with a handle made of stag horn, small enough to fit into the pocket of my breeks.

"It's not much for defense, but it's something a boy would carry, and you may need it. Return it when you come back with the troops."

"I will, Captain Beecher, I promise."

"Bandon has five gates," he continued, "and the river runs right through the middle of the town. You'll come to the southwest gate, which is nearest the garrison. Ask at once to see the commander, and let no one dissuade you. The Bandonians are a rough lot. The militia are more than four hundred, divided into four companies. Nearly all are refugees chased from their farms by the Irish. If they mistake you for an Irish lad, God help you. Just don't lose Sir Arthur's letter. It is your protection."

"Yes, sir."

"One last thing. A mounted troop requires four or five hours to travel from Bandon to Rathbarry, using the main road in daylight. You will be in darkness and off road, the longest of routes, and may have to divert yourself numerous times to avoid being discovered. You have nine, ten hours at the most. If dawn comes and you've not met your destination, dig a hole in the sand and cover yourself until dark. You must survive. If you are captured or killed, so go the rest of us."

"I understand. Thank you, sir."

Sir Arthur stared at me as he passed me his folded letter. I concealed it within the thin fabric of my coat lining. He gave me a few coins to conceal as well, should I need them for food or a bed. "You surely pass as a wretched farm lad to me," he said. "It is so very far from the station I had envisioned for you."

"I'm pleased to hear that, Sir Arthur," I smiled. "I shouldn't delay longer. Jayne will see me off."

By dusk the trench was mostly void of soldiers, the warpipes had ceased, but celebration continued in the camp below the lake and, I assumed, among the encampment beyond the hill.

I was warm in my boy's clothing, my coat secured, a skin of water strapped to my waist, and my belly partly sated with cabbage soup, and partly running on excitement. I had none of the misgivings that vexed me earlier in the day, only eagerness to be free of the castle walls, free of the mistress, free to run without restraint, rich with purpose, and wet faced with the lovely ocean mist. At last I would bring relief to Rathbarry—save so many people, and prove myself and my value well beyond that of maid and companion. My only problem now was that I had lied.

Well, only partly. To cross the Long Strand would be easy, and from there I'd no doubt I could cross the open fields to Clon. It would be as I said, like a deer in the night. But I'd sworn I could get from there to Bandon quickly on foot without being seen. The trouble was, I'd never once been to Bandon. Only one road led to it. I'd assumed once I reached Clon I could run along beside it, in ditches or behind hedges. How difficult could it be? But that was before I knew of Clon's dangers. It was a large enough village that one had to pass through it to get to beyond it. Somehow, I needed to skirt it.

I had also lied, a little to Sir Arthur and a little to myself, about my true purpose. I would make it to Bandon one way or another. I would. But deep in my gut I hoped beyond a wish that I'd discover what had happened to Ty. He was sent in the opposite direction from the one I traveled, but word also traveled, stories were told, rumors were passed on over drink and foolish boasting. My heart insisted he was alive, while my mind told me he was gone, and if that were so I would evermore be alone.

Clouds hung above like sooty rags, parting at times to allow thin beams of moonlight to sparkle on the bay. With any luck, such light would be enough. From the sandy dunes beside Rathbarry I crossed the Long Strand in minutes, staying close to the bluffs and rocks that I might have places to hide if needed. The strand was wide, the calm waves suggesting a low tide, but no one was on the strand nor on the ground above it. A single torch burned at Dundeady, but I was well inland from there. As long as I kept the sound of the ocean in my right ear, I could navigate northward to Clon. As fortune would have it, deer were present in small groups, searching for food in the fields where I traveled. I became one of them, raising no concern. I had a mile and a half to go.

I walked for what seemed like an hour, my legs already growing weary, but I knew I'd reached Clon by the dozens of tiny lights from candles, oil lamps, or torches. An inlet lay before me, the water had drained away with the tide, leaving a wet sand surface parted only by a narrow stream. On the opposite side, a white sand beach. I'd reached Muckruss Head. I could cross here, well away from the town.

I climbed down the rocky edge to the sand. The surface looked deceivingly firm and I nearly lost a shoe in thick, sticky muck, but that was washed away when I came to the stream. The water quickly reached my knees. In seconds I slipped much lower, up to my waist in ice cold water. I pushed across as my strength would allow, praying there be no deeper hole before me. Climbing out was even more difficult, the bluff high and steep. I couldn't let that stop me. I clawed my way over and collapsed on my back to rest, spitting out sand and growing colder by the minute in my wet clothes.

Before me lay another wide-open strand. Such good fortune! I ran across it, but I congratulated myself too soon, for on the opposite end a second inlet ran faster and deeper, likely to swallow me over my head. I trudged through the mud along the edge of the island until it curved west and the inlet split into three, the white sand fingers pointing in different directions. I chose my path and crossed easily, the deepest part rising no more than two feet. I was on solid ground again, with Clon over my left shoulder, the sea over my right, and dark hills before me. I could not see the road.

This meant real trouble, for the inlet had brought me further from the sea than I'd intended, and I could no longer count on its sound as my guide. Coming up out of the water, I would have been facing east. If I could keep that direction, I'd find my way to Timoleague, or at least the road leading to it.

I moved through dense forest. There could be woodkernes hiding within, ready to cut my throat. The cold tremble in my hands and chatter of my jaw increased with each step. The moonlight shone only occasionally, and I might easily walk myself in circles. That's when my throat tightened and my heart began to pound in my chest. I was starting to panic. How arrogant could I be, to think I could do this alone and in the dark, with no knowledge of my destination? What sort of fool insists on such a thing? And in war time? Why did I not plan better, ask more questions instead of pretending I knew more than I did? I ought to just dig myself that hole Captain Beecher talked about, climb in it and stay there forever. But it was no good to keep fretting, I would only cripple myself. What would Jayne say? "Merel, it is simple. *Ye cannot think of discontent while singing.*"

Right. It was a long road ahead, and I would finish it. My best advantage lay in perfect adherence to the direction I was facing. If I veered at all it would be the end of me. I should just sit down, catch my breath, become aware of my surroundings, and wait for something to happen. Something always did. Happen. And to calm myself, silently I sang the first church hymn that came to mind:

> *A Lamb goes uncomplaining forth...*
> *none else the burden sharing...*
> *It goes its way, grows weak and faint*
> *to slaughter led without complaint...*

About a quarter of an hour passed, and if nothing did happen I should soon fall asleep. But then came the clop of horse's hooves, and as I moved closer, a rustle and creak of leather. I must have been near to the road after all. I moved quick and low toward the sound, and lay on my belly to peer about. Two riders passed close by my head, traveling in the direction I'd been facing: east. I kept to the brush as much as possible and followed them all the way to Timoleague, a town I had once passed through in Lady Carey's carriage. I knew it only by the black spires of the old abbey that rose against the blue-black sky.

There was little activity except in the direction of the castle, a five-story tower house whose battlements stood tall and black just to the south of the church. The town had been burned; the sad destruction was clear even in the moonlight, but it meant the inhabitants had either departed or moved into the castle, making it easier for me to pass unseen. I waited in the brush for the proper moment, then reset my direction, heading north and keeping the road at my side.

I had nine miles yet to travel, over ridges and through valleys, across a bridge, and through rocky and ruined farmlands I had never seen or imagined. I was tired and sore, yet the journey would take the rest of the night. I wouldn't stop. I'd been given a true purpose after all my begging and I could not fail. At the end of my path lay the answer to everything. No matter the obstacles that might hinder me, I wouldn't stop.

57

Rubbish

City of Bandon

It was well past dawn when I approached the walls of Bandon. The skies were wonderfully clear, the air smelling like wet soil, the gray stones and towers rising before me. I was beyond weary, staggering with heavy limbs, and my feet so wet and sore I feared I'd find them bleeding. Once I stumbled over rocks and fell, so weak I struggled to rise again. Low branches had torn my breeks about the shins, and my coat across the shoulder. I'd scratched my left cheek on a thorn. But I was here, wasn't I? I told them I could do it, and I had—I'd traveled the entire way without being discovered. So if I'd lied to them, I'd made a truth of it.

Curs slept about the base of the castle walls, and people as well, but enough movement was about that they paid me no heed. I passed bundles, carts, and a couple of dozing mules. I approached the gate with as much purpose and importance as I could muster. The two guards looked me over, one of them tall, the other with a bent knee, leaning on a crutch.

"Wot's this, then?" the tall one asked.

"Sumthin' fer the rubbish heap," the wounded one said, and the two of them laughed.

"I am a messenger, to see the garrison commander."

"Of course. And I am King Charles, sproutin' wings. I've only just flew over," Tall said, and they laughed again.

"I have a letter from Sir Arthur Freke of Rathbarry Castle, for the commander of Bandon Garrison," I said.

"Well, the commander ain't here. Let's have it then." The tall one reached for me and I jumped backward.

"It is for the commander only. Sir. If you please."

"I'll tell you what I please, ye little squeak-voice ragamuffin," Tall said. They both came at me and before I knew it my back was to the wall and I was waving my pocketknife at them. After all of my travels, I'd never once used it, and now I found need of it at the Bandon gate.

"Get back, swine! I swear I am from Rathbarry. The people are desperate for help. Please. I must see the commander."

Had not a soldier approached at that very moment, I might soon have had my neck broken and my body tossed in a ditch. The rider dismounted before me and shouted in the faces of the unruly guards. "What's this boy done?" he demanded.

"He's just another beggar, sir, claiming to be a messenger. He called us swine," the wounded one said.

The soldier turned to me. "What message do you bring?"

"A letter from Sir Arthur Freke, from Rathbarry Castle, sir. Our castle is besieged by the Irish army."

This soldier was more finely dressed than the guards. He grabbed me by the arm and swung around to them. "Fools! Do you not recall that a company is to march for the relief of Rathbarry Castle? If any harm has been done here, Sir Charles will have your heads. If I don't lop them off first."

"Sir," the guards said in unison, and quickly made way for us to pass through the gate. The soldier didn't release me but dragged me behind him, gesturing angrily for his horse to be cared for. He walked me to the end of a narrow lane, scowling, and finally banged his fist on a door.

"Come!" a voice shouted from within.

The soldier opened the door and shoved me inside.

"Jephson. Where have you been? I've found those maps I wanted to show you, of the lands at Mallow." The man sat at a large desk, with similarly large papers spread across it and curling up at the corners. He dressed quite formally, his black and gray hair combed straight back from his forehead and ears. His face was long, his chin square, and his eyes black and shining.

"Good morning, Sir Charles. I just returned from my morning exercise to find the guards on the gate bearing down on this boy, and him waving a little pocketknife like some mad bandit. He says he's a messenger sent by Sir Arthur Freke. I thought we ought hear him out."

"Rightly so, Captain. Take a chair and we'll do just that."

I remained standing in front of the desk, but I'd started shivering, my legs trembling,

"State your name and purpose, boy. Be clear," Sir Charles said.

I hadn't thought to give myself a boy's name, or that anyone might ask, so I just blurted the first thing that came to me. "I'm Tynan."

Captain Jephson scoffed. "Is every male in your castle named Tynan?"

Sir Charles grinned. "Well then, Tynan. Your purpose?"

"I've brought a message for the commander from Sir Arthur, requesting help from the Bandon militia, sir."

"The Commander, Sir William Hull, is away at present, but we are assigned his responsibilities in his absence. You may produce your letter."

I dug inside my jacket, ripped into the lining and pulled out Sir Arthur's folded letter. It was a bit battered despite the protection of my coat, but it was dry. I handed it to Sir Charles, who unfolded it quickly.

He glanced at Captain Jephson. "It's a fine hand. On that basis we shall assume it is genuine. Sir Arthur says the castle has been under siege for several months, saw no relief from Lord Forbes—little surprise there—and he has eighty inhabitants on the brink of starvation, facing Irish troops of roughly 200 under command of John Oge Barry."

"Yes, we've crossed swords with John Oge before, in a skirmish, but he retreated before we could do much," Captain Jephson said.

"Sir Arthur says they are holding out under daily fire, he and Edward Beecher in command. Beecher's a good fellow. He begs that we hasten to his relief, and that we give a care to his messenger, who serves his own family." Sir Charles looked up at Captain Jephson, who nodded agreement.

"Young Tynan, I am Sir Charles Vavasour, commander of the Bandon Militia, and Captain Jephson is my second. Did your Sir Arthur send out a previous messenger for help?"

I nodded. "He did sir, a month ago, by way of Glandore. But that messenger has not returned nor sent word." I bit into my tongue that I would say no more, nor allow any feelings to show. The mere mention of Ty caused my empty belly to twist and burn. I pinched my hand with all my might that my eyes should not fill with tears. It would never do for a boy to cry before men.

"The messenger was here, several days ago. Said his name was Tynan. He slipped past the guards who I suppose would not admit him because he was Irish. When he found us we nearly hanged him on the spot, but he got our attention with Sir Arthur's letters—three of them, in fact. He'd been on quite a journey before he finally reached us from Kinsale. On the strength of those letters and his apparent fortitude, we initiated a relief effort for Rathbarry. We couldn't send notice to Sir Arthur because all messages between Bandon and Castlehaven have been intercepted. Our mission to Rathbarry would have rooted out that problem also."

"Oh sir, thank you sir," I blurted, and my strength started to fail me, but then his words passed from my ears to my mind. "Please excuse, but did you say 'would have'?"

"That is correct," Sir Charles said. "Provisioning was halted."

I dropped to my knees. "But why? Is...is he here, this Tynan who came to you?"

"In fact he is not, and we would like very much to know where he's gone. As soon as we started organizing the relief mission, he vanished. That is why we postponed further preparations. We thought it was the Irish setting a trap for us, that we might ride straight into an ambush. But now you say he was legitimate for Sir Arthur. If he left the city walls, he may well have been captured. The Irish would hang him as a traitor."

58

Provisions

City of Bandon

My throat closed up and the room seemed to sway around me. My head was too heavy and lolled uncontrollably as if a wave inside my skull swelled and surged in circular motion.

"You are quite feeble, boy, and you ought clean yourself up," Sir Charles said. "Our Madeline can help you. *Maddy!*"

A middle-aged frowning woman opened a side-door. "Sir Charles," she said.

"Take this little fellow to a place where he can wash. He seems dizzy. Get him a bite to eat. He'll need a bed for a few nights, I'd say."

"Sir," she nodded.

"Yes, he'll need a bed." Captain Jephson said. "We march in one week's time."

The words shot through me, arresting even swooning, my legs unable to move, my mouth falling open. "One week? But...people are starving and there is no...people will die. My mistress is heavy with child, sir."

Sir Charles just shook his head, and glanced to Captain Jephson.

"If John Barry besieges Rathbarry with 200 men," Captain Jephson said, his voice more harsh than before, "we shall not march into conflict without proper artillery, ammunition, supplies, and provisions, to best him. We march at dawn on eighteen, October."

The image of all the people of Rathbarry lying dead of starvation and musket fire blasted through my mind. I'd succeeded, yet I had failed, for I could not move an army any faster. I cried out when Madeline grabbed my arm and hauled me from the room like a sack of laundry and closed the door behind her.

"Quit ye wailin', ye little mite." She jerked me across a room and out through a back door that led to an open shed in the yard. "There's yer soap, an' yer water. Wash yerself. Yer clothes'll ha' to be brushed, an' it's not fer me ta do." She grabbed the back of my coat collar and yanked it from my shoulders and arms, then snatched away my cap. I yelped and fought, but it was too late. My hair came tumbling down to my waist.

Madeline reared back, staring, her mouth wide with surprise. "Why, ye deceivin' little whore! Jest who de ye think yer foolin' with?"

I smeared the tears from my cheeks and grabbed for my cap but she held it from my reach. "Please," I said. "They wouldn't listen to a girl."

"And rightly so. Ye ought be cleanin' my clothes and not me yourn," she said. She shook my coat, then tossed it to the ground and grabbed my shoulders. She shook me hard. My head rocked back and I bit my tongue, tasting blood, but she squeezed my arms as if her hands were of iron, and kept shaking me until we both heard the sound she'd been looking for. The clink of coins in my breeks.

She gasped, shoved me to the ground and held me there—her knee on my arm that so I could not break away though I twisted and kicked—while she searched my pockets. She let me up only when she came away with the few coins Sir Arthur had given me. She stood, tossed the cap upon my belly, and sneered. "The cost o' my silence about your little secret." She returned to the house while I struggled to stand, and then she returned and tossed a crust of bread to the dirt. "There now, your breakfast. Ye want some dinner, ye'll find the mess at noontide, 'round the corner."

"I need...Sir Charles said I would need a bed."

"So he did, and so ye will. Pity. There's a horse blanket on the fence o'er there. Let me see ye' again and I'll sell ye to the soldiers, won't I?" She stomped back into the house and slammed the door closed. So far, Bandon was not a place to my liking.

I washed as best I could, brushed the caked mud from my clothing, and wound my hair into a tight knot to tuck into my cap. I sat on an upturned bucket to eat my bread—stale and crunchy with sand, and tasteless. I soon lost my appetite, fearful that Ty could have been hanged. If he was lost, so was I. I cast the bread to the birds and left the yard.

As soon as I looked about the town, it was little wonder Ty should have vanished from it. Likely he, being Irish, received even worse treatment than I. Wandering, cold and aimless, I found a spot that reminded me of Rathbarry: a line of fruit trees beside the curtain wall. Their limbs were bare, the ground beneath them covered with large brown leaves. I made a bed of them behind one of the tree trunks, curled up with the blanket, and allowed its horse scent to comfort me. I couldn't rest, tortured by thoughts. What if Ty truly was hanged? How could I go on? How would I learn the truth about him? He could be anywhere.

And what was happening at Rathbarry while I waited a week in this hellish place? Would all the horses be killed? What would happen to poor Sarcen? Would he too be slaughtered and eaten by those vicious garrison soldiers? What if Mistress Dorothy birthed her child and had nothing to feed it? And what if Jayne should be overcome by fever with no one to help her? And then the unthinkable could happen. All could be lost to the Irish while I languished. All the people killed. I'd be best served if I could just lay here and die, no longer having to suffer loss after loss after loss: my birth home, my mother, my father, Lady Carey, Ty, Jayne, Sir Arthur, and everyone else in the castle. They were all my family. I willed myself to a fitful sleep, the darkest part of me hoping never to awaken.

But I did awake, to something shaking me. A boy tugged at my blanket, trying to steal it from me. I still had my pocketknife. I grasped the blanket and flashed the blade at him. He ran away. I'd have to find a better place to sleep if I'd survive the days ahead. I rubbed my eyes. The scent of food reached my nostrils. It did nothing for my sorrow, but urged the pure animal within me. I pulled myself together, wrapped the blanket about my shoulders and I followed the scent to the mess.

In an open hall, no fire to heat it, dozens of rugged-looking men lined up for food while others sat wide-legged on rough-hewn benches eating beans and meat with their fingers. My stomach cramped and my mouth watered, but when I tried to join the line one of the soldiers shoved me to the floor and pointed to a corner. There, a number of boys sat cross-legged, leaning against a cold stone wall and waiting. When a soldier finished his meal, one of them would run up behind him to scavenge his leavings and lick his bowl or trencher, nothing more. And for this bit of nourishment, I had to wait my turn.

I watched from shadowy places as the soldiers built up their supply train for the journey to Rathbarry. One company of 100 soldiers would go, most of them infantry, but about a fourth of them cavalry from the number of horses being groomed and the tack being cleaned and oiled.

Soldiers rolled from their sheds two wagons carrying light cannon, and set them into their positions in the train. Behind those came crated balls and the powder to fire them. Then crates of muskets and more powder and balls. Canvases covered large wagons filled with camp tents, hardware, bedding, and medical supplies. Several carts carried just two days of rations for the soldiers, including salted meat, butter, cheese, bacon, tobacco, dried fish, vegetables, bread and biscuits, water, and firewood. Behind those came two days of fodder for the horses. And added to that, there was bread, milk, fruit, vegetables and meat for the starving souls of Rathbarry.

Soldiers added to the train stacks of litters for carrying sick or injured people, and three fine carriages that looked like those sent out by Sir Arthur before the siege began. I s'posed Sir Arthur thought he'd never see those carriages again, but they'd be useful to carry Mistress Dorothy back to Bandon to give birth under the care of a midwife or physician. Perhaps they'd leave men to restore the garrison until the war ended.

At supper on October 17, a soldier found me waiting on the floor of the mess, and summoned me on behalf of Sir Charles. I followed the fellow through a maze of men rushing about in every direction, shouting at each other, lifting and shoving and heaving the last of the supplies into their wagons.

We entered through the open door where Sir Charles and Captain Jephson were again poring over a map spread across his desk. "It is vast and lovely, this tract, and I think you could win it if you submit your petition early."

"Why not ask for it yourself, then?" Captain Jephson asked.

"Oh, no. I have considered it, but my wife insists on remaining in England. Her family's estate is quite large and demands my attentions. I'll return there when this rebellion is quelled."

The two men, engaged in a war not over but just begun, already were carving up for themselves the richest lands in Ireland, as if the native gentry were just vermin to be swept away. I approached Sir Charles at his desk. "Sir," I said, bowing. "I'm Tynan, of Rathbarry."

"Yes, Tynan. I wanted to inform you that there is a cart prepared for tomorrow's march, just behind the mounted officers. You are to ride there, that you will be quickly available to report to Sir Arthur upon our arrival at Rathbarry. You'll not be late, for we will leave exactly at five o'clock."

"Thank you, sir," I said, my disdain for them quickly giving way to the excitement boiling up from my belly and into my throat. "I'll not be late." In fact, I knew exactly where I'd be sleeping that night.

59

The Eerie Quiet

Rathbarry Castle

Had it been only the week passed that I'd crept in darkness all the way from Rathbarry to Bandon, fearing with each step that I might be discovered and killed? It hardly seemed real anymore, for the way back was as if through a different world.

I'd passed the night in the cart to which Sir Charles had directed me. The boards were hard and my body sore when I awoke, yet my blood stirred to extremity when the trumpet sounded at five o'clock, and I forgot my pain. The gates opened and the company moved out amidst the clamor of horses clopping, officers shouting, equipment clattering, wagons creaking over cobblestones, and the cheering people of Bandon who turned out in the still-dark morning to watch the grand procession. Only a few moments past the city walls, the lands grew quiet, a fine white mist woven low among the black trees, the dark sky awaiting the first blue tint of dawn. I closed my eyes and inhaled deeply, as if to smell the sweet salt air of the Long Strand, but in truth I smelled horsehair, manure, the soil we turned up by our passing, and the stench of my own horse blanket.

Before long, the sun ascended behind us, encircled with a wide gray ring. It foretold a storm that would come upon us in a day or so. Hadn't we enough of storms and terrible omens for one year? Could we not see an omen of joy, especially on the day we would set Rathbarry free? Among the meadow grass and weeds I sometimes glimpsed yellow buttercups awaiting the sun's warmth. That would be my omen, then, and when I thought of joy, I could hardly wait to see Jayne, who somehow found joy in every day. I hoped against probability she'd be well, and that Ty would be there, too.

About an hour after our departure, the company turned southwest, and then south so that the sun, what remained of it, warmed my left shoulder. Graying clouds soon shielded us from that most welcomed light. After two hours marching the officers called a rest halt. In another hour I expected we would reach Timoleague, and then put the sun to our backs once again. The road was now familiar to me, though much more interesting by daylight when the ridges and thickets that had so troubled me were clearly visible. No early-rising travelers stood by while our company passed. No farmers worked in the fields, for there was little to be harvested, and much had been burned as we neared the coast.

The army halted again at Inchy Bridge. Timoleague was before us, where a week ago riders had entered and people were present. Officers shouted orders and soldiers made ready in case of confrontation or ambush, the castle being in Irish hands, but we continued through without encountering a single soul. The eerie quiet unsettled me. Something had happened here. But the Bandonians in their proud formation kept marching on.

Clouds veiled the sun completely as we traveled west toward Clonakilty. Surely there would be a meeting of some kind as the army passed the burned fields and houses that lined the road. No one showed a face, nor were any sheep or cattle grazing. The lanes through the main part of town were deserted. An icy hand ran its fingers up my spine. After what I'd heard, something should be occurring in the town. Something was wrong. Truly, dangerously wrong. But we were on the last portion of the trip, and there would be no stopping.

To reach Rathbarry we had to travel the road toward Irish-held Ross, and then pass through the hills where the Irish camped and where Mr. Millett was killed. If we made it that far, then down past the trenches to Rathbarry's gate. We were a company of one hundred. If the Irish assembled the army of 800 that first marched on the castle, they could close in from all sides and we'd be crushed.

The road to Ross was as deserted as Clon. When we turned south into the hills, no animals grazed, no people walked or rode. If soldiers watched from the forest, they made neither movement nor sound.

The mist thickened as we approached the last hill. The ocean's roar reached my ears, and gulls called in the distance, igniting a fervent long-ing. We were very near, yet I couldn't see the castle. The company climbed with the same relentless pace they had held the whole day through. I wished for speed. I trembled. My heart raced, fearing the Irish would rise out of the brush with all their might and numbers, to cut us off before we reached the castle. We moved with excessive clatter up the hill. Yet, there was no sound from around us, no movement, no barrier. As we crested the hill, the great white spheres of the outer gate posts appeared within the shifting mist, then the outlines of the Irish shooting houses and trenches. At last a break of sunlight revealed Rathbarry, her towers and the keep still standing as tall and beautiful as ever, the azure ocean tranquil at her back. My heart could've exploded, such was my joy to see it.

The trumpeter sounded a blast so near it convulsed me and yet I wel-comed it. Cheers from the men and women of Rathbarry rang all the way to the top of the hill. And as we descended, men appeared along the north wall. I began to recognize them: Sir Arthur, Captain Beecher, David Hyrst and several others of our garrison. But not Ty. Then the boom and bang of hammers, mallets, and iron crows, which meant the furious destruction of the mason's wall behind Rathbarry's gate.

My tears gushed forth, there was just nothing for it and I didn't try to stop them. These were the best kind of tears, even if they should be bitter-sweet. As much as I'd wanted to be free of it, Rathbarry was my home and I rejoiced to return. I wiped my cheeks with the grimy sleeve of my coat, leapt down from the cart and ran like a deer under chase. Had I wings I could've outflown even the swiftest falcon. The men cheered again when they saw me, and I was first to break through the gate as soon as the guards had cleared away the broken bricks enough to open it.

The men came down off the wall to welcome the Bandonians. I ran for Sir Arthur and hugged him as if he were my own father.

"Merel!" he said, the tears brimming in his eyes. "You have done it, truly. You've saved us all. Welcome home!"

I hugged David, and even Captain Beecher, but no one could blame me for it. I was home. We were alive. The siege was finished.

Inside the gates, the court filled with everyone well enough to walk. I searched for Jayne, but could not find her among the crowd, and Da-vid was outside the gate assisting the company with horses and wagons.

I pushed through the people and ran toward the stables, open because there was no door, but void of any people. Ty's cot remained where it had been, empty and unchanged. I ran to Jayne's house in the garden ward. I bolted through her open doorway, but her room was dark and cold. I went to her bedside and found her there beneath her blankets. Thank God, she still breathed.

"Jayne! Wake up, please. We are saved. The siege is broken." She opened her eyes, smiled slightly, but did not lift her head. "Oh, Jayne. What has happened to you?"

"Fever again. All right. 'Twill pass, love."

"Jayne, the Bandon troops are here, the Irish army gone. No battle, no one killed, no more bloodshed. It's over. We've got to get you well."

"I was afraid you...were lost, like Tynan."

I stopped, my breath caught at my throat. My punctured joy suddenly flattened, a broken egg with the yolk drained out, and by Jayne of all people, my queen of joy. "You are right, Ty is not here." I said. "Ty is lost, isn't he?"

She frowned, lifted a weak hand to touch my cheek. "I'm so sad for you, love. But you are home, t'anks be to God. And I'll...be better in a while. Go and see...mistress needs you."

I touched her forehead, warm and damp. "I'll go, but I'll be back very soon with food for you, I swear it. And with something from Elinor for that fever."

She tried to lift up higher. "No, don't..." she said, but her head dropped down again. So weak she was. I could only leave her knowing I'd soon be able to care for her. I tucked the blanket around her and ran for the keep.

Jenkin opened the door wide for me. "Welcome home, miss," he said, his smile wide but his head cocked a little strangely, as if I was unexpected. I ran past him and straight for the stairs to Mistress Dorothy's bed-chamber. She was sitting up in bed. At first she jerked the bedclothes up to her cheeks. I had frightened her, then she softened and let her hands back down to her lap.

"Merel. Welcome home," she said softly. "How filthy you are, and what on earth are you wearing?

I'd completely forgotten that I wore boy's clothing, and that the Bandonians still thought of me as a boy. I supposed things would have to be explained. I went to her bedside and took her hand. Her face was even more thin and pale than when I'd left her, and her eyes were dull with weariness, but the bulge at her belly told me the babe still grew.

"I'm sorry Mistress. I'd intended to be gone only a few days, but the militia...well, they're here now and that's all that matters. They're going to rescue us, to end the siege. We'll have a fine meal this very night."

She raised a brow. "The Bandon militia? They have such a violent reputation."

"I s'pose so, for they've frightened away the Irish from our door. How is the baby?"

"She moves about. I don't know how she does it, I can barely move myself."

"Things will be better now. We've brought milk. I'll get it for you, shall I, and Elinor will fix you something to eat."

"Yes. Elinor," she said.

I ran downstairs again with nothing but energy moving my legs, for I'm sure I'd little strength, and doing something for the mistress took my mind off everything else. I ran through the hall and down into the kitchen. The light was dim and no fire burned in the hearth. Elinor was not to be found, just a kitchen boy with Cal sleeping beside him. I ran up the side stairs to the court, where Jayne and I used to listen to conversations. The court was filling with men, horses, carts and carriages from the supply train, and people crowded in every direction. Sir Charles was speaking to Sir Arthur on the steps.

60

Edge of Sunlight

Rathbarry Castle

I stopped running to hear what was said. By now I was as much a part of the rescuers as the rescued, and wanted to hear what these two leaders, Sir Arthur and Sir Charles, would say to each other.

"It's been quite the strange journey," Sir Charles said, "to be crossing enemy territory and not encounter any resistance, nor even any enemy sightings. It's as if the Irish have moved off the land."

"I've puzzled as well," Sir Arthur said. "They'd taken all my stock from me, and still used my land for grazing. Two days ago they drove all the sheep and cattle from my land. And once the stock was gone, the Irish army pulled back as well. The camp below our lake has vanished. Yesterday was quiet, strangely so."

"Your fellows Tynan are to thank," Sir Charles said. "We understood Lord Forbes had left you quite abruptly, and took some of your men with him, but we'd not realized how dire your situation. After the battle at Clonakilty, word had it that the Irish army was quite weakened. We thought at that point you had the advantage."

"In fact, things only worsened, but we never stopped fighting. Excuse me, Sir Charles. You said 'fellows' Tynan?" Sir Arthur said.

"Your first, Irish Tynan, was quite convincing once we got beyond his being Irish. An impressive man, certainly. Has he returned to Rathbarry?"

"No, Sir. We've not seen him in over a month. I've been quite concerned that he was taken captive or killed."

"As have we. He made his way to us from Kinsale, but after delivering your message he couldn't be found. I admit it raised some doubt in our minds and delayed our coming. But the second Tynan, the boy we returned this morning. He made clear your urgency."

"Ah, the second. Oh yes, you mean Merel. She is quite a wonder."

"Merel?"

I concealed myself among the crowd until I could find the food wagons. One of the officers directed their placement near the kitchen entrance, and soldiers had started to unload. I begged from one of them a jug of milk for the mistress. He shoved me away at first, but then recognized me as the messenger to Sir Charles. I ran to the kitchen with the jug, and found Jenkin waiting there as the soldiers brought in their crates.

"I need Elinor," I told him. "Have you seen her yet?"

Jenkin wisely took the milk jug from my hand and set it on the worktable. "Merel," he said. "We've lost her. We've lost our Elinor."

"No, she's just...I'll go and find her."

He grasped my arm. "What I mean is, she has passed." He looked deeply into my eyes, making sure he had my attention. "She wasn't eating. She gave every bit of food to everyone else, that's how she was. Takin' care o' everyone else but herself. She just...collapsed. I found her here on the floor, as if she just kept working until her very last breath. We buried her in the garden two days ago. Everyone in the castle came to pay their respects."

A heavy, sick feeling came upon me, as if my breast was filling with an ugly black tar. I struggled to breathe. At the same time, my hands, my feet, my legs, all seemed to have turned to ice. "I loved Elinor," I said, as if that should make it impossible for her to die. "She was good and sweet to me. The heart of this place. How...she can't be gone...how will we manage without her?" He put his hand on my shoulder until I met his eyes and he knew I'd accepted the truth.

"The mistress did this to her, didn't she, always demanding, making Elinor run up and down the stairs, running her to death," I said. "I should have been here to handle it, to look after the mistress, and to help Elinor. I should have done."

Jenkin shook his head. "Mistress Dorothy didn't harm Elinor. It's not anyone's fault, Merel. She died. All of us were dying, don't you remember? And now we will survive, because of you."

"Because of me," I scoffed. Ty was dead because me, also. He'd gone outside the castle to prevent me from doing so. He sacrificed himself in order to save me, and it was all of my doing. And I'd hated him for it.

I'd pushed him away. Now Elinor was dead, too. If only I could have convinced the soldiers to come sooner. A few days could have made such difference. She might have survived. But Ty was gone, and now I'd never see dear Elinor again.

I looked toward kitchen door where the dull ochre light puddled on the floor, and men kept stepping upon it, marking it with dirt and mud. Then one by one the women started arriving. Maids from the castle, mothers and daughters from the ward, and boys, too. They unpacked the crates and boxes, and started the process of preparing a meal. It would be a feast, no matter how miserly they had to divide the portions. It would be a lifesaving feast, and Elinor would not be here to prepare it nor enjoy it. Rathbarry would never be the same. I poured some milk into a glass.

"Jenkin, would you please take this to Mistress Dorothy? I must carry the rest to Jayne. She's quite ill with fever."

"Yes, I will. And Merel…Elinor is next to Mistress Rosgill."

Jayne was sitting up when I returned. She sipped the milk slowly, but in minutes it improved her color. She examined my face as she wiped the milk from her lip.

"Ye know about Elinor, then."

I nodded. "Jenkin told me."

"An' ye are heartbroken, aye? I know. She was loved, an' that's the best ye can say of anyone."

I had nothing more to add, and even if I did, I wouldn't be able to speak it. I shrugged. We sat in silence for a few moments. "The women are preparing a meal from what the Bandon soldiers brought. Will you come to the court?" I asked.

"David will bring me something. My legs are so weak, and I grow dizzy. Best I stay here a while longer."

"We should move you into the castle."

"Please don' bother. For me, it's far warmer out here, ye understand my meanin', don't ye?"

My eyes filled, and I could barely see her through the darkened blur. "Oh Jayne. We will laugh again, won't we?"

"One day," she nodded. "Very soon, I promise."

When David came in, I left her to rest and walked out into the garden ward. It was filling with soldiers overflowing from the garrison to set up camp for the night. I never expected to be so comforted by having more garrison soldiers in Rathbarry. I didn't care who they were or for what cause they fought, only that for this night at last, I had no trembling, no ringing in my ears from constant gunfire, and no hunger. I'd sleep again in my own hated little trundle bed. I was fortunate, wasn't I? Fortunate, though a stone weight had found my chest and pressed upon my heart.

I found Elinor's grave at the northwest corner of the ward. There was no marker, because there was no time and no artisan who could make it. It was the only fresh grave. The sun was setting quickly, but still the yellow-orange rays cast shadows upon the mound, like a miniature mountain range with its peaks and crags. I sat beside it, my jaws clenched against the anguish. *I am sorry, Elinor* I wanted to say, but I couldn't speak. I grasped a handful of the soil, smelled the richness of it, and pressed it back down gently and carefully into its place. I watched the shadow edge of sunlight move inch by inch across the mound from left to right, until the sun disappeared behind the curtain wall, and then the forest beyond.

On my way back to the castle, I passed the stables. There were soldiers there, setting up camp beds, and the horses that belonged to the cavalry, but none that I recognized as Sir Arthur's. Not single one. Not even Sarcen. Without Ty there to protect them, had all been killed?

61

A Deep Sea

Rathbarry Castle

At the castle steps, Sir Arthur formally welcomed the Bandonians and thanked them for the first full meal we'd been offered in months. I noticed for the first time the new strands of gray in his hair. "And, good people of Rathbarry," he said, "before you eat, be warned that you must eat slowly, bits at a time and not too much, else our tortured stomachs will most certainly rebel." Some ignored him and ate greedily. I suspected they would learn what Sir Arthur had meant. I tugged on the sleeve of his doublet.

"Merel, you're still in the guise of the messenger. Don't you wish to change back into your gown?" Sir Arthur asked.

"Soon enough, sir. Only I have been to the stables, and find that all of your horses are gone. What has happened? Were they..."

"The horses. Yes. After you left, we had to seal the opening at the tower again, lest the Irish come through. We couldn't gather grasses, and so one night we turned all of the horses loose outside of the gate. Some stayed near the castle for a while, but when the shooting recommenced, they ran off. You mustn't worry, dear. Horses know how to take care of themselves."

"Won't the Irish take them?"

"Perhaps. But at least they'll not starve to death. It's better, don't you agree?"

"Sarcen, too?"

"Sarcen, too. He's not the horse he once was to me. It's best to let him go." He turned to Sir Charles and Captain Jephson, and I was dismissed. While nearly everyone sat in the court to eat—on walls, on the ground, on buckets or whatever could be found, our tables and chairs having been cut up to build the battlements—Sir Arthur, Sir Charles, Captain Jephson, and Captain Beecher took their meals in the stateroom. I brought Mistress Dorothy's meal to her bedchamber, then made sure to eat mine on the stairs, hoping—as ever I did—to hear something useful. My appetite should have been strong, now that there was good food of substance after months of thin soup. But my sadness made chewing even a portion of bread both painful and laborious.

"You can see Rathbarry is a fine castle. Her position is excellent for defense from the sea. Do you not agree, Sir Charles? That she is worth fighting for?" Sir Arthur asked.

"I can agree, she is a fine castle, indeed. But these are not normal times, and the enemy is not at sea, but within our borders. As we understand," Sir Charles said, "the Irish have control of the seven castles around this head of land, from Rosscarbery Bay to Clonakilty Bay. Is that correct?"

"It is, sir, and they still hold the village of Ross, just above us."

"And to the west, Downeen and Glandore castles, as well?" Captain Jephson asked.

"I'm assume so, Captain, but I've had no word to confirm that either way."

There came a moment of silence, and then a scraping of chair legs. How I wished I could see their faces. Someone cleared his throat loudly, I guessed perhaps it was Beecher, but Sir Charles was the next to speak.

"Sir Arthur, we do understand your desire to hold the castle," he said. "However, I must tell you the decision already has been made. It is difficult to envision from your current position, but in truth you are a small island in a deep sea of Irish dominance. We've been allowed to pass through today without obstruction or conflict, perhaps to do what they could not—to dislodge you from this castle without massacre. It is clear the Irish have designs on this region. We suspect, were we to strengthen a garrison here, they would quickly build their numbers as needed to take this final asset at any cost. Bandon hasn't the resources to protect you or defend the castle.

"You must be advised, however, that larger battles are being won in the province. The Irish will be defeated, but not here, and not now. We must evacuate you, your family and all of the inhabitants tomorrow morning. There truly is *no other option.* If you have valuables, we suggest you pack them and be ready to go by dawn."

"Sir Charles, I must beg you to reconsider..." Sir Arthur said.

More chair legs scraped the floor. "I am truly sorry."

I hurried down the stairs to the bedchamber, my heart pounding in my breast. Mistress Dorothy was waiting, a strange gleam in her eye. "We are to leave, aren't we?" she said.

I nodded.

"All of us? It must be all of us."

"Everyone, Sir Charles said."

"Well then. I am delighted. You must start packing my gowns. And go take off that monstrous garb you have on. It's time you were a maid again. Hurry up."

62

Lovely Castle

Rathbarry Castle

I put on my ill-fitting skirt, my ridiculous apron, my stiff and uncomfortable shirt and bodice, and my ugly little coif. Who really cared what I wore or how I wore it? What difference did it make to anyone, except to those who would put me in my place and keep me there? I'd no wish to go back to Bandon, nor travel with Mistress Dorothy complaining and scolding in my ear the entire way.

Why could I not be more charitable toward a woman eight months with child and living in such hardship? I'm sure it was wicked and sinful of me, but I was just angry enough that I didn't care. People I loved were gone. Sweet Jayne was sick and I could do little to help her. And I was just as trapped as ever I had been before. After all I had done to prove myself, to try and help, nothing had changed. It was just an aberration, soon to be forgotten.

I did what was required of me. I packed all of Mistress Dorothy's belongings into her wooden trunk. I packed what I could from the stateroom, the solar, and Sir Arthur's bed chamber. Most of the valuables had been sent away before the siege, but I packed what remained in the hall, buttery and kitchen. The garrison soldiers packed the tools and tack from the stables into their respective crates, and dismounted the cannons from the hexagonal tower. Jenkin packed what remained in the chapel. *The chapel!* How does one pack up the memory of what happened there? And as the memory came forth, so came my cold, sad emptiness for Ty, and the pain of not knowing what had become of him.

We were ready by midnight, and even at that hour the soldiers came through the castle, collecting crates and bundles to be loaded onto carts. I climbed into my trundle. The mistress already slept, a dreamy smile upon her lips—and why wouldn't she have so? In Bandon she'd be treated like a noblewoman again, surrounded by midwives who could soothe her, pamper her, and help her through the birthing. But for me, sleep would not come.

I tossed about, wondering where my place would be in a town like Bandon? Would I still be licking my meals from someone else's leavings? Would Jayne be cast out when they learned she was Irish? And what if Ty was still alive and one day came home to an empty castle? How could anyone do it? How could *I* do it, leave Rathbarry without really knowing? Life still held promise as long as there was the slimmest hope he was coming back. But what good was survival if life held only sorrow? Then it was only existence. People were singing in the garden ward. They had something to celebrate, but this time I'd no wish to join them.

When the dark of night paled as the first indication day, the garrison clatter made sure no one else should have another moment of sleep. I dressed myself and the mistress, and gathered up the last of our bedding. We made our way slowly downstairs. Sir Arthur was already on the steps. The supply train in place, the infantry moved into formation. Sir Arthur directed loading of passengers and belongings into carriages.

He assisted Mistress Dorothy into the largest and finest of them, and I was seated beside her as her companion, opposite from Sir Arthur who would enter once he ensured all of Rathbarry's people were accounted for. The mistress hummed and tapped her fingers on her belly as we waited. She was the thinnest pregnant woman ever I had seen. The evening meal had done much to strengthen her, assuring me that after all, she and the baby would be fine.

"I think I shall name her Elizabeth. Or Mary after my mother. What do you think? Or perhaps Elizabeth Mary. Arthur would agree to that," she said.

"You're quite certain it will be a girl?"

"Well, yes. I've had quite enough of boys. Percy has not written to me even once."

"We can't be sure. No letters have come through since the siege began, except those coming from the Irish."

"I suppose that's true, yes. Nevertheless, it wouldn't surprise me if he had not."

She continued humming and I leaned out the carriage window to watch the rest of the people climbing into carriages and onto carts. Captain Beecher stepped into our carriage to sit beside Sir Arthur when he joined us. Jenkin climbed into the carriage behind us. Jayne was brought from her house on a litter, David beside her holding her hand as she was lifted into a cart, and he took the seat as its driver. The remaining castle residents filled the carts to capacity because all lacked the strength and endurance to walk the distance to Bandon.

As the first crescent of sunlight touched the horizon, officers shouted and our train moved out. The carriage jolted and swayed, the noise of all the movement terrible at first, and when we passed the Irish earthwork I marveled at the depth of the trench, the height of the mounds before it, and the hard labor it must have required. I looked back toward the castle gate thrown wide, and our train still coming through behind us. When we reached the great hill, where the Irish army had first declared their siege, I looked back toward Rathbarry as it must have looked to them: a huge fortress with every advantage, ocean access, and grazing fields as far as the eye could see. Her immense stone walls still gleamed in the light, and with guns silenced, the birds returned, flitting over the walls and calling to one another among the trees.

When all conveyances were clear of the castle, our train halted again. A cavalry detail returned to the castle while we waited. I peered out the window, curious of what they were doing. Quite soon a billow of thick smoke issued from somewhere within the court, and then another from the garrison ward. Then the garden ward. Soon a bright flame leapt from the walls where the stables had been and my heart began to race. Sir Arthur stood, and in his haste accidentally banged his forehead on the top of the carriage. He leapt out onto the ground.

"Sir Charles! You're firing the castle?"

"Yes, of course. We cannot leave it for the enemy's convenience. I thought you understood that. It is quite basic."

"But, why did we not discuss it? It is my home. I intended to return as soon as...."

There came no answer. Beecher stepped out of the carriage beside him, and I watched out the window. Soon more flames shot up as the chapel started to burn, and the servants' apartments. The soldiers were walking a ring around the castle from ward to ward, torching anything that would burn. Bright yellow light flickered from the windows of the keep where the wooden floors would burn through. If the fire became hot enough, the mortar between the stone blocks would fail, the walls would become unstable, the castle itself could crumble. I screamed, and my sound was joined by others, for many among us had been cradled within Rathbarry's walls.

Sir Arthur was stunned, his face as white as his shirt collar. He vomited on the ground, Captain Beecher beside him with his hand on Sir Arthur's back. I wretched in sympathy for him, and watched helplessly as the flames grew higher, the smoke darker, and soon the roaring sounds of it overcame the sounds of the sea.

Sir Charles ordered the train to move out. Sir Arthur and Captain Beecher returned to the carriage, Sir Arthur fuming, and Captain Beecher's face was dark and solemn, sympathetic to Sir Arthur's loss but more likely in accord with the military tactic. I offered him the pocket knife he had loaned me, but he refused it. "You may keep it, in case you need it someday. I'm sure I will not," he said. I nodded and turned my face to the window, watching poor Rathbarry burn, the flames sending bright orange spikes above her walls.

"Arthur, dear," Mistress Dorothy said. She leaned toward him as much as her belly would allow, to touch his hand. "We shall miss our lovely castle. It is a deep loss, and quite painful, I know. But remember this, that the preservation of life is of far more importance. God has sent us this deliverance, and all has happened in his will and his mercy. We could neither doubt nor judge the good work of God."

I believed not for an instant that these words came from her heart. She said what the church men would say. She said what would make him feel wrong for mourning the castle, so that he would turn away from it. And in truth, there was nothing he could do about it anyway.

But I could.

As our train moved forward, putting all but the smoke of Rathbarry behind us, the sway of the carriage eventually lulled Sir Arthur and Captain Beecher to sleep. That is when everything that had happened before was over, and that is when I began.

"Mistress," I said. "Do you remember, months ago when I first became your maid within the keep? You asked me to be your eyes and ears, to help you make sure you wouldn't be sent away from Rathbarry. It was a favor, rather heavily backed by threat, but a favor nonetheless. You agreed a favor would be owed at a time of my choosing."

"Did I? Well, much has happened since then, and we'll have new lives at Bandon. I don't really need that kind of service anymore."

"Perhaps not. But you still owe the favor."

She looked at me, her brow furrowed, her mouth slightly open. "All right," she said with an air of caution. She hesitated, then sighed heavily. "To be fair. What do you ask?"

"To be free. I ask you to set me free."

Her brows lifted. "Free? Whatever does that mean? You're not a bird in a cage. Do you mean to leave our family? Where would you go? How would you manage? Who would feed you and look after you as Arthur and I have done?"

I shook my head. She would never understand. "None of that is, or would be, your concern. You only need to agree, as was our arrangement, and then you owe nothing more."

"Merel, you know I need your help. The baby. And who knows what troubling circumstances may arise in our new living arrangement. I..."

I nodded. "You will have more help than you can imagine when you reach Bandon, and I lack birthing and childcare experience anyway. You will become fully engaged with people there and will hardly notice I am gone."

"But I would miss you. We've shared many secrets."

"It's so. But, as you said, you don't need my kind of service anymore. I think you quite understand what I mean, to set me free."

She stared at me, her lips moving slightly as if she struggled for the next thing to say that would grant her continuing power over me. But she couldn't find the words, and at last her countenance seemed to sag. "All right then, Merel, if it is what you want. You will regret it, but you are free."

"Thank you, Mistress." I sighed, and could feel a tightness around my chest lift with the air I exhaled. Free. I was free. And suddenly I questioned why I'd ever needed her to say it.

We spoke no more until the officers called the next rest halt, near the ridge leading into Clonakilty. The moment our carriage came to a stop, I stood. I touched Mistress Dorothy's hand and nodded. I quietly opened the carriage door, and stepped out.

I walked along the edge of the road, back the way we had come, past the horses and infantrymen, past the supply carts and baggage carts, past several of the passenger carts until I found David and Jayne. She was still on the litter in the back of the cart, but she was sitting up, awake and alert. I kissed David on the cheek, and took both of Jayne's hands in mine. I told her what I had done.

"My God, I am proud of you! But what are you going to do? How will you eat? Rathbarry is burned."

"I don't care. I'm going back. I'm going to live at Rathbarry. Maybe once I'm settled I'll take up sketching again, and sell my work to Lady Carey. I'll make my way somehow."

"I believe you will," she said.

"Find Lady Carey. She will give you both jobs and look after you. She'll see you back to health, Jayne."

"We just may do that," she said. "Then it would be easier for ye to find us, should ye happen to have that notion. In the meantime, Merel, remember this, that ye're the most courageous woman I've ever known. I'm proud ye are my friend. And no matter what happens, when you feel troubled *don' forget to sing.*"

I hugged her, feeling her arms strong around me, and knew she would be well. How I would miss her, my precious and only friend.

Our paths parted. I walked at edge of the train as it began moving forward again. I continued southwest as the gap widened between me and the train heading east. When I reached the fork for Rathbarry or Ross, I could smell the smoke, and see the black cloud rising and spreading beneath the already dismal clouds. I turned south toward home.

The nearer I came to the castle, the more I began to question my decision. Here was I, awash in my own pride and my eagerness to get to Rathbarry, hoping to salvage anything I could, but I had left the train without taking food, bedding, money, nor even that old horse blanket for warmth. I had no tools, matches, or rope, no net or twine, and no cup from which to drink except my own two dirty hands. But when I crested the hill and could see her towers, my choice was reaffirmed. The only thing I needed, I had in abundance, and that was determination.

I needn't have worried about warmth, for heading down toward the castle the keep was engulfed in flames, the roof of my old garret burned away, the wood floors below still burning and the windows blown out by the yellow fire. The heat reached my cheeks as I passed the Irish trench. Yet I moved closer. The gate was wide open, mostly burned away except for charred planks and glowing embers beneath them. I peered inside at the court filled with burning debris, the roof over the well broken down, the chapel in ruins and the stained-glass window in blackened and glistening shards on the ground.

I could move no closer without risk, so I resorted to my old place of comfort among the oak and ash trees opposite the lake, the heat still reaching my cheeks but not so hot as to burn. There I must have fallen asleep, for by late afternoon a terrible explosion alarmed me. The floors of the keep collapsed, causing an enormous rumble crashing to the earth, the flames and sparks soaring into the sky.

The fire raged on through the night. Rathbarry moaned and whined in helplessness, the cruel flames burning through the floors of her guard towers, and along her curtain walls. I kept my place though I could offer no comfort. I cried for her, my beautiful Rathbarry, and let the tears flow freely with no one about to observe me or judge me. I could think of nothing more worthy of my tears. By morning she still burned, but not enough to keep me out.

63

Desire and Courage

Rathbarry Castle

Gray smoke rose in spirals from places all around the castle, and hot coals still glowed red, at times reverting to leaping flames fueled by a hearty gust of wind. I walked through the open gate into Rathbarry's court, now a hellish place of charred wood and stone, collapsed structures, broken glass, and things contorted to strange black shapes that once had purpose and value.

Around me was a place I recognized only by its structure and size. The outer walls of the keep where I had lived, and the steps to the door that I'd climbed every day remained in place, but a volume of black and gray ash blanketed the steps, and the door was burned away, the interior fire still eating at the heart of Rathbarry's existence. The collapse had filled the hall so fully with charred and burning wood, and fire still consumed the thick beams that had supported the floors. Smoke filled the air, causing me to cough at times, but it was far less than the day before, and I had no fear or hesitation. Rathbarry still embraced me. I had work to do.

My first concern was for the well. Beneath its partially burned roof that leaned upon the stone surround, the rope and bucket had been sheltered and could still be used if the water wasn't spoiled. The windlass was gone, so I had only my arms to let the bucket down and haul it back up. The first try I retrieved with terrible effort. The water held ash and bits of charred wood. It might take many pulls to get clean water again, but I would have to do it. Near where the stables had been, I found a partially burned feed bucket and used it to collect sand from outside the gate to douse some of the red-burning embers.

The north and southeast towers burned on and I couldn't enter them, but the west tower seemed to have cooled. The stone spiral stair was blackened but intact, and half of the guard room floor had burned through, with the center support beam still smoldering. Beneath the stair was an empty space that offered cover, protection against wind and rain, and a feeling of safety. I'd make my shelter beneath it, and here would be my new Rathbarry lodgings until I could find something better.

I found a partially burned and sodden blanket among the debris. Once it dried it would be just enough to lay across my shoulders, leaving my knees and feet to cramp with the chill. With nothing to eat, the curs had left the castle, but I could hear the howl of wolves in the woods not too far distant, and me with no gate to lock them out.

That night the foretold storm arrived, with winds howling and gusts that sought and found every crack and crevice to chill me so deeply I could only curl and shiver. Then came the sudden and booming thunder that startled me like a quick knife to the spine, followed by bright white flashes of lightning shrieking and crackling across the sky. Heavy rain whipped against the walls all around me. It flogged, beat and bent the trees and broke branches with a horrible cracking sound. So frightened was I that I sought the very deepest, darkest corner beneath the stair, my arms and legs drawn in, my back exposed to the elements. The top half of the support beam cracked and fell, still smoldering, to the ground just behind me. Just a few inches closer and I'd have been killed. In that moment a curtain of sorrow descended over me, and my heart raced at the realization. How alone I was, more so than ever I'd even imagined before. How I missed Jayne. How I wished to have Ty's arms about me.

I'd got what I wanted, hadn't I, to be free and to live at Rathbarry? I had demanded my freedom and received it. Every minute of desolation I now experienced, I had purchased willingly with my selfishness, my false pride, my fantasies of freedom and independence. In truth I knew nothing of it, what it meant to survive and sustain a life alone and to oneself. I had never considered what loneliness might be, because I had never really experienced even a day of it.

What was this emptiness, this new anger at myself? For turning against Ty? For leaving Mistress Dorothy? Was it shame? A growing conviction that such a fool as I had no right to breathe the earthly air, nor to walk among the ruins of so wondrous a place? Death seemed to dance around me now, laughing at what easy prey this thoughtless waif would be. I had cast off all my protectors.

I was nothing. Should I die this night, I'd never be missed or discovered, until one day someone might uncover my bones while clearing the way for something new. I should only hope they'd say they mine were the bones of a proud warrior who'd fought valiantly for his castle—instead of a woman who was lonely, foolish and lost. I rocked, shivered, and rocked myself until the worst of the storm passed over, leaving only the endless rain. In that steady drumming of water, my poor mother's words came back to me, a warning what the lines of my fingers had foretold: *"Never push so hard for what you want, that you push away what you love."*

I awoke in the morning to gentle drips of water amid the still silence. The rain had drowned the last of the fires, quenching even the flames at the north tower. At last, Rathbarry could rest, her injury suppressed, her wounds calmed, her walls rinsed of ash. The morning sun sent softened beams to bathe those wet walls in lustrous silver. The cool autumn wind chased away the tainted air. Sodden black mud and grotesque forms filled every corner.

I was cold and sore, my clothes damp, but the light of day lifted my senses. I'd survived the night, and had been given another chance at life, to prove my value, or at least to use whatever meager powers I retained to restore bit by bit all that was Rathbarry.

I pulled the back hem of my skirt between my legs and tucked it into my front waist band, as if I wore a baggy pair of breeks. I tossed my bodice and coif aside, allowing my shirt to flow freely and my hair to fall in damp, twisted ropes down to my waist.

I found a fallen oak branch that I used to sweep aside the debris so that I could walk through the court to every ward. All the blackened bits filled me with sad scorn until it dawned on me that each bit I passed was not debris, but charcoal. I walked in an artist's workroom with abundant supply of a perfect medium. I found a good solid piece, and tried my hand on a broken board. I drew some lines and sketched the ruined brick arch near where the stables had been. It came easily, and it pleased me. On broken boards, on bare walls, and on flat stones I passed, I tested and tested my art. A sketch of a tree here, a horse's head there, a mountain top, a sleeping dog, a laughing child. I was cold, wet and filthy, and yet the most joyful I had ever been.

The following morning I could no longer ignore my need for food. I passed through the court carrying my bucket, intending to harvest some small cabbages by the lake. I stopped cold at the sound of crunching gravel at regular beats, like footsteps as if someone else walked through the castle. My back and shoulders seized, and my stomach leapt up from its normal position. I pressed myself against the wall of the keep behind blackened, fallen debris, my heart thumping. The song came to me as if Jayne stood by to quell my fear, and I heard it repeat in my head: … and I'll die an old maid…and I'll die an old maid…and I'll die an old maid in the garret…

The song did calm me enough that I peered around the corner toward the open gate to see what occurred. Through the charred entrance a horse stepped gingerly among the scatterings. A horse! Only a horse. I gasped with relief. But no, it was not just a horse. It was Sarcen—beautiful, graceful, beloved Sarcen covered with gray ash, turning his head warily from side to side, walking through a once familiar place so strange and altered. It was as if I could see what he saw and hear what he thought. I stepped into view slowly so as not to frighten him.

"Sarcen," I whispered. He alerted and backed a few steps, prepared to run. "Sarcen," I said again, and he became more curious than frightened. His ears pointed toward me. After a moment his curiosity won out and he stepped forward. I met him halfway. He raised his head and pushed his muzzle against my hand, and then my shoulder, then let me hug his neck. I inhaled the earthy smell of him, stroked his coarse mane, pressed myself against the warmth of his coat. He'd been expelled from Rathbarry as I had, and now like me he'd found his way home. We were both alive, safe, and exactly where we wished to be.

He swished his tail and then one of his hears flicked back. He turned his head toward where the old gate had been. Both of his ears twitched. There was something he heard that I could not. And then, the snap of a twig. A crackle of scattering leaves. Something rustled and there came a new sound. Another horse, maybe. But no, it was not footsteps this time, but voices. I had no time to run away, for already someone entered the gate while I still embraced Sarcen's neck.

A man stepped over the burned timbers. He was tall and muscular with shoulder-length hair once blond but graying at the scalp. He started, seemingly not surprised to see the horse but quite astonished to see me. His pale blue eyes bore into mine, not threatened but as curious as Sarcen had been. These were the learned eyes of a scholar or a nobleman—patient, cunning, and tempered by a spark of humor. His lips parted and he spoke, but too softly for me to hear clearly, as if he dared not scare away the wild animal before him. His mouth lifted slightly in a half-grin. I waited, still as a bird before flight, and then another man stepped through the gate. My legs nearly gave way beneath me.

Ty. I ran to him, and he to me. We clung to each other until we could not breathe, then we parted just enough to kiss with the hungriest lips and thundering hearts pressed together. I spoke against his jaw. "Ty. I thought I'd never say your name again. Please forgive me."

He held my face and looked into my eyes. "I thought I'd lost you."

"I thought you'd been killed. For so long there was no word." My voice trembled. "At Bandon they said you'd disappeared. I'd never see you again. But... it was you who warned them all, the Irish army, wasn't it? That the Bandon militia was coming. And because you did, we were allowed to pass. We were never attacked. You kept us safe."

"Aye, we've both survived, and I've words for you that I've been savin' up for the day. 'Tis I who must beg forgiveness. You were right, that day in the tower, about bein' the one to go for help. I believe ye could ha' done it better than me, and I believe ye'd mebbe have been more successful. I thought I was doin' the right t'ing, an' I'm sorry to have hurt ye so." He took a gallant bow. "May I be forgiven?"

"Just to see your face is all I need now, and all I'll ever need. I wonder had we come together from the beginning, had we known each other's hearts, had we worked together instead of...but it's no matter now. You're here."

"Aye. I'm here because you were right about another t'ing, as well. Ye remember when we talked about the Tuathal, the mighty high king of the mountain? An' it was me wanting to keep to my own, do my job an' avoid the clash and strife. I had no wish for change, but everything changes anyway, does na? Tuathal has tortured me from the time I left the castle—made himself quite a nuisance until I listened—and then I knew in me gut I had to rise like all the others. I had to own what was in me blood."

The tall man stepped closer. "This, I gather, is Merel."

Ty turned. "Aye, sir, this is my splendid, enchanting, brilliant and wild love. Merel, this is my lord, Teige O'Downe, or rather, Tadhg-an-Duna MacCarthy. He is chieftain, the Prince of Dunmanway. He owns the seven castles along the Carbery coastline, and now he retakes the ancestral castle of Rathbarry."

"I'm glad you did, my lord," I offered a rather lame and uncertain curtsy to O'Downe as I untucked my skirt hem from my waist.

"My lady," he said with a gentle bow of his head, and kissed my hand. "I know who ye are, and the things ye've done, starting with the release of some very special prisoners. Your man Tynan has told me. My soldiers captured him a while back, intendin' to hang him. But I took one look in his eyes and knew him better. Aye?

"When we talked, he struck a clever bargain, did he. Should I set him free to arrange the relief of Rathbarry, he would get me my castle without a battle, without bloodshed. And when all was done, he'd stay on as my horse marshal. It was a fine plan, and he's kept his word, though this is not the Rathbarry I'd counted on."

"No sir," I said, smiling. "It is bittersweet. She is quite wounded, yet she is proud."

"It's right ye are," Teige said. "My men will restore her, if not to glory, at least to a habitable place. 'Twill be my headquarters. You, Tynan, and our Sarcen here, are welcome to stay with respect and honor. Can ye live wi' an Irish host, after servin' an English household?"

I hesitated a moment, unsure of the proper response, but then it seemed honesty was the only right path. "Sir, I think you will understand this. I have been owned for most of my life, depending on others, having nothing that was truly mine, and no choices. I have no quarrel with you, nor with Sir Arthur Freke. It's freedom I've longed for, mine and Ty's. I knew I'd not find that at Bandon. There I saw an army rooted in greed and oppression. Here I've seen an army rooted in pride and liberty. It's more to my liking."

Teige nodded. "Well then, freedom is my own aspiration as well, for my family and especially my wife and sons, and in fact for all the Irish clans. I should think on such common ground we'll manage admirably."

A sudden gust swept through the court, and above the strand a flock of birds flew in murmuration, of such size that it darkened the sky, and so perfect they moved like a single being flexing and spiraling in a warming air. In gathering so, they flew high and joyfully. Interdependence, individual expression, and utter magnificence. Was that not the vision of freedom itself? It kept them safe from predators, and yet, they flew together perhaps for something even greater that I'd not considered before. Belonging. Not in a sense of being owned, but being a part of something that functions because you are there. An empty space is filled that was meant only for you. Belonging in the sense of being loved. Ty squeezed my hand and I became one of them, light as a bird, a beautiful starling, my heart soaring over the sea.

"Ah, the starlings. A most strange and inspiring sight," Teige said. "To move as they do must require trust and communication, each bird in tune with the next, each committed to the whole. It succeeds, and no predators can break it because they cannot understand it. I fear it may be a long time before we humans learn its magic."

"Perhaps it will, sir," I said. "But I've come to believe that even a plain little starling—if she has a deep desire and the courage to follow it—will find her true place in the world among like-minded friends. When that happens, the whole world becomes something greater."

Teige gazed at me with a lifted brow. "Something greater indeed, Merel. Something much greater."

Epilogue

The Irish Rebellion was declared a just war in May 1642 by the Catholic Bishops, who established an alternative government called the Irish Catholic Confederacy. The rebellion became known as the first stage of the Irish Confederate Wars, 1641-1653.

Sir Arthur Freke was son of William Freke, Esq. of Shroton Manor in Dorset, England; grandson of Sir Thomas Freke, MP; and great grandson of Robert Freke, auditor of the treasury for King Henry VIII and Queen Elizabeth I. Sir Arthur purchased Rathbarry Castle from David Barry in 1641. After it was burned, the family eventually returned to the area. Sir Arthur died in 1707. The Freke family still owns the Rathbarry lands.

Cormac (Charles) MacCarthy Reagh may have turned to a wandering life after the loss of Kilbrittain. In 1657, he served as a colonel leading the Duke of York's regiment and his own regiment in France and Spain. He was reported still living in 1667. One quoted description states the MacCarthy Reagh was "a humane and just man, hating cruelty, and severely punishing it at times."

Teige-an-Duna MacCarthy was Lord of Gleanna-na-Chroim, Prince of the Dunmanway branch of the MacCarthy Reagh dynasty until 1648, and died in 1649. He is believed to have inhabited Rathbarry Castle briefly after it was burned and had possession of it until July 1643. He had two daughters and four sons, but was the last of his line to maintain the rights of his hereditary position.

Donough MacCarthy, 1st Earl of Clancarty, 2nd Viscount Muskerry, was a leader of the Irish Confederacy formed at Kilkenny in 1642. As general of the Confederate Munster Army he continued to fight against the English Protestant troops and later against Parliamentary troops. He embarked to Spain and lost his estates under Cromwell's rule, but regained them in 1662 under King Charles II. He died in London in 1665.

General Garet Barry's strong military reputation was irreparably damaged by the defeats at Cork and Liscarroll. He died in Limerick city in March 1646.

Author's Note

This novel is based on the true story of Ireland's longest siege, at Rathbarry Castle in County Cork, from February 14 to October 18, 1642. It was the beginning of a decade of war that ended with the Cromwellian Conquest starting in 1649. The siege is described in detail in an account by Sir Arthur Freke, owner of the castle at the time (dates provided in his report would have been from the Julian calendar).

I have maintained a close adherence to the timeline but have altered or skipped a few minor things in the interest of moving the story forward. Freke was English, and during the siege he protected mostly English settlers. I found no similar account that provides the Irish side or viewpoint of the siege, so I have created that based upon my research.

Many characters are named for real people mentioned in Sir Arthur's account, but of course any dialogue, physical description, or interaction with other characters are purely fictional. There was a Lady Carey and a Mistress Coale; as well as Dorothy, Sir Arthur's wife; and some of those working with him including Beecher and Millett. In addition, Donough MacCarthy (Lord Muskerry), Cormac MacCarthy (MacCarthy Reagh) and other military figures are gleaned from various historical sources. I have kept their names in the interest of maintaining Sir Arthur's circle of contemporaries. Some of their actions also come from Freke's account, but any personality traits, speech or interactions with others are fictionalized. My biggest departure from truth was in replacing William Jennings and Thomas Carbery, the individuals Sir Arthur sent to Bandon in October 1642, with the protagonist Merel de Vries.

Sir Arthur and Dorothy had three children, Percy, Mary, and Agnes. They are listed in various sources, but without birthdates. Sir Arthur mentions Mistress Dorothy's pregnancy during the siege. If my sources have the birth order correct, then that baby, Elizabeth Mary, would have been born in November after the siege ended.

The story of Rosgill and Tantalus is reported in Sir Arthur Freke's narrative. For the sake of logistics, I have their executions taking place near the home of Robert McShane, rather than at the village of Ross.

Merel, Jayne, Tynan, David, Elinor and a few others are invented characters, but some of their actions are based on events in Freke's account. Teige O'Downe (Tadhg an Duna Mac Carthaigh) was an important person in Ireland's history, but I found little to inform his background, personality or appearance, and so he is mostly invented as well.

In some places I have rearranged the sequence of events to make more sense in terms of timing and plausibility. None of these changes significantly alter the overall story. Sir Arthur Freke's account was written after the fact, when he knew things he could not possibly have known at the time they occurred, because of his containment within the castle and lack of correspondence. For example, he provides a seemingly eye-witness description of an ambush he could only have learned about later, possibly even after the siege ended. I refer the reader to Sir Arthur's actual account of the siege for the original sequences (Siege of Rathbarry Castle, 1642; Journal of the Cork Historical and Archaeological Society, Series 2, Vol. 1, No. 1, Jan. 1895).

Rathbarry Castle was burned by the English soldiers after Freke's family and others were rescued. There is indication that the McCarthys briefly inhabited the castle in its' ruined condition following the fire. The Freke family still owns the land and built a new castle on the grounds in the mid- to late-1700s, and restored it in 2013-2019. I visited the ruins and saw partial walls, the spiral stair down to the lake, and the stone arch that was part of the stables.

In James N. Healy's remarkable book, *The Castles of County Cork*, there is a partial description of the castle ruin and a sketch, but I have taken some license with it to situate living quarters, stables, chapel, and so forth. The actual position of the castle in relation to the Long Strand may have been different in Freke's time, altered by the Great Lisbon Earthquake of 1755. A blog post on my website provides more about the earthquake, images, and more history about this castle ["Tracking the Prince: Rathbarry and the Red Strand, 11/29/2016]

About the Author

When Starlings Fly as One is Nancy Blanton's fourth novel taking place in 17th century Ireland. Each of her books has won literary medals and favorable reviews. Her blog, My Lady's Closet, focuses on writing, books, historical fiction, research, and travel. She was born in Miami, Florida, earned degrees in journalism and mass communication, and continues to live in Florida with her husband and two cats. Her love of Ireland stems from her father and grandmother, and her own unforgettable experiences on the Emerald Isle.

www.nancyblanton.com
www.facebook.com/NancyBlanton.author
@nancy_blanton / Twitter
blantonn17c / Instagram

If you've enjoyed this book, please consider leaving a positive review on amazon.com, barnesandnoble.com, bookshop.org, goodreads, or any of your favorite bookseller or social sharing sites.

Thank you!

Made in the USA
Las Vegas, NV
13 September 2021